GRANDMOTHER'S
HOUSE

GRANDMOTHER'S HOUSE

(FARMOR'S HOUSE)

by *Soya*

Translated by
Agnes Camilla Hansen

English Translation Revised
and Edited by
Alan Moray Williams

TAPLINGER PUBLISHING CO., INC.
New York

First published in the United States, 1966
TAPLINGER PUBLISHING CO., INC.
29 E. 10th Street
New York, New York 10003

PT
8175
.S66
P65
1966
may 1995

Library of Congress Catalogue Card Number:
65-26941

This book was published in Denmark under the title
FARMOR'S HOUSE

Printed in Denmark
by A. Rasmussens Bogtrykkeri
Ringkjøbing

FOREWORD

The memoirs which follow were written by a businessman, a director of a large Danish insurance company. I first met him at a private social gathering where he confided to me at dinner that he had written a sort of novel covering a period of his youth. He said that he had not submitted the manuscript to any publisher because after writing it he had grown rather doubtful about whether these private memories of his were of sufficient interest for publication. He also felt reluctant to put his name to them because of his social position. As he expressed it, "I couldn't very well have the three hundred people who work for me poring over my family life and my intimate confessions."

Naturally, I became curious and asked if I might borrow the manuscript and read it. He sent it to me. And after reading it I came—rightly or wrongly—to the following conclusions:

The contents were interesting both from the point of view of psychology and as a period-piece. The period about which he wrote—the early years of the twentieth century—will in a few more decades no longer be in living memory. At the same time, the manuscript revealed serious faults from a literary standpoint. The sentences were excessively long and involved. The style was sometimes too dry and businesslike, making the context dull or unintentionally comic. Too many details of little or no general interest were included. And the book's organization—or lack of any—was chaotic.

These facts I communicated to the author. He countered with the surprising proposition that I myself put the manuscript to rights, or, as he wrote me, "make it fit for publication." With true generosity he offered me a free hand in editing it.

After some consideration I was rash enough to agree to his suggestion. The undertaking was by no means a simple one. Of course, if I had taken advantage of his permission and just ruthlessly rewritten what he had written, few difficulties would have arisen. But I regarded it as a duty to preserve as much as possible of the author's own turn of speech, and to leave as little trace as possible of myself upon it. In other words, what I have attempted to do was to write the book as Director X would have written it had he been a man of letters as well as a business executive.

I believe that this delicate assignment has been accomplished successfully. At any rate I base my belief on the satisfaction and pleasure which Director X evinced when I read him the manuscript in my revised version. He said, to my gratification: "It is exactly as I would have wished to write it had I known how."

Despite my pride in this, which I hope is justified, 99 percent of the credit for Farmor's House belongs to the anonymous author himself. These are his experiences, his views, his commentaries—not mine. On the other hand, I have to acknowledge my share of the responsibility for its publication. If it proves the consensus of opinion of the critics and the reading public that the novel did not merit putting into print, it will have been my own judgment that was at fault.

Director X has asked me to state that even though the memories he recounts are true ones—as true as memories ever can be, that is—all names in them have been altered and all places mentioned, disguised. And I can personally add that in my opinion he has been so thorough in this respect that it is hardly possible that anyone could ferret out the author's real identity.

The original manuscript, in accordance with Director X's wishes, has been destroyed.

1

"Soren, wake up! Wake up! You have to get up now!"

I protested peevishly and tried to pull away from my nurse's hands which were laying hold on my inmost being. My spirit was already on the way back to my body, back to the peeling iron bed, back to my combination bed-room and nursery ...

"Does Mother want me?" I mumbled—rubbing my eyes with warm, moist fists.

"Not now, little man." The voice was mournful, sad. Sad because of the sympathy in it. "You have to go to your Farmor's." The voice changed, grew brisk, persuasive.

"There will be Victoria kringles when you get there and your Sunday ten ore."

My nurse stood me on my feet, seized the hem of my night-gown, and pulled it up over my head.

It is horrid to be awakened at night—much worse than any grown-up can imagine—but it is torture to have a nightshirt, too tight in the neck, pulled up over the head. Your chin gets caught in it, then your lips, your cheeks, your nose, your ears! And it isn't just these things but one is frightened of what seems to be impending.

Still blinded by the shirt, I began to hit out. My small fists drummed against Johanne's fat bosom. It was my usual point of attack whenever her will and mine clashed. But the result was negative—as negative as always. She did not hit back. She let me hit unrestrainedly as if her bosom was proof against all life's blows.

She only said, "Don't fuss, Soren. We'll get it all over within a minute. Now then ..."

Dressing began. First the little undershirt was whisked down on me. That, fortunately, buttoned across the breast and up to the neck, so it slid over my head without touching my face as it emerged, and without discomfort. Then came the garter-belt with its two elastic garters, still attached from the night before. And finally my stockings—two blue-black snakes, ribbed inside and out, lying coiled at my feet before they crept up over my legs.

I had my own particular feelings toward each article of clothing. I liked my shirt. It was manly, and in its snowy whiteness aesthetically appealing. It also smelled nice, especially after being freshly laundered. By contrast, the garter-belt was repugnant. It was the most hateful of all my garments. Everybody knows that garter-belts are only meant for little girls, or what is worse, baby-boys. Besides, my garter-belt fastened in the back—and is there anything more humiliating than a piece of clothing one can't put on or take off by oneself? I also hated my stockings. My objection to these lay in their length. They were drawn up over the knees, and, of course, any regular boy wears socks. Stockings require garters to keep them from falling, and something told me they were intended solely for females and similar weaklings. Did one ever hear of an Injun with garters?

Johanne now lifted me over the high side of my crib and set me down on the floor. Stooping, she held my pants for me to step into by myself.

"Your nose is red," I said.

It annoyed me that it was red. It especially annoyed me now because I noticed that her nostrils were wet. And, being a merciless aesthete, I did not conceal my disgust.

Johanne sniffed.

"Well, I've been crying," she admitted.

"Then Father must have been scolding you!"

I did not say *Mother*. I knew that Mother was in bed and much too tired to scold anyone.

"Your father has other things to think about than scolding," Johanne said.

"Why have you been crying then?" I asked.

Johanne lifted me up on a chair—the one on which my clothes had been lying—knelt in front of me, and worked my foot into a boot.

"You will learn why later, Soren," she said.

Although the voice was motherly and sympathetic, there was something disconcerting about it, something dark, foreboding.

She finished buttoning my boots with her fingers. When buttonholes in boots have not been much stretched, this is a long and difficult process, but the buttonhook was in the Master's bed-room and Johanne would not think of going in there under any circumstances.

"Are they asleep?" I asked her.

"Yes, they are asleep," she said.

But her reply sounded so strange as if she was thinking of something distressing. The shirt-front was a blue, stiff piece of cloth which snapped at the neck. I had a friendly attitude toward the shirt-front. I was old enough to know that an undershirt is something immodest, something to be seen only by parents and nursemaids.

Then darkness again. It was my blouse with the sailor collar which was being dropped down over my head. The blouse was to my liking, too. It was properly masculine.

Now the comb descended on my head. I immediately began shaking my head from side to side. A comb is something grown-ups have invented with which to plague children. Still—in spite of my wrigglings—Johanne succeeded in making a parting, that neat parting so essential to a little gentleman.

Then she tiptoed away to fetch my overcoat.

I made good use of the time I was left alone. A collection of possessions were slipped under the elastic of my blouse. Something told me that Johanne would object if she saw the things—but what is a boy without his treasures in his blouse and pockets? There was a tiny damaged mechanical toy which I could not live without. There was a little puzzle—a mouse which had to be shaken into a mouse-trap. There were a parrot's feather taken from a duster, a stamp rescued from Father's wastebasket, a whistle in the shape of a locomotive (it was made of *pure* gold) and, most thrilling of all, a little paper book with traceable pictures. The remnant of a pink peppermint stick went the way of the other things. Johanne returned before I had time to collect any more.

Johanne had put on her coat and hat. The coat was mother's old fur coat, and the hat was one from which mother had removed the trimming and given Johanne because the shape was out-of-date.

More clothes for me, and still more. There was a hybrid garment—the upper part pants, the lower stockings. They might have been all right if they could have opened in front instead of having an elastic waist-band. After them came mittens, mittens with fingers. These were especially horrid. I always had the sensation that an attempt was being made to break my fingers when they were being forced into the fingers of the mittens. As a rule two were crowded into the place for one, so we had to begin all over again. After the mittens, came my coat. Johanne ordered me, "Hold your arm still," whereupon I beat my way into my winter top-coat —the thick dark winter coat with its fur collar and braid trimming. Then at last came my hat. It came dangling down from above, coming to rest on the back of my head like a halo. The stiff hat-band pressed a little, still we were friends, my hat and me. It had a little feather on the side, and a little curlicue of felt on the top.

Johanne went to the wall and pressed the switch. It became dark. The light in the bulb hanging from the middle of the ceiling under a green shade disappeared. Now only the blind, with a cross in black silhouette, let in a pale moonlight.

She caught hold of my hand and led me down the corridor in the direction of the kitchen stairs.

"Why are we going this way?" I asked in surprise.

"We are going down the kitchen way so as not to wake up Father," she explained.

Johanne began going down the steep, unlighted stairway. She went backwards, with one hand on the rail, and the other clutching my arm so that I should not fall.

I began to be afraid. In the daytime I liked the back stairway. With the maids hurrying up and down, it was more entertaining than the broad, elegant front stairway. But now, in the pale moonlight and on the creaking steps, it was almost too exciting.

"I want to go back," I said, on the point of tears.

Johanne appealed to my sympathy.

"Just imagine how disappointed Farmor would be," she said. "And you wouldn't want to disappoint her, would you?"

I did not answer—not because the argument worked. I was indifferent with respect to Farmor's disappointment, but I lacked words. I chose another way out: I began to cry.

Johanne stopped and picked me up in one arm, and continued steadily descending the stairs backwards, the other hand on the bannister.

Not for a moment did it occur to me to wonder. Never before had I been awakened in the middle of the night— except when I had fallen asleep in a tram—nor had I ever visited my father's mother at this time of the night. But when grown-ups do something, even if it disagreeable, it rarely stirs a child's wonder. It is something happening just because it's got to happen, like the rain and wind and snow.

At last we were at the bottom of the stairs. The outside door closed silently behind us—silently because of a small buffer.

It had snowed very lightly. The flagstones of the court were hidden under a kind of soft, blue-white down. There was bright starlight now and scattered, drifting clouds, and a moon was floating up there in the sky like a silver boat.

I stopped crying. The court-yard was lighted up and friendly, just as I remembered it in the daytime. Besides, the crunching of snow makes a nice and harmless sound— not frightening like the creaking of stairs.

We went through the porte-cochère, past the entrance stairs. I vaguely perceived the bronze lady holding the light-globe, on the first landing.

A cab was waiting. The coachman stood by the side of it beating himself to keep warm, now with the right arm, now with the left.

When the gate was opened he discontinued this exercise and doffed his cap politely. But as we came closer he put it on again.

"That isn't your child?" he asked, looking Johanne suspiciously up and down.

"What business is it of yours?" Johanne said shortly.

"One has to be on the look-out," he retorted goodnaturedly. "There are so many people running off, you know, with the children of the rich."

Of course he was joking, but Johanne bridled with rage. Her only reply was Farmor's address.

The coachman applied himself to removing the covers from his old nag. Johanne had to open the door herself. When I drove out with Father and Mother, the door was always opened and closed for us.

We crawled into the covered two-wheeler. It was dark in there and smelled musty—both of man and horse. Johanne took the rugs lying on the seat facing us. One of them she wrapped around my legs and the other right up to my chin. None was left for herself.

Now I felt the coachman climbing up on to his seat—the coach squeaked and tipped heavily to the side. Then I heard a couple of cracks of the whip—and the cab started to move.

I enjoyed driving—especially on asphalt. On cobblestones, the carriage rumbled and rocked so that one got all shaken

up and down, and one's ears ached. Every time we drove
on cobblestones I wished we would get back to a piece of
asphalt.

The noise of the horse's hoofs caught my attention. It
sounded as if drops of rain plumped into a cask of water,
only it was much louder and in a different tempo. I both
liked and disliked the sound of it. It was at one and the
same time dismal, exciting, festive, and a little sad. I listened
so long the monotonous rhythm of it that I began to get
sleepy.

Johanne gave me a worried look.

"You mustn't go to sleep," she said. "We shall be there
in a few minutes."

"Don't you think Farmor may be asleep?" I asked.

Johanne shook her head.

"She knows we are coming."

"How does Farmor know?"

I knew that she did not have a telephone as we did. She
was fearful of that kind of modern apparatus. Hadn't she
read in the newspaper of somebody who'd died of an electric
shock?

"Your father sent a messenger—with a letter."

Whereupon I stopped asking questions. Instead I applied
myself to watching the gas-lamps which came and went. It
was so late that every other one had been put out. I dimly
saw the light long before we came to a street-lamp. Little
by little the light grew brighter until one was abreast of
the whitish-greenish-bluish Welsbach burner, when the whole
cab was lit up. Then the light dimmed again—in the same
slow way that it had grown bright—until it became almost
dark inside the cab, but then in an instant it began to light
up again, this time from the opposite window.

I began to think about the fun a lamp-lighter had. Yes, a
lamp-lighter—that's what I most wanted to be when I grew
up! Imagine, to be allowed to go from lamp-post to lamp-
post, lightening them by means of a long stick! Imagine,
being able to make light and darkness whenever one wanted!

The carriage began to slow up, and, all of a sudden, we heard the coachman's "Whoa! Whoa!"

We stopped and stepped out on to the side-walk's thin layer of snow.

"How much is it?" Johanne asked.

The coachman turned down the little flag over the meter and put his face close to the glass.

"Exactly eighty ore, little lady."

"That is a lot," remarked Johanne—in a suspicious voice.

"That's the night-rate," he shrugged.

Johanne had fished up one krone from her worn black purse and the coachman at the same time opened up a large leather pouch which looked like nothing so much as Mother's sewing bag. The pouch was filled to the brim with money. I had never seen so much money at a time, not even when my savings-box was opened. He must have been a very rich man, that coachman!

"You can give me ten ore change," said Johanne.

"Many thanks," said the coachman, a shade more civil than before.

Johanne fumbled in her coat pocket for the key, unlocked the street-door and we slipped into Farmor's house.

Just inside the door there was something they called a "vestibule", a huge hall, at least as large as the inner of a church. The ceiling was round like a barrel. There were colored pictures on the wall, and the floor was of black and white squares of marble. I liked the pictures, especially one of dancing ladies. Their legs were bare and they held a strange instrument in their hands, something my Mother called a *tambourine*. But the most exciting thing about it was a blue mountain in the background. Fire and smoke came out of the top but the ladies did not seem the least bit frightened. I always found it hard to get through the vestibule, partly because I wanted to look at the pictures, partly because it was ordained—according to my own private code—that I step only on the black flagstones.

At the other end was a pair of glass doors which could

swing in and out. Here at the swinging doors it was especially hard not to step on the white squares. First one had to step backwards to open the door, then one had to hurry through and forward so that the door should not knock one down. All this maneuvering was terribly difficult. Still I took care, even now, to obey the unwritten law. It delayed me a bit, naturally, so much so that Johanne burst out suddenly,

"What in the world is the matter with you, Soren? Hurry up now."

I realized, then, that in spite of all her insight, Johanne ignored the important code of behavior: never to step on white.

The main stairway was just inside the glass doors. There was a dark cave under the stairs the ceiling of which was the stairway itself. I loved this cave. It wasn't really a cave, but a hollow space that changed me into an Injun every time I ran in there. Once someone had used it as a privy. On that occasion I flew upstairs and burst out without any preliminaries,

"Farmor, someone has made gaga in the cave."

Farmor was furious. It was easy to see that she was, though she tried to hide it under an air of long-suffering. Her anger had a peculiar effect upon me. Every time after that when I visited her I always ran into the cave to see what I could see. If I found anything there—and it happened sometimes that I did—I flew and rang her bell and shouted triumphantly,

"Farmor, there is a dirty mess down in the cave."

I have to confess I even shouted it to her sometimes when it wasn't true.

We soon arrived at Farmor's door. As owner of the property, she lived on the most desirable floor, that is, the second; and in the best apartment, that is, the corner one.

I hurried to get there first so that I could press my finger on the little bell-button, but I pressed it so long that Johanne protested,

"Now, now, Soren. You mustn't ring any longer."

A long time passed—I figured ten thousand years. Finally we heard the familiar dragging footsteps. And a moment later we heard Farmor's piping voice,

"Who is it?"

"It's me," I shouted.

And Johanne said in a hushed voice,

"It's the young master and Johanne."

The key on the inside began to turn. I knew it would be a long process—another ten thousand years, at least. Farmor's door had, to wit: a yale-lock, two ordinary locks, a burglar-chain, and an iron hoop. The hoop went around the door-handle, and its two ends fitted into an iron key-hole. The idea was to prevent burglars from turning the key from the outside. She had protected herself in other ways too. There were wooden shutters on the inside of the glass-door, and I knew that she kept a little pistol in the console-table drawer.

Finally the door opened a crack and Farmor peeked out with one eye.

"Is it you, Soren?" she piped, and when I said Yes, she continued,

"Just a minute now and you can come in."

Then the door was closed again—it was a necessary procedure in order to release the burglar-chain. Farmor was accustomed always to peek out before she removed the burglar-chain. She even did this when Mother and I came for our Sunday visits. For who knows!—it might be thieves or murderers imitating Mother's and my voices!

At last the door was opened a crack and Johanne and I squeezed into the hall. I received a damp kiss on the cheek, and then the locking-up began, just as thorough a process as the unlocking had been.

So as to avoid lighting the gas in the entry, Farmor had brought with her a little oil-lamp. It was a kitchen lamp with a green glass base, and a round, shiny brass reflector behind the chimney glass. The lamp was standing on the floor, and though Farmor was unusually small, she cast a gigantic shadow not only on the wall but way up on the ceiling. It seemed strange to me that the shadow was hunch-backed.

While Farmor locked up, Johanne peeled off my outer garments. As usual we had the greatest trouble with the leggings. I had to stand now on one foot, now on the other, with my arms around Johanne's neck while she tugged with all her might, now at the one leg, now at the other.

The hall was short and narrow, yet it had four doors: one to the dining-room, one to a little den, one to the sitting-room, and the fourth, the wide door to the main stair-way. On the other hand, the architect had been niggardly with sources of light. There were just the windows in the entry-door, thick, milky panes of glass, and these Farmor invariably kept covered with heavy wooden shutters. Thus the hall was always enshrouded in darkness, unless lighted by gas or oil-lamp.

On the two longest walls of the hall were pegs. On one of the pegs, just opposite the entrance, hung a man's high hat, and beneath it, a man's overcoat with a velvet collar. Both hat and coat were the remains of my Grandfather's wardrobe. They had been arranged so adroitly that they caught the eye when the entry-door was opened. Farmor had the idea that beggars, thieves and murderers would be restrained from violence when they saw that there was a man in the house. On the same theory she had also changed the nameplate on the door when Grandfather died. In his day it had always been *S. K. Jensen*, whereas now the name of the occupant read *Soren* Jensen.

"Now you must come in and have some coffee," piped Farmor when she had finally locked all the locks, "coffee and Victoria kringles."

She tried to make her voice sound cheerful and inviting, but its natural pitch—sad, resigned and plaintive—was as clearly perceptible as the cheap metal of a silver-plated spoon.

We moved quickly into the dining-room in single file, I in the lead, then Farmor, and last, Johanne. The gas was lighted in the chandelier and the oval table in the middle of the room was set for coffee, only half covered by the table-cloth—we were just the three of us. Here on the white damask I saw the familiar service: the Royal Copenhagen porcelain with the mussel pattern. Only the sugarbowl and the cake-dish did not belong to the set. The sugarbowl was a half-sphere of blue glass, set in a silver holder. And the cake-platter was of red glass, with a shiny metal cover, with an eagle on the top. I did not like the china service with the bevelled edge and its blue shells. It was too cold, too common, too unromantic for me. On the other hand I adored the cake-platter and the sugarbowl—not just on account of their contents either.

We sat down. Farmor began to pour.

For the first time I observed that her clothing was unusual. She had on a white jacket. The front of it was fastened with cords tied in long loops. Below it a pink flannel petti-coat spread its fulness. And her head was covered with a white cap. The cap had a bow under the chin, and its edges were folded back from her face.

It was the first time I had seen Farmor in night attire, and I did not like her appearance at all. Father wore a long white night-shirt and Mother a long white night-gown, but neither of them wore anything on their heads when they slept. So to me, Farmor's clothing was all wrong.

Farmor had finished pouring, and now put a Victoria kringle on my plate. She herself took none—was it because they cost too much?—and nobody, of course, gave a thought to Johanne, not even Johanne herself. In those days no one would be so out of his mind as to put cake in a servant's mouth!

The Victoria kringle was something very special. It was bought from a baker who lived several hours away, in the opposite end of town. He was the only baker who made the *real* Victoria kringles. Indeed, rumour had it that he had gotten the recipe from Queen Victoria's own master-cook himself. At Farmor's kringles were only served to very special guests. Thus, fortunately, there were frequently some left over, and these Farmor kept under lock and key until there were prominent guests again. I had often heard my father and mother make fun of her kringles on our way home. They said they were both rancid and mouldy. Once my father said, laughing,

"I'm sure they were left over from Queen Victoria's wedding."

But all their criticism failed to alter my own judgment concerning them. I always fell upon my kringle with delight and relish.

The two women sat as silent and immobile as mice, enjoying the pieces of cake vanishing into my mouth. I had a feeling that, thus, their enjoyment in these pieces was greater than if they had put them into their own mouths.

Suddenly Farmor broke the silence.

"Does he know yet?" she asked in a hushed voice.

Johanne shook her head.

"I couldn't bear to tell him yet," she said unhappily. And I saw her eyes fill with tears.

Farmor pondered this. Then she observed with a slight nod,

"Perhaps it would be best if he slept first."

I had a presentiment that they were talking about me, but I wasn't clear what it was they were referring to. As usual I was glad to be the centre of interest, but at the same time, I felt as if something dark and menacing were lying in wait for me.

"When do I get my ten ore?" I asked outright. Perhaps there was an association of ideas here, some inarticulate thought-connection between what I anticipated with joy and what I feared.

"It isn't Sunday today," Farmor answered, trying to be coy.

"Oh, but Johanne said if I came here I would get my Sunday ten ore."

Johanne interrupted here with an explanation. I had cried so heartbreakingly when she had wakened me, that in order to comfort me she had gone as far as to say that about the Sunday's ten ore. But she would gladly give it to me herself if—

Farmor shook her head and smiled. Then she said playfully,

"Well, if Johanne told him that, then there is nothing to do but give it to him."

She rose and with a heavy step glided into the bed-room.

Sunday's ten ore was an old tradition. And at bottom a kind of bribery. If I would go and see Farmor, I would get ten ore; if I didn't go to see her, I didn't get it. Perhaps Farmor had an inkling that I did not care about her, and that she had no other means than bribery to awaken my softer feelings. But for ten ore I could go to the baker's and buy two whipped-cream cakes, and get myself a huge bag of sweets. I could even get a whole box of colored crayons; or, what was still better, a note-book with a glazed paper cover, a black crayon, ending in a piece of rubber, and a halfsheet of scraps. No, indeed, I did not neglect my Sunday visits.

Farmor came back from the bedroom with another bunch of keys, different from the one for the entry-door, and glided over to the den.

I knew where she was going. She was going to her moneybox which was in her desk, in the lowest drawer on the righthand side. That money-box was her holy of holies. I had often, of course, begged to have it to play with, but the box was, together with her keys, the little pistol in the consoledrawer, and a razor which she also kept there, the only things I never succeeded in getting my hands on. However, if I plagued her long enough she would eventually let me play with her glasses, the pin-box, and her collection of cancelled leases.

Sunday's ten ore piece which was always new and shiny, was kept in a little silver cylindrical container. There was a spring in the cylinder which pressed the money up and out. When a ten ore piece was shot out, another immediately took its place. I liked to imagine that the silver tube was a magic apparatus. I was *almost* convinced that it never could be emptied—that a new coin would always come forth no matter how many were taken out.

Farmor returned. She held the little cylinder out to me. I was to be permitted to press the spring myself!

I grew warm with happiness, but my joy was not nearly so much because of the money as because of the magic I might work.

I pressed out my ten ore. Then I bowed from my chair and murmured my thanks—just as mother had taught me.

"Well, well," murmured Farmor, and stroked my cheek with her cold, crooked forefinger. "The little man seems mighty fond of money."

I nodded assent gravely. The nod was to a large extent hypocritical. I reckoned that it meant a plus for my character if I showed her that I liked money. Maybe I would get more of it from her by seeming to like it.

Johanne nodded pensively.

"Some are born to riches," she said, "and some to poverty—and no one knows which is better."

Farmor tried to look severe—severe and haughty. It was hard for her to achieve such an expression—to such lengths had she cultivated her mask of melancholy and humility. However, she succeeded in saying with some asperity,

"One must not let the child hear such things, Johanne. Of course it is better to be rich than poor."

Until now Johanne had been treated as a kind of guest. This remark reduced her in rank to what she was, a *servant*.

"It was just something I remembered," she murmured apologetically. "I had an aunt once who was always saying things like that."

"She couldn't have been in her right mind, that aunt," answered Farmor with conviction.

"Well, no—she *was* a little strange-like," Johanne obligingly agreed. Then she added,

"One wouldn't want things any different. If one was rich one wouldn't be a nurse-maid, and then one wouldn't ever have had Soren, and then what would one have done, Mrs. Jensen?"

"No-o," said Farmor thoughtfully. It was evident that she understood Johanne's point of view.

Johanne proceeded, encouraged by Farmor's response,

"I don't know what in the world I'd do if I ever got a lot of money ... Well, yes, I do though—I'd buy little Soren a clockwork train."

I understood at once what Johanne was thinking about. Just before Christmas we had seen a wonderful train in *The Children's Bazaar*—a train which ran under its own power through tunnels, over mountains and past stations, switches and signals. I had vanted it passionately—but I did not get it. Still I did not suffer from undue disappointment—there had been so many other gifts that Christmas that I forgot all about it.

Farmor tried again to look severe.

"If Soren is to have a train, my son is the proper person to give it to him."

I realized that poor Johanne had once again said the wrong thing. I did not understand why it was wrong, for what would't I have given to own such a train!

Their coffee cups were by now empty and Farmor and Johanne sat and mumbled something about its being bedtime, especially for at little man like Soren.

"Am I going home now?" I asked.

The two women looked at each other and were silent for a moment. Then Farmor said plaintively,

"Not tonight ... Tonight little Soren will sleep at my house."

"No, I'm going with Johanne," I burst forth with an energy born of fright.

"Well, Johanne is going to stay here too," answered Farmor. "You shall sleep on the box-couch and Johanne on the sofa."

My troubles were over. If Johanne was with me I was willing to sleep anywhere. Not even a gypsy's hut, which is entirely without windows, could have frightened me.

Farmor got up, and in her slow, noiseless fashion took from the buffet a stick lying behind the tea-urn—a long stick with a hook on one end. I was very familiar with it. It was what she used both to light and to extinguish the gas. I was sometimes permitted to play with it on my Sunday visits. It was ideal for stabbing to death one's enemies.

Johanne fetched some blankets which were lying on the sofa, brought them over to the box-couch and began to make up my bed. Her quick skilful hands wrestled with the pillows and the blankets, opened the folded sheets, smoothed them out, tucked them under.

Farmor had lighted the candle in a little brass candlestick which usually stood on her night-table. Then she lifted the gas-extinguisher in her trembling hand, fitted the hook into the ring which hung below the fixture, and began to pull it slowly and carefully. The gas flickered a couple of seconds, there was a little pop—and then the light was gone. It immediately became quite dark all around us, but thanks to the little blue-yellow candle-flame which threw some light between the red walls, I gradually began to make out most of the furniture.

Farmor, who heard Johanne stirring about, asked anxiously, "What are you doing, Johanne."

"I am getting a couple of chairs to put against his bed, Mrs. Jensen; so that he won't fall out."

Farmor was fumbling her way towards me. Her cold hand brushed against my face. Then she pressed a kiss on my forehead, almost without having to stoop.

"God's angels watch over you," she whispered. She spoke

with the same voice that some of the old fairies in my glossy pictures might have used, but the words sounded somehow wrong coming from her lips. I couldn't bear it. If Johanne had said the same things I shouldn't have been surprised, nor have felt any embarrassment. My embarrassment now probably sprang from lack of trust in Farmor's having any connection with God's angels.

"Goodnight," said Farmor to Johanne. The tone was not unfriendly, but not nearly as good-fairy-like as her words to me had been. And she added, almost tearfully,

"Remember to put it out—candles are expensive."

Then she was gone, seeming to vanish right through the door without opening it.

Johanne began pulling my clothes off. It was a process which took time because every garment had to be folded neatly and artistically before being placed on a chair beside my bed.

I examined the box-couch. I liked it. Yes, it was actually more appealing to me than my own bed at home. The couch reached right down to the floor, whereas my bed stood on six thin iron legs and there was a lot of space between its legs, a thing which was wrong—wrong because every night all kinds of strange animals could crawl under the bed— spiders, centipedes, lady-bugs, frogs, earwigs, cockroaches, caterpillers, and others even stranger. And they were not the small creatures which are visible by day either. No, they were the size of little puppies, hens and parrots. If they had only been content just to crawl back and forth down there—though that could be bad enough—but some-times they tried to climb up the wall beside me, or to push their long sharp claws up through the mattress. Johanne often wondered why I screamed for her at night. Of course, I could have told her, but as soon as she lit the light, the animals vanished. And if I had told her, she would only have said there were no animals, that little Soren had been dreaming, and all that sort of thing.

Suddenly a frightful thought popped into my head.

"What is inside there?"

"In there ... ?"

"Yes—in there."

"In the couch?"

"Yes," I nodded.

"There are sheets and pillows and—"

"Are there any animals?"

"Animals? What in the world do you mean—*animals!*"

"Animals."

"What an idea. Why should there be animals?"

I used my most wheedling voice.

"Johanne, please—can't you lock them up?"

For a long time Johanne refused to do anything. She was afraid to disturb the bed linen, but my persuasive powers were great where Johanne was concerned, and she finally folded back the bed-spread, ran her hands over the blankets and even lifted off the sheets.

I brought the candle-stick over to the couch. "Watch out, child, you'll set the place afire!" she exclaimed in alarm.

The box below was full of sheets, bed-spreads, and woolen blankets. They all lay in the most perfect order and smelled deliciously of fresh laundering. And there were no animals there—not a single one.

"There are no animals," I said.

"Of course not," said Johanne, full of wonderment, and closed the box.

We resumed the undressing.

I had to crawl into bed in my day-time shirt. Johanne had not brought any of my night clothes along. "But I shall fetch it tomorrow," she said consolingly.

"Shall I say my prayers?" I asked.

Johanne was obviously confronted with a difficult problem. I had already said my prayers once that night. I assume she reasoned that one can't perform a good deed too often, for she said,

"Yes, do just that, little Soren."

I sat up, my back very straight, and put the palms of my

hands together, just as Mother had taught me. Then I began:

> "Now my eyes are closing tight.
> Oh, Father, in the sky so high
> Guard my home with all Thy might;
> Put sin, and grief, and wrong to flight."

The words "to flight" took me suddenly far away—back to Father and Mother, especially to Mother. There was something inside me ready to fly home; only that part of me which I could see and touch was sitting here in a strange bed in a strange house. But even that tangible part of me yearned homeward. It was as if suddenly something inside me split asunder into countless pieces of longing. And a cry, wild and despairing, burst from me,

"I won't stay here. I'm going home to Mother."

Johanne who was sitting on the edge of the bed, threw her arms around me. She pressed me so hard against her that my nose fitted into the hollow between her breasts.

"Soren, little man," she whispered—and I had never heard her voice so sad—"Little Soren, *your mother is dead.*"

Mother dead!—then she was up which that old man in Heaven. I knew there was something good about being up there. Still I much preferred having my mother down here on earth with me. Heaven is so high up—so terribly high—

It made me mad. Mad with Mother for going away from me. Mad just as I used to get mad when Father and Mother left me to go out of an evening. But what hurt me most at that moment was that Johanne held me so tight I couldn't breathe.

Suddenly I became aware of something wet on the back of my neck, just below my hair. Drops of water were oozing right down my back, right under my shirt. I knew at once what it was: Johanne was crying.

And whenever Johanne cried, I cried. I always did. But just why we sat there and cried and cried and cried—that question I could not have answered.

All this happened when I was five-and-a-half.

2

Farmor's house was situated in one of the new quarters which sprang up in the 70's when the city's old ramparts were demolished. It was a pleasant, urban house, provided with all the modern comforts. True, it had gas instead of electric light—which we had at home—but electric light had not yet proved itself: it was controversial and dangerous to life. It was only found in places where people thoughtlessly ran after the latest thing. Nor were there flush toilets —but their installation had only been introduced in Denmark seven or eight years earlier. Still there were gas and running water, and two elegant main stairways; and the two streets at the intersection of which the house stood, were broad, open boulewards, one of which was even of asphalt.

The house was really three houses built together. One looked out on a beautiful park—one of the parks the city had laid out to replace the old ramparts which had been torn down. The second house faced a wide street. A tramway ran in front of it. Directly across the street, a newly built church towered, and a little beyond the church a spacious hospital could be glimpsed from the windows. Each house had its own entrance and stairway. The third house was in the rear of the other two. It began at house number two, and paralleled number one. To enter it one had to go through the vestibule and glass doors of house number two, then out through another door at the foot of its main stairway, and across the court-yard. It was always called the "garden house", with no other authority than Farmor's and God's, for there wasn't a spear of green near it except the moss which grew between the cobblestones.

The three houses had been carefully classified: number one was the finest. It was the one with the corner windows. Still it was not so fine that the occupants of number one and number two could not associate; number three on the other hand ranked far below the others. The idea that one could have anything to do with number three's tenants never occurred to those of number one and number two. I doubt if there was even a bowing acquaintance between those in the front houses and those in the rear.

There was a basement-shop in number one—a little green-grocery—whose proprietor was also the houses' caretaker. As far back as I can remember there was only one and the same man who held that position, Lillelund, and he was no taller than a ten-year-old. To improve God's handiwork he had grown a full beard, a regular Russian beard which reached way below his belt. Lillelund's cheeks were always ruddy, somewhat the color of roast-beef.

Here at number one, up on the second-floor, was where the houses' owner lived.

But now I open the door and walk into the apartment— the home of my father's mother.

As I cross the threshold I experience a strangely bitter-sweet emotion. It is sweet, I think, to summon up the memory of one's childhood. And at the same time it is bitter, because such a vision is but a figment of the mind, not a reality. O Time, mysterious Time, thou riddle of riddles, thou who stealest our joy and releasest us from suffering! What hast thou done with my Farmor's rooms, my childhood, the people I knew and loved? Do they exist anywhere but in my imagination—or are they but a strip of film stored away in my brain?

But be silent, my heart. Control your emotion and let us proceed.

The apartment is composed of four rooms—all in a row; all with windows looking out on the street. Besides these there are a vestibule, a corridor, a den, a kitchen and a maid's room.

Farthest in, is the bedroom, a little room with a bay-window.

As I enter, I experience a little discomfort—my sense of

smell has caught a sour odor, such as meets one so often in old people's sleeping-rooms.

Here everything is as it should be: a bed, a wardrobe, a washstand, a night-table and a medicine chest. All the wood-work is painted brown to resemble mahogany.

The bed is short and broad and it bulges with heavy down comforters which in the day-time are hidden under a white, crocheted bed-spread. The head-board is unusually high. Farmor does not sleep lying down but sitting up. A bed-staff leans against the wall. At night when she gets into bed, she lays it lengthwise on the outer edge of the bed. She has heard of people who while dreaming have fallen out of bed and broken their necks and legs. Fastened to the two knobs at the foot of the bed is a white, crocheted harness. By holding on to the "reins" she can pull herself into the bed at night and ease herself out in the morning.

The night-table stands next to the bed, a little in front of the head-board. On its marble top, in plain view, are: a low candlestick; a milky-white carafe with an upturned glass over its neck; a table-clock; a couple of medicine bottles and pill-boxes; an expectoration cup, and a Bible. I am doubtful if Farmor ever read the Bible. At any rate I never saw her do so. On the other hand she certainly couldn't have dispensed with the round white vessel with a handle enthroned in the little table's interior, standing on a mat of white paper with a lace-like edge.

The wash-stand is topped with an icy-cold marble slab, and shelves rise from the back of it. The wash-bowl and jug lord it over the stand, bulging out as if they were pregnant. False hair is hidden in the drawer underneath as are a razor and a set of extra teeth. Oh yes, little Soren has peeked!

The big medicine-chest also holds secrets. But for me they are *not* secrets. With a child's all-embracing curiosity, I rummaged through it whenever Farmor went to town. Here are to be found remedies for coughs, bronchitis, asthma, rheumatism, insomnia, nerves—all authentic medicines pre-

scribed by her nice old family doctor. There are also im-
portants things here like corn-plasters, adhesive tape, linen
bandages, pieces of gutta-percha, cottonwool, an ear syringe,
a medicine-dropper and an eye-cup. And here, too, are a
bottle of Brama's Elixir of Life, a box of Keating's throat
lozenges and another of Dr. Williams's pink pills for curing
arthritis, rheumatism and all kinds of stomach ailments.
Also in one of the drawers are hidden a copy of St. Cyprian,
an amber cross, and a little knob which looks like the finger-
joint of a child.

My good Farmor, who was, as a rule, so niggardly with
everything, was not so where medicines were concerned.

I proceed into the dining-room which is the largest of all
the rooms. The dining-room has two bay-windows, and four
doors, two of which are folding ones.

In the center of the room the oval table stands. It is the
kind of table that can be extended for guests. At full length
it reaches from the windows to the stove. When she has
guests Farmor always has the stove heated so high that the
door in front of the grill goes red with heat. The result is
that guests who sit near the stove gasp as if in hell while
those sitting at the other end of the room shiver with cold
thanks to the draughts from the den and the sitting-room.

The cylindrical iron stove is set in a niche. Between the
stove and the wall behind it, there is a narrow, rounded
space of floor—specially designed as a sleeping spot for
Farmor's dog-of-the-hour.

Along the walls are a red box-couch; a buffet; a sofa,
upholstered in the same material as the box-couch; and, over
on the other side, Farmor's sewing-table and wicker chair
and an armchair which stands between the two vindows.
The wood-work is painted to resemble oak; the walls are
dark-red—Pompeian-red. The most elegant object on the
buffet is a copper tea-urn.

Farmor sits as comfortable as ever in the wicker chair.
Every time I evoke her in my imagination I see her sitting
there with her expectoration cup and the open sewing-basket

before her; with a piece of knitting or crocheting in her hands; with the canary's cage in the window and the reflecting street-mirror just outside.

The dining-room ... A misnomer. Of course we eat in the dining-room, but a thousand other activities take place also. Farmor sews here, she reads her newspaper here, she takes her afternoon nap here, and here also she receives visitors. To me the dining-room is play-room and sleeping-room. Here Johanne mends my clothes. In here the maid irons and folds the sheets and polishes the silver and the copper. In reality it is the one room in which we live during the winter; the only room which is heated—unless, of course, Farmor gives a large party. Parlor or sitting-room would have been a better name for it.

Next to the dining-room is a little cabinet or den which has only one window. Nevertheless it has three doors, of which two are double: the first is a folding-door into the dining-room, the one by which I have just entered; the second leads into the sitting-room; and the third, a little single door, connects with the hall.

This den is used practically only when Farmor collects her tenant's rent. Then she sits at a little writing-desk in it, with her cashbox in front of her, receives their money, gives change, and hands out receipts.

On such days the folding-doors into the dining-room are left wide open, partly in order to allow the heat from the dining-room to enter and partly so that the maid can sit in the dining-room and be on guard. One can never be sure but that one of the tenants might be tempted by the sight of so much money!

How often I have played there on the floor with counters from the games-chest. It occurs to me now that I was especially invited to do so on such occasions. Perhaps Farmor thought that any tenant with murderous intentions would think twice about it if a small boy was on the premises.

On the days on which Farmor collected her money her voice was always particularly pitiful and melancholy.

If a friendly tenant asked,

"And how goes it with Mrs. Jensen?" her answer was likely to be,

"Not good. I cannot sleep at nights."

Or,

"There's something wrong with my heart. I am not long for this world."

If one of the apartments became vacant she would explain with tears in her eyes that her property was in the red. If anyone mentioned repairs, she could produce plain figures to show that taxes and upkeep were in excess of rent.

She would also discover pretexts for complaining about payments which were still due; or about money she owed and her not knowing where to lay hands on any. She made it all sound very plausible and touching. I was almost grown up before I learned that she raked in far more money on such occasions than she ever had to pay out.

Why then all that plaintiveness and whining? Undoubtedly it was a means of self-protection. By claiming to be sickly and in money difficulties, by appealing to people's sympathy, she aimed first to be spared requests for repairs, and second, to avoid arousing envy. Envy is a dangerous thing. You never know what an envious person may do!

The den has another function as well. When Farmor has company, the card-table is set up in there—the lords of creation can only be entertained with whist or l'hombre.

The room bears the imprint of its use. It has but little furniture: the desk and two chairs, one for Farmor and one for the tenant; a pedestal with a palm; a mahogany folding card-table which is pushed up against the wall. And there is also a corner what-not with Thorvaldsen's Christ on the top-most shelf, and a collection of porcelain dogs on the other shelves. I have a suspicion that Christ also was put there to help protect Farmor.

On the half-opened card-table is a carved wooden box, a games-chest. It is flanked by two brass candelabra.

I do not need to open the chest for like a magician I can

see right through the dark, carved, pine-wood, and what I see is this: in the middle section, four decks of cards, together with a soiled incomplete loose pack. Two sets are for whist, two for l'hombre. All are of cheapest kind. The incomplete pack is for the possible demands of Mrs. Jensen's grandson.

I look further: there are four small wooden boxes, containing chips to be used with the cards. The chips are made of bone and are of four colors, white, red, yellow and green. Among them are some imitation gold pieces. On one side of these is an engraving representing either Queen Victoria as a young girl or else Napoleon III at his zenith. On the reverse side is inscribed, within an oak-leaf wreath, the word: *Spielmarke.*

One other object is in the dining-room, a gilded plaster bust of the actor Zangenberg of the Royal Theater. It stands on top of the stove within a little circular iron grill. Since I am quite sure that neither of my grandparents sought diversion in the theater, it is a mystery to me how Mr. Zangenberg ever strayed into this room.

There is still something else I must stop to look at before I leave the room. It is one of the door-posts at the entrance to the dining-room. There are scratchings of horizontal lines on it, bearing dates and ages. The lowest is about eighty centimeters from the floor and was inscribed there by Grandfather on my second birthday. The uppermost figure I had to put there myself on my twenty-first birthday. Farmor couldn't reach that high.

The last room is the living room. The shape of this is somewhat irregular. The floor is a square but two opposite corners have been cut across diagonally. There are three windows and two doors. One window looks out over the park, another is in one of the two obtuse corners and has a view of the church and the hospital, while the third looks down the asphalted avenue and the tramway. The doors are, one a folding-door into the den, the other a single door which is in the other, obtuse, corner of the room diagonally across from the window, and opens into the hall. The panels in both doors are painted with representations of violins, flowing bowknots and bunches of field-flowers.

The round walnut table fills a large part of the room. Farmor is very proud of the table-top which is inlaid with many different kinds of wood in various designs. Unfortunately one sees hardly anything of her source of pride because it only comes to view during the semi-annual house-cleaning. Every day and on company-days it is hidden, covered by a lace doily, a couple of photograph-albums, a receptacle for visiting-cards, four or five glass and china bowls, and twenty to thirty framed photographs.

The four legs of the table—greyhound thin but with feet like badgers'—are bound together, a little above the floor, by two cross-beams. Where the beams cross there is a knob. This knob was a master-piece of the cabinetmaker's art. It is that knob I see the most distinctly today and in greater detail than anything else in the living-room. But that is not to be wondered at—when Farmor entertained, my favorite place was underneath that table.

Six or seven chairs stand about the room, besides a sofa, all in red plush, and with tassels below the arms and seats. The living-room is the only place in the house where the chairs are comfortable, with perhaps the exception of the wicker-chair and the armchair in the dining-room, but here they are, in contrast, luxurious. They are almost enervating, almost suffocating. It is especially true of the two "lady-chairs," in which the seat is especially low and close to the floor, and the back slopes dangerously backward. It was seldom that anyone sat in them, least of all women. There were still many people in those days who thought that a woman of good family and with self-respect should sit so erect that she never touched the chair-back.

But the tassels!

Yes, the tassels! They characterize a whole era of culture. I used to call them "ringers", which was my own private appellation for bells, for they were in a sense a kind of bell.

When one pushed them and then listened carefully, one could really hear them tinkle, ring in different tones—just like sleigh-bells. It was amusing, too, to push a number of them at the same time, so that they all swung, each in its own way; or, what was still more fun, to get the whole set moving with a single push of the finger. If one tassel stopped swinging, one had lost. What it was one had lost, I don't know, but the skill required to set them all going at once was not so slight.

Between the windows there are two tall mirrors, framed in walnut, almost reaching from the floor to the ceiling.. Oh you mirrors! How well I remember you! How often you must have admired me at full length—especially when I had armed myself with the gas-lighting stick for a sword and with a three-cornered paper-hat à la Napoleon, and a handtowel for a sash.

Beneath the mirrors are marble console-tables, and on one of them is an atomizer with an absinthe-green stopper. I know that well, too. Many is the time I pestered to be allowed to press the rubber bulb so as to see the spray shoot out like a vaporous cloud. "Oh, please, Farmor, just this once!" And in Farmor's soul a bitter conflict was fought out between her housekeeping instinct and her understanding that an heir apparent should once in a while be privileged.

A book-case stands against one wall—the one between the living-room and the den. It has glass doors and can be locked—yes, it not only *can* be locked, it *is* locked—*continually* locked. Still there were a couple of times in my student years when I was permitted to borrow the key. There were mostly *Collected Works* there, collections or selections —all in fine bindings and less intended for reading than for display in a book-case. Farmor hardly ever touched a book other than the Bible, the psalmody, almanacs for rural folk, and her book of expired leases, and I find it hard to believe that my grandfather was any more of a reader either. Andersen, Bjørnson, Lie, Hertz, Hauch, Mrs. Gyllembourg, Carl Bernhard, and *Letters from the Underworld,* all give

the appearence of never having been opened. That is not
true, however, of the stack of old school-books piled together at the bottom of the book-case—the bottom which
can't be seen through the glassdoors. They belonged to my
father, head of his class during the years he attended a fine
and learned school in a provincial town: the Cathedral
School. The Latin dictionary, in two thick, dull bindings,
is full of underlinings and notes, and is all dog-eared.

Still another piece of furniture arrests my attention. It is
a foot-stool; but it is no common foot-stool. The surface on
which one's feet rest is angled so that it is a little higher on
one side than on the other, and one's legs rest against the
longer side. What innumerable times I have galloped in
warfare on that foot-stool, clad in silver armor; or streaked
across the prairies in combat with Injuns.

I turn toward the albums on the walnut table. They are
two fat blocks, bound in leather and decorated with gilt
edges and metal clasps. Both volumes are covered with imitation leather, but the style of each differs: the one is
"rococo" and the other "renaissance." The albums are what
is called "*insert* albums". Here are inserted large and small
photographs of long since deceased men and women, re-
spectable, dignified citizens whose names I am unable for
the most part to recall. Indeed many of them do not evoke
the slightest recognition. No wonder: many of them were
laid in their graves before I was laid in my cradle. But
there are two groups there which I can easily identify. The
one is of myself at many different ages; the other is of my
playmates: Farmor's dogs.

There I am, new-born, in my mother's arms, immersed in
a cloud of white. I am there at the age of two in a hand-
embroidered dress, and bow-legged. Here I am at four
years of age, with long golden curls reaching to my shoulders,
and with a doltish expression around the mouth, which makes
me look like Oscar Wilde. I am here at the age of six, in
the clothes in which Johanne dressed me the night my mother
died. Here I am in a sailor suit with long trousers. Here

again in shirt-sleeves and baggy trousers; and in class pictures. I am here in a smock with a broad open collar and an artist's flowing tie; there I am in a Tyrolean outfit; in a fur-coat; in a school uniform with a knapsack on my back; as a young boy just confirmed, in which I look like a young fowl which has just been plucked. And I am here as a student with my white student-cap cocked to one side, wearing a bright expectant look like someone bound for a big banquet. It was generally assumed in our home that the best gift we could give Farmor was a photograph of me. It was probably true.

There are almost as many pictures of dogs as of me. Generally the dogs are either fox-terriers or pug-dogs—but rarely pure-bred. An undiscerning person might think that only two dogs had been photographed, to such a degree do all the pugs resemble one another and all the fox-terriers seem one and the same; but there are at least ten different ones. Farmor's dogs did not live as carefully as she did: some over-ate; some got run over, either by boys on bicycles or wildly galloping horse-trains. How many times did Lillelund come up to Mrs. Jensen's apartment bearing the mortal remains of a dog in his arms! Once I was present at such a scene and saw her tears (they came easily, for her eyes were always watery) and heard her pitiful complaints about the traffic's increasing wildness.

Not only did all the fox-terriers and pug-dogs resemble their predecessors outwardly; they also bore their names. Every pug received into my Farmor's home bore the name Fie and every fox-terrier, the name Vips. As Farmor had pug-dogs and fox-terriers alternately, the names Fie and Vips succeeded each other just as the names in the royal Danish dynasty alternated between Christian and Frederik. In one respect only the dog dynasties differed in order of succession: all the Fies were female.

Fies and Vipses are photographed sitting on a table, their bodies in profile, their faces looking direct at the spectator. Their only ornament is a collar with a padlock, with the exception of one of the Fies, who wears an embroidered coat. I remember that one well. She was accustomed to lie in the niche behind the glowing stove shaking all over with cold— until one morning she shook herself out of existence. The veterinarian diagnosed the cause as fatty degeneration of the heart ...

A visiting-card receptacle lords it over the center of the living-room table. It has a metal stand on which rests a dark green porcelain bowl in the shape of an oversized fig-leaf. I rummage a little in the bowl: it contains the visiting-cards of distinguished guests; some photographs of members of the royal family, with royal autographs; a ball of yarn, with knitting-needles stuck in it; and a spectacle-case containing glasses which Farmor can no longer see through. To tell the truth, Farmor never received any photographs from royal personages herself. They are only some that she had wheedled out of her son, Dr. Viggo Jensen, dentist by appointment to the royal household. But Farmor is reticent on this point. When guests, full of respect and curiosity, rummage in the pile, Farmor suddenly becomes modestly silent. But her grandson, with childish mischieviousness, has now and again burst forth with the truth.

"Living-room" is a still more unreasonable name than "dining-room." The room so-called is actually only used three, four, or five times a year when Farmor has important guests. At other times it is an ice-box into which the house's inmates only enter for cleaning purposes.

Despite its infrequent use, Farmor wouldn't have done without it for anything. It is what lends one position and prestige. It is what distinguishes one from the lower classes, those who have only a dining-room and a bedroom, if they have even that much! Farmor is also proud of her furniture—so proud that she is constantly impressing upon me that I shall have it all when she is dead. Even if my father is living, even if I should have a step-mother, it is to be mine, only mine. She has taken care to have her lawyer put that in her will.

Alas, dear departed Farmor! The one generation ordains, and the next does just exactly as it pleases. When you died, I, like most young people, detested what you found beautiful. Walnut was hideous, tassels unhygienic, and all your knick-nacks ridiculous, clumsy, superfluous. I let the entire contents of your drawing-room which you so handsomely bequeathed to me go, with the rest of your furniture, under the auctioneer's hammer. If it will give you any pleasure wherever you happen to be now—I am a little uncertain as to your address—I almost regret it. Today my rooms could do very well with that round walnut table from the sitting-room, a couple of those tasseled armchairs, the dark-red cake-platter, and the deep-blue sugar-bowl.

I cast a farewell look about the room with its "ringing chairs"—and go back through the den to the dining-room.

Just opposite the door to the dining-room there is a door which opens on a corridor, a little prison-like hole without light of any kind. In spite of its limited space, four doors open on it. One of them—the one I have just come through—is to the dining-room; that on my left leads into a bed-room; the one on the right, to the kitchen; and the one in front of me, to the dwelling's most private room of all.

In spite of its privacy, I will open the door, and strike a match.

Here right in front of me is the room's most important object, the toilet with a cover on it. The wood is painted yellow with streaks of brown—apparently with a view to imitating fir—which it probably really was. As the seat is high and Farmor small, a wooden footstool stands in front of it. Next to it is a wooden box, which looks like a coal-scuttle lying on its side. The likeness is enhanced because the handle of a shovel sticks out of the open end of the container. But if one looks closer, it turns out to be a bucket containing not coal, but sawdust. The idea is that the user of the toilet is supposed to sprinkle saw-dust after his use of the thing. But not too much—saw-dust costs money, a fact which Farmor is accustomed to impress on every new maid.

Two bundles of paper hang on the wall, each on its own metal. One bundle consists of pieces of newspapers; the other of tissue paper, pink wrapping-paper, and bags from the bakery. The first is for the use of the maid; the other for Farmor and her guests. The pieces in both bundles are cut into nice neat squares.

Permit me to close the door quickly. Farmor would have died of mortification if she had read this description; and even my parents would have thought me tactless. A toilet is essential, but of course nothing anyone needs to talk about. Even if one must go there, one must not let it be apparent. One says, for example, that one must go to the kitchen for a glass of water. And if the place has to be mentioned at all, then it can only be paraphrased: "the little room," "the retiring-room," "the place where one can't send a substitute" —or whatever else one can hit upon. Ah yes! In those days the smell of the place frequently came into the other rooms but never its name ...

The kitchen is small and looks out onto the court. It has three doors: one to the corridor, one to the maid's room, and one to the kitchen-stairs. The wall facing the court has three connecting windows. On the same wall as the windows are the kitchen-table, a built-in affair; a cupboard; a sink; and a pump. The kitchen stove protrudes from the opposite wall—a fine range which burns both wood and coal—a stove with an immense number of jingling iron rings, with a water-boiler in the rear, with shiny copper kettles, and an always newly polished brass railing around it.

The pantry is also here—one might think it was a safety-vault, so well locked is it kept! When Farmor wants to get some article of food out of it, it is a very long process. First she goes to the cabinet adjoining the dining-room. There she lifts her skirt, and a red petticoat comes to view. This is also lifted, and still another is seen, matching the first. But in skirt number two there is a pocket in which rests a bunch of keys. With the aid of one of these, she unlocks a drawer in her desk, and from here she takes another key, a key to which is attached a little wooden label. Then she locks up the desk drawer, puts the bunch of keys in her petticoat number two, and trips back to the kitchen. The key with the wooden label is for the pantry. When she has brought out the food, the same procedure ensues, but in reverse order. It is tiresome, but is is necessary. Nobody knows how much a maid would stuff herself with if she had free access to the pantry—to say nothing of little hussies who have soldiers courting and visiting them!

For practical reasons, however, Farmor keeps certain things constantly in the open; for example the sugar-bowl, the tea-caddy, the cake platter, the butter-jar, and the cruet-stand. But these are kept in the dining-room, inside the buffet, on which Farmor keeps a vigilant eye from her wicker-chair in the window.

The maid's room is the smallest of any in the apartment indeed—it can hardly be called a room. There is an iron bed there which lacks a leg; a rusty stove which is never lit; and a wash-stand; a flowered, rust-stained curtain in one corner provides a wardrobe. If the maid brings a wooden chest—and in those years it constituted her trunk—the bed and chest would have to stand so close together that one had to crawl on to the bed to get past. There is no chair either in the maid's room or in the kitchen. And indeed why should there be! Maids are paid wages to work for you, not to sit around and be lazy! To make the dreariness complete, the wallpaper in the room is here and there in tatters. In some places large pieces have come loose from the wall. If one touches the places where the paper has come away there is a rustling sound behind the plaster.

The maid's room reflects lots of servants in my Farmor's home. A maid-of-all-work was usually paid at that time sixteen to eighteen kroner—in some places as much as twenty kroner. Farmor, however, never went higher than ten or twelve. As a consequence she got inexperienced girls or in any case very very young ones. Sometimes her girls were not yet confirmed. But maybe Farmor preferred them that way. Young girls are easier to order about than older ones.

Farmor's maids never stayed long. One month, perhaps two—one year at the most; and now and then they departed after only a fortnight—an event Farmor by no means regretted since she was thereby spared paying their wages. The girls left for different reasons. Some probably thought that a position with a single lady would be easy and pleasant, but they soon found otherwise! Farmor took good care that her maids should not fall into slothfulness. Others possibly dreamed of a gay life after the day's work—dancing at *The Chain, The Bird* or *The Evening Star,* followed by a little loving in doorways or on stairs. But they, too, learned differently. When darkness fell Farmor locked the kitchen door, and it was not opened again until she got up in the morning. It is not impossible either that some of the girls suffered a blow to their dignity—were offended by Farmor's monstrous suspicions. She not only suspected them of stealing food and money—girls got that way in most homes —she also suspected them of harlotry, lice, all manner of diseases, lying, eavesdropping, and gossiping. I remember a scene played out not infrequently in my innocent presence. Farmor sits chatting with a caller. Suddenly she rises, and while the caller continues the conversation, moves slowly and soundlessly to the door leading to the corridor. Suddenly she throws the door wide open. The whole thing occurs with a phenomenal speed of which she is now and then capable and which always gives me an uncomfortable shock. To what purpose this peculiar performance? Why, she simply wanted to catch the maid eavesdropping. As I have said, I witnessed this scene a number of times; but on the other hand I never saw anyone caught listening.

The kitchen stairs are steep and falling to pieces. The steps are worn thin and their centers are grooved. One must be young and quite sober to use those stairs, especially after it begins to get dark, since naturally no light is provided. As a boy it was comparatively easy for me to go up and down them, but Farmor would assuredly have fared better jumping out of the window than descending them. The walls are scrawled and scribbled over. One of them gives the information in pictures that Mrs. Jensen, on the second floor, gives money to beggars. For Farmor, in spite of her corroding stinginess, in spite of her love of lucre, in spite of the sign on the front door: *No hawkers, beggars, or wooden-shoe traffic permitted here*, always has a two ore piece ready for anyone who comes mumbling his need. However, it is not Christian charity which dictates her act. It is fear, that fear which constantly chills her blood—fear of the stranger who in a twinkling will prove to be a robber with murderous intentions.

That is the reason why a copper-piece is always handed out through the narrow crack made by the chain's remaining fastened when the door is opened . . .

I have finished. My passage through the house is completed. My alter ego—he who is my subconscious self—has, like a spectre, passed through Farmor's rooms; has seen her things, touched them; has caressed the vanished treasures with his own hand. And now he turns homeward—home to the desk in his own room—that part of him which is not solely a subconscious spirit, but made of flesh and bone. We both feel relieved. Coming once more face to face with the forgotten rooms and vanished things was becoming more and more moving, more and more painful. It was not a longing for Farmor which caused the pain—for I never loved her, was never even fond of her—nor was it longing for her things, for things are after all just things. That which caused my heart's disquiet, which so weighed it down, was the realization of the passage of time. But there is a certain felicity mixed with sadness in the knowledge that once time has vanished, it can never again return—neither with its joys, its boredoms, nor its sufferings.

3

It is forty-two years since my nurse late at night brought me to my Farmor's house. It is twenty-one years ago since as a young man I closed her door behind me for the last time. I was there then to select what I might want from the house of death. This wasn't very much.

Nevertheless those rooms are just as vivid to my inner eye as the ones I live in today. Yes, even more vivid. I have lived in the same house now for about ten years, yet it happens sometimes, in the dark, that I stumble against a chair or a cabinet; that I stand fumbling for a door-handle on the right when it is on the left side; or have a feeling that I have come to the foot of the stairs in the hall when there is really one step more. But that sort of thing would never happen to me if by some miracle I found myself in Farmor's house at night without a light. My body would know just where the furniture stood. My hands would know just where the door-handles were. My feet would know just when they should lift themselves for a door-sill. I could find my box of toys under the sofa in the dining-room and fetch my cards from the games-chest in the den. Yes, even without smashing anything I could open a door in the buffet, remove the cover from the cake-platter and fish out a vanilla cookie. And it is not only the shape of things and where they are that I remember, but also their color. At this very moment, sitting at my desk in my own home, I can not recall the color of the walls of my office, where I sit five to six hours every day for twelve months of the year. But I remember the red color of the walls of Farmor's dining-room, I remember the pattern of the wall-paper in the den, and I remember the panel decorations on the doors of the living-room.

The explanation presumably is that a child's brain is blank and sensitive, so that everything that is impressed on it in its early years goes deeper and remains more indelible than anything that follows.

4

But it is not only things I remember so clearly, it is also people; it is also events that happened and words that were said. I have but to close my eyes to witness again the trifling events of those distant days—see them, hear them, smell them. Sometimes, especially when I lie in bed at night, they come back to me uninvited—come back bringing me the sensation of taking part in a play.

There is something else, too, which I think that I remember clearly; but here I am in doubt as to my memory's reliability: I refer to feelings and thoughts I had at that time. It is not impossible that I am subject to self-delusion. Although I have repeatedly in this book reproduced events and conversations from those days, it is quite possible that maturer years have sometimes added lines of reasoning and an understanding of the behavior of grown-ups which at the time I did not possess. I repeat, it is not impossible. On the other hand, a child's power of reasoning and understanding are not to be under-rated. Children are both logical—as one can perceive from their mistakes in speech—and good psychologists—as can be seen from their attempts "to get round" grown-ups. They are just not so, as a rule, in an articulate way.

There is, however, one respect in which my memory absolutely fails me, and that is, generally speaking, everything that is inherent in the concept *time*.

I can remember whether something happened in the daytime or at night; I can remember, as a rule, whether it happened in the winter or the summer, but then—period. The whole first part of my life—I can say with assurance the first ten years—were spent in a time I call "the morning of life." And in this "morning of life," there are no years, no dates, no clock-hours. There is no such thing as chronological order. Everything that happens is at sixes-and-sevens. The utmost resources of my memory are incapable of saying what happened before what ... Did Farmor strangle the pigeon before Hoppensach burst my balloon? Or did Hoppensach burst my balloon before Farmor strangled the pigeon? I honestly don't know.

I could easily find out the exact years and dates—the year, for example, when I moved from my parents' home to my Farmor. I know, of course, like all normal people, in what year I was born. I know, moreover, that I was five-and-a-half when the move took place. To fix the exact date when my story begins would require but a very simple problem in addition. And if I were still uncertain, I could verify the year by telephoning the tramway company, for it was while I was living at Farmor's that the tramway in front of her house changed from *a horse-drawn* vehicle to an electric one. It would be even better if I were to go to my parents' graves at the cemetery—there I would find not only the year, but also the exact date of my Mother's death.

But I don't choose to do that. My memories from those years are unchronological, and I have set myself the task of telling things as I remember them, not as if I were compiling an historical record.

It would be hopeless to try to date most of the events. Could I possibly fix the date when Aunt Constance first began reading Grimm's Fairy Tales to me? Or when I scared the life out of Farmor by telling her that there was a man in the den, or when Lillelund rescued me from the thrashing the "garden-house" boys intended giving me? No—it would be impossible, wholly impossible.

So I relate my adventures in Farmor's house not only without dates but also without any attempt to record them in the order of their happening. The order I choose will depend upon the order in which memory evokes them, as I write.

5

I said a little while back that children are psychologists and logicians. But they are so inarticulately. They are so, for the most part, without words.

I feel impelled to write about this phrase "without words" before I embark on recollections of my experiences in Far-mor's house.

Once I gave some trifle to a four or five years-old girl—a little note-book which was lying on my desk. Her immediate reaction was to ask a question—a question full of suspense and unconfident joy,

"Can I have it the whole day?"

The expression startled me, until suddenly I understood it. Her meaning was "Is it something I can only borrow or something I can own?" Her vocabulary lacked the word *own* so she had to paraphrase it. The *concept*, however, she knew.

A child's world is word-poor.

I am certain that when I was five or six I could not have said, "The shell-pattern set from the Royal Porcelain Factory"—not only because my tongue could not have managed it, but because I did not know what "shell pattern" meant, and did not know of the existence of any Royal Porcelain Factory. I should have been unable to use the terms "album," "renaissance," "rococco"; the expression "merciless aesthete," words like "premonition," "the centre of interest," "association of ideas"—these were all far re-moved from my comprehension. Indeed even an expression such as "a creeping sensation in my stomach" was probably not in my vocabulary nor yet formulated in my mind.

But it was *only* words that I lacked.

The dinner-service with the fluted edge and the peculiar blue wavy pattern I saw as distinctly as any grown person might—yes, even with a keener sight and a more receptive mind. The two photograph albums, each with its distinctly different ornamentation, were registered in my mind's eye, though I did not know the words "album," "renaissance" or "rococo". Even though I did not know the meaning of the words "presentiment," "centre of attention," "association of ideas," I often had presentiments, loved to be the centre of attention, and my brain experienced what we call the association of ideas. Even though the expression "aesthete" couldn't be found in my private glossary, still it was an aesthetic discomfort I felt when I saw the moisture in Johanne's nostrils. And as to "a creeping sensation in my stomach," well, I experienced it every time I was frightened—and I often was in those years.

It was the same with numbers as it was with words.

I could only count up to five and had not the slightest acquaintance with the four branches of mathematics; still, I could perceive that there were more spots on a domino with six spots than on one with five. Just as I could tell which of two armies had the most tin soldiers.

Thus many of the figures the reader will find in the following pages were not arrived at during those days, but are the result of my brain's retaining so accurate a photographic impression of things seen that I have been enabled at a later date to describe and enumerate them.

In the adult's world, too, this lack of vocabulary is not unknown. When a peaceful landlubber goes aboard a man-of-war he sees everything as well as the captain who shows him about. But the captain knows the names of things, whereas the landlubber—if he should dare to open his mouth—has to get along with a few general terms, or paraphrases, just like the little girl I have mentioned. The same holds good for the man in the street who goes botanizing with a specialist in botany. He will discover that he not only lacks the names of countless trees, shrubs and flowers but also that he has to make the words, "flower," "leaf," "root" cover a great multitude of different phenomena. And even the botanist's supply of words is poor in comparison with the myriad phenomena existing in the plant world.

So what I experienced in Farmor's house was experienced in a world with a limited supply of words. Yet if these experiences are to be communicated to others, it can only be done with words. A word-poor world must be described to a world swarming with words. I know the picture is out of focus, incorrect in many ways, but there is no other practicable way of presenting it. I am like a composer who has seen a remarkable piece of natural scenery and now wants to impart it to others in the form of a musical composition.

6

I could hear Father and Farmor whispering in the hall—I had been hearing them for a long time. But I wasn't interested. I was too occupied with my own affairs.

We were sitting at the table in the dining-room, Johanne and I. I wasn't really sitting. I was kneeling on a cushion which had been put on the chair for me. We were each attending to our own business: Johanne embroidering monograms on my linen and I building a fort with Farmor's dominoes.

Suddenly the whispering ceased, the door to the hall was opened and Father came in, followed by Farmor.

Johanne rose respectfully. I, on the contrary, remained kneeling, not lifting my eyes from my building.

Father came right over to me and lifted me so that I stood on the cushion. We were then almost of the same height. First he took my cheeks between his hands, then he kissed me, then he threw his arms about me and pressed his face against mine. Of course I liked his being affectionate but the pleasure was not unmixed—his cheeks and his moustache tickled and scratched me.

"My boy," he said. "My poor little boy."

I understood from the tone of his voice that I was an unfortunate being. This resulted in my being suddenly overwhelmed with such great pity for myself that my tears started to flow. I had a vague idea that I was unfortunate because my mother had been taken up to Heaven. My sorrow was not lessened when my father too, began to weep.

We stood there for a minute until Farmor interrupted our grief.

"Now then, you must have a cup of coffee, Viggo—and a Victoria kringle," she chirped, at one and the same time admonishing and sympathetic.

Father let me go.

"Thank you, but I don't want anything," he answered with a gesture of rejection. "I have no appetite."

I understood that his grief was so great that he could not even eat!

"Oh but one can always drink a cup of coffee," observed Farmor hospitably, and fetched the coffee-tray from the buffet. "It will give you strength too, my boy."

Johanne, who had been gathering up her sewing, took the tray and went out into the kitchen.

My eyes followed her longingly. I would much rather be with her than in here with Father and Farmor. Something told me that there was going to be a scene.

"Now you must hurry up and pack away the dominoes," said Farmor in a wheedling voice. "I want to put the cloth on ..."

I scooped the dominoes back into their box—not without some irritation.

Farmor spread the cloth and began to set out the coffee service.

Father blew his nose—the noise positively shook the little room— then he sat down in the armchair which stood between the two windows.

"And you are really serious about wanting to have him?" he said.

Farmor nodded affirmatively but made no reply. It was obviously a matter that had been debated for some time.

"It would undoubtedly be best." Father sighed. "Henceforth my own home will be a house of sorrow ... not the home for a child."

I had resumed my game of fortress-building on the floor. Now suddenly my hand came to a standstill. I understood that they were talking about *me*.

Father continued,

"How can a man bring up a child by himself?"

There was a moment's silence. I held my breath. The silence was so very strange. I could almost feel Farmor poised, ready to spring.

When she finally spoke, her voice was innocently inquiring, "Have you ever thought of marrying again, my boy?"

The inflection of her voice made it clear that this, of course, was wholly *his* affair—that it would never occur to her to interfere.

Father rose excitedly.

"Of course I shall not marry again," he said emphatically. "Anyone who had a wife like Anette could never love another!"

I knew, of course, that Mother's name was not only Mother, but also Anette.

Father continued,

"And what is more I'd like to be spared that kind of ... question."

I understood by the pause before "question" that there was another word Father wanted to use, but did not utter.

He began striding around the table—as vehemently as the space allowed. When he reached me he lifted me up and held me close to him, tightly and tenderly.

"You shall never have a step-mother. Never! I promise you that, my son."

Then he set me down again—down to my fortress building.

I felt a little uncomfortable. I didn't like all these things he was saying and doing. He was so strange to-day—not at all like his usual self.

"That is wise of you, my boy," came from Farmor. "There is a proverb: 'A good wife is always followed by a bad one'."

Father reseated himself in the armchair, and threw one leg over the other. Father's trousers were so elegant—striped and very narrow.

A pause ensued. Farmor continued her table-setting. I

resumed my fortress-building ... "But what about the money side of it?" Father inquired ... and studied his nails.

One of Farmor's cups was poised in mid-air.

"I don't understand, Viggo," she said mournfully.

Father fumbled for words.

"We ought to ... I mean, you certainly can't ... I must pay something, naturally, mustn't I?—that is only reasonable."

Farmor brought the hanging cup to rest on its saucer. Then she seated herself at the table. She sat so as to face her son.

"You mustn't be offended," said Father, blushing a little, "but I know that you are very interested in the financial aspect of things—that is only praiseworthy, understand me —it is a good thing that you have a talent for managing your own money—but it is just for that reason that I am unwilling for you to go to any expense on my account."

I understood very well what Father really meant. He meant "You are greedy. And if you give me something gratis now, I shall hear about it all the rest of my life. So I much prefer to pay for it."

I must interpolate here that my understanding this was not the result of any unusual psychological insight. It was due solely to my long ears. Father and Mother had often discussed Farmor in my presence—presumably in the naive belief that I wasn't listening.

Farmor sat for a while, smoothing the table-cloth with her hand and not saying anything.

When she began to speak it was as one conscious of her own insignificance, her own worthlessness.

"Of course I don't want you to give me anything, Viggo. Surely you can understand that. If I attach any value to money, it isn't for my own sake—it is for yours. It means nothing to me whether you give me money—I shall soon die, and then you will get it all anyhow."

Father laughed curtly.

"You! Die soon! You'll live to be a hundred! You will outlive us all!"

Farmor put her hands up to her breast and shook her head.

"My heart—it is very bad."

Farmor's voice expressed as much anguish as if she already lay on her deathbed.

Then she rose and lifted the cake-platter from the depths of the buffet.

I knew it was going to be the cake-platter before I saw it. I recognized it by the clink of its handle.

So did Fie. Half asleep she raised one ear; remained so an instant, then the little ear-phone dropped. It was still a bit too early to leave her warm corner behind the stove.

"Well then, it's agreed," said Father. "The boy is your guest—for the present. And I thank you, Mother."

His voice was a shade more hearty than before.

"It is nothing to thank me for, my boy," Farmor said plaintively.

"But what about Johanne?" continued Father. "Is she to remain here?"

"The boy can't do without her."

"No, it's true. She might spend the day here, and at night she could sleep in the nursery at home."

A horrid fear arose in me—

"I am going to stay with Johanne," I burst forth. Father looked down at me in surprise. He realized for the first time that I had been listening.

"Devil take the boy," he exclaimed. "That youngster hears and understands every word uttered."

"Soren can't do without his Johanne," said Farmor. "Especially at night. Johanne can stay here."

For a moment I felt like flying over to Farmor and kissing her, but then I remembered her cold lips. I stayed where I was.

Farmor and Father continued talking. About Johanne's wages; where her clothes could be put; about what tasks she should perform for Farmor, and similar matters. I understood that Father was to pay Johanne's wages and he was also to pay Farmor for her board. But I confess, I hardly listened to that phase of the arrangement. It did not interest me—now that I was assured that the only thing that mattered had been settled: Johanne was to stay with me.

Farmor finished setting the table. Then she slipped into the den to get the key to the pantry.

Father looked down at me—

"Well, what do you say to living with Farmor—of course only for a little while?"

"I want to live with Johanne," I answered.

"Oh, you and your Johanne!" he exclaimed with some annoyance. "One would think you cared more for Johanne than you do for your Farmor and me."

And, in truth I did. I honestly was fonder of Johanne than I was of Farmor and Father. I liked Father well enough, except when he got mad and slapped me; but for Farmor I had not even a lukewarm affection. I believe it was an instinctive understanding of human motives which dictated my affections. I was instinctively aware that Farmor's and Father's love was, for the most part, a kind of vanity, a phase of selfinterest: I was one source of their vanity; I figured in their plans. I knew on the other hand —without words—that Johanne's love was unadulterated selflessness.

I did not reply to Father's outburst. I was silent and continued playing. I said nothing because I was, first and foremost, completely at a loss for words to express my feelings. Yet even if I had had words at my command, I should not have used them. I was, at five-and-one-half years of age, an ingenious diplomat. When Father and Mother used to ask me which one of them I loved the most, I always answered—though I loved Mother most—"I love you both the same."

After this, I would throw my arms around my mother's neck and kiss her.

So on this occasion I made no answer, and Father began addressing himself to the ceiling.

"Man is a solitary creature," he muttered bitterly. "He is loved but by few, and Death takes those away from him."

Then he heaved a heavy, mournful sigh.

By this time Farmor had finished her clatter in the den and glided through the dining-room into the kitchen.

"That might do for a theme," murmured Father; whereupon he took a little red note-book from his pocket and began to write in it.

I was well aware that when Father wrote, it was something called *poetry*. To write poems was considered very distinguished. I had arrived at this conclusion from something in Mother's voice. Whenever she alluded to *"My Husband's Collected Poems, 'Violets and Violins',"* her voice sank low and her back straightened. And the faces of the ladies around her assumed expressions of respect and admiration.

I was much relieved that Father had found his notebook. I knew that as long as he wrote poetry, I should be left to attend to my own affairs without interruption. And for the moment there was nothing on earth that interested me more than these magical pieces of bone which could be simultaneously dominoes and fortress walls. They worked such magic that I saw them—*clearly* and *distinctly*—as little bone counters and yet at the same time as mighty, sky-high stone walls. And that, too, without my two worlds—reality and fantasy—interfering or conflicting with each other.

So coziness descended on the room. Father composed poetry; I built; and Piphans (the canary) jumped audibly about from one perch to another. We were happy, yes, and not one of us bothered about his companions.

But in an instant that happiness vanished. The door to the corridor leading to the kitchen opened and Farmor glided in, followed by Johanne. Farmor carried the cake-platter with Victoria kringles. Johanne, who towered above Farmor, carried the coffee-pot in one hand and in the other a platter of buttered French bread ... I observed that the coffee-pot was not the same as the one we had used in the evening—that is, the granite one—but was the one which belonged to the mussel-pattern set from the Royal Porcelain Factory.

"If you please—both of you," murmured Farmor, invitingly.

We rose simultaneously—Fie, Father and I. Fie seated herself at Farmor's feet, and struck the floor a couple of thumps with her copper-colored tail. That meant, "Don't forget *me!*"

Johanne poured out.

"Something has just occurred to me," said Farmor. "Soren must have some black clothes."

"Yes, so he must," said Father, a bit hesitantly. "Still I don't really believe much in mourning. Those who go in for mourning most often have least in their hearts."

"But one must always take into consideration a little what people will say."

"Excuse me, Mrs. Jensen." It was Johanne who entered into the conversation. "But Soren's winter coat is black and he also has a dark blue suit. I could sew a black arm-band on it—"

"Yes, I think that would suffice," said Father.

"Of course," murmured Farmor. "You are the one to decide."

Her voice emphasized again her humility, her acceptance of her complete lack of influence. Perhaps there was also a slight shade of reproach in it, as if she were saying, "My opinion is never taken into account."

Johanne had finished pouring, and went back to the kitchen to refill the coffee-pot.

"I don't know any place where one gets such delicious buttered French bread as here," said Father, and reached for another slice. "I don't know why it is so, for we have often got it from your own bakery—but it never tastes the same as yours."

"Now you are flattering me," murmured Farmor, visibly pleased.

"No, I'm not. There really is something about your food —Now, take, for example, your squab—they are so firm and yet just ripe. And no-one in the world can make such good squab sauce as you do."

Father's face was all aglow with gustatory pleasure. He looked as if he were envisioning a squab on the very plate in front of him. He reached for another slice of bread.

"Farmor," I said, as affectionately as I could, "Won't you make a squab stew?"

Farmor melted.

"I can't today, Soren," she said sadly. "We are going to have hasty pudding and hash for dinner—we must use up the roast we had yesterday. But you shall have squab another day—I promise to remember."

"Anette tried to cook squab, too," continued Father in a melancholy voice, "but the sauce was never quite right."

He took another slice of French bread.

Johanne came back with the china coffee-pot. After peering into our cups to see that we had enough, she placed the pot on a porcelain stand.

"May Fernanda and I have what is left in the pot?" she asked. By "pot" she meant what was left in the granite coffee pot in the kitchen.

Farmor answered,

"You may have a full cup, Johanne, but Fernanda must be satisfied with half-a-cup. She can fill it up with hot water."

"Yes Ma'am," said Johanne, and closed the door to the corridor.

"Good Lord—one wouldn't believe you were living in the twentieth century!" Father remarked. "Deuce take it— you can't treat servants like that! Not, at any rate if one wants to keep them."

Farmor refused to discuss the question. She directed her gaze to me, and piped,

"Would you like my ring?"

She was accustomed to cut away the crust of her bread all in one piece so that the crust formed a "ring." This was on account of her teeth. Afterwards she ate the crusts—for the sake of economy, though she camouflaged the reason as ethical and religious. "One must not let God's gifts go to waste," was one of her numerous pet sayings. This amusing illogicality—taking the crusts off and then later eating them—she dispensed with when her grandson was present. He regarded them as a delicacy.

I stretched forth my hand for the shiny, light-brown crusts.

"Won't you have a kringle?" This time she directed her question to Father.

"No, thanks," he said. "I prefer your buttered bread. And besides I can't eat any more." Father shook his head and added in sober earnest,

"I have no appetite."

Farmor dipped a piece of sugar in her cup, then reached the brown, dripping little coffee-fish down to Fie. Fie signified thanks with a thump of her tail. The sugar began to crunch in her mouth.

"Whom have you invited?" Farmor asked.

"Invited? To what?" Father said in surprise.

"To the wake . . ."

"Heaven forbid. I can't conceive of anything worse—anything more tasteless—than wakes!"

"Why, Viggo?"

"Why? Why? Well, if you can't imagine why yourself, it's useless to explain. There they sit after the funeral, those who really loved the person who's died, miserable, unhappy—and yet they have to smile, be polite . . . And there sit the others—the indifferent ones—and pretend to be sad, bereaved, full of sympathy! Then little by little as the evening wears on—and the wine begins to work—jollity bubbles forth among the callous ones and the bereaved become more and more unhappy, more heartbroken! And . . . No, it is a devilish performance!"

"But, Viggo, it is customary. You have *got* to invite *some* of the family at least."

"Don't you believe it. I don't intend to invite a single soul!"

"I have never heard of a funeral that was not followed by a wake."

"Well, of course, you're thinking of those country wakes you've been acquainted with, where people celebrate just as at christenings and weddings. In the country, I know, there is more grief over the death of a cow than of a human being. The death of a cow means loss of money. But here in the city—here among cultivated people—one has gradually gotten away from all that sort of twaddle.'

Father stirred his cup quite violently.

Then he said derisively,

"You can be quite at ease, Mother. Your son knows perfectly well what is right and proper for him to do."

Farmor paused as usual before answering.

Finally she said querulously as if she were yielding a point,

"I understand you very well, Viggo. You have so much on your mind just now that you can't be bothered with having guests. I do understand, my boy, you must not think otherwise. So *I* shall give the funeral party for you—even if it *is* a little more than I can afford."

Father halted, and stared at her, a puzzled expression in his face.

Then he said, rather angrily,

"All right, all right. Do as you like. But *I* won't be there."

"Do you really mean to say that you won't come, Viggo?"

"Absolutely. Because I am unhappy, that's why. But you for whom Anette's death means nothing—*you* can give a party for others."

"What do you mean—that it means mothing to me?"

"But it does. It's the truth. Yes, it doesn't only mean nothing—the real fact is that you are delighted that Anette is dead!"

Farmor tried to interrupt him, but Father pounded the table-cloth with his knuckles. "Yes, now it is *my* turn to speak. Delighted, yes, that's what you *are!* Because you could never stand her! Why, I don't know. Perhaps her dowry wasn't big enough; or perhaps you are one of those mothers for whom no daughter-in-law is ever good enough. Why, I repeat, I don't know. I only know that you always objected to her; that you persecuted her and said awful things about her—and unhappily Anette knew it, too. The first year we were married she used to come back crying every time she visited you—crying over all the malice you'd heaped on her. She used to cry until I comforted her and persuaded her that all your meanness was powerless—"

"*I*, who was always so nice to Anette?" Farmor whined, deeply wronged.

Father rose.

"You—nice to her! You who never showed her anything but cruelty—sweet, charming, innocent cruelty—from the first time she came, naive and open-hearted, to visit you, until the last night when, weary and grieving, she closed her eyes forever! No, no, Mother—God may forgive you your sins toward Anette, but *I never* can!"

Father put down his napkin and strode toward the door. There he turned and shouted in his deep, powerful voice,

"And you can hold as many funeral carousals as you like, but *I won't come!*"

The door banged shut.

The slam was such as to make the tea-urn rattle.

Apparently it had been Father's intention to make his exit in this dramatic manner, but in his excitement he had forgotten his mother's locking-up system. I could hear him rattling the burglar-chain, wrestling with the iron prong, shaking the outer door furiously—yes, kicking it, just exactly as I would often have liked to do!

Farmor slipped down from her chair and moved furtively toward the door.

The door was thrown open. Father stuck his head in, his face very red.

"Will you be so kind as to open up this damned door!" he cried furiously, but embarrassed too.

"My little Viggo—" Farmor began in her most placating voice, but I heard no more—the door shut behind her.

Whispering began again—violent, excited; now and again, hurried. It sounded like a ball of paper being rubbed against the floor.

But the whispering did not interest me. It was nothing new for me to hear Father and Farmor quarrel—or rather to hear Father rail at Farmor. Farmor did not rail, she only whined, whimpered, wept; became pitiful and wronged. How often I had witnessed such scenes! Father and Mother rarely quarreled, but when Father and Farmor came together the meeting ended more often in squabbles than in peace and forbearance.

But I was not concerned. In truth, I even found it rather funny. Only the times when Mother wept, had I minded it. And when Father got really mad I took good care to be well-behaved and to keep my distance, for sometimes his wrath with Farmor had something to do with me.

The whispering ceased. I looked around, snatched a Victoria kringle, and once more got down on the floor back to my fortress-building.

7

Fernanda and I were alone in the dining-room. Johanne and Farmor had gone to the funeral.

It was Johanne who had managed it that I should remain at home. She thought it was a sin that a five-year old boy should see his mother put in the ground, and she had fought so long for this view of the matter that Farmor had finally capitulated. Of course Farmor did not understand what dictated Johanne's feeling—such human subtleties were beyond her—but she had probably given way chiefly because Johanne knew of a certain member of the government who had not taken his own children to their mother's funeral.

I know that it sounds incredible that Johanne should have dared to oppose Mrs. Jensen in anything, but nevertheless it is true. Naturally it was not something that happened often —Johanne knew only too well her station in life. But where her little Soren was concerned she was as fearless as a veritable lioness.

Fernanda was peeling potatoes. She had been allowed, contrary to custom, to do the peeling in the dining-room. It was no kindness to her, but simply on my account. I was not to be left alone. I don't know whether it was to supervise me or to keep me amused, but it was well understood that the young master could by no means be relegated to the kitchen. So on newspapers spread out on the table there were two mountains: one of potatoes, the other of peelings; and next to them was the household's second-fattest pot, to hold the potatoes when peeled.

I was seated on one side of the table with a game of lotto. It consisted of a set of cards with pictures—twelve to a card —together with a stack of small square disks each wearing a picture matching one of those on the cards.

The rule was that, as each disk was drawn, the one who drew it read aloud its caption and covered the corresponding picture on the big card with it. To an onlooker it would have seemed as if I was playing alone—which I was not. We were quite a party—me, Johanne, Father, Farmor, Fernanda, and Lillelund. The reading feature of the game I omitted—for a very understandable reason. But I was always able to fit the little disks into their proper places, thanks to the pictures on them. For some reason or other I nearly always came out first when we played and Johanne came out second. Fernanda, on the contrary, usually came out last, and if she looked disappointed or annoyed when this happened, I used to feel particularly pleased and laughed triumphantly.

Was I not thinking at all about what was happening at

this time? No, I had forgotten about it. Lotto had made me forget. But I *had* thought about it. The horrid black clothes; all the talk about the burial, the coffin, the cemetery, the location of the grave—all that had brought home to me what was taking place. I understood that when a person dies he or she is placed in a wooden box, the cover is closed and nailed down, and it is buried deep in the ground. The thought was horrible, terrifying; it turned my stomach, especially when I imagined myself in the box in place of the dead person. But there was something incredible about the whole thing, something meaningless. Why should somebody whose destination is heaven be put down in the ground? However, I hit upon a kind of explanation for this. The dead person obviously crawled up in the night, was undressed by the angels—even down to his shirt—a pair of wings were attached to his shoulders, and then he flew up to the old man in Heaven. This all happening at night was a hypothesis based on there being a kind of connection between night and undressing; and then, too, the fact that no one ever sees the dead when they fly, reinforced the idea.

For one moment the pain had seemed unendurable. For a moment it had seemed as if a stinging arrow had pierced my very heart. This was when Johanne and Father—silent and dressed in black—came into the room to bid me good-bye. In that moment it was as if what lay ahead was revealed to me in all its horror. *Mother—my own Mother—* was to be put down in a hole, deep down in a dark, dismal hole—and dirty, heavy, disgusting earth was to be heaped upon her. How could she ever—with all that earth on top of her!—have strength to come up again? All that Johanne had told me about Heaven was a lie—it was something she had made up just so that I should not be unhappy! No, indeed—I understood what was going to happen. It was the grown-ups, all the other grown-ups, who for some reason or other were being cruel and wicked to my own little mother!

And my anguish had found expression in a wild shriek for her they were taking away from me.

Johanne came up and put her arms around me to comfort me. But I did *not* want to be consoled. I squirmed and fought to get away, and when that didn't help, I hit out at her. "There, there—don't cry, little Soren," she whispered tenderly. "If you will stop crying, you shall have a package." The word package interrupted my grief. I loved packages. Almost the best thing about them was the unpacking. "Unpacking" is the wrong word. I used to tear them open. I floundered in the paper, I hauled frenziedly at the string. And if the knots were stubborn, I howled with rage until a grown-up came with a pair of scissors. There was nothing to a gift if it was not wrapped.

Then Johanne lifted the cover of the box-couch, and fished up a little package, wrapped in pink paper. And when I finally got it open, there I stood with a picture lotto in my hands.

It wasn't my first game of lotto. I had had one once before, and Johanne had taught me how to play the game and knew that I loved it. But due to my childish handling, the forerunner of this one had long been only a collection of unmatched, tattered bits of cardboard.

The instant I held the box in my hands, my grief was assuaged, the vividly imagined burial-scene began to fade, and my only sorrow was that Johanne could not stay and play the game with me. But even for this grief she had a solace: she would tell the coachman to drive fast so that she could get home quickly to her Soren.

Ah, you, my second mother, you who, thanks to your great heart, were so understanding, now, many years later, I realize what you did then in all its wisdom and foresight. You had foreseen that the moment would probably come when I, even at five years of age, would sense what it would mean to lose my mother, and for that moment you had an anodyne ready. With more cleverness than many a physician, you had provided that little pink box with its picture cards and disks, paying for it yourself out of your meager servant's wages.

It is from my childhood's nurse that I first learned what all my later experience confirmed: if you would seek the most tender of heart, search for them among the most lowly.

We had been alone, Fernanda and I, for half an hour. Suddenly she burst forth, without any kind of preliminary, with the words,

"Do you like sand?" And at the same time she grinned at me in a foolish kind of way.

I had had a toy mill at home—a little water-mill made of wood. When sand was funneled into the top, a wheel revolved and two hammers clattered inside the mill. When all the sand had run out, the drawer into which it had collected was emptied into the funnel again, and again the mill began to run.

"Y-e-s, I do," I told Fernanda.

"Then you shall have some," she said. This time she grinned not only foolishly but furtively.

She went into the kitchen and returned with a saucer and a teaspoon. I noticed that they belonged to the luncheon service and had not been washed.

"Where is the sand?" I asked.

"You're going to get some," she said with the same smile.

She walked over to the window—to Piphans's cage. There she pulled out the tray at the bottom and tipped a little sand from it into the saucer. She spread out what was left in the cage with her fingers, evidently to prevent Farmor's noticing that any had been taken.

My eyes followed her full of curiosity and wonder.

She came back to the table with the saucer and held it in front of me. The sand was repugnant—strewn here and there with bird-droppings and empty seed-shells. She evidently knew nothing about my esthetic nature if she thought that I would play with sand like that.

Besides there was not nearly enough to play with.

"Help yourself," she said, offering the saucer to me.

"What shall I do with it?" I asked.

"You said you liked sand."

My diplomatic instinct came to the rescue. If she couldn't herself see that the sand was disgusting, I would not hurt her feelings by telling her it was.

I said, "I haven't got a mill."

Now it was her turn not to understand.

"A mill? What do you want with a mill?"

"To put it in," I said.

I did not say "naturally"—that word was too difficult—but it was implied in my tone.

"I thought you wanted to eat some," she said.

There was a pause. A sudden suspicion that she wanted to commit me to some kind of act of naughtiness entered my head. Fernanda was probably one of those bad people I had heard about—one of those who tempted children to do wicked, sinful things.

I straightened my back and answered with dignity,

"That sort of stuff can't be eaten."

I was proud of my ability to resist temptation. It did not occur to me that as a matter of fact I was not experiencing any temptation at all.

Fernanda had now realized that I was a novice in the matter of sand-eating.

"Oh but you can't imagine how good it tastes!"

"Ugh!" was my only reply.

"Well, if you won't have it, I'll eat it myself."

She took tight hold of the saucer and spoon, returned to her side of the table, and sat down, the saucer in one hand, the spoon in the other. Then the meal began. Spoonful by spoonful, Piphans' sand disappeared between her pallid lips. Her face beamed with satisfaction. Now and then after swallowing a mouthful, she sighed,

"Ah-h-h!"

My eyes grew wide with amazement.

At the same time I had the sensation of my stomach's rising as if it would force its way through my lips. I knew instinctively that if I remained there, I should end by vomiting. I scrambled down from my chair and rushed through the den into the living room. There I crawled under the walnut table and clung to the round ball in the middle of the cross-beams between its legs. My gorge rose so that I had a hard struggle keeping down my lunch.

I sat huddled there for some minutes. The room was quite dark—it was not late enough to light up for the company.

After a while I heard Fernanda's voice.

"Come back, Soren. I've finished eating."

I crawled forth from my hiding place and peeped cautiously through the dining-room door. Fernanda had resumed her peeling of potatoes. The empty saucer stood beside her with the cleanly-licked spoon in it.

I climbed back on to my chair.

"You are a thog!" I said with conviction.

I wasn't quite satisfied with the way I had pronounced the word, and tried again.

"You are a hog!"

This time I got it right, but to give it more force I added, "You are a *dirt-eating* hog!"

Fernanda grinned, not the least ashamed. But suddenly a look of anxiety crossed her face.

"You mustn't tell your Farmor or Johanne about it."

An evil spirit took possession of me.

"I shall tell them that you are a thog!" I said.

"Then I shall tell them about your making wee wee in the kitchen yesterday!"

This threat made me thoughtful. I silently weighed and considered the matter.

Then I answered in a somewhat subdued tone,

"Alright, I won't tell!"

Fernanda smiled complacently.

Then she picked up the saucer and spoon and carried them back to the kitchen . . . .

I did not keep my promise.

The next day I told Johanne, and a couple of days later, Farmor.

Both times I had the satisfaction of hearing them express their disgust for Fernanda and their admiration for myself; I had been a good, sensible boy not to make a pig of myself eating sand!

I don't believe either of them said anything to Fernanda then, but a couple of months later she was no longer with us. I can still remember how I loathed her after that day. I howled as if I were being murdered if she so much as touched me. Even looking at her made me feel sick.

Childhood experiences are indelible.

Much water has run under the bridge since that afternoon. Nevertheless, even today I cannot look at a game of lotto without growing depressed, without remembering that man's last dwelling on earth is a narrow coffin in a dark hole in the ground. And whenever I attend a funeral, sooner or later, I start feeling sick. It is because in my mind's eye I see a servantgirl—a poor, miserable little slattern—shovelling into her mouth spoonful after spoonful of grimy sand that she's filched ... from a bird-cage ...

8

"Such a pity your own son couldn't come," Mrs. Agerlin exclaimed suddenly. She sat at the end of the table opposite Farmor, and shouted her remark the length of it.

The conversation came to a halt. Silence descended on the company.

Farmor waited a moment before making a reply. There was a tiny, tiny pause.

Then she said, "Yes."

Only "Yes." Nothing but "Yes."

But there was so much implied in that one word that Pastor Moller felt obliged to defend Father.

"I understand your son perfectly," he said. "His grief is

so deep, so personal, that he craves solitude. Maybe at this very moment he has gone into his study to commune with his God. We must not forget, Mrs. Jensen, that he was the one closest to the deceased and so, of course, the one who suffers most."

"There is no one who can express such things so beautifully," said Farmor tearfully, "as Pastor Moller!"

But Mrs. Agerlin was not defeated.

"Even so, I believe no one has the right to cut himself off from others," she continued in her hoarse screech. "No matter how much one may suffer, one owes something to the living, I think."

"Give him time—give him time, Mrs. Agerlin." The pastor waved his big bear-like paw. "Wounds require time to heal, so do sorrows."

We were sitting in the dining-room at the extended table, ten people in all, ten people all in black, grey and white.

I had been placed at the end nearest the stove. Merciful heavens (a popular expression at that time)—what I had to put up with! To be sure, some of the blasts of heat were diverted by a screen, but I still felt like a roast in an oven! I don't know whether I was seated there because Farmor thought that as son of the deceased I should have the seat of honor, or that as the youngest present, I could best endure the roasting. It may well be I was simply placed there to emphasize my Father's absence.

Farmor sat on my right. In other words, she was my dinner partner. Probably there was a reason for that, too. Perhaps it was according to some rule of etiquette of which I was ignorant, but it could also have been a practical arrangement. The chair she occupied was nearest the door leading to the kitchen, and during meal-time she was accustomed always to be more in the kitchen than in the dining-room.

On Farmor's right sat Dr. Agerlin. He was father's medical partner. At one time he had been a provincial dentist, then later he'd moved to the metropolis to establish a practice

there. In the course of time my grandfather had bought his
son a partnership in the practice, and it was my clever father
who had made it famous by one fine day getting himself
appointed dentist to the Royal Household. Ever since it had
been fashionable to have one's bridges put in by the firm
of Viggo Jensen and Agerlin.

Dr. Agerlin was an old man now, and according to Father
no longer good for much. He had difficulty in running his
drilling machine; his hands shook so much that he used to
spill mercury all over the floor; he knew so little about anti-
septics that he dusted his instrument-table with his pocket
handkerchief; and his sight had become so bad—according
to Father—that he even had difficulty in locating his patients'
mouths. "But there is one advantage about him," Father
used to say. "While he is standing beside them half asleep,
I am allowed to narcotize my patients!"

Dr. Agerlin's manner of speech was strongly at variance
with that recommended in the New Testament. He never
said just, "Yes, yes"; or "No, no," but "Yars" and "Naow"
and "It is paw-ssible". His affirmations were so vague that
he could in one and the same remark glide from Yes to No.
How often I have heard him say,

"Yarss ... Yarss ... Naoh ... Naoh, I daont really think
saoh."

The switch from affirmation to negation frequently followed upon a lightning glance from his wife.

I liked him. When I was taken to the dental clinic Father
was always short-tempered and in a hurry. "There's no
need to drag the boy up here ... I really haven't got time ...
The waiting-room is full of patients," and so on. But
with Uncle Agerlin it was different. Nobody was ever too
busy—neither he nor his woman-assistant. With him I was
permitted to raise and lower the patient's chair, to work the
treadle of the drill, and squirt the atomizer—the one with
the bent spout; and in fact there was not a single instrument
he would not hand over to me if I asked him. Why, he once
even sat down in the patient's chair and let me play dentist!

Uncle Agerlin had as his dinner partner Aunt Laura. She was certainly the strangest of all the strange people I remember from my childhood. But it was strange that she should be strange. On the surface she was frank and straightforward and not in the least evasive or secretive. She had a forthright and unaffected personality; her character was strong and self-reliant. Furthermore she was kind and helpful to people without being the least bit sentimental. In fact Aunt Laura was usually the one sent for when any of her acquaintances became ill—especially those who wanted nursing service gratis. Her dresses were unconventional— she wore mannish collars and cuffs; she cut her hair short, smoked cheroots, rode a bicycle, and was on the committee of the Danish Women's Club. To Farmor and Mrs. Agerlin she was an unfailing source of gossip, gossip given a sad and compassionate expression, but at bottom carried on with enjoyment and zest. Yet for all her straightforwardness, there was something in her very candidness that excluded one—like a hedged-in spot in a park to which there is otherwise free access. It was as if she knew something which she would not confide to her fellow-humans—and maybe not even admit to herself. Perhaps it is significant that I do not remember her surname—perhaps never knew it. Yet I can remember the first and last names of all those other personages who trod the stage of my childhood's theatre. But Aunt Laura still remains Aunt Laura to me to this day. I don't know whether she was a Mrs. or a Miss, whether she was related to me or not, or what her financial situation was. And her death, which occurred only a few years later, was shrouded in mystery. One morning I was informed that the previous night Aunt Laura had gone on to Our Lord—nothing more was told me at the time, but later I discovered by listening to my elders that something frightful had happened: her bed had caught fire and she had been burned to death.

I never hated Aunt Laura, but neither did I care very much about her. The aesthetic and masculine in my na-

ture found her lacking in charm. Furthermore, she had
an annoying manner of greeting me whenever we met:
she did not say Hello or just greet me in a friendly way,
but would run the flat of her hand down my face, saying
with a serious expression, "This is conforming," after which
she would run her hand up in the reverse direction and say,
"and this is non-conforming." Then she would wipe from
her hands the dampness caused by the "non-conforming"
gesture. She did this with such a serious expression that I
was quite grown-up before I understood that the act was
intended as a joke and an expression of friendliness. As it
was, I learned in course of time to take a long sniff just
before she said the word "non-conforming".

Farmor had placed on Aunt Laura's right the widow
Tychsen. She had been married to a provincial doctor but
he had died at an early age—in fact he was an incurable
morphinist—and she and her daughter had moved to the
city and into Farmor's apartment house where they were
now living on a modest income.

Mrs. Tychsen was religious. She always wore black
dresses with high collars, above which peeped a narrow
white ruching. Father used to say that she looked as if she
were wearing a budding parson's dog collar. She went to
church twice every Sunday, and bore the impress of a number of the Christian virtues such as quietness, mildness,
spiritual purity, and lack of humor, and she never criticized
anyone. In contrast to Farmor's sham religiosity, Mrs.
Tychsen's was uncomfortably genuine.

Farmor and Mrs. Tychsen were accustomed to see each
other occasionally—usually for a game of bezique. Even
so I had only seen her once or twice before, probably because my visits to Farmor had for the most part occurred on
Sunday afternoons. But I knew her by reputation—down
to the last detail. Their friendship did not prevent Farmor
from telling people a number of things about her. Of course
Farmor always did it very sweetly and with deep feeling.
Her voice brimmed with sympathy and her eyes with tears

when she discussed Mrs. Tychsen's poverty. She was aghast when she described how meagerly they lived, and sighed heavily when she recalled how long it was since either mother or daughter had had any new clothes. But I, who knew Farmor's heart, was aware that under the hypocritical layer of sympathy there was only contempt—the contempt of a rich woman for a poor one. Still, Farmor was fair enough to inform everyone that Mrs. Tychsen always paid her rent promptly every quarter. This bit of information was always introduced with the words,

"Still one must admit . . ."

Mrs. Tychsen's company was always especially painful to me and I kept myself as far as possible away from her aura of piety. It was not because she had ever done any harm to me—on the contrary her manner bore the imprint of the Master's words, "Let the children come to me, do not hinder them," but she somehow filled me with a nagging feeling that I was not what I ought to be. In daily life I was successful in overlooking the fact that I could hardly be regarded as a good and well-behaved child, but this comfortable state forsook me when I came within Mrs. Tychsen's magic circle. What did it avail me that my face assumed an expression of innocence or if, for an afternoon I behaved like a little gentleman! I knew in my heart that I was cheating; I felt self-contempt for behaving like a despicable hypocrite—like Farmor's own grandson!

I never experienced this sense of guilt in Farmor's presence, nor, for that matter, in Johanne's. Is it to be wondered at that I felt more at ease with bad people like Farmor, than with the strong, the pious and the well-behaved?

The seating of guests at table is a matter provocative of considerable thought. First and foremost it reveals a great deal concerning the degree of esteem in which said guests are held by their hostess and how she compares their social positions. But psychological conclusions of another sort may be drawn from the seating arrangements also. When today, many years later, I recall that funeral banquet, I am perplexed by the way in which Farmor—intentionally or not—seated Mrs. Tychsen. She was not escorted in by Pastor Moller, which would undoubtedly have demonstrated a recognition of their common interest—the Christian church. But why was no other male escort into dinner assigned her? Was it because she possessed only a modest little income and so had to give precedence to other ladies in better financial circumstances? Or had Farmor, with fiendish cunning aimed to let everyone know that she regarded Aunt Laura as a kind of male?!

At the other table-end—directly opposite me—bulged Pastor Moller. He was a large, broad-chested man, with a long, nut-brown beard and thick scarlet lips. He had early brought into the conversation the fact that he had also had an invitation to a wedding dinner; but, as he expressed it, he couldn't let Mrs. Jensen down. Farmor had a deep respect for him—wasn't he a clergyman, the best-known in the district, and in addition, a kind of sorcerer, a man in league with supernatural powers? For all her domestic economies, Farmor was not niggardly with contributions to his church expenses on occasions. But despite her respect for him, she was not exactly respectful when she discussed him behind his back. I have often, from my place on the floor, heard her accuse him of adultery, drunkenness, untrustworthiness and blasphemy.

As for myself, I couldn't stand him. He was too big, too domineering, too coarse. And even though he was friendly enough toward me, he never gave me any sign of admiration. Whenever we met, two self-centered personalities collided— and it was usually his which emerged unscathed. But I never let him see my enmity. On the contrary—I stood in holy terror of him. Like Farmor I understood that he represented partly orthodox morality, partly certain mysterious powers—two forces it would be dangerous to be at odds with. Perhaps this fear contributed a good deal to my enmity.

Pastor Moller was in the habit of making frequent pastoral

calls on Farmor. My Father maintained he always turned up around meal-times.

The Pastor had as his table companion Mrs. Agerlin. She was the better-half of Dr. Agerlin—or if not the better, then the more imposing, the more authoritative, the more vocally gifted. Her complexion was as brown as cocoa, her hair was partly sable black, partly chalk-white; her eyes were deep-set, with heavy eyelids; her nose had an aristocratic arch to it, and her military back turned stiffly, always erect. Her voice was at once hoarse and screeching. But I don't know whether she screeched because she was hoarse or was hoarse because she screeched. When she wasn't talking she pinched her lips together into an unnatural pout. It was the custom in those days for ladies of quality to hold their lips as if they were about to say "rur."

Mrs. Agerlin loved colors. Her dresses, which were usually magenta, cerise, or yellow, were embellished with ribbons and scarves, the most colorful on the market. Father used to say that she was an asset to the dental profession, because it gave one toothache simply to look at her . . .

I could not stand Aunt Agerlin. But I was also afraid of her—afraid of her making me the object of her witticisms and sharp tongue. As for her, she was not charmed by me either. This childless woman did not care in the least for children. Nevertheless she treated me, as a rule, with over-whelming sweetness. She knew what I meant to Farmor, and for some reason or other she wished to remain on good terms with Mrs. Jensen. I think I hit the nail on the head when I say that there existed between us an armed neutrality.

It was quite evident that the adults did not care for her either. At any rate Johanne used to call her in my very presence a cheat and a swank, two epithets I applauded without exactly understanding what they meant. But between Farmor and Mrs. Agerlin a kind of friendship did exist. It was not particularly warm. It was what develops between certain people who meet only to gossip. These two ladies were past masters of the same art: *Slander*.

On Mrs. Agerlin's right was Station Superintendent Billen-stein. His mother had been Farmor's sister, so that he and Father were cousins, though he was quite a bit older than Father.

He was a thin man in a Prince Albert coat. His eyes were grey. His nose, which was long, flattened out toward the end. There was a slight cleft at the tip. He had a broad mouth with narrow lips, which gave him the appearance of a Jesuit priest. His voice grated. His was an amiable personality, almost deferential—at any rate he never contradicted anyone. He was always affable, but his affability did not go deep; he was disposed to take life easily and cheerfully but the quality that could share another's grief and pain and could sympathize with cares which prevent anything like a wholly joyful existence—this he could hardly be said to possess to any marked degree. If anyone came to him with sorrows or anxieties he could always dismiss them with a joke. In general, a certain irony, a certain clandestine mockery underlay his courtesy and amiability, as if he were, at bottom, inclined to be amused at his fellow-humans.

He was in his element when, uniform-clad, he strode up and down his station platform. The station of which he was superintendant was in one of the richest coastal suburbs, and he was extremely popular with the leading merchants, manufacturers, directors, and professional men who came and went. He was ready to laugh at their witticisms, and when the occasion called for it he was always ready with a clever repartee. He could also be relied upon to hold back a train if he caught sight of some delayed dignitary hurrying to catch it. But his popularity was not less among other and broader classes. The always obliging station-super-intendent, always in holiday spirits, was also a familiar and popular figure among the numerous city-folk who went out to the country in summer.

He was a widower, and had been so for many yers. Reputation had it that he was not blind to feminine beauty, but whether it was anything more than that he used his eyes and now and then presented flowers to someone to whom he shouldn't, that I do not know. In childhood one's not interested in the erotic enterprises of adults. If I know anything at all about that side of his life it is only because I could not close my ears. Whenever Farmor and Mrs. Agerlin got round to the subject of her nephew, it was always this aspect of it that Farmor brought up first.

Why then did Farmor—despite her virtuous contempt for him, despite her conception of him as a shameless Don Juan —let him take into dinner the only young and pretty woman present? Was it because, after all, she wished him well? Or did some abysmal devilry lurk behind this act also?

This only young and pretty woman was Constance Tychsen, daughter of the widowed Mrs. Tychsen whom Farmor had placed next to Aunt Laura.

It was the first time I was in her presence. The few times I had met Mrs. Tychsen before, her daughter had not been with her.

I shall never forget my first impression of Constance. We were awaiting the guests, Farmor and I, in the little cabinet, when the hall-door opened and Mrs. Tychsen glided in, followed by her daughter. Miss Constance walked in bent a little forward from the waist as was fashionable in those days (I wonder if the expression "to sail in" to describe a woman's walk was not invented at that time?) Her movements were so graceful and elegant, her whole person of such altogether heavenly loveliness, that I forgot to bow and extend my hand, but instead, stared at her, open-mouthed. At last Farmor gave me a push and asked,

"Have you fallen in a trance, my boy?"

I answered angrily, "No." My anger sprang partly from being jerked away from fairy-land, partly from the fact that I did not know what *trance* meant.

Miss Tychsen was a brunette. Her hair was arranged in three tiers, but, let it be well-understood, not in a hard, sharp-edged, architectural manner, but in a pile of soft, round cushions. She also wore two curls, one at either temple, and there were no loose wisps hanging down her neck. This last fact I had hurriedly established. The esthete in me—or love of order—detested the straggling neck-wisps which were so prevalent in those days. One reason that I couldn't stand Mrs. Agerlin was because of the thick bristles, some black and some white, which stuck out sharply above her collar.

Miss Tychsen's mouth was a strawberry; her nose, a charming little projection. She was so thin that she looked as if she might break in two; and her hands and feet were tiny. I found this diminuitiveness adorable, thus sharing contemporaries' conception of feminine beauty.

In contrast to her elongated elegance, her face was round like that of a porcelain doll. Even her eyes were round and full. In this respect too she complied with what was fashion's decree of that age.

She was the loveliest thing I had ever seen—there wasn't a doubt about it. Of course I was busy eating most of the time—eating with unusual zest in fact, for Farmor's food was always of a particular quality—but during the time I wasn't stuffing myself I stared at her fixedly and unashamedly. I liked her simply because she was pretty. And I longed for the privilege of sitting on her lap.

She did not have much to say during dinner. Of course silence is most befitting an unmarried young woman of twenty years; moreover she wasn't called upon to speak very often: Uncle Billenstein saw to it that the flow of his gallant, grating conversation went on uninterruptedly.

I knew that she and her mother lived in narrow circumstances, a fact, I had gleaned, as I have already said, from Farmor. As I sat and looked at her, I could imagine her dressed in rags, lying on a miserable bed in a tumbledown hut in the forest. The vision touched my heart so sharply that several times my eyes filled with tears. It's true I could see that her white silk dress, under a black scarf, was new and elegant. I knew, too, that she lived up above us on the fourth floor; but this did not interfere with my fantasy. In those years I kept a kind of double-entry book-keeping. An embroidered foot-stool could be to me at one and the same time both a fiery steed and a foot-stool.

The last guest at the table was Cousin Christian, who sat between Miss Tychsen and me. He was Uncle Billenstein's son, so in point of fact only my second cousin. He was between seventeen and eighteen; thin; rather tall for his age and with narrow shoulders. He was pale, with bright red spots on his cheeks. His grey eyes usually had a sad expression in them. I rarely saw him—I believe there was a little career jealousy between Father and Uncle Billenstein—but when we did meet, he not only did not tease me, as big boys usually tease smaller ones—or assume a superior or disinterested air, but on the contrary used to play with me in a patient, good-natured, and rather melancholy, way. I was fond of him.

We had finished the first two courses—soup with meat-balls, and salmon—and Johanne and Fernanda, who were both wearing white caps and white aprons, were beginning to serve the roast. What kind of a roast it was I haven't the faintest idea. In those days I did not know the difference between roast-beef, veal and pork. Roast was roast, and roast was good.

Farmor's dinners were always tremendously orthodox. They consisted of soup, fish, roast and dessert. The dessert was usually apple-cake. As drinks, she served tepid sherry with the roast and cold burgundy with the dessert. Her wines, according to Father, were as bad as her food was good. But as Father said,

"One can't expect anything better than ink if one buys burgundy at 90 ore a bottle!"

When Johanne came to me, she rested the platter on the table, selected the best slice and cut it up into small pieces on my plate. She did the same with the potatoes. Then she mixed it all together, and covered it with gravy. I was a little embarrassed at her doing this for me and glanced over at Cousin Christian to see if he had noticed it. Fortunately he was just at that moment talking with his father and Miss Tychsen. Goodness, there were two things I especially longed for in those years. One was to be allowed to use a knife myself, the second was that my legs could reach the floor when I sat on a chair.

Before she moved on, Johanne whispered to me,

"Be careful now not to touch your food with your fingers, Soren."

She knew my appetite for Farmor's food.

I had only swallowed a few mouthfuls when Pastor Moller tapped on his glass and rose. The guests grew silent, put down their knives and forks, and looked towards him. Their expressions were a mixture of solemnity, expectation and irritation. Of course they tried to conceal the latter, but it was visible nonetheless—not least in the face of Uncle Billenstein. Well, it isn't particularly pleasant to let your food get cold after it has been served. As for me, my reaction was the same as theirs, though what I put down was only a spoon.

"Ladies and gentlemen," said Pastor Moller, "We all know the sad occasion which has brought us together ..."

Pastor Moller began with a discussion of the tragedy of life. We see healthy young people, separated in the flower of their youth from their consorts, their parents, their children. We see Death with his sharp scythe cut through the most tender and intimate bonds. How many bitter tears have fallen at the sight of the empty room, the vacant place at table, the empty bed ...

But the tragedy is only an illusion. A delusion that springs from our sinful human outlook, which is weak and mortal. The Greeks knew it long ago. They said, "Those whom the Gods love, die young." Today we know better. We don't say "the gods." We say God. We know there is only one God, one true God, the Holy Trinity. But in another sense, we are in agreement with the wise Greeks. We, too, can say, "Those God loves, die young." For we know that those who die young, with a spotless past—like that of the one we are gathered here to commemorate—such enter straight into the Kingdom of Heaven. So we really should not grieve for the dead. We know that he or she is well off—has come into a happiness that passes all understanding. No, indeed, we should really grieve for ourselves, because we must still tread the realm of sorrow and sin ...

I sat and endured it.

I endured it because I had a feeling that the speaker up at the other end of the table frequently turned his eyes in my direction. And this pastoral glance filled me with shame and remorse. I had been made to feel all too often before that my past was not spotless and would not bear Christian inspection.

I had to put up, too, with a steadily rising temperature. Not only was one of Hell's furnaces roaring behind my back but the gas lights from the ceiling, the candles in the two brass candle-sticks on the table, and each and every guest, were all sending forth waves of heat. The soup I had eaten was a source of inner heat; and the plates which had been heated out in the kitchen, wafted the heat of the food up in my face.

But I was suffering most of all from a sensation in the region of my stomach—and further down—that unmentionable sensation that gives warning that the undigested part of one's food is threatening to leave its host. What a very inopportune time it had come, that warning! I knew very well that one must not "go to the little room" when one sat at table. It wasn't proper. It wasn't well-behaved. And I wanted very much to be a well-behaved and proper boy. That was why I kept in my mind a secret list of everything that was forbidden or improper: one must not pick one's nose in other people's presence; one must not let one's undershirt, suspenders, or underpants be seen; and linen buttons were also a little unseemly—especially when the linen had worn off them. I knew that women's underskirts and legs were not meant to be looked at; that the iron coffee-pot must not,

when guests were present, be taken from the kitchen; and
that if people put plain, undecorated flower-pots in the
window they must be very poor. But, of course the worst
things of all had to do with the natural physical functions.
To make any kind of bodily noise was a catastrophe. At
best, it was only permitted if one was alone with one's nurse;
and if with one's nurse that was only because she was not
so refined as others. One must never say that one "had to
go somewhere" except to one's parents, one's farmor or one's
nurse; and to use other expressions than "the retiring room,"
or "the little room," was very naughty ... Therefore there
was nothing for me to do in the present distressing situation
but to sit still and hope that the sensation would pass off ...
So I assumed a hunchback position, pulled my insides together, and struggled to the best of my ability to control
the part of my body I was sitting on.

"Shall we all rise then and drink a glass in memory of
the beautiful and noble woman who has gone from us—gone
to her heavenly Father?"

There was a scraping af chairs. We all rose quietly and
drank—Christian and I our soda water, the others their
sherry.

We all sat down again. A painful little pause followed.
Nobody dared to break the silence or to resume eating.
Uncle Billenstein was the first to take up his knife and fork;
the pastor followed suit, then the rest of the company.

The next few minutes were passed in eating. Appetites
had been rekindled during the little pastoral intermezzo ...
Besides, the roast had to be eaten before the gravy hardened
and it was preferable to have an empty plate before the roast
was passed around again.

I, too, was ready to stuff myself again. The threatening
sensation, thank goodness, had passed.

In a short time the conversational orchestra began again.
Everybody began to talk at once, and only when Pastor Moller or Mrs. Agerlin raised their penetrating voices, did the
others respectfully stop to listen.

"As for as I'm concerned, I simply can't stand this modern literature," said Pastor Moller. It was evidently in answer to some one or other of Aunt Laura's opinions. "I often start reading a book that's in fashion—I believe one should know what their highnesses, the authors, have on their minds—but usually it makes me so angry that I never reach the end. For example yesterday, I began reading a new novel and in the very first page I found that the man had spelled *captain* with a K instead of with a C! If they are going to make foreign words Danish, then they ought to be consistent about it and write *cigar* with an S or *contour* with a K; and spell *odeur*, odor; and *cycle*, siggel. But just imagine how it would all look in print! And they go even further sometimes ... I finally got so disgusted that I threw the book away! ... No, really, it ought to be forbidden by law to do violence to the language like that, for what they are really doing is to trample on their mother-tongue instead of holding it sacred!"

Both Mrs. Agerlin and Mrs. Tychsen expressed their agreement with him.

As for me, I didn't know what *captain* with a K meant; nor did I know what spelling was. But this I did know, that when I grew up I would myself spell *captain* with a k, or whatever it was, in the way Pastor Moller could not stand!

Uncle Agerlin cleared his throat.

"A thing that I find rather trying," he began in a shy and diffident manner, "is that they use dashes instead of quotation marks and periods. It's so hard to make out the sense. One can never tell when people are talking and when they stop. At least that's the way it appears to me, but, of course, perhaps it is I who—"

I did not know what dashes or quotation marks or periods were. But this I did know that when I learned to write, I would write in the way Uncle Agerlin found it easier to understand.

"There *are* some exceptions," said Mrs. Tychsen, "There is that young writer, Johannes Jørgensen ..."

Pastor Moller conceded that he was among the better ones.

Cousin Christian turned to me,

"Aren't you looking forward to going to school and learning to read?"

I nodded. Nodding was partly being dishonest. I didn't really look forward to going to school at all. The thought of spending the whole day away from Johanne, together with strange people, struck terror into me. Moreover, Father had a habit of pointing out every school that we passed, ("It is a school, that building there,") and up till now I had never seen a building in that category which did not look severe and menacing. Even their facades seemed to whisper to my imagination that behind those walls the spirit was tortured and the body mishandled! A victim in the Middle Ages must have felt in the same way at the sight of a torture chamber that I felt at the sight of a school.

But learning to read—that was another matter. I desired nothing better than that. I knew very well that thrilling stories of all kinds were to be found in books; and that as soon as one learned to read, one could get to know them all. As the case now stood, I was dependant on a middleman, either Father or Johanne, to read to me. And neither was entirely satisfactory. Father was an excellent reader, of course, and he read me exciting stories about knights and Injuns. But it was difficult to get him to do it. He was usually either too busy or too tired. Johanne, who was willing to read, did it badly. She stumbled along, with the aid of her forefinger, and her reading was so slow and choppy that it was hard to get the thread of the story.

"I like to read very much," said Christian, dreamily. "Especially Sherlock Holmes, Jules Verne and Darwin."

His father's voice cut in,

"Take that young fellow Herman Bang—now there's a fool, if ever there was one!"

"If he would simply be content to be a fool," rumbled on the pastor, morose, pompous and sullen, "but he is also a thoroughly depraved man—a man who is leading the youth of our day into unspeakable immorality . . . !"

"As for the youth, I can vouch for that," said Uncle Billenstein in his harsh voice. "Especially when it has got a sense of humor!" His voice changed and became sharp and bitter. "He wrote the other day something about a station and a stationmaster, and the whole thing was utterly and ridiculously wrong!"

A sad expression came into Christian's grey eyes.

"One can never be happy again after reading Darwin. Everything appears evil and repulsive. Promise me, Soren, that you will never read him."

I nodded. Christian was always so clever. And I promised myself that as soon as I could read, I would get hold of the story of this Darwin. Was he a knight or an Injun?

Farmor came in from the kitchen, followed by her rearguards, Johanne and Fernanda. Each of the latter carried a platter, and on each platter were the remains of a roast accompained by newly cut slices. Farmor had decided the time had come for second helpings.

The sensation in my stomach returned. This time more strongly than before. It is possible that my distress might have been seen on my face if everyone's attention had not been focused at that moment on the maids and Uncle Billenstein. Uncle had just begun on an anecdote about a member of the royal family.

The second helpings had hardly been served when Uncle Agerlin struck his glass and stood up. He began stammering and stuttering—at first the words would not come. The discomfort in my stomach diminished, but a new fear took its place. It was a fear that Uncle Agerlin would not be able to remember what he was going to say; fear that he might sit down and cry while the others laughed at him.

He spoke of the one whom such a death as this would strike hardest. Pastor Moller had said something about its being the husband who lost his wife, but he was not quite in agreement with Pastor Moller. Pastor Moller must not misunderstand him, it was no criticism of him, he only meant—ahem—of course it was frightful to lose one's dear wife, of course he understood that, er—er—Now if he should lose his wife—er—er ... he only meant, that grief is really borne better by grown up people than by children—er— He had himself at the age of fourteen lost *his* mother, a loss from which he had never recovered. Even to this day he suffered when he thought about it ... what he meant to say was just that there was no loss so unbearable and so bitter as that of a child who loses its mother—

Aunt Laura broke in,

"You are quite right, Doctor."

Her voice was resolute and not without sympathy for Uncle Agerlin.

The terrifying sensation in my stomach had returned. I felt half-crazy with terror—soon something would happen if I did not struggle against it. And struggle I did; I struggled with all my might. I must have looked queer, but although many were looking at me, there were none who understood what was taking place. They must have interpreted my grimaces and the sweat on my brow as grief over the loss of my mother.

Uncle Agerlin continued,

He would not propose any toast—nor ask those present to empty their glasses—he would only tell little Soren who was sitting there at the other end of the table, and looked so unhappy—he would only tell him that everybody present was his friend. He could depend on them. If he should ever be in trouble, or life's difficulties overwhelmed him— great ones as well as small ones—he had only to turn to one of those who were present here tonight ... He himself ... he himself would always stand by—er—er—I only had to come to old Uncle Agerlin and he would—er—er—

Johanne, who was standing over by the door, wept unashamedly.

Suddenly Uncle Agerlin sat down—clumsily, unexpectedly.

No one had suspected from the tone of his voice that his speech had come to an end.

There was an awkward pause.

Then Pastor Moller saved the situation.

"It doesn't make any difference what the Doctor man says," he shouted cheerfully, "We shall all empty a glass just the same, to little Soren's health."

"Hear, hear," came from Uncle Billenstein.

All stood up. I was also going to stand up, but Farmor indicated with a hand on my arm that I was to remain seated.

Johanne came to me and whispered,

"You must lift your glass and look at all of them and then drink your lemonade . . ."

I tried to include as many as possible in one look, as told, and then drank my lemonade which had become rather cloudy in the course of the meal.

The grown up people lifted their glasses of sherry and gave me a hearty look, then there was again the scraping of chairs.

"That was a beautiful speech," said Mrs. Tychsen.

"Absolutely," answered Pastor Moller.

The pain in my stomach passed again. I breathed more freely.

Then Aunt Laura stood up.

"I am not going to make a speech," she said. "There are many people so benighted that they can't bear to hear a woman talk in public. Well, I can ignore that fact—I am accustomed to people's not liking what I say or do—but if I don't like making speeches the chief reason is that I am not nearly so glib of tongue as certain other womenfolk we know . . ."

"Ha, ha!" laughed Mrs. Agerlin shrilly. "Is that a hint at me?!"

"It wasn't meant so," said the speaker, "but when one strikes at a pack of dogs, the one hit is the one that yelps . . . Well, I simply want to thank Aunt Kirstine—to thank her for having gathered us all here this evening. I understand

Viggo very well—his sorrow is so great that he cannot bear the thought of company and no one can reproach him for that. But I also understand Aunt Kirstine. She believes that when something is proper—things like funeral wakes and mourning—then one must have the strength to go through with it. I admire you, Aunt Kirstine, for your strength and your will. Even if you are, as we all know, always complaining of ill-health, there is something solid and sustaining and robust in your nature. You possess a resiliance, a tenacity, a primaeval strength which even many of the crowd who call themselves *menfolk* must envy you."

My torture had begun anew. I knew miserably what would happen even before it actually took place. For the fraction of a second I felt a prodigious relief, then terror invaded me, terror of its being found out. Imagine what it would mean if it became known! I would never survive the shame of it!

Aunt Laura had finished her speech. I stood up cautiously, together with the others, to drink to the health of "Aunt Kirstine."

"Shall we not all have another helping?" piped Farmor, after the toast.

Johanne moved towards the platter on the buffet.

But before she reached it, the guests all protested laughingly,

"We couldn't eat another bite!"

"Even a poor station superintendent," chuckled Uncle Billenstein, "strikes bottom!"

"Well, then, we must serve the dessert," said Farmor in her plaintive voice.

Johanne began to gather up the empty plates. As she approached me, she stopped with a jerk. Her nostrils vibrated, then she bent over me and whispered,

"Don't you need to go to the little room?"

"No," I answered. I tried to look surprised, as if I couldn't understand why it should occur to her to ask such a question, although inwardly I was in mortal terror.

"Are you quite sure?"

I did not answer. The question was too foolish to require an answer.

"You must say so if you need to ..."

She added my plate and spoon to the pile she was carrying and hurried on.

When the apple-cake arrived, I was able to attack it with restored power. What had happened had renewed my appetite.

My mood brightened also. I almost forgot the catastrophe. Now I only had to behave so that the others would not notice anything. The idea that sooner or later discovery was bound to come never entered my mind.

At last the meal came to an end. We pushed back our chairs and went around shaking hands. We said to Farmor, "Thank you for the dinner;" to each other, "Velbekomme."

The coffee-cups were already set out in the living-room, and Johanne was on the way in there with the coffeepot, cream and sugar. The ladies gathered around the walnut table, while the men took possession of the sofa and the chairs by the window. I crept under the table. From this vantage point I could view the guests from their knees downwards.

"Socialism is utter madness," boomed Pastor Moller, who was sitting on the sofa. "It has been worked out that if everyone in the country was to have the same amount of money, nobody would get more than six kroner!"

"You cast off 108 stitches on three needles," Mrs. Tychsen was explaining, "and knit six rows, knit two straight and purl two."

"But next day when one man found he had twelve kroner, and his neighbour nothing, what then? Should we have to start all over again?"

Suddenly Farmor's mournful voice piped:

"I think I must have stepped on something," she said. "Something smells nasty."

She lifted her foot, and examined the sole of her shoe.

Whereupon the others also examined their footwear; and I understood then what was in Farmor's mind: she was much too courteous and considerate to accuse any of her guests themselves of smelling nasty. From my place under the table I watched the movement of their legs. I realized that the smell which Farmor could trace was emanating from me—from what had happened a little while ago at the dinner. Anxiety began to torture me again. But still I was not completely terror-stricken. I reasoned, subconsciously, that if I just remained very quiet and pulled myself together, nobody would think of me.

They had finished their self-examination. Nobody would admit guilt.

"Then I must have been mistaken," murmured Farmor humbly.

There was a pause.

As usual it was Uncle Billenstein who had the courage to break it.

"Such odors," he chuckled, not unlike a naughty boy, "sometimes emanate from other parts of the body than the soles of the feet . . ."

I could see by his broad, flat shoes, with their many fine cracks, that he was sitting on the sofa next to Pastor Moller. Pastor Moller wore shoes with elastic sides.

"There are ladies present," Mrs. Tychsen reprimanded him.

Mrs. Agerlin's coarse voice was heard,

"One can always tell when a man becomes a widower. It makes men so *rustique!*"

Uncle Billenstein only answered with a boorish laugh.

Then Farmor asked sweetly and innocently, "Where is Soren, I wonder?"

Mrs. Agerlin answered mercilessly,

"He is sitting there under the table as usual."

I crouched like a frightened rabbit. Horror froze my blood. Farmor lifted a corner of the laced tablecloth and tried to look under the table.

"Soren," she called, "little Soren."

I could tell from her eyes that she could not see me, so I kept still.

"Isn't he there?" Farmor asked peevishly.

"Of course he's there," cried Mrs. Agerlin, sticking her purplish red face under the table. Oh, how I hated her!

Farmor coaxed,

"Come on out now, little Soren. Come now."

I didn't stir. I kept a stubborn silence.

"Is there no one who will get him?" she asked—in her most helpless voice.

Mrs. Agerlin stuck her shoe forward, as if to kick me out. Fortunately I was sitting on the opposite side of where the bars crossed, so she could not reach me.

"Well then, I'll get hold of the sinner," roared Pastor Moller cheerfully. I could see from his shoes that he was standing up.

Uncle Agerlin stirred uneasily.

"It is almost a pity . . ." he murmured. "I only mean—er—that . . ." but nobody paid attention to him.

"Human nature is contrary," remarked Mrs. Tychsen, with feeling.

"Oh mother, can't you understand—he is just frightened."

There was so much sympathy in Miss Tychsen's voice that it went to my heart.

At that instant an enormous brown beard came in view under the table.

I stiffened with fright. I was mute with terror, the same terror which seizes a small animal when it stares into a big animal's open mouth.

But when a body with a broad, thick-lipped mouth, surrounded by long brown hair reached out for me, my muteness vanished. My body stiffened and shook, while prolonged shrieks of fear burst from me in rhythm with its convulsions.

Johanne who had been clearing the table in the dining-room came flying in. She stooped beneath the table.

"Soren, little Soren," she called, and every "Soren" was like an embrace, a caress.

I stumbled out on my knees, stood up, threw my arms around her legs, and pressed myself against her skirt as if I wanted to crawl into her lap and hide myself there.

Behind me I heard Mrs. Agerlin saying,

"Too bad it should happen just on his mother's burial day!"

Johanne wrapped me into her apron—and fled.

9

And then I stood in the bed-room, in Farmor's basin. The basin had been placed on a chair. I leant against the chair-back, so as not to fall; and all I had on was a short woolen shirt. Johanne was all around me, armed with a large sponge; one minute its mass was dipped and squeezed; the next it was scrubbing my legs and behind. The luke-warm water gurgled, splashed, bubbled ...

My weeping had ceased. Johanne had stopped it. But shame had replaced shrieks and tears—for now they all knew, of course—all Farmor's guests—that I, who wanted so much to be regarded as a big boy, made messes in my pants! The thought rounded my back, and made me close my eyes.

The worst thing was that Pastor Moller knew it. He was a priest and therefore might regard this sort of thing severely. Besides he had called me "the sinner." Maybe he would stand in the doorway of his church and forbid me to enter it on Christmas Eve; maybe he would see to it also, that I should never be allowed into Heaven.

No—it was still worse that Mrs. Agerlin knew. The priest would probably only cause me trouble in church and in Heaven, but Mrs. Agerlin would take charge of all the other, more wordly, fields of life. For I knew her too well to think she would hold her tongue. She was never one to throw the cloak of charity over others' faults. No, indeed, she would cry out my shame to everyone she met. And whenever she came to see Farmor in future, she would come out with a remark about it. One of those *remarks* which sound so kind, so indulgent, but none the less bore deep down to where it *hurts most*.

But no—the worst thing of all was that Miss Tychsen knew—she who was so lovely! She who was so good and fine and sweet! I must be disgraced for ever in her eyes ... But I would probably never see her again. If she called on Farmor, I would hide. I would hide myself in "the little room" and not come out till after she'd gone.

For an instant a dreadful wish took possession of me—a wish that they would all die, the whole lot of them, except me and Johanne. If they all died, then there would be no one who knew that I had soiled my breeches on mother's burial day. No one but Johanne, and she would never blab.

But I quickly revoked this wish. The thought occurred to me that the dead do not just lie quietly in the ground but hover up there in the air. They are invisible and can see everything that goes on. All that the living Pastor Moller and the living Mrs. Agerlin could discover was bad enough; but it would be simply indescribably awful if they were suddenly struck dead and then were able to keep track of everything I did. The thought of having the whole company flying around me in the air was, on the whole, still more frightful, positively gruesome, in fact. No, it was better, really, to have them all alive ...

Johanne must have been reading my thoughts, for suddenly she said,

"Now you mustn't grieve about it any longer, Soren. It just happened because you were a bit sick in the stomach. Don't worry. I'll explain that to everybody."

What a more clever person would not have understood with his mind Johanne understood with her heart.

A few moments later I was lying—smelling of almond soap and in a clean white night-shirt—in Farmor's bed.

The buzz of the funeral party came from far away. Then the sound ebbed out of my consciousness.

10

I know but little of Farmor's family background. I only know that she was born in the country and christened Kirstine Rasmussen. While quite young she married a farmer. But her husband was no ordinary peasant. He was skilled in accounting and reading, knew a good deal about conveying and mortgaging property, was a born businessman, and instead of making the soil bear fruit for himself and others, busied himself with something much more fruitful to himself, namely, estate brokerage. How he got into it, I don't know; nor from whom he got the necessary initial capital. But he made money, and ten years after their marriage, Soren and Kirstine moved into a nearby provincial town, where he established himself in the real estate business.

There were three things which drew them away from their home: it was considered in those days more "refined" to live in a city than in the country; the city offered wider opportunities for increasing their income; and last, but not least, there was Viggo. Viggo, their only child, should go to the best school they knew about—the Cathedral School: he should become a student, go to college, attain a higher social level than the one they had reached. This was also the reason why they moved to the capital when Viggo was ready for college. For just as it was more refined to live in a provincial town than in the country, so life in the capital was more elegant than that in a provincial town. One had to go to the capital if one really wanted to rise in the world. And so grandfather eventually procured for himself a good, substantial corner-dwelling in the metropolis's newest quarter. And by that time he did not need to work. The rest of his life was spent in leisure, as property-owner and landlord.

I ought, however, to mention one other thing: a few years

ago somebody told me that my grandfather sometimes engaged in usury. But it was told me by a man whom I had outstripped in life's race and it was told me in anger and envy, so it was very likely not true.

Father's father died shortly after my birth, and I can not remember him. However, his pictures suggest his career. The face is broad, powerful, intelligent; it is evident that its owner had his roots in the soil, but at the same time the peasant traits in him had become polished by city-life and the consciousness of financial security. The face could easily have belonged to a professor of peasant extraction or to one of the country's ministers. Curiously enough, he looked not only like a cultivated man, but also like an upright one.

In addition to the other things revealed in his face, there was also a certain self-reliant contentment. But then he had all possible grounds for being both self-confident and contented with existence. He had risen from nothing to be a wealthy man, he had seen his son become head of his university class, and later a poet and dentist to the royal family.

Still, his happiness may not have been unadulterated. Some years ago, on the death of an old lady, I received a package of letters and photographs. The letters were written by my mother, and some of the photographs were pictures of her as a young girl, and when just married, while others were of myself in the first years of my life. The old lady had been a friend of my mother's, and after she had married a secretary of some foreign legation and gone to live abroad, the two young women had continued their friendship by correspondence. From one of these letters I learned that my grandfather had died under slightly disreputable circumstances. He had had a heart attack while visiting a woman of unsavoury reputation. His son had had his body brought home in a cab, however, and no one except the writer ever knew where he had died.

On his death Farmor inherited his house and his fortune.

Farmor was small of stature, always dressed in black, always looked as white as wax and always wore a cap. Her hair was white, but only part of it. The rest was a greenish-yellow color. She wore it parted in the middle, pulled straight down over her temples, and drew it over a hair pad on the nape of her neck into a modest bun. She always wore glasses; the lenses were elliptical, framed in a cheap metal; and they were often so blurred that existence must have seemed rather dreary to their wearer. She had three pairs: one for reading and sewing, one for conversation, and one for the street. The glasses she was not wearing she would usually put somewhere that she could not later remember ... She must have spent not a little part of her life hunting for her glasses. Her eyes were greatly magnified through them, but not dilated: for they had a rather flat surface and were so anaemic that they appeared colorless. Her nose was a chapter in itself. It was quite broad when seen in profile, particularly the bridge curved inward instead of outward, while the end of it was wide and shapeless —"amorphous", to use a mineralogical expression. It suggested, because of its pallor, its lumpy structure, and its pitted surface, the unripe side of a strawberry. Her mouth was broad and the upper lip always blue from diligent shaving. She had lost her upper teeth. If I had not been aware of this before it was impressed upon me so that I shall never forget it when I saw her on her death-bed. No one had thought to remove her plate, and during her death struggle it had gradually loosened and fell out with a plop. Her hands were pale, she had thin fingers with blue worm-like veins. When I was at the fairy-tale stage, they always made me think of the witch in Hansel and Gretel; when I reached the stage of nature-study, they made me think of tadpoles' feet. Farmor's hands were perhaps that part of her which inspired the greatest fear and revulsion in me. What her body was like underneath her black garb, I did not, thank Heaven, know.

Farmor was hardly what could be called "a nice elderly lady." Whereas grandfather, to judge from his photographs, had been quite a handsome old gentleman, Farmor was neither handsome nor charming—her physiognomy was far too toad-like for that; nor could she be called *elderly*—she was simply *old*; and she was so palpably of peasant origin that it is doubtful if any of her neighbours would have described her as a *lady*.

She was always old in the years that I knew her. When I look back it seems to me that she looked the same age in all the time she and I were in touch with one another. It must, of course, be a trick of memory. My brain tells me that at one time she must have been a child and young like everybody else, but as I remember her the idea of her ever having been a child who had playmates or a young girl who fell in love and was beloved, is simply inconceivable.

Many years after her death a certain photograph of her fell into my hands. It was then that I realized who it was on whom she modelled herself. In those days, it was not film-actresses whom women imitated, but royal personages. Consciously or unconsciously, directly or indirectly, Farmor had modelled herself on Queen Victoria. To be sure, Farmor did not possess the Widow Queen's protruding eyes, nor her finely-shaped nose, nor her arrogant mouth; but the resemblance was there nevertheless—in the manner of wearing the hair, in her maggot-pale skin, in her melancholy expression, in her headdress—yes, in every article of her clothing. There were probably several hundred thousands of little widows at that period, not only in England, but all around the world, who imitated this widow above all widows.

Farmor's health was always vacillating. She suffered from dizziness, asthma, and ringing in her ears; her hearing was bad, very bad; and she slept poorly. I imagine much of this was hypochondria and some, craftiness. She made good use of her ill-health. People were considerate and helpful when she complained of her asthma, her cough and her mucous condition. Envy melted away when she spoke of her approaching death. If, through her back-biting, she'd sometimes got herself into an awkward situation—like the

time when she'd told everyone that Pastor Moller got drunk
on altar-wine—she was able to save the day by talking
about the ringing in her ears, her headache, her dizziness,
her being obliged to lie flat on the sofa. Also, like so many
other more or less hard-of-hearing people, she could hear
considerably more than she admitted. She would sit in the
midst of company and pretend—with a melancholy expression—that, due to her bad hearing, she was left out of
everything. But she was really listening intently, listening
in the hope that people might begin talking about *her!* She
used her difficulty in hearing in another way also. When,
in company, she learned that someone was to be away on a
certain day, she would invite this person to her house for
that particular day. When the person in question had
to decline her invitation, she would register great surprise and disappointment. But no invitation followed for
another day. In this manner she showed hospitality without
its costing her a single ore. Thus she could accept a second
invitation to the same household without having returned its
earlier hospitality—since a declined invitation ranges as
high as an accepted one! I believe that there were not many
who saw through this form of economy—probably no one in
fact, but her unnoticed, long-eared grandson.

But Farmor's invalidism was not all imagination or pre-
tence. I had sufficient proof of that after her death. She
was unable to take many steps before she had to stop
and gasp for breath. How often I used to imitate her
with youthful mercilessness—her open mouth, her short
choking breaths, her left hand pressed against her side and
the right reaching out for something to hang on to. Yes,
unhappily, I even mimicked her in her very presence. She
was never angered—on the contrary, she regarded it as a
roguishness which bespoke a high degree of genius. "What
that boy Soren won't hit upon!" she would pipe admiringly.
My father was amused by it, too, which was really rather
wrong of him. Thanks to this reaction, there was fostered
in me no little skill in mimicking Farmor. Many years

later I happened to meet at some social gathering a physician who was a specialist in allergies. I told him about Farmor, and I enacted for him the acts which I remembered from my childhood. To my surprise he informed me that the person I mimicked had undoubtedly been, notwithstanding her dramatics, genuinely asthmatic, authentically and typically asthmatic, probably from childhood. I admit this gave me a different conception of her invalidism.

Farmor had two outstanding traits: distrust and fear.

She distrusted everybody. Every living person, according to her belief, was bent on cheating her, stealing from her, deceiving her, plundering her and murdering her. Even I was not exempt. When I was quite small she suspected me of filching sugar and small change. It was unjust—among other reasons because I would not have known how to steal things and money which were always kept under lock and key. Later she accused me of altering my school reports, which was likewise unjust—I would never have had the courage to commit such a crime. When I got to a secondary school, she spread it abroad that I was seducing young girls there: another thing that never happened—also, unfortunately, because my courage failed. And in her last years, she was convinced that I went about longing for her early death so that I should inherit her house and fortune. It was probably this charge which came nearest the truth. But, strangely enough, there was nothing particularly shocking to her in the accusation—she found it quite in order that I should wish her dead. If I had proved to be extravagantly attractive to women, she would no doubt have been simply pleased. So far as sex was concerned, only two things would have caused her displeasure: if I had married a girl without money and if I had been sued for alimony. And if, as a child, I had really succeeded in altering my reports, or robbing her of sugar and money, I believe I should have aroused, in the depths of her soul, only admiration and pride.

Ah, spirit of Farmor, I call upon you to come forth and

solve your myriad riddles! Was your monstrous distrust a personal trait bequeathed to you by nature when seed and cell first united in you? Or was it a normal characteristic which life developed to sickly proportions? And, if the latter, would "life" betoken "Grandfather?" His erotic escapades? His work as estate agent and real-estate broker? Alas, I am only too well aware that neither the grimy bones in the family grave at the cemetery, nor the picture which my mind projects on memory's slate can ever yield me the slightest answer.

The simplest explanation af Farmor's fear is that it was a consequence of her distrust. When one believes every maid servant is a thief, every tenant a cheat, every beggar a murderer; when one awaits death by strangulation within twenty-four hours, it is natural to live in a realm of fear. But I am not even sure if this line of thought is tenable. Mankind knows so little of cause and effect. One can easily reason that fear came first; that, for example, it was aroused by some glandular secretion, and that suspicion followed in an effort to rationalize it. If one is afraid, must there not be some cause? So one always looks for a reason, and little by little it could appear that one's fellow-man was plotting to get possession of one's property, honor and life.

Farmor not only lived in terror of being robbed, cheated, and murdered, there were other malignant forces which aroused her fears. I remember a little scene which was enacted shortly after I came to live with her. I had been playing on the floor and while doing so I happened to see that she was sitting cutting her nails. The odd thing about it was that she carefully collected the cuttings in a little piece of white paper she had torn from a notebook. I was surprised. When Johanne cut my nails, she cheerfully let them fall where they would; as a rule they fell into a wash-basin, from which they disappeared with the water down the drain. Farmor's method not only surprised me, it disgusted me. I hated nails—especially hers.

Suddenly I burst out,

"Farmor, are you playing a game with your nails?"

I had got the idea that if she saved her nails so carefully it must be because she wanted to use them as playthings.

But Farmor looked at me with an air of mystery, and said in a hushed voice,

"Soren, promise me that when you cut your nails you will always burn them, otherwise you can never know what may happen."

And, sure enough, when Farmor had finished, she wrapped the nails carefully in the paper again, glided over to the stove, and put the package in.

At that time I did not grasp the motive for her procedure, and I did not waste much time thinking about it. Understanding came later on when I read, in my schooldays, a book entitled "Daily Life in the North in the 16th Century." From this I learned that witches and sorcerers could work their spells with the aid of human nails and hair-combings. Among Farmor's many other fears was that of being bewitched!

If there was a connection between her distrust and her fears there was also one between her distrust and her back-biting. It is natural, of course, for people to talk about their fellow-men; and if one suspects others of all possible evil, then it is also a logical necessity to engage in what is called back-biting. But Farmor's fears and perhaps also her idea of good manners gave her back-biting a peculiar character. It was what you might call *sympathetic* back-biting. She never said,

"Pastor Moller is a drunkard. He always gets tipsy on the eucharist wine he drinks behind the altar."

No, indeed. Instead, she would say, sadly,

"I hear that somebody happened to see Pastor Moller slightly intoxicated behind the altar. People say that he often gets drunk on the eucharist wine. What a shame they should say such things about him ... One can only hope that it isn't true—that it's just slander ..."

However, Farmor's defamation was, of course, not exclusively composed of mistrust. It contained an element of malignity, too. Let me add— in favor of Farmor—that it seems to me that women with a wicked tongue were far more common in those days than they are to-day. The cause may be that the women were still waiting for their emancipation; or, maybe, that many women were sexually starving. Perhaps it originated from the "abdominal diseases" which so many young women got as morning-gift at their wedding. Or was the cause to be sought in their sedentary life?—I can't tell. I can only guess.

There is yet another trait of Farmor's that I must mention —one which was not particularly noticeable. I only understood it in its full significance after her death. She was an ideologist. She lived for an idea. All her actions in both big and small affairs were motivated by one and the same idea—and truly a grandiose one—an idea worthy of a queen —that of founding a dynasty.

Farmor, so small and frail physically, possessed an enormous will-power ...

11

Before I proceed further I must forewarn my readers that there will be little continuity in these memoirs. As I have already said, I do not remember events chronologically and therefore I have to record them for the most part just as they come to mind. The worst of it is that they float before me as sharply outlined phenomena, as absolutely disconnected experiences. What I actually find in my brain is a varied assortment of stories, happenings, moods, scenes, and speeches—and the only real link between them is a small group of recurrent figures, with first and foremost the chief protagonist, MYSELF. If I were to jot them all down just as they occur to me, this book would become like a tray of miscellaneous food served up higgledy-piggledy-fashion.

Let me give an example of what I mean by this "slice of life" method of recollection.

I am sitting at the window in Farmor's dining-room, my

elbows on the window-sill, my cheeks resting on my closed fists. I am looking out on a wintry sky which is grey and dismal. Outside the window seagulls are uttering sharp, complaining cries. I sit there and feel thoroughly glum. I am as sad as a child can be without actually bursting into tears. One of the panes of glass in the window features in that memory—a pane with a flaw, a little air-bubble in it —and so does a yellowish-colored tree, grained with brown stripes.

And then there it nothing more. Nothing goes *before* or *after* that memory. There it not even any recollection of my reason for feeling unhappy. On the other hand the mood of it is intense and painful, and it still comes to mind to me whenever I hear seagulls' cries ....

My memories abound with "happenings" of this kind. Some are not so clear-cut; some are, for example, only memories of a conversation, one that I cannot even connect with any particular person!

I offer this as an excuse for the fictional character of my book. And in particular as an excuse for the following: there are two conversations which have persisted in my memory which absolutely have no connection with anything else. All I can be sure of is that they were between Farmor and Mrs. Agerlin, and that they took place in Farmor's dining-room. Despite their complete lack of beginning or end, they seem so characteristic that they ought not to be omitted.

I hear Mrs. Agerlin shrill,

"Don't you think the boy is rather backward, Mrs. Jensen? It isn't natural for a child of his age to make a pig of himself like that."

And I hear Farmor piping,

"O no—it's very common. Common with boys, that is. Boys dirty their clothes much more often than girls do."

Mrs. Agerlin again,

"Is that so? I never heard that before. Don't you think

your memory fails you, Mrs. Jensen? He's going on for six now, isn't he, that young man?"

"Yes, that's right. But of course, you wouldn't know about such things, Mrs. Agerlin. You've never been blessed with children."

And she added sympathetically,

"Believe me, Mrs. Agerlin, I have often felt so sorry for you ..."

I suppose this little dialogue took place a few days after the funeral dinner. Probably Mrs. Agerlin had been paying Farmor a thank-you call—that was often done in those days. But, as I said, I remember nothing more than that.

In the other conversation I recall, it is Farmor who holds the floor. But for some reason I am certain that it was again Mrs. Agerlin she was adressing.

"I have the boy living here, and do you suppose Viggo gives me a single ore for it? He has not so much as offered to pay anything! Of course, I like to let Soren live here for nothing—he's the very apple of my eye, that boy!—but his Father could at least thank me for it ..."

A hand strokes my hair.

"Soren will never be so ungrateful, I'm sure."

The final remark transformed me in an instant into two conflicting personalities: the one was proud that I was considered better than my Father; the other was angry on Father's behalf because Farmor had spoken ill of him. And the second had also a feeling that what she'd said about him was untrue and unjust.

But that memory goes no further either!

12.

"To-day you shall have that pigeon we promised you," said Farmor, in her squeaky voice, at breakfast. "Lillelund knows someone who has a pigeon-house on his roof ..."

An hour later I was sitting at the kitchen table peering

down into the courtyard. Fernanda stood beside me washing out some trifles. Farmor was in the dining-room . . . enthroned as usual in her wicker chair beside the window with the street-reflector, and Johanne had gone home to fetch a suit of clothes for me. My eyes were busy following the antics of some boys playing below, when suddenly I heard steps on the kitchen stairs. The steps stopped and there was a pull at the door-bell. A second later the bell rang shrilly. Fernanda wiped her hands on her apron and went in search of Farmor.

The rattle of her keys announced Farmor's entrance. She began the slow, involved process of unlocking.

When the door was finally opened, Lillelund was seen standing outside on the kitchen-stair landing.

"Here are the pigeons, Mrs. Jensen," he said in his sing-song voice.

He held a wooden box in his hands. When he had placed it on the table I saw that the side which had been turned inward had a wire screening with a door in it. Behind the screen some pigeons were strutting, looking rather frightened.

"He wouldn't kill one hisself," said Lillelund, "so as Madam should choose the one she wanted!"

One of the pigeons was pure white; another was many shades of blue and grey. I thought them all wonderful— but the *white* one, that was simply the loveliest thing I'd ever seen! That beautiful, helpless bird touched something tender in my child-heart. And I could plainly read, too, in its one eye that it was also drawn to me!

"Oh how sweet the white one is," I cried, clapping my hands. "Can I have that one? Oh, please, Farmor!"

I crawled down from the kitchen table to see the birds better. They had quieted down now and were walking about their wooden cage, pushing their heads back and forth.

"Shall we try the white one?" asked Lillelund.

Farmor nodded affirmatively. Lillelund opened the door a crack and stuck his hand into the cage. Again fear seized the pigeons; they fluttered around in the narrow space so that their feathers fell out. Lillelund felt around in the cage until the white one was driven into a corner. Then his hand came down over it. And the pigeon was pulled out.

"It's a little hard to get hold of 'em," said Lillelund with his good-natured smile.

"I want to pet it!" I cried, "I want to pet it!"

Lillelund who held the bird, tucked it close to him and arranged his hands so that I could touch it. I carefully petted it with my finger tips from the neck downward over its back. I was certain that this was the only way one was supposed to stroke animals. It was "conforming", the opposited way was "non-conforming."

The pigeon sat perfectly still, accepting the inevitable. Perhaps it liked my loving fingers.

"I wonder whether it is any more than bones," Farmor said, pushing my hand gently aside, and herself began poking the bird here and there with her index finger. Suddenly she pinched its breast with two fingers.

"It's only a young one," said Lillelund.

"I want to have *that* one!" I screamed.

"Yes, I think it will do," nodded Farmor.

"It's quite a nice one," said Lillelund.

The pigeon was carefully slipped from Lillelund's hands into Farmor's.

I was happy. I understood that I was going to be given the white pigeon as a present. I was so filled with happiness, even down to my legs, that I could not stand still. Hopping and kicking up my heels, I sang out shrilly,

"It's my pigeon! it's my pigeon!"

Then something happened. Yes, suddenly something had happened. My slow-moving Farmor, who could sometimes surprise one with an act of lightning speed, had with an imperceptible movement done something extraordinary to the pigeon, something that filled my blood with horror.

"Farmor!" I began, my voice trembling with anxiety ...

Farmor laid the pigeon on the kitchen table. It lay there without moving.

My breath stopped. My heart stopped. At least that is the way I felt then anyhow.

When I found my tongue at last, I moaned,

"Why is it like that?"

I stood staring down at it, my eyes round with fright and wonder.

"Like that? What do you mean 'like that'?" whined Farmor, pretending not to understand.

"Madam has only killed it," explained Lillelund in a friendly way. "Otherwise the young Master couldn't have it for supper to-night!"

Suddenly I understood—understood the whole horror of it.

"You have made it dead," I shrieked, a fury of despair spreading all through me. I rushed at Farmor and gave vent to my hatred. I pounded at her stomach and her breast, I kicked her shins. Simultaneously I cried,

"I hate you! Oh how beastly you are! I hate you."

Farmor did not budge. She just stood there, weakly defending herself and whining,

"But little Soren – little Soren! It was only for your sake, little man!"

And behind Farmor Lillelund mumbled, puzzled and frightened,

"Oh but little Sir, don't—don't!"

It was Fernanda who rescued Farmor. She came up behind me, seized my arms, and pulled me backwards. I kicked her; I struggled; I flung myself about; I tried to bite her—but in the end she was the stronger.

Then all of a sudden, my fury was over; it ebbed slowly away from me like gas from a balloon. Only despair remained. Despair that the little white pigeon could no longer move.

My violent fit of weeping diminished; became first a long drawn-out sobbing, then a kind of hiccup.

"I think we'd better try and put him on the sofa," wailed

Farmor, "and then we must see if we can get him to go to sleep."

A procession started through the little corridor. First went Fernanda, who held my wrist as in a vice, although I no longer struggled against her; then Farmor; and at the end came Lillelund—the latter possibly to protect Mrs. Jensen if I should get violent again.

I heard Farmor mumble behind me,

"What a pity Johanne isn't here."

Farmor and Fernanda got me to lie down on the sofa; a down pillow was put under my head, and Farmor's crocheted rug was spread over me. I still whimpered; water from my eyes and from my nose dripped on the pillow ... and then everything began to slip away—farther and farther away.

Even grief.

I ate roast pigeon for dinner with an excellent appetite.

The three women ate the left-overs.

13.

I had been sent out with eighteen ore, wrapped in a piece of paper, to buy a loaf of French bread. The expedition had been successful, and I was on the way home and had gotten as far as the foyer. But crossing the marble floor was taking some time—I had to take care not to step on the white squares, you remember.

Suddenly I heard the street-door open behind me. I looked round—and there stood Miss Constance.

I was filled with fright and shame. Not for anything in the world would I meet Miss Constance after what had happened on Mother's burial day. I could well imagine how the loveliest woman I had ever seen or heard of must despise me, must look down on me.

I realised from the warmth of my cheeks that I must be blushing. I quickly turned my head and started to run—without paying any more attention to black or white squares.

Then the glass-doors stuck. The two horrid things were so heavy, so almost impossible to pull apart!

In my struggle to open them, I dropped the bread.

Miss Tychsen came hurrying up, and picked it up.

"Why it's Soren, isn't it?" she exclaimed.

"Yes," I mumbled, feeling desperate.

"Don't you remember me?"

I stared at the floor and answered "Yes," even more weakly than before. She drew off her glove and patted my cheek.

"Have you been out buying a French loaf?" she asked.

I nodded.

"You *are* a big boy to go into town alone and buy things!" Her voice cast a little sunshine into my despair.

"Shall we go upstairs together?" she asked.

With a hand stretched above my head she opened the swingdoor.

"How old are you now?" she asked.

"Five-and-a-half," I answered.

"Why you *are* tall for your age! And you're a handsome boy, too. I'm not surprised that you're your Farmor's darling!"

She said these pleasant things quite without a grown-up's usual saccharine mode of speaking to children. They came straight from her good heart and were as melodious as music. And she was as gay as people tend to be on a Sunday morning when the sun is shining. The shame in me began to diminish a little.

We were half-way up the stairs:

"Do you really know who I am?"

"Yes."

"Well then, what is my name?!"

I knew very well, but I also knew that my tongue and lips would refuse to say it. So I kept silent.

"You don't *really* know!" she teased.

"I do—but it's difficult to say," I said miserably.

She grasped the situation at once.

"Then call me 'White'," she said. "It's short for "Snow White". That's what I used to call myself when I was a little girl. It's my pet-name. As a matter of fact I was almost grown up before I could say Constance Tychsen. You can say 'White,' can't you?"

"White"—I said cautiously.

"Do you know the fairy-tale about Snow White?"

"No—o," I said. Then suddenly I remembered what Mother had taught me and corrected myself:

"No, thank you."

"Don't you? Don't you really?" she exclaimed. "Do you know what you must do, Soren? One day you must come and visit me. And then Aunt White will read to you the story of Snow White."

"Thank you," I said. The well-brought up child that I was gave me orders to bow. But it is difficult to bow at the same time as you're climbing stairs, so I was a little awkward in doing it. My clumsiness embarrassed me.

"Do you like stories?"

"Yes, thank you," I answered politely—but also very truthfully.

We had stopped outside Farmor's door. I pressed the bell-button very hard so that Farmor would come quickly to my rescue. It was at the same time both wonderfully nice to be together with Miss Constance and frightfully painful. How could one reach the heights of somebody who was so fine and clever and sweet and beautiful and noble! Certainly she could only look upon me as a second-rate being.

"What sort of stories have you heard?" she continued.

"Some about Injuns—and some about knights."

"Did your Farmor read them to you?"

"No."

"Was it your nurse—what is her name, now?"

"No."

"Then it must have been your Daddy?"

I had gotten into the habit of saying No, so this time I said it again.

"Well, who *does* read to you then?"

"I read myself."

The words burst from me—absolutely without forethought. I realized what I had said only after I had pronounced them.

"But Soren, surely you can't read yet!" she exclaimed, amazed. I could see she was pondering whether it really could be true.

Farmor's keys were rattling in the door.

"Yes, I can," I said. For now I had told a lie and now I had to stick to it. My honor required it. "Yes, I can. I could read when I was two! ... I've read hundreds of stories ... all Father's stories ... and I've read all the newspapers in the world!"

It was not quite such a whopping lie as might appear. I had often been sitting with a book or a newspaper in front of me and Father and Mother used to call it in fun *"reading."* "Well, look—there sits Soren reading" they would say! In my vocabulary, therefore, "reading" meant to sit with a book or paper in front of one. And yet I suspected even as I spoke that what I was saying was not quite accurate, that it was even what grown-up people called a lie.

"Do you know what, Soren," said Miss Tychsen with a broad smile, "you're making things up!"

Then she grew serious—and started talking like her mother.

"Really it's not like a nice boy like you to say things that aren't true ..."

At that moment the door was opened.

I darted through the entrance without even saying goodbye to her—dashed straight to the red box-couch and buried my face in its cushions.

What must Miss Tychsen be thinking of me! Now, she not only knew that I'd made gaga in my pants—she also knew that I told lies! Perhaps she had gone straight up and told her mother. And her mother would tell Pastor Moller, and Pastor Moller would speak of it in church ...

Everybody in the whole world would despise me! I knew it only too well—I would be despised now and forever more.

And I writhed under a sole desire—a desire to sink down into the couch and remain hidden there for the rest of my life ...

Out on the landing Farmor and Miss Tychsen were whispering together. It could only be about me they were whispering: I knew it. Only too well!

14

Farmor and I were alone in the dining-room. Fernanda, for once, was off for the evening, and Johanne had had permission to go to a dressmaker who was altering one of Mother's dresses for her.

It was evening—past bedtime. I knew that I was only waiting up for Johanne to come back and put me to bed. But up to now I had been allowed to build houses with that mixed pack of cards which was always at my disposal.

Fie was snoring softly and peacefully in the niche behind the stove; the clock hanging on the wall was ticking low and muffled; the coke in the stove was crackling; high in the ceiling the blue-white gas-flame was fizzing weakly and monotonously; and now and again Farmor's knitting needles clinked against each other. That was all this serene world knew of noise and disturbance.

We rarely spoke. There were long pauses between each exchange of words.

Suddenly Farmor piped out, in the midst of the silence: "Don't you need to go to the little room, Soren?"

Perhaps I had been fidgetting rather a lot. I was kneeling on my chair, and that is something that tends to make you tired.

"No," I answered with some irritation. I was angry at being interrupted in my task, which was very important and required all my concentration. Besides it was a sign of lack of confidence on her part. Why remind me of a function which I could perfectly well take care of myself?

Farmor said plaintively,

"You must remember what happened on the day of your mother's funeral."

My house of cards wobbled and collapsed. And I had just succeeded in getting two cards on the second story!

Farmor's words awakened my sleeping shame. I had almost forgotten that terrible event. But now memory returned to disturb my quiet evening's pleasure and invade every cell of my body with the pain one feels when one knows one has disgraced oneself ...

I did not answer her. My soul bowed down, I began the rebuilding of the fallen cardhouse.

And Fie snored. The clock ticked. The fire crackled. The gas bubbled. A long time passed. A very long time. Perhaps ten thousand years!

I began to feel bored. My body craved relaxation. Besides, it was irritating that all my houses fell down when I began on the second story. Angry thoughts possessed me.

Finally I couldn't be bothered with card-houses any more, but just sat and scattered the cards with the flat of my hand while I tried to think up a new game—a new amusement.

Suddenly I started listening—my neck stretched out, my eyes staring.

"Farmor!" I whispered in pretended fright, "Farmor, there is somebody in the den!"

I knew very well that this wasn't true. But *why* I was lying I did not know. Nor did I ponder the reason. Perhaps it was something I was just saying in fun—as one does on April Fool's Day.

There was a few seconds' pause before Farmor stuttered, "W-what's that? ... D-did you say? ..."

Her voice was pitiful. Plainly, I had succeeded in frightening her.

It was too tempting not to follow up the victory,

"There's somebody moving about in there"—I nodded towards the den. "It must be a burglar!"

Farmor tried to pull herself together.

"Nonsense, Soren. I don't hear a thing."

This argument was easy to quash. I lunged out heartlessly, triumphantly:

"But *you* are *deaf*, Farmor!"

But Farmor still wouldn't be quite persuaded:

"How could anyone have come in? The door is locked."

"He may have crawled up on the roof and along the drain-pipe, and in at the window," I said. The answer burst from me without forethought, to my own surprise and even admiration.

I climbed down from my chair and tiptoed over to the closed door. Then I put my whole soul into an act of mimicry.

"He's over there by the desk," I whispered. "He's putting a key in the drawer—the one with the money in it!"

I had so immersed myself in the rôle I was playing that in my mind's eye I actually saw the man. He had a black beard all over his face.

So as to seem very convincing, very dramatic, I bent my back and pressed my ear against the door.

At that instant I suffered a real shock.

I had heard a slight rustling sound in the room!

I put my ear again to the door and listened, straining every nerve. Wasn't there a sort of scraping noise at the desk? Wasn't there a sound of rummaging around, exactly as if— ?

Yes, someone really was in there ...

Suddenly I could hear the sound of a key being slipped into a keyhole, and a second later there was the clicking noise of a key turning in a lock.

So I really *had* heard something right from the beginning! There was a bad man in there—a burglar!

I stiffened—a jittery feeling in my stomach and in my head.

All at once I could hear steps coming toward the door on the other side of which I was listening.

Paralysis left me. I dashed over to Farmor, grabbed her arm, pulled her, and whispered urgently,

"He's coming, Farmor! He's coming to take me away!"

In spite of my terror I had presence of mind enough to keep my voice low.

"O Jesus! Jesus!" moaned Farmor.

She, also, had sufficient presence of mind to do her moaning softly.

I pulled at her arm as if I would wrench it loose.

"Let us run, Farmor! Let us run!—Come *on*, Farmor!"

"Sh-sh!" she whispered, softly, warningly.

My body was shaking as if I were in a cold shower. The trembling communicated itself to Farmor, and she, too, began to shake all over.

Suddenly she got up and rushed into the bedroom. I followed at her heels. In a second she had locked the door, turned the key and drawn it out. Trembling feverishly, she also locked the door leading into the corridor.

There was no light in the bedroom except that which shone through the blinds from a street lamp; but now she struck a match and, with trembling hand, lighted the candle on the bedside table. The wick caught. A little sigh of relief escaped her lips.

"Well, in God's name, let him take the money," she muttered. "Now at least he can't murder us!"

A sly smile crossed her blue-shaved mouth.

"Most of it's in the bank, anyway ... He! He!"

At that instant, a loud bang sounded from the den. It sounded as if some evil spirits were simultaneously knocking over the stove, upsetting the pedestal on which the palm stood, and smashing the furniture. Then the noise died away in a long rumble.

Our new-gained sense of security vanished. Farmor shook and moaned. I shook and howled. There was no longer any talk of lowering our voices for caution's sake.

Farmor was the first to regain some sense.

"Help me, Soren," she whispered.

For the next ten minutes we busied ourselves barricading ourselves in. With our limited strength we pushed the bedside-table up against the door to the dining-room; then piled chairs, the looking-glass and the big wash-basin against the door leading into the corridor. Then we added to the other barricade material the water pitcher, the basin, the bed-staff, the medicine cabinet, the down comforter, the pillows, and various band-boxes which Farmor brought out of the wardrobe. We gave up the idea of moving the heavy wardrobe and the wash-stand—Farmor hadn't the necessary strength on account of age and I hadn't it on account of youth.

Then we sat down on Farmor's bed and waited. Farmor had her razor in her hand, but the blade was shut, and I doubt if she'd ever have had the courage to use the thing.

On the floor in front of us was the brass candlestick-holder; Farmor had brought it from the bedside-table. The blue flame of the candle flickered in the room's confusion.

We sat listening. We tried to be as quiet as mice, but it seemed to me that my heart was clattering like the wheels of a train.

Suddenly I heard something again. It was certainly steps. Steps stealing nearer and nearer to the bedroom ...

"Farmor!" I cried, and my nails dug into her wrist.

"What is it, Soren?"

"He's going into the dining-room! He's coming in here!!"

The razor slipped from Farmor's hand down to the floor. The clatter of it increased my terror.

"If he takes hold of the door," gasped Farmor in my ear, "smash the window and call for help."

I nodded dumbly.

She bent down, took off one slipper and put it into my hand.

"Break the windows with this,' and don't hurt yourself!"

Then she was silent. We listened in strained silence.

Suddenly I heard a sniffing noise outside the door. It sounded like a dog.

"Farmor, I think there's a dog out there."

"A dog?"

Her piping voice expressed amazement. "Aren't you mistaken, Soren?"

I listened again.

The sniffing sound had stopped. But it was followed by a scraping noise, low down on the other side of the door. I was no longer in doubt. It *was* a dog.

"Yes, it *is* a dog, Farmor. It's scratching at the door. All the time!"

Farmor listened. I could see from her expression that she, too, could hear it. Suddenly a look of relief came into her face.

"Then it is Fie," she said.

"No," I answered, "Fie is under the bed."

Investigation proved this to be the case.

When we fled from the dining-room, Fie had left her niche and slipped between our legs into the bed-room. She always liked to sleep in company. She lay under the bed now and grunted, half-asleep, quite unaffected by the terrors surrounding us.

Now it was *Farmor* who seized *my* wrist.

"Then it's the Devil," she whispered. "He can change himself into a dog and ..."

Her voice caught. Horror robbed her of speech.

I knew the Devil by reputation. He was very red and very nasty. He didn't like the good old man in Heaven, and the good old man in Heaven didn't like him either. When bad people died he came and fetched them and put them down in the earth in a place full of fire and boiling water, because it was only good people who were allowed to go up to the good man in Heaven.

Perhaps the Devil had come to fetch one of us, either Farmor or me. But which one of us? Was Farmor really bad?

No; true, Farmor was not nice, not like Johanne; but neither was she really bad. A Farmor can't be bad any more than a father or mother.

Well, then, it must be *me!*

A long series of my bad deeds rose before me with magical clarity. There was, that one yesterday for example, when I'd told Miss Tychsen that I could read books and newspapers. There was that night of the burial when I'd made gaga in my breeches. There was that time when, in a fit of naughtiness, I'd thrown a handful of gravel in Mother's face and hit her in the eye. There was that time I'd, in a fit of temper, spat at Johanne. There was that time I'd stolen some butter from the pantry without anyone's finding out. There were all the times I'd gone with my hands in my pockets, picked my nose, hit Johanne, made we-we in bed ...

An icy fear pierced me. It was *me* the Devil had come to fetch. ME! Any doubt was excluded.

Suddenly I threw myself down on Farmor, hid my head in her lap, and howled—howled in mortal terror and fear of the Devil.

And what happened then? What came next? To tell the truth, I don't recollect. It has disappeared from my memory—like a fragment out of a mosaic. But I think I fell asleep for a while, my head in Farmor's thick, black skirt. At any rate it would have been like me. All my life I have possessed that gift from heaven: the ability to sleep away my cares. When sorrow, depression, or physical pain have become too hard to bear, I have found escape in sleep; and when I have awakened, if not wholly relieved, at least I have traversed suffering's tunnel and come out on the other side where hope is again shining.

Someone was knocking on the door—someone was continuing to knock.

"Mrs. Jensen! Open up, please! It's me!"

It was Johanne! I jumped up. All fear left me. I cried jubilantly,

"Farmor! It's Johanne!"

But Farmor had not yet come out of the tunnel.

"Johanne," she called out, "There's someone in the sitting-room—a man or ..." She stopped dead. Perhaps her theory concerning the devil embarrassed her. Anyway, she continued in a lower voice,

"Or something or other."

"I'll go and have a look."

Johanne's voice sounded as calm as if she had said she'd go and see if the water were boiling.

Doors opened and shut. It was Johanne going through the hall-door into the dining-room, and beyond into the den. Farmor and I listened with anxiety and suspense. Suppose The Man should kill her? Or his dog bite her?

It was not long before she was back, but this time she came to the door leading into the dining-room.

"There isn't a soul there," she called.

"Has anyone been there, any burglar?" Farmor asked.

Johanne's reassuring voice sounded from the other side of the door,

"Don't be afraid, Mrs. Jensen. Everything is in perfect order."

Farmor considered.

Then she muttered,

"Wait a minute—I'll unlock."

Farmor and I cleared the way. We shoved the bedside table a little to the side; the band-boxes were stuck in the bottom of the wardrobe; the pillows and comforter were put back on the bed; the chair and medicine cabinet were returned to their places.

Then Farmor turned the key ... and opened the door a crack ... She was still not wholly reassured. It might be the Devil assuming a woman's voice!

Johanne stood there in the gas-lit dining-room—smiling—wearing Mother's former coat—and with a key in her outstretched hand.

I squeezed through the opening crack of the door, flung myself at her and hugged her knees as if she had been away for years. She had to take a step backward, so violent was my embrace.

Johanne put her free hand on my head, and stroked it

down to the neck. At the same time she said in a friendly and cheerful voice,

"Thank you for letting me have it, Mrs. Jensen."

It was the key to the back-door she was handing Farmor. She had been permitted to take it when she went to the dress-maker's.

"Thanks," said Farmor. "Hasn't there really been anyone in the den?"

"Not a mother's soul," answered Johanne gaily.

Then she added in a respectful manner, "Not so that any-one can see, that is."

I thought I saw a little smile play about her mouth. I was in no doubt that if she really was smiling, it was at us —Farmor and me.

Farmor took the candle-stick, and, with her hand shielding the flame, she sneaked across the room into the den. Johanne followed, calmly and fearlessly. I came last, with a hand clutching a fold of Mother's coat.

There was nothing to be seen in the den. The fragile desk stood in its accustomed place; also the palm on its pedestal, and the what-not with Christ, and the porcelain dogs, the card-table with its game-chest, the stove with Zangenberg . . . Not the slightest harm had been done to the drawers of the desk—

Farmor turned to Johanne,

"And there was no one in the entrance hall?"

Johanne shook her head.

"I was out there. The door is locked and the safety chain is on."

"How strange," said Farmor slowly. "We heard someone in there quite plainly. We both heard it, Soren and I. And afterwards there was a crash, as if someone had knocked over both the stove and the writing desk."

"It was probably the wind," explained Johanne. "Maybe a windowpane broke or a tile fell off the roof. It is rough out tonight."

There was a pause. Farmor tripped back into the dining-room and put out the candle.

Then she said, closing the subject,

"Then it must have been the storm we heard."

But I could tell from her voice that she did not really think it had anything to do with the storm. In her heart of hearts, she was still of the belief that it was the Devil who had haunted the house. But of course one doesn't always say what one thinks or believes.

15

Every time Mrs. Agerlin came to visit Farmor—and it happened often—I received a vague invitation to go and see her. I don't know if these invitations stemmed from Uncle Agerlin, who perhaps remembered his talk on Mother's burial day, or if they really originated from Mrs. Agerlin, who for some reason or other cultivated Farmor. I only know that they were tendered—regularly. And just as regularly, I used to bow formally and answer, "Thank you very much," in the way I had been taught by my dear Mother. But just as regularly I used to pray to the good man in Heaven—pray him secretly—to make Farmor and Mrs. Agerlin forget the invitation; for the idea of going to the home of the Agerlins filled me with shame, embarrassment, fear, and aesthetic discomfort. I was ashamed because they knew what had happened on Mother's burial day. I was frightened of Mrs. Agerlin's sugar-coated malice. And my aesthetic discomfort arose from the bristly hair-wisps on her neck and her ugly, screeching voice.

But one day the calamity became a reality. Farmor and Mrs. Agerlin did not confine themselves to a vague invitation, but went so far as to fix a day and time. And the worst of it was that I was to be *alone* with Mrs. Agerlin. Johanne was to take me there and fetch me back at a certain hour. I shuddered.

And alas! The hours passed, the days passed, and that singular thing we call TIME rolled on so mercilessly that the day of the visit came around. I began being depressed in the morning. And when the appointed hour approached, Johanne first had to catch me because I led her a chase round the rooms, trying to escape my fate. Johanne's legs were the longer, however, and so the great preparations began. My captor scrubbed my face, my hands, my feet; put clean linen on me inside and out; and mauled me about until I stood imprisoned in my dark suit. She put a stiff white drooping tie round my neck and tried to strangle me with a kind of four-in-hand knot. Then she curled my hair with a sizzling curling-iron, a thing that always filled me with fear and pain—fear because I was afraid of being set on fire, and pain because I had to stand still for such a long time. And on top of that: my arms had to be twisted into the sleeves of my black overcoat—the one with the fur collar—and my hat had to be cocked rakishly on one side over my freshly curled hair. Only then was the first ordeal over. And Johanne stepped back a few steps just as I imagine the Lord did on the day of creation—to admire her handiwork.

"Now you are the pink of perfection!" she said admiringly.

She put on her coat—which for me would always be Mother's coat—seized the sacrificial lamb by the hand, and off we went.

The Agerlins lived in a milk-white palace in a broad, quiet and fashionable street. A large part of the apartment was given over to the dental clinic—the one Father and Doctor Agerlin ran—but I had learned from Father and Mother that there were more than enough rooms there for this childless couple to live in as well. I really liked the fine house, where I had come but seldom: liked it because of the thick red runners on the stairs; liked it for the gleaming brass rods that held the runners in place; liked it for the marble plaques on the walls, and the grey-painted iron balustrade embellished with gothic patterns. But to-day when I was being dragged up there to something unknown and disagreeable—I didn't like it at all. On the contrary, I was filled with a cold, gnawing apprehension. I clung on to the hope, however, that when we rang the bell, the maid would come out and tell us that Mrs. Agerlin had died.

A maid came all right—one with a neat white apron and cap—but, alas, she did not say a word about Mrs. Agerlin's decease. On the contrary, she threw the door wide open, and said in a welcoming voice,

"Yes, please come in!"

Johanne silently removed my overcoat, loosened my curls with a comb and said goodbye.

I felt a strong, ardent desire to cling to her, to let my tears flow, and to scream as loudly as I knew how for her to take me home again. But I knew what was expected of me. I was expected to conduct myself like a man who was unacquainted with cowardice and like a diplomat who used words to conceal his feelings. And, strangely enough, my fear of not fulfilling the behavior excepted of me was even greater than my fear of Mrs. Agerlin and the terrors awaiting me. And things went their relentless way. The door closed behind Johanne; the maid in the fine lacy apron, said, "If you please," and led me along a corridor, knocked on a door, and opened it . . .

Mrs. Agerlin sat in her den at a writing-desk, elegantly supporting her chin with one hand. But she got up quickly and came toward me with outstretched arms.

"Welcome, little darling!" she cried enthusiastically and stooped to kiss me on both cheeks.

Something whirled inside me, but I remained standing, without turning my head the least bit. The ethics of the time that politeness and beauty exact a toll had already left their deep mark on my behaviour.

"Now you shall see my children," cried my hostess, and taking me by the hand she led me importantly into the living-room.

The living-room was a huge place, a room for giants. However, there were no giants living there, but parrots. The room was absolutely starry with parrots. Not only along the walls, but all over the floor, row upon row of cages; and the cages were on pedestals. The room was intersected by avenues of pedestals. There were pedestals of all types: round ones, twisted ones, fluted ones, four-cornered ones, octagonal ones; there were mahogany pedestals—and pedestals of oak, walnut, birch and ebony, there were also pedestals of marble, porphyry and alabaster ... but the most elegant ones were those gilded.

Mrs. Agerlin called out something to me, but I couldn't hear what she said. There was a tremendous amount of shrieking and hissing, flapping of wings, and scratching of claws, against wood and tin-plate.

The scene was a surprise, an agreeable and lively one. Among the horrors I had been expecting had been that of boredom. Now I knew that I shouldn't get bored. If only Mrs. Agerlin would let me spend all the time here among the parrots, then—why, I even did not wish Johanne to come back for the present.

Mrs. Agerlin began showing me around.

"This one is called Lora," she shrieked in her hoarse voice. "She is a cockatoo—I won her in a raffle at the Zoological Gardens."

She stuck her crooked nose against the cage and whispered lovingly, "Lora!—Sugar!"

The bird, which had been sitting at the bottom of its cage, picking up sun-flower seeds, hooked itself up to the cross-bar by its claws and beak. Suddenly it let go with its beak, and shrieked, in a distinctly human voice,

"Lora!—Sugar!"

My delight found expression in my hands and feet—I had to jump and clap my hands.

Then I stopped suddenly, a little thoughtful.

"Isn't there a person inside it?" I asked seriously.

"No, there isn't a person," answered Mrs. Agerlin just

as seriously. "But there's a soul. There is a soul there."

I could tell by the tone of her voice that I had risen in her opinion. "Parrots are just as clever as human beings—and much nicer!"

She stuck a long-nailed finger between the bars, and scratched Lora's neck.

"Can I do that, too?" I asked.

She shook her head.

"You'd better not. Parrots don't care for strangers. You'd risk being bitten—and goodness how hard they bite!"

She took a lump of sugar from a pocket in her skirt, and stuck it in to Lora. Then she held me by the shoulder and dragged me on.

"This one is Jakob. He's a real aristocrat of a parrot. He comes from New Guinea ... Say something, Jakob!"

Jakob was bright green all over except for some dark red spots. He sat and wobbled first on one leg, then on the other. The movement made me think that maybe he needed to go to the little room.

Mrs. Agerlin stuck her cocoa-brown face close to the cage and screamed loudly and coaxingly,

"Say something, Jakob—then you shall have a kiss!"

"Hello," said Jakob cheerfully. "Hello, old boy."

"That is English," explained Mrs. Agerlin. "The captain who brought him from New Guinea was English."

She put her mouth right up against the cage. With one flap of his wings, Jakob flew over to the bars of it, and, gracious! if he didn't make a gentle peck at Mrs. Agerlin's lips. The sight disgusted me. True, Jakob was lovely—in his own way—but to kiss him!—mercy, no!

"Good little parrot-man," cooed Mrs. Agerlin, pushing her finger in among Jakob's neck feathers and scratching him tenderly.

Jakob gurgled his thanks, jovial and affectionate:

"Old bitch! Old bitch! Old bitch!"

She gave him his sugar.

And we went on again.

"This one is Alexandra. She is a cockatoo also—like Lora. But Lora is a rose cockatoo and Alexandra is a yellow-crested one."

Alexandra was chalk-white, but with an elegant little yellow comb. Her body was round and plump, her feathers were soft and choice. She looked like warm glowing snow. My hands positively ached to caress her. The aesthete in me would have fallen even more in love with her if she had not suddenly opened a little hole in her rear and shot out a long greenish-white worm. The sight caused me both distress and embarrassment.

"Alexandra can't speak," Mrs. Agerlin informed me, "but she can laugh."

Mrs. Agerlin sputtered forth an artificial "Ha-ha-ha!" A pause followed—then suddenly the bird answered with a shrill and hysterical burst of laughter which sounded like that of an insane person. I jumped a step backward. The strange laughter first gave me a shock, then seemed to stab through me unpleasantly.

Alexandra climbed up on the bars. She knew she was going to have her neck scratched after her introduction. And Mrs. Agerlin duly did scratch her neck and rummaged in her pocket for sugar.

The next cage was large and square and occupied by a number of tiny parrots no bigger than sparrows.

"These ones are all sweethearts!" explained my hostess. Oh how sweet they were—how very sweet! I was seized with a wild and painful longing to hold one of them in my hands—to own one of them.

"Will you give me one like that?" I asked meekly and appealingly.

"I never give animals to boys," she answered with unpleasant firmness. "Boys mistreat animals."

I was not offended. I did not have time to be. The birds had enchanted me so much that what I was seeing, hearing and thinking were all mixed up together in me. Then I remembered how Lora, Jakob and Alexandra had talked when they had been presented to me, and asked,

"Can these ones say anything?"

Mrs. Agerlin shook her untidy locks.

"No, they can't talk," she answered. Then she added, to save their honor,

"But they are so adorable!"

She was right. In one place a pair were sitting, crossing beaks as if they were kissing. In another, one was pecking at the neck-feathers of its beloved, gently and carefully. And they were all sitting around in pairs, and pressing themselves lovingly together. In only one spot was there sorrow and dissension. But perhaps even that was an expression of love. It looked as if one bird wanted to sit very close to another and a third one did not want it to ...

I would have liked to see the conclusion of this interesting quarrel, but Mrs. Agerlin drew me on.

"Now you are going to see one of my real showpieces. He's an Inca-cockatoo. They are very rare. They haven't even got one in the Zoological Gardens."

This cockatoo was grey-white and pink—almost like Lora. I could not see why it, in particular, should be regarded as a special showpiece.

But Mrs. Agerlin picked up a little stick which was lying beside the cage and pushed it between the bars and towards the cockatoo. The bird tried to catch hold of it with its beak, but Mrs. Agerlin was too quick and strong. It was evident that she was trying to tease her beloved child. And suddenly the cockatoo began raving. It let out a loud hiss, spread its wings, ruffled up its feathers—and raised its crest. At the same moment I realized why it was a showpiece. From its eyes up over its head and down to its neck rose a gigantic jagged comb, white, red and yellow in color. It was a head-dress that any Injun would have worn with pride. Before we had got close to the cage, the bird had looked so self-important—now I acknowledged it had a right to feel superior to the others.

Mrs. Agerlin pulled out the stick and replaced it by a piece of sugar—the comb subsided.

We went further, from cage to cage. Always new colors, always new works of art. Mrs. Agerlin shrieked, the birds chattered and blustered, and I myself screamed with delight and enthusiasm. The noise made me giddy.

Finally we reached the centre of the room. Here I found a chair, the like of which I had never seen. At first sight it appeared to be just a big, comfortable armchair with upholstered back and arms; but between the arms there was a little table with hinges enabling it to be lifted up or down, and below it there was only a single leg, a thick, heavy leg which was grooved like a screw. The leg fitted into a kind of cone-shaped plate which was fastened to the floor.

"Why is it so strange?" I asked.

"It can turn around, you see. I can sit in it and turn it round so that I can look at just whichever of my children I want to."

"May I try it?" I asked.

"Yes—if you are careful."

On the little table between the arms were a coffee-cup with a drop of coffee in it and an ashtray with the end of a cheroot. Beside them were a newspaper and a piece of crocheting. Mrs. Agerlin removed these to the floor, beyond the reach of the chair. The crocheting she put on top of the newspaper.

Then she lifted the bar between the arms of the chair. I crawled in and settled myself.

"Take care now," she said, as she let the bar down, "that you don't get sea-sick!"

I began to turn. First slowly, then more and more quickly.

"Stop, stop," cried Mrs. Agerlin. "Don't turn that way any longer. Now turn it the other way!"

She stood frozen with fright. It was too late. Suddenly I was thrown up in the air . . .

When I came to my senses again, I discovered that I was not dead. Not even hurt. I had fallen over together with the chair and was lying on my back; but thanks to the good upholstering, I had fallen softly and comfortably. Strangely enough, the chair had not hit any of the parrot cages either, although the nearest ones were well within its range.

I began to crawl out, feeling that strange blankness one experiences after a shock.

Suddenly I heard a voice, a deep mannish voice screaming with rage,

"Scamp! Rascal! Throw him out!"

I reacted by throwing up my elbow to protect my face— but no blow followed. I looked about me in bewilderment. Where was he, this angry man who was shouting at me in such a way that my boyish sense of sin overwhelmed me? Then I realized that the screaming came from a gaudy-colored macaw sitting in the nearest cage.

"Now you really must help me to set it up again," hissed Mrs. Agerlin; her rage matching that of the angry bird. "Why didn't you stop when I told you to? Haven't your parents taught you to obey? You can thank God that nothing worse happened!"

Very conscious of guilt, I took hold of the chair together with Mrs. Agerlin. My help, however, was of little service —the monster was deadly heavy. Fortunately the dentist's wife was strong and muscular. The chair was righted; the grooved leg was stuck down in its screw-hole again and the apparatus screwed to its usual height.

Our work was accompanied throughout by the macaw's scolding:

"Scamp! Rascal! Throw him out! Flog him!"

"Why is Rodolfe scolding so?" I asked, crest-fallen. From the earlier introduction I knew his name was Rodolfe.

"He has no use for little boys," answered Mrs. Agerlin.

"Then I have no use for him!"

It was with a bleeding heart I returned evil for evil. I would have liked to love all parrots.

"You mustn't say that. He is my favorite child. He has my father's voice."

"Have you a father?" I forgot to close my mouth, such was my amazement.

"Have had," she answered sadly. "He died in '67—from a disease of the bones. But Rodolfe was in my childhood home. So it is always as if I heard my father's voice!"

I felt a deep and honest indignation against Mrs. Agerlin's father—who, I was convinced, dwelt in Rodolfe's stomach.

"But now you shall see something!" she said, mysteriously and triumphantly. "Now I shall make him stop."

She picked up the coffee cup and went up to Rodolfe's cage. I followed a few steps behind, expectantly.

Rodolfe, who was big and long—the largest of all Mrs. Agerlin's parrots—was robed in a feather costume which shrieked red, blue, yellow and white—but mostly red. His black eye and his yellow eye—I could as a rule only see one at a time—was set in a piece of white skin shaped like a prune stone. It was a rather uncanny arrangement. And its uncanniness was increased for me by the fact that the eye appeared to be staring at me with concentrated spite.

But at the sight of the cup, the macaw became affectionate.

"Coffee!" he cried, "Rodolfe, coffee!"

He stuck his beak on the wires, and hauled himself along the lattice-work of the cage.

Mrs. Agerlin dipped the coffee spoon in the cup, filled it and held it up to the beak which Rodolfe opened wide. I stood on tiptoe to watch. The tongue, which was black, round and repulsive, looked like a little animal, a maggot that had an existence of its own inside Rodolfe's maw. With a turn of the spoon Mrs. Agerlin poured the drop of coffee down Rodolfe's throat, and the macaw snapped its beak together, put back its head and swallowed.

"Good coffee!" he cackled. "Rodolfe, good coffee!"

Although I disliked Rodolfe because of his dislike of small boys, I had to admit that he was the cleverest and the best speaker of all Mrs. Agerlin's "children."

Another drop of coffee was taken from the cup and poured into Rodolfe's beak. Another half-spoonful, and the cup was empty.

Suddenly I remembered the cheroot stump on the ashtray. "Shall we give him that?" I asked.

Presumably I reasoned that if a parrot could drink what was left of her coffee, it could also smoke what was left of her cheroot.

"Dreadful boy," exclaimed Mrs. Agerlin, getting quite angry. "Do you want to kill him?"

"Would he go up to the old man in Heaven if he got a cheroot?" I asked in amazement.

Mrs. Agerlin, realizing evidently, that I had meant no harm, answered a bit more gently,

"Parrots can't smoke. If you gave one a cigar it would eat it and die."

Then she added,

"But now you must come in and have some chocolate. Come along, my friend . . ."

Although I liked drinking chocolate very much, I left the parrots with great reluctance.

I don't know how long I sat in the dining-room, drinking and eating—and being watched by Mrs. Agerlin!—but it was a long, long time. At last the maid stood in the door-way, bringing the message that the little boy's nurse had come to fetch him.

"Show her in here," was the order given.

Johanne came to view in the doorway—bowing deeply. I was sorry she had to bow so humbly—according to my protocol, which was dictated by my heart, it was *Mrs. Agerlin* who should have been bowing to *Johanne*. After her bow, Johanne closed the door and took a step into the room. I had a passionate longing to fly to her, to touch her, but some power outside myself, which controlled my will, forced me to remain seated. Just like Mrs. Agerlin.

Madam and my nurse said How-do-you-do and exchanged

some remarks about the weather. Johanne scrupulously agreed to Mrs. Agerlin's views about the climate.

Suddenly there burst from me,

"Mayn't Johanne see your parrots? You can't imagine, Johanne, how pretty they are!"

Although this was all one outburst, the first part was directed to Mrs. Agerlin, and the latter to Johanne. This was not without intention. First, I knew unconsciously that to get anywhere with Mrs. Agerlin, one should begin by praising her "children". And, second, if I was so keen that Johanne should see the birds—the chief reason, really, was that I was dying to see them again myself.

Mrs. Agerlin took it under consideration for a moment.

"Well," she said. "Have you time, Johanne?"

Yes, indeed, she had time.

Mrs. Agerlin rose and led the way. I followed, but it was all I could do to stay behind her, so great was my eagerness to get back.

"This one is called Lora," began Mrs. Agerlin. "She is a cockatoo—I won her in a raffle at the Zoological Gardens. Can you say, 'Lora! Sugar!', darling?"

"Lora! Sugar!" came back the answer.

"W-e-l-l!" said Johanne, her mouth hanging open.

While Mrs. Agerlin and Johanne moved on from cage to cage, I ventured on a voyage of discovery for myself. There were certain parrots that attracted me more than others. Moreover, I cherished a dream of making one of the birds talk. It would be both a triumph and lots of fun if I could make the spirit residing in the stomach of one of them answer me.

"This is Alexandra," I heard Mrs. Agerlin shriek, in the midst of all the other shrieking. "She is a cockatoo, also, but has a yellow crest. Lora there is a rose cockatoo."

I observed that she not only led her guests around in the same quadrangular spiral, but also, like a phonograph, used exactly the same words.

I drew near the centre. That devil-red Rodolfe drew me

like a magnet. I was aware that Mrs. Agerlin looked anxiously back at me, but as long as she didn't say anything nothing could stop me. And her harsh voice did not call me back. Evidently she did not dare to tell me off or give me any orders within earshot of Johanne—not because she was afraid of Johanne, but because she was afraid of what Johanne might report to Farmor.

Scarcely had the black and yellow eye caught sight of me than Rodolfe began to screech out his abuse.

"Throw him out! Rascal! Scamp! Flog him!"

I cast a lightning glance at the two women. They had their backs to me and were quite taken up with Poppe-Boy, a grey parrot who could sneeze explosively. In an instant I had reached out my hand, snatched the cheroot stump from the ash-tray, and in the next second it lay in the bottom of Rodolfe's cage. Then I moved away, slowly and with dignity—knowing instinctively that quick movements always look suspicious.

Rodolfe was instantly silent. He clung with his beak to the wires of the cage and then hooked himself by beak and claws down to the bottom of the cage. His long red feathered tail swept over the sand and tinplate. He put his head to one side and with one eye, which at one and the same time looked spiteful, distrustful, inquisitive and lickerish, stared at the cheroot stump. Then suddenly his upper bill snapped down to the bottom of the cage. When he lifted his head again, there sat the cherrot stump clamped between his upper-bill, lower bill and tongue. Then it was tipped upwards. While climbing he held it only in the tip-end of the upper beak— this interesting object he had just acquired evidently had to be treated with care ...

And now he is sitting on his perch. He pulls the stump apart with his claws—stares at it—stares now with one eye, now with the other—then, all at once, begins to bite at it—!

I stayed only long enough to see the first brown leaves crack and crumble—then I walked with long steps and an innocent expression toward Johanne and Mrs. Agerlin. They had only gotten as far as the cage with the parakeets.

"Aren't they lovely?" exclaimed Johanne. "Don't you wish you had one yourself?"

Mrs. Agerlin, who suspected a hint, remarked sullenly, "I never give away parrots to boys. Boys maltreat animals."

When we reached Rodolfe's cage, the stump had disappeared. But he was not dead yet, that Satan of a bird, but was flouncing around on his perch and muttering angrily,

"Rascal! Flog him!"

Then Johanne and I twittered our good-byes—"Thank you for a lovely time!"

I was never invited to Mrs. Agerlin's again, nor did I ever again hear her talk about Rodolfe at any time. So to this day I do not know whether he survived the cheroot, or whether, with the aid of it he was transformed into a parrot-angel and flew up to the good old man in Heaven.

16

I did not always play on the floor or sit at the dining-room table. Not a little of my time was spent at the window, which is to say either the kitchen window or that of the two dining-room windows which was not appropriated by Farmor. I liked the kitchen window best, because from that I could see boys playing, while from the dining-room one I could only see grown-ups walking. It was not, however, the view which determined my choice. It depended on where Johanne happened to be.

I remember from these window observations that one day I saw some boys in the street who looked curiously different. They were stumbling about in long trousers and turned-inside-out coats; had soot on their faces; and wore false noses. There were even some flopping around in women's clothes, with windmill hats or women's hoods! All without exception were carrying little boxes or tin cans, and when a grown-up person came by, they rattled the boxes or cans in front of them. Now and again they stood still and sang a bit of a song at the tops of their voices. I noticed too that there were many more boys in the street than usual.

Johanne explained to me that the whole fuss was due to its being Shrove Monday. At Shrove-tide it was the custom for poorer children to dress up and go around begging. The boxes they had were collection boxes and occasionally somebody would drop in a one-ore piece, or even a two-ore one.

In spite of the expression "the poorer children," I felt a twinge of longing to be down there with them. But I didn't ask for permission. Not even the slightest hint passed my lips. I understood only too well that I was too "genteel" for that sort of thing. Neither Farmor nor Johanne would ever let me go around with a coat turned inside-out, or blacken my face, or take money from strangers.

It was not only on Shrove Monday that I experienced that twinge of longing. I often felt it. And I felt it hardest when I sat, half-hidden by the white curtains, at the kitchen window, and watched the boys tumbling about down in the court-yard. I felt the want of playmates. Johanne's love and Farmor's sweets and Sunday's ten ore piece, were not enough. Boredom, yearning and melancholy were frequent intruders.

It became worse as spring approached. When I looked down through the slightly dusty panes and saw the courtyard house bathing in golden sunlight, it was as if something gnawed at my stomach. And it would continue to gnaw until it was dinner time or the sun disappeared behind a cloud.

One day I asked Johanne if I couldn't go down in the courtyard and play. Johanne looked doubtful and mumbled something in reply—it was still too cold; I might fall into the area-opening and become a hunchback for life; the boys down there were not genteel or well-behaved. However, she went into the dining-room to hear what Mrs. Jensen's opinion might be. But the idea did not meet with Farmor's approval at all. The boys playing down there were from the gardenhouse, and her little Soren was much too sweet and of much too good a family to mix with that type of street Arab!

I asked again the next day—with the same result. It went on for a week, but by that time the spirit of mutiny arose in me. My answer to everything said to me was simply, "I *will* go down and play in the yard." I put on a hunger-strike at luncheon. When it was time for me to take my walk with Johanne, I refused to go, and when she tried to put my coat on me, I threw myself down on the floor and kicked.

At last, after a whispered conference with Farmor, my two guardians gave way. Farmor said that if I would be good for the rest of the day, I might go down and play—"tomorrow."

I *was* good—right up to saying my prayers when I went to bed. And when the next day came, I remembered the promise.

"Yes, yes," sighed Johanne. "But you must wear your overcoat, Soren—it is very cold out to-day."

I was washed and combed and enveloped in my overcoat, and my hat cocked on the side of my head. Then the back door was opened.

"Now take care that you don't get dirty," were Farmor's last words. And Johanne called after me, "Be careful not to fall into the area-opening, Soren."

I went carefully down the steep stairs. The right leg always in advance. When it had a fast grip, the left leg followed on to the same step. At the same time I held on to the bannisters with both hands.

My heart was throbbing. It trembled with anticipation but also with fear of the unknown. The boys' games had looked such fun from up there, but suppose I couldn't learn how to play or they wouldn't want me to play with them, or ... For a moment I almost turned back.

The door to the courtyard clanged behind me. I stood on

the doorstep and my eyes blinked from the strong light. The three boys stopped their play and turned toward me and stared. The largest of them looked at me in such a way that I wanted to turn and dash back upstairs.

Half the courtyard lay between us, and I truly wished that the distance would not diminish; but suddenly one of the boys started to come closer, and the two others, sticking their hands into their pockets, followed. I noticed that they wore neither a hat nor a coat, and I experienced that painful embarrassment one feels when coming into a social gathering incorrectly clad.

"Fre'erik," said the foremost of them, with a certain deliberation. "Get an eyeful of that—will you? Take a look at a *count!*"

The boy who spoke was of about my own height. His skin was grey-white in color with the exception of his big protuberant ears which shone bright red as if they had just been pulled.

From his gesture when he said, 'Fre'erik', I could see that it was the tall one who had that name. "Fre'erik" looked severe, with two brown eyes that pierced right through me, and with a broad mouth pressed tight shut which made me feel scared.

The third boy was the strangest. He was chocolate brown around his eyes, and the eyes themselves shone bright as mother of pearl. His nose was small and round—it resembled an owl's nose. His mouth was small, but hung open, so that you could see his teeth—they were all sharp and pointed, as if he had only eye-teeth. His hair had been combed back with a wet comb—while the two others wore theirs boy-fashion, that is to say, in bristling disorder, but with the remains of an earlier parting visible.

The three fellows faced me. I was glad that I stood up on the door-step.

"What d'you want?" the tall one asked. Absolutely unfriendly.

"Can I play with you?" I asked. I was on the point of

bursting into tears, but I felt sure that if I didn't act like a man, I would be knocked down and ill-treated. Unfortunately my voice betrayed the state of fear in which I found myself.

"What's your name?" asked Fre'erik.

"Soren," I said.

I thought I owed it to my position not only to let myself be interrogated, but also to ask questions myself.

With false courage I fixed my eyes on the tall fellow, and asked,

"What's *your* name?"

"Fre'erik," he answered. He spoke abruptly, as if to imply that he wasn't obliged to answer and if he nevertheless did, it was a piece of magnanimity.

I turned toward the other two.

"Haralt," said the one with the ears. It came out promptly and good-humoredly. Owl-nose, on the other hand, stuck his head forward and whispered, "My name is Sophus, and my father has a million."

"He's a louse," commented Haralt, interrupting him. Then he added as an explanation to the newcomer,

"Don't take any notice of what Sophus says—it's all nothing but lies."

So the introductions were at an end. There was a pause. Suddenly Haralt punched me in the chest and said "It!"

Then he was off like lightning. A second later the others ran also.

Suddenly I realized that it was the introduction to a game of tag.

A feeling of joy sprang up in me: I had been accepted! I was included in their game!

I started to run—to tag one of the others.

Alas, I soon discovered that they were quicker than I. Perhaps they knew how to run better, maybe it was my overcoat which hampered me. After a few attempts I realized that I could neither tag Haralt nor Fre'erik. My only chance was Sophus, so I concentrated on chasing him.

All at once I was close to my prey. Sophus could not escape me. He turned sharply at the out-house door, and before he could get away, I touched his back, crying "It" with a victor's jubilation—and dashed away.

"But this is base," he gasped, out of breath.

"That's a lie," shouted Haralt. "We haven't any base. You're 'it'!"

Sophus stood a moment, still gasping, then he raced after me. He, too, had discovered that he did not stand a chance with the others. Fre'erik was too quick in the legs, Haralt too quick in the head.

I stayed out of his reach for a long time, but he caught up with me in a corner from which I couldn't get out. So it was my turn to be "It" again.

Haralt amused himself teasing me. Several times he ran close up to me, but each time I thought I could reach him, by a sudden twist of his body he got out of my reach. Finally I gave up trying to catch him, even when he danced right up to me.

During this time Fre'erik stood leaning up against the wall. I noticed from time to time that he was glowering at me, hate and contempt in his eyes.

I was again on Sophus's heels. Suddenly he fell down. It was a mere nothing to tap him on the shoulder and cry "It!"

"That don't count," he bawled. "It don't count if someone falls down."

"Yes, it does," yelled Haralt. "You just don't have to fall down, you idiot!"

The congenial feeling I had developed for Haralt increased considerably.

Sophus got up, rubbing his scratched hands and knees.

Then he came limping toward us.

"I don't wanna play any more," he said.

"That's 'cause you know you play worst," jeered Haralt.

"I don't want to either," said Fre'erik sullenly. " 'Taint worth while. Them two idiots there can't catch us."

"What shall we play then?" I asked.

We all stood a little at a loss.

"We could play chuck-a-luck," suggested Haralt.

"Accepted," said Fre'erik.

I gathered that any game we played had to be approved by him.

Haralt looked at me.

"Have you any buttons?" he asked.

"No," I answered, ashamed.

"You can just take off some of those!" It was Fre'erik who spoke, pointing to the buttons of my overcoat.

I imagined Farmor's and Johanne's faces if I came back with my coat minus any buttons.

"I mustn't do that," I exclaimed, terrified.

Even as I spoke the words, I realized that what I was saying was stupid. I ought to have said that I *would* not do that.

"You are a sissy," announced Fre'erik with contempt.

Suddenly he pointed to a boardfence between our court and the one adjoining.

"D'you know what that is?"

My eyes followed the invisible prolongation of Fre'erik's forefinger. At the place where it reached the fence there was a drawing, scratched with chalk. The drawing was a kind of square, with one corner pointed up, the opposite one down, and the two others to either side. In the middle of the square was a vertical line, and from each end of it ran streaks like those one draws to represent the rays from a star. I had seen drawings like that before, but had no idea what they were meant to represent.

I was just about to reveal my ignorance, when I caught a glimpse of Haralt's face out of the corner of my eye. He was grinning—grinning jovially, chummily, naughtily and precociously, but in a way that made me shiver.

In that instant I realized I must not betray my ignorance. Why, I do not know, but somehow or other it penetrated my mind that if I were to maintain their respect, if I were to

keep them as future playmates, yes, if I did not want to
have them fall upon me then and there and tear me to pieces,
I must let them think that I knew the meaning of the drawing.

I nodded. I nodded without saying anything. It is easier
to lie with a gesture than with words. And at the same time
I put on a grin as much like Haralt's as I could muster.

"Have you got any chalk?" asked Fre'erik.

I had, in correspondence with the truth, to answer "No".
Fre'erik pulled a piece out of his pocket.

"This is real chalk," he said importantly, and handed the
stump to me. "Take this and make another drawing like it."

For some reason or other I knew that it was naughty to
draw such a picture. And I imagined standing there and
drawing one on the boardfence while faces from all the
windows on the court stared down at me.

I tried to hand the chalk back to him, but he didn't take it.

"I won't," I said.

My intention was to make my voice sound firm and de-
fiant. Unfortunately it sounded more of the whimpering
order.

"So you're scared, eh?"

"No, I'm not scared; but it's forbidden to draw on board-
fences—Johanne told me so."

Fre'erik came close up to me.

"You take it and do what I say! This instant!"

I was dreadfully afraid of him, but I was still more afraid
of those faces in the windows. Perhaps I was most afraid
of all of showing my fear.

I took two steps backward.

"I *won't*," I said with desperate manliness.

Fre'erik came toward me. He fixed his eyes, which were
as brown and round as chocolate pastilles, on mine. It was
as if he wanted to hypnotise me to obey him.

Then he grabbed me by the lapel of my coat.

"You want a hiding, eh?"

I seized his wrist and tried to unloose his hands.

An ugly grin appeared on his face.

"So you think you're smart, do you? You think you can get away from me!"

Before I really knew what was happening he seized me around the waist and flung his weight against me. I fell backward on the cobblestones; then he threw himself on top of me.

Then he began to beat me. His fists hit me in the face, on the shoulders, on my chest. I didn't feel any of it very much. In the fury of battle blows and wounds go almost unnoticed.

I tried to free myself, but he held me down with his body's weight, pressing one knee on my belly.

Then I began to defend myself. I pulled his hair, tore at his ears and tried to bite his nose. At the same time I kicked and jabbed at him with both my legs.

My resistance increased his rage. Suddenly he stopped hitting me and, instead, grabbed my neck with both his hands.

His clutch on my neck was much more painful than all the blows. And he kept on squeezing it so hard and desperately that I couldn't breathe. Suddenly millions of black spots appeared in the air. Then I really was frightened . . .

Deathly frightened.

But all of a sudden the clutch grew less tight. His hands gradually let go. It seemed as if he were floating up into the air above me. At last he was so high up that his hands couldn't touch me.

"You dirty scamp! You rascal! You—!"

A voice was screaming. All at once I recognized it. It was Lillelund's.

Then I understood what had happened. Lillelund was freeing me from my attacker.

"I'll teach you to attack Mrs. Jensen's grandson!"

I got up slowly, still a little dizzy after the strangle-hold.

Lillelund, who was always red-cheeked, was at the moment a bluish-purple. Suddenly he began smacking Fre'erik. He was not much bigger than the boy, but evidently the stronger.

At any rate, Fre'erik did not attempt either to resist or to escape. He just stood and tried to parry the blows as best he could—now with one elbow, now with the other, for Lillelund rained blows with both hands.

"He began it," he wailed.

"That's a lie"—smack—"I saw the whole thing from my window"—another smack—"But even if Soren did hit you, you had no business to hit him back—" a final smack.

Lillelund seized the boy by the ear, pushed him against the wall and got right up close to him—

"Mrs. Jensen owns this house, I'd have you to know, and Soren is her grandson. And if you so much as touch him with your little finger again, I'll tell Mrs. Jensen, and you and your parents will be thrown out of here—and don't you forget it!"

Lillelund turned toward me.

"If they ever do you any harm again, Soren," he said, respect and devotion in his voice, "you just come and tell me. I'll teach 'em—you see if I don't!"

He smoothed his beard a little, straightened his blue apron and walked over to his cellar-steps.

There he turned and shouted back,

"Soren is a little gentleman—remember that, you three rascals! And do whatever the young gentleman says."

Then he disappeared down into his cellar, like the devil on two sticks in a puppet-show.

Silence descended on us.

Haralt stood grinning a little—apparently there was something that amused him. Sophus stared hard at me, his mouth hanging open and his eyes shining. Fre'erik had gone scarlet, and it was probably not only the beating which made his face red, but also his humiliation. Humiliation that he, whose strength had made him the courtyard's overlord, had now been dethroned.

And I, too, felt ashamed: ashamed at realizing my physical weakness—my inability to hold my own among other boys.

I was just as helpless as Piphans, the canary, when he got out of his cage.

To be accurate, I'm not sure whether it was already at that time that this analogy between Piphans and myself occurred to me. Quite possibly it is something that memory has added. But I record it nevertheless because it so accurately describes the emotions that filled me when I stood there in the courtyard after Lillelund had rescued me.

I knew the extent of Piphans' helplessness because once he had flown out—once when the maid had forgotten to fasten the wicket after taking out his bird-bath. My goodness, what a fuss Farmor made about closing all the windows and doors! And when the little creature finally did flutter back into its cage she explained to me that a canary cannot survive if it flies out into the street among other birds; that it is incapable of finding its own food, and will probably freeze to death. It was also possible, she said, that the other birds would peck at it—and perhaps continue doing so till it fell to pieces. Or a cat might come along; or a larger bird might devour it. A poor little Piphans could only live in a cage, where some human being who loved it would take care of it and provide it with food ...

Alas, I had been just as helpless as that. I couldn't catch anyone in tag—anyone but Sophus, that is, and he was a poor wretch himself. I was so ignorant that I didn't even know what that picture on the boardfence represented. And in a fight, I was the one who would always get a walloping. Instinctively I felt that not only Fre'erik could wallop me, but also Haralt and Sophus.

If only one of them had been weaker than I! But even Sophus—! Even that miserable Sophus—!

But even in the midst of these painful feelings, a new feeling awoke in me, *haughtiness!* Even if I was inferior in all respects to the others—and that knowledge continued to fester despite the new feeling of joy—I was, in a certain sense, the strongest. Unseen powers protected me. Thanks to these unseen powers, Farmor ruled over Lillelund, Fre'erik,

Fre'erik's parents, yes everybody living in any of her houses. It seemed strange indeed that Farmor, small and nervous and weak as she was, was all the same the strongest of them all. Everybody did what she told them. If she said to someone, "Move!", then they moved; and if she said "No-one must strike Soren!", no-one struck Soren. And this magical power which Farmor possessed also helped *me*— helped me because I was her grandson.

And I was not only the strongest in this way, I was also the most genteel. How had Lillelund put it? "Soren is a gentleman"; and he had spoken of me as "The young gentleman". He certainly would never have said that either to Haralt or to Fre'erik—just as he would never have called me a "dirty rascal."

But why was I the most genteel? There must be some reason for it. And how had it been decided? Let me see: how was it Farmor expressed it: "Everything rests in God's hands." Perhaps it was the good old man in Heaven who had selected me—selected me maybe because I was nicer and more handsome than the others? Well, at any rate I was handsome—I had learned that from Johanne.

Still, the joy of pride was not unmixed. I realized that my gentility would make me lonely. I wanted so much to play simply and naturally with the three others—play with them as if I were their comrade, their *friend*. But the fact that I belonged to gentle-folk would prevent that. There would always be a little chasm between us, perhaps just a little gutter, but a gutter not to be crossed—

And a cold little shudder ran over me. I felt as if I stood alone on the roof of a tall, tall house—Farmor's house.

Did I really think all this as I stood there in the cobble-stone courtyard? No, of course not. Naturally I didn't think much of anything. For thinking, in the usual meaning of the word, requires words, many of them, and my vocabulary at that age was meager; and besides I was inept in making the most of it. Still something or other must have been registering reflection in me, thoughts of a kind corresponding to those set forth here. Why, otherwise, should I first have felt crushed by my ineptitude, then afterwards experienced the gratification of pride—even though the sense of unfitness continued to prick it—finally beginning to shiver with loneliness?

It was Sophus who first broke the silence.

"You can beat *me* up, if you like," he said, turning to me.

He might as well have been speaking a foreign language—I couldn't understand what he meant.

"You can beat me up as much as you want," he continued, "I won't tell a soul on you."

When I still did not react, he added impressively,

"We can go down in the cellar, so that no-one can see us!"

"Idiot!" hissed Haralt. The tone was concentrated contempt.

It gradually dawned on me that Sophus was giving me a free hand to thrash him, but why I did not understand. He seemed very strange to me.

But he had not finished.

He stuttered anxiously, saying with shining eyes,

"I get beat up very often, I do! When Pa and Ma are away, a big, black man comes and pulls my breeches down and flogs me with a big stick till I bleeds!"

Fre'erik put his shoulder against Sophus, and gave him such a push that he stumbled several yards away on the cobblestones.

"Shut up with that nonsense!" he said angrily.

"You don't need to pay any notice to what Sophus says," explained Haralt. "He's got a screw loose!"

I was glad the others had relieved me of Sophus's pestering. His curious offer had given me a rather uncomfortable feeling.

Lightly and cheerfully I said,

"Shall we play something?"

"Yes," they said.

Fre'erik added eagerly, almost servilely,

"You choose what we play."

"Let's play Injuns."

"What's Injuns?" Haralt asked.

I explained that they were some red people who lived far away. They rode horses and fought with the white people.

But none of them knew anything about Injuns and they did not seem to get anything from my explanation. I perceived that it was a game best played alone—then too, I could be a flock of redskins and a regiment of American soldiers all at the same time.

"Then let's play hop-scotch," I suggested.

"In a square?" asked Fre'erik.

I nodded.

"Ugh, that's a sissy game," objected Haralt.

But Fre'erik decided for hop-scotch. He was very anxious now to please me. I think, if I had proposed it, he would even have agreed to play papa, mama and child.

Haralt drew a hop-scotch plan on the paving-stones, and Sophus found a little stone which was acceptable to everybody.

We played for a while. The game was too peaceful really to appeal to Haralt and Fre'erik. But they loyally put up with it for my sake.

Then all of a sudden Haralt stopped in the middle of a hop. He put his foot down in one of the compartments—something absolutely against the rule—and turned to me.

"Say, you—have you got any pocket-money?"

His white face positively beamed with eager cordiality.

"Yes," I answered, and stuck my hand down under my overcoat, into my trouser-pocket. My handkerchief came up like a snake, bringing the pocket-lining with it. In one corner of the handkerchief was a knot, tied by Johanne, in which was a ten ore piece.

The three boys watched my every movement, silently but with greedy eyes.

I fumbled with the knot, bit into it, but could not undo it. Finally, by tearing the linen with my nails, I got the coin out.

"Satan! If it isn't a ten ore!" exclaimed Haralt.

The three clustered closer to behold the miracle. All at once Haralt cried out,

"Will you let me go and buy you something with it?"

His eyes were bright with eager helpfulness.

"I know a place where you can get a heap of things for ten ore."

"Better let *me* do it," said Fre'erik sombrely. "Haralt is a thief—his own mother says so!"

"Oh let *me!*" pleaded Sophus.

They stood there begging, while I kept silent—in a quandary. I wanted to give the ten ore to Haralt, but didn't want to hurt the feelings of my other new friends.

Suddenly Haralt burst out, "It was *me* asked first—so there!"

That settled it.

I said, dignified as a judge,

"That's right. It was Haralt that asked first."

He got the ten ore. In less than no time he was through the little door leading into house number two, then through the glass-doors beyond it and out into the street.

Fre'erik plunged a hand down into his pocket.

"Do you want a button?" he asked.

"Yes, please," I said. From habit I was on the point of bowing, but fortunately I braked the movement before it was too late.

He handed me a button—made of lead or tin and with four holes in it. I knew it was one of the kind the boys played jacks with. I also knew that one could buy them at the chandler's and in small toy-stores, three for one ore. Still, I had never owned one—possibly because the streets were forbidden territory for me, and therefore I had never thought I'd have a chance to play the game. But, now, there I stood with a jack in my hand, one of my very own. How beautiful it looked to me! I felt quite radiant inside. At that moment the jack was my most treasured possession.

"Here's another one."

It was Sophus holding out another button, a second and larger one.

"Are you crazy?" Fre'erik burst out. "That one's no use."

The button was a big brass one, gilded but a little scratched. On the back was a single shank which was pressed down to the level of the button, probably with a view to its new use: jacks. I realized that the button had originally adorned a soldier's uniform.

I said "Thanks," and shook hands with both of them— a procedure which evidently astonished them. However, Fre'erik said nothing: even the expression on his face did not change. Evidently he had decided to accept my behavior, however peculiar it appeared to him.

We stood about for a while and then agreed that we would not play hop-scotch any more, but instead play jacks. Now that I owned two jacks I could take part.

Suddenly the door leading out of house number two flew open and Haralt came bursting through it. I saw he had his hands full of sweets: shiny black, grooved, licorice strings and fat pink peppermint-sticks, all in a piece of thin, yellow paper.

The sight of the licorice delighted me. Neither Farmor nor Johanne could bear to have me buy licorice. It made one so dirty, they thought—nobody could eat it without getting black around the mouth. To frighten me off it, Farmor used to tell me that licorice was made from the blood of negroes, and Johanne that it was made out of horsedung, but as neither of these things frightened me in the least, they had finally resorted to absolutely forbidding me to buy it.

Distribution began.

I was amazed at all Haralt had gotten for ten ore, and Sophus seemed to be equally so. At any rate, he said, deeply impressed,

"If all that licorice was sewed together, there'd be a million miles of it!"

The remark was allowed to hang in mid-air. I had already learned that one did not have to answer anything Sophus said, nor make any comment on his observations.

"You've cheated," burst out Fre'erik suddenly. "That's only eight ore's worth."

He had been silent until now—his brow wrinkled—probably working out the difficult computation.

"No, I haven't—there's ten ore's worth there," answered Haralt, angry at the accusation. And he went on very hurriedly,

"Work it out for yourself, you fool. Peppermints cost two ore, that's four ore. Licorice—that's one ore a stick, and that's another four ore. And four and six make ten. Ain't I right, you blockhead?!"

Fre'erik hesitated. Haralt's calculations seemed completely unassailable, and yet when he'd tried to work the sum out himself he'd made the total eight. I could tell from his look that he was on the point of yielding, but had decided to make one more attempt. He first took one of the peppermint sticks and laid it on his outspread, dirty palm (he was unquestionably the dirtiest of us four), at the same time counting:

"Two ore!"

Then he put the other stick on top of it, mumbling,

"Two and two make four."

Then he took the licorice strings, one at a time, and hung them over the peppermint sticks, at the same time counting slowly and laboriously,

"Five, six, seven, eight."

He stopped and looked up quickly—

"You *have* cheated! There's only eight ore's worth there!"

"It's a lie," screamed Haralt. "The devil take me if I haven't bought ten ore's worth!"

He recommenced his accounting from the beginning—and, see, the result was the same as before—ten ore.

But now Fre'erik had turned stubborn. He took my hand, put the sweets into it, one by one, and counted at the same time. And it came to eight ore.

Then he counted further on his fingers—nine, ten. There

were two fingers left over. Harsh and threatening, he pronounced the result.

"Two ore are missing—and you know it!"

Haralt mumbled,

"I don't understand—they must have cheated me at the
shop."

Up to now I had believed in Haralt's innocence—out of
sympathy, of course; for I was unable to verify his figuring
—as yet I had only learned to count as far as five. But now
I knew he was lying. His look, his voice betrayed him.

Nor was Fre'erik in doubt.

"Come on, cough up that two ore!" he said.

His pastille-like eyes stared at Haralt with such brutality
that I felt more sympathy for the sinner than for the law's
defender.

Haralt squirmed.

"I haven't got two ore, I swear it."

"If you don't cough 'em up this second, you'll be hearing
snakes hissing—just wait!"

Haralt did not answer; his ready wit had disappeared.

He just stood and stared down at the cobble-stones, while
red spots gathered in his face.

Suddenly Fre'erik grabbed one of his protruding ears, and
began to twist it—twist it with such lack of caution that I
thought the ear would come off . . .

Haralt danced up and down in pain.

Suddenly his hand plunged into his pocket.

"Alright, then—take them," he wailed, "Let me go, blast
you!"

Fre'erik seized the two ore, and let him go.

"You're always cheating," he said contemptuously. "You're
a regular sneak-thief."

He pushed the little copper-piece into my hand.

"Here's your two ore!"

Surprised, I took the coin. I had taken for granted that
Fre'erik would keep it—because of his strength. At any

rate I did not feel that it belonged to me. Fortunately I had an inspiration.

"We can take it and buy more sweets with it when we've guzzled these," I said.

I felt pleased with myself. My suggestion was generous and elegant; it softened Haralt's defeat; and furthermore I had had presence of mind enough to say "guzzled" instead of "eaten."

"Soren!"

I felt a little shock. It was Johanne's voice that came from above, and consequently I supposed I had done something wrong. I bent my head back and looked upward.

"All right," I answered, guiltily.

Johanne had partly closed the window. I could see her face in the opening.

"Soren," she called again. "You must come right up. Your father is here."

"All right," I answered.

I was hurriedly given my share of the booty—a whole string of licorice and half a peppermint stick. I buttoned up my coat, stuffing the sweets under my blouse. Then I hurried to the door leading to the kitchen stairs.

"Will you be coming down again?" shouted Haralt.

And the two others yelled almost at the same moment,

"You'll be coming back, won't you?"

"Yes. Sure," I called, walking backwards toward the kitchen stairs. "I'll come back just as soon as Father goes."

I was happy. I had gotten some playmates—playmates who desired me to come back and play with them.

That the two ore in my pocket may have influenced their desire never occured to me.

Not at that time.

17

After that I usually got permission to go down to the courtyard to play—if, at any rate, I plagued Farmor long enough about it.

But it always had to be before noon—or, more rarely, between three and seven. In the afternoon, that is after coffee had been drunk and Farmor was taking her customary little nap, there was no time to play because of the walk I had to take.

The walk was a part of Johanne's duties. A nursemaid in those years had not only to watch over the treasure entrusted to her, to dress it, wash it, curl it, clip its nails, and so forth —she also had to drag it around for an airing. Victorianism was on the way out and the significance of exercise and fresh air was beginning to dawn on civilized people.

There were plenty of places to walk. Farmor's house lay in a quarter where thirty years earlier had been the city's ramparts and moat. The growing city had found its girdle too tight and with a little breath of relief had done away with it. Fortunately the girdle was not transformed into buildings and pavements. The city fathers had with unusual foresight laid out a part of the old rampart area in parkways—a green ribbon worming its way through the city. It was at a corner of this green worm's middle section that Farmor's house stood.

We had only to cross the street, Johanne and I, to be in one of the parkways. If we walked farther in the same direction, it led into another park or, if we went in the opposite direction, we only had to pass three blocks of houses before we arrived at another green strip. If we turned to the right, it was only two or three minutes before we came to an old park, with a fairy-like little castle in its depths. If we turned to the left, we could walk around the "lakes", long, rectangular lakes, with elegant broad bridges, small, plashing row-boats and gulls whose cries made me feel sad.

As a rule we walked hand-in-hand. Often very serious, now and then chatting cheerfully. Fortunately, it sometimes happened that Johanne sat on a bench and let me wander about on my own. But never without first warning me:

"Now you mustn't go out of my sight."

We were nearly always alone. Only on some occasions were we accompanied, and then always by the same person. Our escort was a gentleman, a very elegant gentleman, whom Johanne seemed to know intimately and of whom she also seemed to think highly. After a while I gathered that his name was Hoppensach—Emylius Hoppensach—and that he was a hairdresser.

Hoppensach was very elegant indeed. His collars were as high as Father's cuffs were wide. His little moustache was curled tightly into points like pigs' tails, and his yellow, pomaded hair curled on his brow like the undulations on a scrubbing-board.

Hoppensach accompanied us on special days, that is on his so-called "days off." I didn't know what "days off" were. The only "day" I knew about was Sunday, that tiresome day when Farmor went to church to hear Pastor Moller and all the stores were closed so that one could not buy marbles or scraps. On these so-called days off we usually met him in front of the limestone gate leading into one of the parks, though I remember that once we met him at the barber's where he was employed. It was a little shop with three plush-upholstered chairs, hair on the floor and a copper cuspidor beside each chair. Hoppensach was in a white coat and had a comb stuck in his hair, but after having finished curling a customer's moustache, he went behind a screen, and after a little while came out again dressed in a black jacket, with a flower in his buttonhole, a straw hat on his head, and a bamboo cane in his hand.

When Hoppensach was around, there was always something exciting and festive in the occasion. Exciting, because Johanne had forbidden me as strictly as could be to say anything about him to Farmor or Father, and festive, because he liked to take us into a cake-shop or a garden restaurant and order us cakes and drinks. "Drinks" for me meant either lemonade or red soda-water.

I believe they were by way of being sweethearts, Hoppensach and Johanne, or that at any rate he was, as they used to say in those days, courting her. But whatever stage their courtship had in fact reached, one day the balloon burst (another expression common in those days) both literally and figuratively—and the cause, curiously enough, was simply my existence!

One summer day—I think it was at Whitsun week-end—we met Hoppensach as usual in front of the limestone gate. It should be mentioned here that I couldn't bear that gate. Its greyish white color was not sufficiently clean in my eyes, and I thought the many small holes in the stones made it look shabby. This should be mentioned because the connection in my mind between the barber and the limestone led me at the time to transfer some of my dislike for the limestone to the barber.

We had been walking for a long time till we came to a park which I had not seen before. A man selling balloons was sitting at the entrance and naturally I couldn't look at the dancing red and blue clusters without immediately wanting one of the "long ones". I expressed my desire for it in my most appealing tone of voice, yet with just a hint of a threat in it that if I did not have my wish fulfilled, there might be dire results. Hoppensach was immune to this. His red, hairy hand pulled firmly at my wrist (I walked between him and Johanne as if we were playing Papa, Mama and child)—it was obvious that he wanted to hurry quickly on, out of reach of the red and blue "long ones". Fortunately Johanne was more sympathetic toward the idea. She stood for a moment, then fished up from the pocket of her coat—she had mother's coat on her arm—her black purse, and asked which one I would like to have.

"That one," I said—and pointed to a red one.

The balloons were pulled down and the red one was detached and tied to one of the buttons of my blouse, so that it would not escape from me. Hoppensach, meanwhile, stood looking on, a rather wry expression on his face.

He vented his feelings as we continued on our way into the park.

"There's no sense to it!" he burst out. "Why the devil do you spend your money on that little puppy? If he has to have a balloon, then let the old golden goose pay for it herself!"

I understood something of what he meant. But it made no impression on me. My joy over the balloon was so boundless that somebody else's sourness could not affect me much.

We settled down in a broad, sunny spot in the garden. The grass was all covered with people. Many had brought picnic-baskets; some had spread cloths on the grass, and the cloths were covered with sandwiches and bottles.

I observed that many were wearing their best clothes, but their appearance did not satisfy me somehow. Their clothes were fine in a different way from those of Father's and Mother's friends—there was something wrong about them.

Hoppensach had brought a rug, which he had spread out for Johanne. He sat down himself on the extreme edge of it, and there was no place left for me. It was not unfriendliness—at any rate not on Johanne's part: they just expected that I would prefer to run around and play.

But I neither ran nor played. I drifted about. I just drifted about, devouring with my eyes the happy people all about. I felt contemptuous of their clothes; their pleasure made me sad. Perhaps I would have judged them less harshly if I had found someone to play with. But all the children there were playing in groups—private groups which did not open to admit a chance stranger. Especially when the stranger in question was too embarrassed and too much on his dignity to give any hint that he wanted to play with them.

At last I had enough of staring. The people on the grass

bored me. I went back and sat beside Johanne.

Both Hoppensach and Johanne lay on their stomachs in the sunshine. One of Hoppensach's hands smoothed Johanne's hair and cheeks, stroked her back, and now and then went even farther.

His caresses hurt me. They awakened in me a feeling which I—many years later—can only describe as jealousy. Nobody but myself had the right to pet Johanne.

Hoppensach did not seem especially pleased, either, with the presence of a third. Between caresses he cast an embittered look in my direction.

A little while passed in silence.

Then suddenly he burst out,

"You go and play for a while, Soren. Johanne and I are going for a little walk—"

His voice was friendly, surprisingly friendly.

"A walk?" said Johanne—and lifted her head from the rug. "Are we going for a walk?"

Hoppensach nodded.

"Just over there among the trees!"

Johanne looked as if she would protest, but Hoppensach's expression and hands silenced her.

"We'll be back in a jiffy," he added to appease me.

But I wished for more specific information.

"How soon is a jiffy," I asked.

"Just a few minutes—not longer than it takes to count to a hundred!"

I knew that a hundred was a vast number. If it had only been ten thousand millions now! But I dared not be alone up to a *hundred!*

"I'll come too," I said.

"Nonsense, boy. Just stay here and play—we'll only be gone five minutes!"

Johanne and Hoppensach got up. There was something strange in Johanne's eyes, something I did not understand. She looked as if she were walking in her sleep.

"I'll come too," I reiterated.

Johanne bent over me, her cheeks warmly pink, her eyes veiled. She stroked my cheek and said appealingly,

"Just leave us alone for a little while—we'll be back very soon."

I realized that stronger weapons would be necessary if I were to prevent their carrying out their plan. My strongest one was a scream. And I followed it up with a heart-breaking sob.

"There, there, Soren. Be good now!"

I could tell plainly from Johanne's distressed voice that my weeping had hit the mark. But it wasn't enough yet. I continued in a slightly lower key, but also more despairingly.

"Stop now, Soren," cried Johanne pleadingly. "Listen— we are not going *any*where! Do you understand—We are *not* going *any*where!"

"You won't go over among the trees?" I asked.

"No-o," she said hesitatingly. "No."

"It is simply not to be borne the way you let yourself be bullied by that boy!" exclaimed Hoppensach. "Come on now, blast it!"

Johanne gave him a pleading look. But his eyes were the stronger. She turned anew to her beloved Soren.

"Please now," she urged.

I quickly resumed my weeping.

"Why can't you stay here!" I wailed. "Why do you have to go over among the trees?"

Suddenly Johanne seemed to awaken from her somnolent state. The strange, veiled, look disappeared like a film from her eyes.

"Yes, why *must* we go over there?" she said to Hoppensach. "We can just as well stay here."

She spoke and looked as if she did not understand what he meant.

Hoppensach made no answer. Not right away. He took one end of his moustache in his mouth and chewed on it. His face was distorted with fury and chagrin.

Finally he muttered,

"Soren, you shall have a bag of barley-sugar if you'll leave Johanne and me alone for a bit!"

The voice was friendly enough, but an unfriendly sentiment sounded through it.

A bag of barley-sugar was something of an offer. My weeping stopped. I weighed the matter up. But not for long. I was stuffed with the cookies we had brought from home, and furthermore I had kept under my blue-and-white linen blouse a bag of bonbons, cylindrical in shape and decorated with flowers. The offer of a bag of barley-sugar did not tempt me nearly so much as it would have done under normal circumstances. According to my inner scales, the barley-sugar came far from outweighing my fear of being left alone among all the many strange people around me.

"I will go with you," I repeated doggedly.

All friendliness slipped away from Hoppensach.

"Oh how that spoiled brat needs a thrashing!"

But now Johanne was offended.

"You know you mustn't talk that way about the boy! Soren hasn't done anything to you. Soren is a nice well-behaved boy. If you can't be decent, Hoppensach, then we'd better go home ..."

"Let's go then, the devil take it. Expect me to stand here and let myself be ordered about by that little sniveller!"

Our picnic broke up in a hurry. Hoppensach threw the rug over his arm and Johanne, Mother's old coat over hers. As we stalked out of the garden Johanne was in the middle, I on the right side of her, and Hoppensach on her left.

For a long while we hurried along without uttering a word. But the walk dispelled a portion of Hoppensach's wrath, and after a while he mumbled, almost mildly.

"I reckon you're damm well in love with that boy!"

Johanne thought it over a little, then she said quietly,

"It wouldn't be any wonder if I was."

Then she continued in a lower voice,

"Maybe one shouldn't say it in his hearing, but you'd have to go a long way to find another such a handsome lad!"

"What, that little shrimp!" Hoppensach exclaimed, both surprise and contempt in his voice. "My God, he looks more like a girl than a boy! Such hands! They'll never be good for anything!"

For once he was expressing his real opinion of me.

"It's because he comes of gentlefolk," explained Johanne. "It's considered elegant to have small hands. You should see how small his feet are, too—and not one of his toes is crooked!"

Again there was a pause and silence.

Then finally Hoppensach murmured,

"Do you know what I think? I think if you have a child yourself you won't care as much for it as you do for him!"

Johanne gave this some thought. It was obviously a serious and thought-provoking problem.

"Well, no . . ." She spoke hesitatingly. "No . . ."

Then she added quickly,

"But there couldn't ever be a nicer or more handsome boy than Soren."

Hoppensach answered by quickening the pace. I trudged along on tired legs, half pulled along by Johanne. But I wouldn't complain. The weariness in my legs was a mere nothing in comparison with the knowledge that I had prevented Johanne from going off with Hoppensach.

During the rest of the walk, Hoppensach said nothing more. He just blew clouds of smoke with unusual frequency through his cigar with the amber tip. We neared the kitchen steps and began to climb them. We chose that way because Farmor's confidence in Johanne had grown so great that she had entrusted her with a key to the kitchen door. Besides, Hoppensach was with us and there was less chance of his existence being discovered.

Johanne worried the key into the key-hole and turned it.

But before she got her hand on the door-handle to turn it, Hoppensach's arm was around her and his waxed moustache pushed against her face. From their position and the little clucking sound which followed, I realized that he had kissed her. That strange, indescribable feeling of pain filled me again ...

"Johanne," he said in a low voice, "see if you can't get away tonight—and come up to my place ..."

"All right," whispered Johanne, bereft of resistance. She rested in his arms with half-closed eyes and a red flush on her cheeks.

I realized that Hoppensach was trying to get Johanne away from me—that I would have to sleep all alone. Perhaps he would even kiss her again!

"You mustn't go away from me," I screamed, my tears rising.

Johanne aroused herself.

"Yes, but Soren—"

"I'll tell Farmor if you go. I'll tell her you've gone to Hoppensach's!"

"Be good now, little Soren," begged Johanne, but as she saw the muscles of my face tightening in preparation for a yell, she added quickly,

"I won't go out—I promise you!"

"Very well, then," said Hoppensach peaceably, "If Soren won't let you go, then—"

He waved good-naturedly with his hand.

A sudden bang—a bang which shot right through me.

When I came to my senses I saw that my balloon lay on the steps reduced to a crumpled bit of red skin.

My anguish found expression in a prolonged howl.

"The devil," Hoppensach broke out, fervent apology in his voice, "I must have touched it with my cigar."

At the same instant, Johanne struck his cheek—a heavy smack.

"You are a wicked man, Hoppensach," she said.

Hoppensach stepped back a little. He defended himself only by saying,

"But I didn't do it on purpose—I just happened to touch it by accident."

"You are lying, Hoppensach. You burst it because you don't like the boy. But if *you* don't like *him*, then *I'*m not going to like *you* any more—so there!"

She seized me by the hand, opened the door, and drew me quickly into the kitchen.

"You needn't expect to see me again, Hoppensach. It is over between us!"

The door was closed.

The key was noisily turned. And the burglar-chain rattled. Johanne bent over me and whispered,

"Now don't cry any more; then you shall have another balloon the next time we go for a walk."

"Why was Soren crying?" asked Farmor when we came into the dining-room.

"I had given him a balloon," answered Johanne calmly, "But out on the landing, one of my hat-pins pricked it and it burst."

We never met Hoppensach again, and as far as I know Johanne did not meet him when she went out alone either. Forced to make a choice between hairdresser Emylius Hoppensach and myself, she had chosen her little Soren.

18

"There it is!" cried Johanne.

In the next second I also saw it.

"There it is!" I screamed. Joy spread to my hands and feet, I had to clap my hands and dance.

A little pause ...

Then Farmor's voice was heard:

"Yes, there it is!"

Farmor sat in her wicker chair by the window, with her face turned toward the mirror which reflected the street.

The long-awaited landau stopped. I saw the coachman tie the reins, put the whip in its holder, step down, his foot on the wheel, to the street. Then he disappeared from sight under the window.

Both Farmor and I were dressed up to go out. I wore a white sailor suit and a navy-blue sailor-coat. I had objected to the jacket because the sun was shining and it was awfully warm. But the women had taken the opposite view. When one is driving it is always cold, they said. I had been allowed, however, on account of the heat, to wear shoes instead of boots—this in spite of the fact that shoes were not yet seasonally quite *comme il faut*. Farmor was wearing her summer coat of heavy black silk, and her best bonnet. In addition, she sat and clutched her parasol so that she would not forget it. It was lavender in color and had a fringe of lace.

Farmor went into the hall, followed by us, and began unlocking. Before she had finished, there was a ring at the bell.

"Who is it?" murmured Farmor.

"It's Larsen," came from the other side, in a deep, rough, good-natured voice. "Coachman Larsen."

Farmor opened the door a crack and peaked out. What she saw reassured her. She released the burglar-chain and opened the door.

A giant of a man stood there, with a large red nose and small good-natured eyes. He held his coachman's hat in his hand.

"The carriage waits," he said, jovial and yet respectful.

"We are quite ready," answered Farmor.

The giant bowed, and crooked his arm.

"May I be so gallant as to offer Mrs. Jensen my arm?" he asked.

"Thank you," said Farmor, all smiles.

They began to go downstairs, the red-cheeked bear of a coachman and the little black-robed worm. On every landing they stopped for a pause—Farmor had to catch the breath she had lost on the way getting there. My youth and my joy made it hard for me to move at Farmor's pace. Every minute I was stepping on her skirt, which dragged a step or two after her.

"That's right, Mrs. Jensen! You're doing fine," said the big bear cheerfully as they arrived at the street-floor.

"No, no," wailed Farmor. "The next time I go down those steps, I shall be carried."

The coachman hurried ahead to open the glassdoors.

"You mustn't say such a thing, Mrs. Jensen," he remarked respectfully. "There are many much frailer than you, who live to eighty or ninety."

Larsen's studied respect did not surprise me. On the contrary. The remarkable thing about Farmor was that no matter how feeble and helpless and humble she made herself out to be, people always showed her deference and respect. Possibly there were only two exceptions to this: Father and myself.

Farmor crept under Larsen's arm, through the door. The giant held the door until Johanne and I had gone through also, then hurried ahead to open the street door.

It was a landau which stood waiting there. It was an elegant landau, much more distinguished than the usual cabs. What especially impressed me was the doorstep. Just above the step and parallel with it, was a thick plate. It was connected to the carriage-door by a bar, so that when the door was opened, the plate came down. In this way the step came forth without being wet and dirty, whatever the weather.

Farmor turned her head around to Johanne.

"The sugar," she said.

Johanne produced a little white paper bag which she handed to Mrs. Jensen.

Farmor passed it over to the coachman.

"There are four pieces of sugar for the horses," she said. "Give them the first two now and the rest after we have gotten safely home."

The coachman bowed three or four times.

"Thank you kindly, Mrs. Jensen. Thank you kindly."

Farmor was normally as economical with sugar as she was with money. But when it was a question of life and limb like this she could be a regular spendthrift. I gathered that the horses were to get the first lump of sugar as an inducement not to run wild and the rest as a reward for bringing us home alive and all in one piece.

The last point was typical of Farmor's craftiness. The horses wouldn't get more sugar if they upset us, ran us into the sea, or did away with us in some other manner. So they would have an interest like ourselves in coming back to her house safe and sound!

Larsen opened the door and helped Farmor up. She made the ascent successfully though she kept protesting that she couldn't. As for me, I wrenched myself out of Johanne's hands, rather offended at the idea that I couldn't climb by myself.

We sat in the back seat, Farmor on the right, I on the left. The coachman spread the rug over our legs. The grown-ups had decided it might be cold during the drive.

"Remember to put on the burglar-chain," said Farmor to Johanne.

Johanne promised fervently to do so.

Farmor opened her parasol.

"One melts in such heat," she complained.

"Yes, it is warm," said the coachman. There were little bubbles of water in his nostrils which shone like diamonds.

He leant toward the horse nearest. "Just look, Klaus," he said cheerfully, "That nice Mrs. Jensen has brought you some sugar."

He stuck the flat of his hand up under the horse's mouth. I got on my knees and leant far over the side to watch. I didn't want to miss anything. Klaus munched in such a way that you could both see and hear him. Then Larsen went to the horse on the farther side. Mette also munched and scrunched. I enjoyed it. It was always a source of enjoyment to me to see animals eat.

Farmor was busy giving orders to Johanne, who was standing on the sidewalk beside the carriage.

"Don't forget to put the burglar-chain on. And if anyone rings, don't open the door! You remembered to lock Piphans's cage? And be sure all the gas-cocks are turned off."

There were still more instructions, many more. And Farmor had said it all several times already, up in the apartment. But Johanne betrayed no impatience. She just stood and said,

"Yes, Mrs. Jensen," and "You can be sure I'll do that, Mrs. Jensen."

The coachman mounted his box. He seized the whip and the reins, turned around and looked cheerily down at Farmor.

"Now we'll start, Mrs. Jensen," he exclaimed with a grin. It was probably the new word "start" which he found amusing.

"Now, mind—not too fast!" pleaded Farmor.

"No, no. We shall drive at the usual speed."

He smacked his tongue and cracked his whip. The carriage rumbled off.

"Goodbye! Goodbye!" shouted Johanne. "Have a good time, Soren!"

At that moment I suffered a little twinge. How lovely it would have been to have Johanne along too! But it had not occurred to me to ask. When Farmor and I drove out in Larsen's finest carriage—with Larsen himself driving—we couldn't of course take Johanne with us! That was clear somehow.

But I waved to her as long as I could see her.

It was my birthday. Already when I woke in the morning there had been some parcels on the chair placed beside my couch to prevent my falling out. A little later the postman arrived bringing me two picture post-cards! One was from

Cousin Christian and was a picture of the railway station where he and his father lived (a circle was drawn around the windows of Christian's room); the other was from the Agerlins. It was written by Uncle Agerlin, but the picture was that of a parrot.

Later in the morning Father had come. His visit was a short, hurried congratulation-call made between two appointments. He brought me a wooden fortress complete with towers, a draw-bridge, gates and a moat, and a box of soldiers, Danish guardsmen. Aunt Laura also paid a fleeting visit. After the inevitable "Conformity and Opposition" act she handed me a giant chocolate cigar. But what I had looked forward to most of all had been the drive in Larsen's landau which Farmor had promised I should have on my birthday.

And now I had begun it—

The carriage rounded the corner with the new church —the one where Pastor Moller stood in a kind of pencil box high above the heads of the congregation. It rolled past the wide, many-winged hospital with its pale green copper dome; it clattered across a round market-place just as a tram stopped to take in and let off some passengers. It drove past many side-streets, with long rows of building-association houses. Johanne, for some unknown reason, used to call these streets "potato rows," and somehow the sight of them injected a few drops of depression into my happy birthday mood. But on we drove—along a cemetery wall, as far as the cemetery stretched, then sharply round to the right.

Farmor closed up her parasol—and cautiously jabbed Larsen's back with it.

Larsen turned his face half-way around.

And Farmor piped as loudly as she could:

"Will you please stop at the flower-stall, the one just before the cemetery?"

"Yes, Mrs. Jensen—certainly."

Larsen drove to the other side of the road. His hands

pulled the reins tight, while he shouted what sounded like "Brrrrr" to his horses.

The carriage stopped. Larsen got down from his box, threw the carriage door open, and helped Farmor down to the sidewalk. I avoided Larsen's hand—a big healthy boy like me could get out of a carriage without anyone's help!

In the flower-stall Farmor had eight bouquets made up— all of dark red roses and light blue forget-me-nots, and all exactly alike. Then we continued on our way. A few yards more, and we reached the cemetery. It was the so-called, *Dog-Cemetery*.

Covering a space of about three thousand square yards were vast numbers of graves—small, rectangular pieces of ground adorned with marble headstones and marble figures or with blocks of granite, wreaths of white and black glass beads or plaster figures under glass shades. On one grave lay a bone made of white marble, on another were placed two bowls for the deceased, one with water in it, the other with pieces of rye-bread, spread with liver sausage. At the moment it was not the dead who were enjoying these delicacies, but a crowd of flapping, twittering sparrows. There were not only dogs lying in the Dog-Cemetery—there were also the remains of cats, canaries, monkeys, turtles, parrots ...

Although, as I have said, I could not read at that age, I recognized some of the inscriptions—Johanne and I had slipped in there once on one of our walks. On one headstone, for example, stood the words: "Sleep well, little Trutte!"; and for another: "Here lies Fido, my truest friend." Yes, I could even remember others, too—"My little she-cat, Marie Pedersen"; "Goodby Hanseman—we shall meet again"; "Here lies a Saint Bernard—Trusty: he saved a mother and child from drowning." Several times when Johanne read the inscriptions aloud to me, I had felt that clutch in the throat which is the forerunner of tears.

We approached the burial lot which belonged to Farmor. It was larger than the others, but then there were eight headstones on it, and there was also room for more. Eight small, slanting marble head-stones, all alike, each bearing a gilt cross and a name. The names read: Fie I, Vips I, Fie II, Vips II—and so forth. The stones were arranged in two rows, the Fies in one, the Vips in the other. Fie I, first in the one; Vips I, first in the other. Under Farmor's direction I laid down the bouquets, one in front of each headstone.

Then we stood for a little while—with serious faces—and contemplated the graves. Farmor had tears in her eyes, but then she had them so often, especially when she went out-doors, so it is possible that she was not really weeping at all. I, for my part, was having visions. In my mind's eye I saw four small pug-dogs and four small fox-terriers all dressed in white shirts and with wings, flying up to the old man in Heaven. This sight I would dearly have liked to witness in reality!

Farmor's endurance came to an end. The time for mourn-ing had been sufficiently long. When we arrived at the exit, Larsen had drawn up to the gate and was standing by the side of the carriage, ready to hoist Farmor back into the vehicle.

We had not driven very far when Larsen suddenly pulled hard on the reins. "We'll make a little stop here," he said, in his most reassuring voice. Then, turning his face half-way around, he explained to us down in the landau,

"There's one of those chug-chug contraptions coming!"

"Goodness gracious," groaned Farmor, almost in tears, "Won't the horses run away?"

"No, no." Larsen reassured her; "Klaus is much too calm and sensible for that. He's quite an experienced old horse, is Klaus ... No, we'll just have to stay at the side here till the hellish thing has gone past ..."

I leant as far out of the carriage as I could to witness the fearful piece of devilry. I could feel Farmor's hand clutching the back of my coat and hear her warning me not to fall out and be run over by the monster. But she could wail and pull me back as much as she liked—I did not care. And suddenly the thing was there! It looked like a carriage (at any rate it had four wheels like a carriage), but oh, miracle of miracles! no horses drew it. The apparatus whizzed past of itself. In the front sat a man towering over the small wheels. He wore dark dust glasses and a winter overcoat and had a rug over his knees. A slanting stick culminating in a wheel with a horn rose up in front of him. The man was clutching the wheel, apparently so as not to be thrown out. Yet he did not seem to be afraid. I did not get much of a look at him—in the flash of a second the vehicle was past us, and a moment later, out of sight.

I turned around, glowing with enthusiasm and excitement. "Did you see that, Farmor!!"

"No," said Farmor, shaking her head. "It went by so fast I declare I couldn't see a thing."

Up on his box Larsen was speaking quieting words to the horses. They had reared up as the monster flew by, pulling the landau in towards the side-walk, and their out-stretched necks were trembling, so that the old hacks looked like powerful steeds.

"There, there, quiet, Mette," babbled the coachman. "Calm down, old girl. You don't need to go crazy just because there are others who do!"

"It is frightful what people will invent," sighed Farmor.

"Yes, Madam is certainly right there. But that there bit of devilry won't last—that's as certain as amen in church. Folks aint so crazy as to be willing to risk life and limb in that kind of rattletrap!"

My mind was divided. It must be wonderful, I thought, to whizz away at such speed—to whizz past even the fastest horse—and yet I should hardly have had the courage to accept if anyone had invited me to ride in such a machine.

Mette had calmed down. The coachman clucked his lips to her, and the carriage rolled on.

We passed a newly built railroad station, then turned to the left, away from the paved streets, out on an earth road. The jolting ceased; the silence which followed was luxurious.

We came into a new quarter. The broad roads turned this way and that in elegant curves, with trees, ramparts, and small lakes on either side. Other carriages passed us, mostly going in the opposite direction. There was a creaking, a chattering, a tinkling, suggestive of wealth and inherited superiority. Clouds of dust rose up behind every carriage. Once we drove into a thick cloud of it made by a carriage with a crest on it, but it did not annoy me. On the contrary —in the golden sunlight the dust acquired a kind of festive gleam, poetic. Even the smell of it pleased me. Yes, it positively intoxicated me, just as the smell of the soil on a spring day intoxicates a city child.

Larsen turned around suddenly.

"Here comes the Royal Family," he said quickly. His voice was excited, ceremonious; it was the tone in which people speak when they witness some great historical event.

"Bow!" whispered Farmor to me.

She quickly closed her parasol. I assume it would not have been in good taste to sit with an open parasol in the presence of Royalty. Then she began to bow. The bowing consisted of a drawing up of the upper part of her body while she nodded—nodded rhythmically and continuously, just like the old woman in the coffee shop in town. At the same time she broadened her lips into a Pierrot-like smile.

Seeing Farmor's efforts, I realized that I also should be doing something. Although my mother had initiated me into the art of bowing, she had neglected to teach me how to bow while sitting down. So I had to improvise. I began swinging the upper part of my body, forward and backward, deeply and perseveringly, now and again tapping my heels against the woodwork beneath me. In the midst of my efforts I had a feeling that I must be looking rather ridiculous.

But my embarrassment and my bowing did not prevent my keeping a careful watch to the left. I was determined to have a look at the Royalties.

Suddenly another carriage drove by. A big open one. A young woman and a big girl sat in it. They both smiled to us, but their smiles were strange ones—like Farmor's. When they saw our bowings, they nodded their heads in a friendly way—and then the carriage disappeared.

"It was only the young princesses," said Farmor, a little disappointed.

I, too, was disappointed. They were the first royal people I had ever seen and I had imagined royalties to be much more beautiful, much more grand. Their clothes were not the least bit elegant! Constance—who I knew was frightfully poor—even she had been more elegant on the day of Mother's funeral. The most disappointing thing of all was that there had been no crowns! I had learned from literature that princesses all wore crowns on their heads. Only one thing about them had completely satisfied me—the red-clad coachman on the box.

"Farmor," I asked, "Are princesses very poor?"

Farmor opened her parasol again.

"No—they aren't that," she said, smiling a little. "But they have a sensible grandfather, who takes care that the young ones don't waste money. That's why they're no better dressed than the rest of us."

"But why are they ugly?"

Farmor shook her head.

"You mustn't say that they're ugly. They have slender waists, I know, and very straight backs. But it's their busts that are a bit unshapely, that's all."

I, for my part, had looked hardest at their faces. But in Farmor's world, a woman's face was obviously of secondary importance, her body and posture the most important thing.

A blinding light struck my eyes. We had come out from under the shade of the trees. When after a second the pupils of my eyes had adapted themselves, I saw that we had come right out onto the shore of the Sound, and before our eyes stretched a vast expanse of water, calm, sparkling and bluish-white. I was carried away with delight, a feeling of happiness beyond the need of words or movement. It was born of sea-light and sea-air, and was so intense that it actually hurt.

Farmor also became silent. Perhaps she, too, in spite of her age experienced the same smarting happiness.

We drove for a long time beside the sea. Tiny swells churned between the rocks, and from a distant shipyard came the faint strokes of a hammer, like metallic notes from a music-box. The sounds, the heat, and the light together awakened in me a kind of radiant, happy drowsiness. If I could have put my thoughts into words, I would have called on Time to stand still—to remain—immovable.

Then suddenly I became aware that the carriage was rising from the solid earth. I was not really surprised, it was as if I had been expecting it all the time. It glided upward, gradually and carefully until neither the horses' hoofs nor the wheels touched the ground. At the same time all sound was stilled. We continued to rise ... up over the tree-tops ... higher still, above the roofs ... and still higher, above the city's spires and towers. At last we were sailing far away—a couple of small clouds like granite boulders on either side of us. And there, far below us, lay the city. How dear it was—the city! Sweet as a brood of little chickens! with its red tiled roofs, its pale-green towers, its rising smoke columns, its symmetrical trees, and its light ribbons of shining water.

But we went still higher. The horses which had become as transparent as glass, were galloping up toward the sun. Soon we had reached its outer rays, then sailed into that pale golden realm of happiness that surpasses understanding.

— — —

"'Now we must get down—now we are home," piped Farmor's voice.

I had been sunk so deep in my happiness, that I had hardly noticed that the carriage had descended. But now I remembered. A few minutes ago Larsen had mumbled,

"Well, I suppose we must think about getting home."

His voice had sounded so strange—as if it came from the other side of a curtain.

I rubbed my eyes—not feeling quite myself. The carriage had stopped in front of Farmor's house. Stopped on the cobblestones of the gray, melancholy street. Alas, I was back to the humdrum of everyday life. Everyday life with its gravity, its boredom, its irritations, its sorrows, its fears.

Larsen had descended from his box, and was opening the door.

"The young gentleman had a little nap," he grunted jovially. "Well, the air is tiring."

"I haven't been asleep," I said angrily. It was an insult to say I had fallen asleep when I was out driving. I couldn't understand how he had got the idea either. I had been wide awake the whole time. Apparently I had been mistaken in Larsen. He wasn't at all the nice fellow I had thought him before. He was horrid—I hated him!

At that instant the door opened and Johanne came hurrying out.

"Well, Soren," she said cheerfully, "have you had a nice time?"

She did not expect any answer, but she spread her arms wide and wrapped them tenderly about her foster-son. The strength of her embrace communicated her thoughts. It would be a long time before I went away on such a long journey again, if she had any say.

"You'd better come up with me," said Farmor to Larsen. "I will settle up with you in my office."

"Thank you kindly, Madam," answered Larsen, and respectfully offered her his arm.

And so we went up. Up to our chocolate.

19

It happened a few times that summer that I had to take my walk with Farmor instead of with Johanne. It wasn't exactly what I liked to do. That there was no place for her in my heart's little core was a minor detail. What was much worse was that she moved at an entirely different tempo than I. Her movements were not only painfully slow, she had to stop every few minutes, had to stand still on flights of steps or in the middle of pavements or parkways to pant asthmatically for breath. Oh, I could have covered the ground in a tenth part of the time that our walks took us!

Still, we never took any *long* walks together. We just dragged across the street over to the parkway and through a little gate which was only open to a select group. A little way inside was a cleared space, a bright square adorned with trees and brown benches. Farmor settled down there, and there she would remain seated, until we groaned our way homeward again.

On the days I had to walk with Farmor, I was rigged out even more elegantly than usual. Johanne had to put a new white sailor blouse on me, with long trousers à la grown men to match it. A white sailor hat was put on my head, with a navy blue ribbon hanging down to my neck; and in my hand was placed a large net containing three colored balls of different sizes. Sometimes the balls were replaced by a hoop, with its essential stick. Children in the magazines to which Farmor subscribed were pictured with toys of this kind. They were supposed to be chic—indeed quite indispensable if one were not to be exiled from the world of fashion. Farmor assumed, I suppose, that I could amuse myself with the ball or the hoop during the hours she throned on her bench. But her assumption did not correspond with reality. After a few minutes I would toss aside the toys and get down to what the present had to offer —that is to say, down to the gravel path, with its varied flotsam of discarded papers, corks and matches. The clean white garments I wore always had to be washed again after I had been out with Farmor.

One Sunday an acquaintance of Farmor's was sitting on the same bench, a little, fattish lady with a face like that of a rat. The rat-woman was extremely elegant. A huge pancake-hat rested on her coiffure, and a layer of sparkling rings glittered through her transparent net gloves. The two ladies greeted each other with shrieking heartiness (it was, however, the stranger who shrieked the loudest) and Farmor's bonnet and the lady's hat with its cartload of fruits, flowers and trimmings vied with each other in bobbing up and down.

The rat-woman aroused my hostility at first glance. But the feeling changed to a faint liking when she exclaimed that Mrs. Jensen's grandson was an unusually handsome boy. This feeling soon changed again, however, to one of complete indifference.

I was just about to begin my solitary play when the rat-woman set up a sort of trumpet-call.

"Beata!" she cried, "Here is a playmate for you!"

A large fat girl, who had been playing shuttle-cock by herself at a little distance, reluctantly drew nearer. She remained standing a little way off, turning around on the tips of her toes and staring at the gravel. As for myself, I was terror-stricken at the thought of the difficulties involved in beginning an acquaintanceship.

"Can you say a nice good day to the little girl?" said Farmor in a voice as sticky as a piece of candy taken out of the mouth.

"Little girl!" She was a half-head taller than I, and three times as fat! I was tempted to stick out my tongue and say "ugh!"

"Shake hands now," prompted the other woman, impatient at our initial difficulties.

Beata got over being embarrassed more easily than I; she was evidently more accustomed to meeting strangers. She stuck a chubby hand toward me and said,

"Day."

I answered with a careless ditto and an almost inaudible, "Good-day." Mother had taught me that one must not say just "Day" alone. Well-behaved people said "Good-day."

"Go and play shuttle-cock together," said the woman cheerfully.

I felt a strong urge just to walk away. Not because I was afraid, but because the whole situation disgusted me. Of course, it might be fun to play with that strange kind of ball she had—but not at the command of a grown-up. And certainly not with a stupid idiot like her, Beata! The girl's long lumpy nose, her slanting, ferrety eyes, her peculiar red hair, her fatness, the crude color of her dress, her innumerable bows—they all made something swell up inside me like a balloon, a balloon of hatred and rage.

But I had been brought up to dissemble, and perhaps was hypocritical by nature. I accepted the racket Beata held toward me, with a bow. "Thank you," I said, as correctly as any diplomat. Though it was such a long time since Mother had gone away from me that I had almost forgotten her, I remembered her teaching.

Farmor and Mrs. Daversen began talking. At first they twittered a little about the weather; then they bemoaned the sudden death and pitied the poor motherless child—"but it is fine that he has *you*, Mrs. Jensen!"—and finally they began on their mutual acquaintances. I understood very well that the poor motherless child was myself. I felt flattered to be thought interesting and tragic; still there was something in the way they discussed my destiny—for all their tearful sympathy—that aroused my wrath. They became less effusive but more in agreement when they proceeded to the next subject.

Beata and I had in the meanwhile begun our game of shuttlecock. It turned out to be not too boring. I had never played before, and to begin with missed the shuttlecock much more often than Beata. But that did not last long. I quickly learned the technique—naturally I was much more clever than this clumsy, fat girl!

The game assumed new interest when I thought out a variation. This was to aim at Beata's nose instead of hitting the shuttlecock up in the air. My hope was to hit it so hard that she would scream. This new objective I kept to myself—it was my private secret.

At length I almost succeeded—I say: *almost*. The shuttlecock dangled in the air just in front of her nose, yet the effect was almost the same as if it had hit her. She dropped her racket, covered her face with her hands and wailed,

"U-uh!"

Mrs. Daversen commented amiably from over on the bench,

"The ball must be hit up in the air, Soren, not straight across!"

And Farmor added,

"Remember that, Soren."

I hated Farmor. I hated Mrs. Daversen. I hated Beata.

The grown-ups resumed their chatter. Beata and I continued—but not for long. Suddenly I let the shuttlecock fall instead of trying to hit it.

"I'm bored with this," I said.

"So am I," said Beata.

We stood and looked at each other. Then she threw down her racket and said,

"Shall we play ball?"

"No, that's boring, too."

"Yes, that's boring, too. Well, what shall we play then? Father, Mother and children?"

I turned and scowled at the ladies on the bench. Then I turned back and muttered to her in a low voice,

"You are a stupid little idiot!"

The remark did not seem to make any impression on her. She continued unsubdued,

"We could pretend that some stones are the children. Or we could go for a walk."

The idea of going for a walk held more appeal for me.

Anything to get away from the grown-ups—it would make the whole situation more endurable.

"I'd like to go for a walk," I said.

"Can we go for a walk?" shouted Beata to her mother.

Mrs. Daversen stopped short in the middle of a sentence.

"A walk? Why, yes. There's no harm in that, is there, Mrs. Jensen?"

"No-o," came Farmor's hesitant answer. I knew it was just out of politeness that Farmor consented. If we had been alone I should never have been allowed to go for a walk by myself.

Mrs. Daversen added,

"But don't go further away than we can see you."

"All right, Mother," said Beata.

"And don't dirty your clean clothes," came from Farmor. Her grandson did not take the trouble to answer.

Beata seized my hand and we began our walk. I wanted to let go her hand. It was disgustingly damp and warm, but I realized that the grown-ups would think it looked well and would be more at ease if we walked hand-in-hand.

"Now we are father, mother and children," whispered Beata.

"I am an Injun," I said, "and you are an Injun squaw."

"You can play Injuns, if you want to; but I am playing father, mother and children."

This business of holding hands seemed to yield me an advantage. I noticed very soon that Beata was letting herself be led by me. Wherever I chose to go, she went. Perhaps that was a part of playing father, mother and children. At any rate I took advantage of it and went in wider and wider circles. At last I got her by degrees in behind a large green-house.

"But they can't see us," she said dubiously.

Some wooden boxes stood piled up against the house, half-concealed by bushes. They were filled with withered leaves, yellowed papers, cut branches. I steered her there.

"This is our cave," I said.

"We can also pretend it's our house," she answered. "This is the dining-room, and that is the den, and that is the bed-room."

"You are a stupid idiot," I said, irritated. "It's a *cave*."

"*You* can pretend it's a cave," she answered peaceably, "but *I* shall pretend it's our house."

I peered out from the bushes, a hand shading my eyes. In the distance I observed a factory smokestack belching smoke.

"There is smoke among the Palefaces," I muttered in a deep voice.

"Now we are married and you must kiss me," she said. I peered all around me—

"I must have a gun. The Palefaces are on the war-path!"

"You must kiss me, see. That is part of the game when you play father, mother and children."

Sniggering in a slightly suggestive way, she added,

"That's how children come in their mothers' tummies."

I had found a branch that was highly suitable for making a gun. It was straight and thick. I was just lopping off the sidebranches when Beata threw her arms around me and kissed me. Her lips landed on my nostrils instead of my mouth.

The rage which had been mounting in me became with that kiss so violent as to break the dam—that dam of fear and compunction that hitherto had kept it an enclosed lake. The dam had in any case grown less imposing after the greenhouse concealed us from the grown-ups.

I took a step backward, lifted the branch and hit Beata in her face with it.

She uttered a shrill cry.

If she had not screamed I doubt whether I should have gone further, but that cry made me wild, made me lose my senses. I threw the branch away and went for her with clenched fists. I hit whatever part of her I could reach— her face, her breasts, her stomach. Maybe I aimed hardest at her nose, that nose which for some reason or other aroused my enmity. I knew it was a dreadful thing to strike a girl, but my hatred, my disgust, my contempt, were so over-whelming that all my compunctions, all my fear, all my mother's teachings failed to stop me.

Beata turned and fled. I pursued her. She only got a short distance away when she fell full-length. She had stumbled over one of the many bits of rubble lying behind the greenhouse. She lay there, howling so wildly that her back rose and fell convulsively. I rushed at her—pulled her hair, tore at her sash, kicked and spat at her. Even her sobs aroused my fury and disgust.

But my violence gradually diminished. Finally I stopped short—like a mechanical figure. My rage was exhausted, my hate had disappeared, my passion was spent. In their place arose a terror-stricken awareness of what I had done. I had struck a girl; I had used a weapon against a weapon-less person; I had kicked someone who'd fallen; I had ruined her dress. I had pulled her hair; I had spat at her. Fear began to tear at my stomach.

"There! Get up now, you stupid idiot!"

My voice attempted to reduce what had happened to a mere bagatelle and Beata's weeping to an affectation.

Beata ceased crying. Slowly she rose. She was appar-ently no longer afraid of me—evidently her instinct told her that my attack was over.

I began to shiver when I saw her face. Dirt, blood from her nose and tears had all run together in long streaks and stains.

"'I shall tell my mother on you," she sniffled, but there was more sorrow than vengeance in her voice.

A cramping feeling in my stomach made me huddle. Yes, of course. Of course she would tell her mother. I had not thought of that. But *now, now* I did, intensely and pain-fully. All of a sudden I could foresee the consequences, all the inescapable consequences: the exposure, the shame, the reproaches, the sermonizing—why, they might even tell Father what I'd done and he would certainly use the long ruler he kept in his desk! Or perhaps I should be sent to a reformatory, one of those places where they locked up naughty boys in a dark cellar! And I should never again see Johanne—!

I clutched my stomach, so greatly did fear of the consequences gnaw me internally. But oddly enough, the sensation was not only one of pain. What I felt reached far down into the lowest part of my tummy and made it feel lovely there ... in a strange and disturbing way.

Beata was walking away. I seized her by the arm.

"Don't tell," I pleaded. And suddenly I burst forth—with the fire of inspiration,

"I'll give you ten ore if you won't tell."

Beata stopped. A little brightness came into her face. But it quickly faded away.

"You haven't got ten ore," she said. For all the categorical form of her statement a latent question gleamed in her eyes.

I nodded my head vigorously.

"Of course I have ten ore," I said. "It's my Sunday ten ore."

I had received it that very morning and had not yet spent it. The sad thing about Sundays was that the shops were all closed. That was something I had learned from many bitter disappointments.

I plunged my hand into my pocket and brought up the ten ore piece. A lump of wool came out with it.

"Just look!" exclaimed Beata. The brightness returned to her face. It was as if the new and shiny piece of money threw its light there.

"It is a special kind that they make for Farmor," I explained. "Farmor is the only one who can get them."

Although this piece of information was new to me myself, a product of the fantasy of the moment, I was in no doubt of its correctness. If anyone had told me I was lying I should have been surprised—and felt a great injustice was done to me.

"Give it to me," she said and came closer.

I drew back my hand and closed my fist.

"Only if you promise not to tell."

"I won't say anything."

"Do you promise?"

Beata nodded her head.

"You must say 'amen'."

"Amen? What is that for?"

"When a person says amen, then he keeps his promise."

"How shall I say it?"

"Just say:
I-promise-never-to-tell-that-you-hit-me-amen."

I made a gesture with my hand across my neck—something I had once learned from Cousin Christian.

Beata repeated, slowly and uncertainly,

"I-promise-never-to-tell-that-you-hit-me-amen."

Then she asked quickly,

"May I have it now?"

It appeared that she was not quite certain that the ritual had been completed or that I would keep my word.

I handed her the ten ore.

"Now you'll die if you tattle," I said in a threatening voice.

Beata looked solemn.

"I won't tattle," she said.

Then she added with a smile,

"I like you, Soren. When I am big, I shall marry you."

I did not answer. I thought it inopportune to reveal my feelings—but marry a girl with hair and a nose like that! What did she take me for, the little pug-face!?

We reached the corner of the greenhouse.

Beata turned toward me.

"Soren—give me a kiss."

My right hand itched with a desire to hit her again. But it did not move. In spite of the ten ore, I was in her power, now.

I looked at her for a moment—at her dirty face, her big

lumpy nose, her drab, course, squirrel-red hair—everything about her provoked my enmity, evoked my disgust. Unfortunately the antipathy was not mutual!

I shut my eyes and mouth, and put my lips to hers. They touched for just an instant, then I jerked my head away.

She smiled blissfully.

"You are a handsome boy," she said.

Then, fearing, perhaps, that I might become too conceited, she added quickly,

"But it isn't right to hit girls."

We directed our steps towards the grown-ups. I had arrived at the conclusion that I could depend upon Beata not to blab on me, but I still had a creeping sensation in my stomach.

Even at some distance, Mrs. Daversen fixed her eyes on us. Suddenly she screamed,

"But good heavens Beata—how you *look!*"

At the same moment it flashed through my mind that even if Beata had promised not to tell, my crime would still be detected, for her mother could not fail to see that something had happened. Beata's mud-stained, blood-stained face, her disheveled hair, her soiled, torn dress—everything would betray me. This had not occurred to me before, but now I suddenly grasped the situation and all its probable consequences. When Beata was questioned—what then?

I shriveled with apprehension.

"But, child, what has happened?" wailed Mrs. Daversen— tears springing to her eyes.

"Oh, nothing!" Beata began.

"Now don't pretend to me, Beata! You know you couldn't get in a state like that unless something happened. You know you must tell your mother everything."

Beata hesitated.

I stuck one hand down into the gravel and feverishly clenched the fist.

"A big boy came along," began Beata.

"And what did he do?"

"He said I was a gingerhead and a stupid idiot. And then he hit me and ... kicked me and ... pulled my hair and ... spat at me and ..."

Beata was so moved by her own description that she began to cry again.

Her mother drew her down on her lap, pressed her close, and stroked her hair.

"There, there, my little girl. Now you must not cry any more. Life is like that ... Life is like that."

The fat, ugly rat-woman became curiously beautiful all of a sudden as she sat there stroking the hair of her little maltreated rat-child.

"It's dreadful with all these hooligans," whined Farmor. "Even decent folk's children can't be safe from them."

My first feeling after Beata's false explanation was one of immeasurable relief. Now none of the grown-ups would ever know what happened behind the greenhouse. I also experienced a little feeling of gratitude. How easily Beata could have betrayed me yet retained my ten ore! But instead of taking revenge, she had kept her word—yes, kept the law in childhood's code: *Do not tattle!*

But this initial feeling of relief yielded to one of frightful shame. If only Mrs. Daversen had jumped up, if she had screamed or run for the gardener! But instead of that just to sit there and look beautiful and unhappy—and stroke her little girl's hair—and just murmur, "Life is like that" over and over again—nothing could have stung my conscience more painfully. I felt as if I had done something really mean, something quite exceptionally dirty—and that everybody would despise me if they found out.

"Why didn't you defend the little girl," Farmor asked reproachfully.

"I did," I lied, a blush of shame warming my face. "I kicked him and—and—bit him—"

"He was so big," said Beata between sobs, "much bigger than Soren."

"Life is like that," nodded Mrs. Daversen, "The weak are

despised and persecuted though they do no harm. That is the way life goes—so it is . . ."

There was something about Mrs. Daversen's view of life which I could not understand. Now if *I* had been attacked, Farmor would have told somebody in the vicinity to run and fetch the attendant. For all her famous helplessness, she would have set a mess of activities in motion. And if my Father had been there, he would have telephoned for the police, or at least have written to the newspaper—he often did the latter when he was annoyed about something. But Mrs. Daversen did nothing. Absolutely nothing. What is more, she took it as something normal that a stranger should come along and mishandle her child. And the story was not exactly a usual one. I knew that it was by no means an everyday occurrence for boys to go and attack other children in a park. And if the strange boy had really been in a fighting mood, why had he not set on *me* instead of on Beata? It is certainly more usual for boys to fight with boys than with girls. And why had Mrs. Daversen never once asked what was the cause of the attack? Beata had given no other explanation than that the boy had said she was a red head. Even if I myself couldn't stick red hair, I couldn't see that constituted sufficient reason to attack anyone. Yes, there was something rather mysterious about Mrs. Daversen's resignation and lack of surprise.

Beata's weeping ceased. The new flood of tears had not made her face any cleaner, but only added new furrows and streaks to it.

Mrs. Daversen pulled out a snow-white handkerchief, held it in front of Beata's mouth and ordered, "Spit."

Beata bubbled. When she had bubbled enough, her mother set to wiping her face, wiping away the blood, dirt and tears.

"I have a piece of soap in my bag," Farmor volunteered.

"Thanks, Mrs. Jensen, but I shall take her home and give her a bath. This is just to get the worst off."

"Must you go so soon? We were having such a nice chat ..."

"Yes, it's too bad, Mrs. Jensen. But Beata can't run about looking like this."

We said our goodbyes. The ladies with many hearty exclamations and many expressions of hope that they would soon see one another again. Beata and I shook hands, as ordered; Beata curtseyed and I bowed. We were also ordered to say, "Thanks for today," and "Till our next meeting."

Then they went. Their two figures grew smaller and smaller, until they disappeared in the distance behind a rockery with dark fir trees on it. Oh, what a relief! I felt as if I had been down to Lillelund's for a bushel of potatoes and struggled up the kitchen stairs with them and at last been relieved, thanks to Fernanda's hands, of the stone-heavy grocery basket. No-one, no-one, no-one was ever going to know what happened behind the greenhouse! And Beata and Beata's mother—never in the world would I meet them again. The next time Farmor wanted to go over to the park, I would get green in the face from stomach-ache and ask to be allowed to lie down on the sofa. I knew from experience I could do that in such a way as to make the grown-ups go grey in the face with anxiety.

"He! He!" Farmor smirked, "So Soren found a little sweetheart, did he!" She stroked my cheek with her cold, crooked forefinger. "Well, well, you might do worse. She'll be a good match one day—her father's the rich clothes merchant Daversen, him that has that shop around the corner."

She pressed me close to her, and with a secretive air whispered to me, "And they are Jews, too. Jews always have money. Remember that, my boy."

One Monday forenoon I had been allowed to go out as usual to blow my Sunday ten ore. I was part-way up the main stairway when a voice from below called to me,

"Soren! Wait a minute, Soren! It's Aunt White."

I was only a few steps from Farmor's door. I debated with myself whether I should not fly on up and ring, so as to slip in before Miss Tychsen could reach me. But my acquaintance with Farmor's slowness and all her locking-up gadgets made me decide against this. I stopped. I stood at ease—the ease of a bird in a man's hand.

Miss Tychsen's face came to view from the depths.

"Hello, Soren!" the face said—cheerful and out of breath. The rest of her quickly came in view also. She had gathered her skirt in her hand to mount more quickly. When she arrived where I stood, she said with friendly reproach,

"Aren't you ever coming up to hear stories?"

"No," I said hesitantly.

We went up a little further.

"But why? Why have you never come?"

"No-o," I repeated.

I knew very well why I hadn't gone. It was because I was ashamed. I had, indeed, a quite special reason for feeling ashamed in her presence. She not only knew that I had soiled my breeches on Mother's burial-day—so many people knew about that now—but unhappily also knew about something that nobody else knew. It was to her I had said that I could already read when I was two; and I had also tried to make her believe that I had read all the newspapers in the world! But in any case she was so beautiful and lovely, that she certainly couldn't have any interest in a little disobedient boy who was always getting into messes. Her offer to read to me was only a gesture of sympathy, of Christian charity. And that kind of affection I didn't want. So I really had ample reason for trying to avoid her. But *to tell* her why, *to confess* why I had not come—that—that of course, I couldn't do. That would simply have been to pile shame upon shame.

We had stopped in front of Farmor's door.

"Mother has taken a job in the office of *The Christian Daily*," she said. "She's there from 12.30 to 5 every day. You could come and hear the stories during that time if you liked."

Even if Time dims all feelings of shame, it takes a surprisingly long time to do so. Although my various sins already lay quite a long way behind me, their shame still remained with me, and in such a heavy dose that I wanted to get out of Miss Tychsen's readings at almost any price.

"I don't know whether I may," I mumbled.

Miss Tychsen pressed the bell.

"Well, we can ask your Farmor," she said.

After the requisite period of waiting the door was opened a crack, and from the crack came the familiar piping,

"Who is it?"

"Good-day, Mrs. Jensen. It is Constance Tychsen. And your grandson is here too."

Miss Tychsen's voice was as brisk and cheerful as Farmor's was slow and sorrowful.

The door was shut. The burglar-chain rattled, then the door was opened again—opened a little wider than before.

Farmor's maggot-white face glimmered in the darkness of the hall—

"Come in, Miss Tychsen—"

"No, thank you—I won't disturb you. I only wanted to hear whether Soren could come up and visit me a few hours each day. I would like to read some stories to him—and if he likes, I could teach him a little reading and figuring, also."

Farmor cautiously peered through the door-opening, apparently wanting to make quite sure there were no murderers lurking on the steps. The view must have reassured her. At any rate she now opened the door wide ... and stepped out on the landing.

"Yes, indeed," she said. "It would be very nice if he could learn a little before he goes to school. One certainly couldn't say No to such an offer."

It was obviously the idea of the lessons which appealed to her, not the story-telling. And undoubtedly what attracted her most about the offer was that the lessons would be gratis ...

They stood a little while discussing the matter—discussing it from all points of view. Finally they came to an understanding. It was agreed that I should go up to Miss Tychsen's every day from one until three o'clock. I was not to stay longer than three—I had, of course, to take my afternoon walks with Johanne.

Nobody consulted *me!* Nobody was interested in *my* feelings! And yet a new anxiety had descended upon me. An anxiety which, coming on top of my shame, made the forthcoming visit to Miss Tychsen seem a nightmare. The prospect of learning how to read and do sums was the cause of it. Actually I wanted to do both, especially to learn to read. It must be wonderful to be able to read all the stories in the whole world oneself! But suppose now, I *couldn't* learn! It was certainly terribly difficult, and just suppose my head wouldn't take it in! Just imagine—oh horror!— it turned out that I was *stupid!*

And how nasty of her: to first pretend that she was going to read stories to me, and then get the thing changed into teaching me to read and do sums! Why, it was worse than nasty—it was sly, it was mean! I hated Constance Tychsen. At that moment I hated her. Hated her despite all her loveliness ...

The rest of the day and the next forenoon I went around with the anguish of knowing that I was to go up to Miss Tychsen's. But hope mingled with the anguish—hope that

Farmor would forget about the agreement. But, no! Ah no! Farmor was not the one to forget anything that could be had for nothing. As soon as we had swallowed our luncheon coffee, she murmured to Johanne,

"Now you'd better clean him a little, before he goes up to learn to read and figure!"

Johanne inspected my nails and my ears, wiped my mouth clean and passed a comb improvingly through the wisps of hair on my neck. Then she seized me by the hand and led me up to Miss Tychsen's—right up to the door. Possibly she suspected that my journey there would be very protracted if I went alone. But it is also possible that she entertained fears that some evildoer might fall upon me on the way.

Miss Tychsen lived on the topmost floor, or, to be exact, the next-topmost, for the stairs continued past her door, up to the attic.

She came herself to open the door. At the sight of me her whole little round face beamed.

"Well, good day, Soren!" she said happily. "And welcome!"

Johanne gave me a little push forward.

"Well, here he is," she said.

She stood for a moment as if she wanted to say something, something important. But she did not get it out. Instead, she contented herself with the remark,

"Then he will come down again at three?"

Her step was slow and heavy as she descended the stairs. The door was closed. I was alone with Miss Tychsen. She put her hand on my shoulder and led me into the sitting-room.

I don't know whether I was surprised—I certainly had reason to be—convinced as I had been that she lived in penury. The rooms turned out to be just as fine as Farmor's. Perhaps the apartment was a tiny bit smaller; on the other hand, the furniture was more elegant, and the cosy atmosphere that these reddish-brown rooms exceeded far surpassed what one met with in the rooms of the house's proprietress.

There were three things in particular that promoted this heart-warming cosiness.

The first was the carpets. At Miss Tychsen's there was a carpet in every room. They stretched, thick and soft, from wall to wall. At Farmor's there was a carpet only in the living-room; in the den and in her bedroom there were some little hearth rugs—provided for Farmor's always-cold feet; but in the dining-room, where we spent all our time, there was only linoleum—dreary, cold linoleum.

Second: the furniture. Mrs. and Miss Tychsen's furniture not only bore the mark of a higher cultural level than Farmor's. Here the tables, chairs, screens, pedestals and what-nots were grouped much more closely together than ours. There were also many more pictures and photographs—especially photographs. Whereas Farmor kept her photos in albums and on stands, the Tychsen family evidently preferred to hang theirs on the walls. In fact it took some skill to find enough bare space on the wall on which to put so much as the flat of one's hand. This lavish wall-decorating appealed to me. Without giving it any reflection at the time I shared the era's dislike of bare, undecorated walls.

And finally, the potted plants: Mrs. and Miss Tychsen had a great many more flowers and plants than Farmor. Not only were their window-sills filled with them: from the window-frames and the fret-work on either side of them it was as if a shining green light poured down. And in the room itself plants stood on tables and pedestals, one after the other. I had the feeling of being in a cool cave surrounded by a lush green thicket, and I liked the feeling.

"Oh how nice you have it," I said. It came forth spontaneously and honestly.

"Have I?" Miss Tychsen patted my cheek. "I'm glad." Then she burst out in high spirits,

"Well, now, let's begin reading!"

I, too, felt happy and in a working mood. All that unwillingness to make the visit—on account of my shame and anxiety—had disappeared. Indeed, if anyone had told me that a moment ago I had not wanted to come up there, I should have stared uncomprehendingly at him, for not only had my unwillingness, but also my memory of it, vanished.

Miss Tychsen produced a book. There was a picture of a crowing cock on the cover.

"This is an ABC," she said. "Sit down here and I'll teach you some of the letters!"

She piled two or three cushions on the sofa, lifted me on top of them, and stuck a couple more behind me to lean against. Then she sat down beside me, without any pillows, so that we were of about the same height.

Miss Tychsen opened the book—

"Do you see that tower there? That is an A. Can you say A?"

"A," I said. That wasn't so difficult.

"Right, Soren!" She pointed to another place in the book,

"And can you tell me what letter that is?"

"It's an A," I said, a little surprised at her question. Why she had just told me!

"That's right," she said admiringly. "Now we'll learn another."

In the course of a few minutes I had learned the first few letters of the alphabet, together with a little jingle for implanting them in my memory.

"A says a, B says b—A—Be."

"My, but you are clever, Soren!" she said. "Soon you'll know the whole alphabet and then you'll be able to read 'all the newspapers in the whole world.' But now we have done enough studying for today—and you shall have a story as a reward."

She opened the book-case, the glass-doors of which reflected the sky and the potted plants, and took a big book out of it. When she opened it I saw that it contained hundreds of pictures—wonderful, thrilling pictures which made me feel the pound of my heart within me.

And then she began reading ...

21

Yes, and then she began—and she kept it up. She stuck to it day in and day out, week after week, month after month. Every day between one and three a young girl of about twenty-two and a little boy of six could be seen sitting together in a shadowy room on a dark-red sofa, a gleaming picture-book before them.

A new world opened up for the boy—a new and wonderful one—a world full of beautiful princesses and wicked queens; of princes who became frogs, and frogs who became princes; of witches and robbers; of giants and dwarfs; of knights, burghers and peasants; of fishermen, tailors and musicians; of wolves and foxes and flying fishes and talking birds—a world where Death and the Devil, Saint Peter and the Virgin Mary wandered around in the flesh.

The boy had heard stories before. His father had read to him; his nurse also. But his father had done it but seldom, and his nurse, with the common people's veneration for the printed word, had assumed a pronunciation which made it difficult for him to understand what she read. Perhaps, too, he had just at this time attained a more intelligent, more receptive age. At any rate, the stories he listened to now made a much deeper impression on him than anything he had previously heard. Yes, even a deeper impression on him than reality. Certain people—not so few at that—can feel more deeply about characters in fiction than they do about people they meet in everyday life. Of course it is a somewhat abnormal attitude, but the boy about whom this story is told, *had* that kind of abnormal attitude. He loved his devoted Johanne, but it is a question whether he did not feel still more warmly about St. John. To be sure, he had felt frightened of Fre'erik in the court-yard in the seconds before the latter threw himself on him, but it was nothing compared to the terror he experienced when Bluebeard was about to murder the last of his wives. To be sure, he had wept when his mother died, but what was that grief compared to the grief he felt the first time he heard about the Seven Dwarfs putting Snow White into a glass coffin?

These fairy-tales not only became a component part of his imaginative world—so much so that he secretly added to them—but were woven into the actualities of his ordinary life. One of the barred windows in the store-room up in the attic became the cage where the witch had imprisoned Hansel and Gretel. Down in a cellar-room under the house the devil's great grandmother lived and plucked the hair of her sleeping great-great-grandson. Mrs. Agerlin was a witch like the one in Jorinda and Joringel; her parrots were all unfortunate people she'd bewitched. There was no doubt but that Pastor Moller was a giant who gobbled up little children when he had time to spare. And as for the Holy Virgin, well the boy saw her with his own eyes one night when he lay and could not sleep. She came out of the wall, all shining, with a golden crown on her head and looked exactly like his mother. She glided soundlessly right up to him, bent over him, and kissed him on the forehead—and then was gone, vanished like the light in a lamp that some grown-up has blown out ...

As I have said, the boy loved these fairy tale characters, loved them more than the real people he met. But the strange thing was that he did not only love the *good* characters. Of course, he cared most for the good ones. Naturally he wanted the good ones to prevail and the bad ones to be defeated. But nonetheless he loved the bad characters too. His soul was so constructed that let the bad ones only be sufficiently uncompromising and magnificent, sufficiently monomaniac in their sadism, envy, cunning, greed (or whatever else constituted their wickedness)—the door of his admiration would open wide for them also. The result was that, deep in his innermost heart, together with the gentle, the pure, the noble, the self-sacrificing, the valiant, such beings as the wolf in Red Riding-Hood, the witch in Hansel and Gretel, and the wicked queen in Snow White all had a place.

I have a feeling that this dualism was something very characteristic of the little boy Soren about whom this story is being written. In any case the reader must know about it, for only with it in mind will he be able to understand why the boy reacted to his Farmor as he did.

Yes indeed ... the happiest hours of his day were those when his new "aunt" read aloud to him from the book called Grimm's *Fairy Tales*. If sometimes there were things in it that bored him—perhaps because he couldn't quite understand them—he just sat and listened to her voice or gazed into her eyes ...

For her voice was like a caress.

And her eyes like a kiss.

22

Johanne and I were taking our daily walk.

The weather was horrid. There were intermittent showers; the wind howled in my ears and tried to tear off my cap. It was slippery, too—the brown leaves had stuck to the flagstones and paving. It was one of those bad days when one realizes, with a shudder, that summer is past and winter on the way.

In spite of the weather Johanne and I had ventured far from home. We had crossed the parkway opposite Farmor's house, and gone into the adjoining park. The weather was too bad to play or to sit on a bench—besides there were no other children to play with; there was nothing to do except walk and walk. And so we did; and now we had reached a little curving path. It was a rather dark, low-lying outoftheway part of the park: despite wind and weather there were still leaves on the trees and bushes there.

At a·turn in the path I noticed a woman sitting on a bench a little way ahead of us. Under ordinary circumstances my eyes would not have lingered on her—grown-up people were normally outside my field of interest—but she was sitting so strangely—so *crookedly*—that my curiosity was aroused. Perhaps without my being aware of it, there was a certain familiar look about her also.

Suddenly I recognized her.

"Why, it's Aunt Laura!" I exclaimed—and started to run toward the bench.

"Good-day, Aunt Laura," I cried happily, while still at a little distance. My happiness did not derive simply from affection for Aunt Laura but rather from the pleasant feeling aroused on meeting an acquaintance when a long way from home.

Aunt Laura made a slight movement—she had plainly heard my glad shout. But she only lifted her head slightly— then sank back on the bench again in an even more crooked position than before.

I stopped abruptly. What kind of a way was this to welcome me! Why didn't she say, "Good-day" in a pleasant, friendly fashion like other grown-ups? I felt a little offended.

Johanne, who had hurried up, came alongside of me.

"How strange she is!" I whispered.

Johanne took me by the hand without saying anything, so that we reached the bench at the same time.

"Is Miss Laura unwell?" Johanne asked—while a step or two away.

It was a little while before Aunt Laura answered. Then she slowly lifted her eyelids. How strange her eyes looked! Bloodshot and veiled. As if she were looking at us from far away.

"Yes, I am ill," she muttered. And closed her eyes again. She looked queer. Her straw-hat, which should have rested straight on her brow, looked as if it had been smashed in; her pince-nez hung crookedly; her stiff collar was limp from dampness; and her elastic belt had become unfastened and lay carelessly on the bench. I noticed the belt particularly— it consisted of a broad, dark-blue piece of elastic, with a metal buckle shaped like an S—for I had one just like it. She was all wet, also. Her jacket was soaking wet at the shoulders, and the lower edge of her skirt was begrimed with mud and dirt. She didn't have any gloves on, either. But the strangest thing of all was her nails. They were as black as black could be. Never before had I seen Aunt Laura with dirty nails. Nor, for that matter, any of Father's or Mother's acquaintances. As Father now and then pontificated:

"Decent people are known by their nails and their punctuation when writing."

Johanne let go of my hand, and sat down on the bench beside Aunt Laura.

"Wouldn't Miss Laura like me to take her home?" she asked, in a serious and urgent way.

There was a pause, just as before.

Then there came from the collapsed figure, strangely haltingly,

"Why . . . why . . . should I . . . go home?"

"But you *are* ill, *aren't* you?"

Another pause.

Then suddenly Aunt Laura opened her eyes wide and looked at Johanne. Just looked. It was a remarkable look. All-knowing. Full of a deathly despair.

Then her eyes shut again. At the same time she mumbled slowly,

"You know very well that I am not ill."

"Of course you are ill," said Johanne quickly and urgently. "At any rate, you can't remain here."

She put Aunt Laura's hat on straight, smoothed her collar, and fastened her belt. Then she slipped her arm under the sick woman's, and lifted her to her feet.

Aunt Laura responded dully.

"Walk ahead of us!" Johanne ordered.

I had not heard her use that commanding tone of voice before. Or, if ever, extremely seldom. But I obeyed. Johanne seemed in these few minutes to have increased in stature and become another person. In addition, my heart told me that her commanding was dictated by compassion.

I could hear her voice behind me asking,

"Where does Miss Laura live?"

Aunt Laura mumbled an address unfamiliar to me.

"Good—that's not very far," said Johanne, evident relief in her voice.

Then she called out to me,

"Just go on walking, Soren, stay in front of me and go straight ahead—until I tell you otherwise."

I marched on, obedient as a soldier.

Strange sounds came from Aunt Laura. It sounded as if she were whimpering. I was very curious, but did not dare turn around. For some reason I knew that Johanne did not want me to look back.

We came quickly out of the park.

"To the left," came the order.

The left. Yes, indeed, I had learnt where "left" was. The hand one shook with when one said Good-day was the—right hand, so the opposite one must be the left. But then the question arose, which of my two hands *did* I say Good-day with? I practiced a moment with my hands—to get the feeling if I could. Unfortunately, I came to the conclusion that one could use either hand for the purpose.

I turned half round.

Johanne, who instantly knew what my dilemma was, made a little gesture with her head.

"It is that way, Soren."

Her voice was tense and grave. I hurried to turn my head.

So on I marched again.

It was not a pleasant walk. I could plainly perceive that

people were staring curiously at us. A street urchin made a gesture of emptying a glass, at the same time grinning in a very nasty way. A woman who passed us with a basket on her arm put a finger to her forehead—I could see that she thought we were crazy. And a man in working clothes with a wooden hand-cart, turned it round and followed us along the gutter, gaping open-mouthed at us. Before very long, too, we were being followed by four or five children.

I felt dreadfully embarrassed. In spite of being only six I had a keen understanding of what a person could and what he or she could *not* do. A person couldn't fall ill in the streets, and a person couldn't look as Aunt Laura was looking. But nor could one be seen in company with a person who looked as Aunt Laura did. So I hastened my steps, hoping to increase the space between me and the two women so much that no one would suspect I was part of the procession.

Unfortunately Johanne increased her tempo also. It seemed, moreover, that she was not sorry to go a little faster. Maybe she too—for all her compassion—was feeling a little uncomfortable in Aunt Laura's company. The result was that in spite of walking my fastest I continued to hear Aunt Laura's desperate moanings just behind me.

We approached a corner where two streets crossed.

"Look sharp before you cross," I heard Johanne's voice behind me.

I stopped short at the edge of the sidewalk. I looked around—and saw a large, pot-bellied policeman striding toward us.

Fear welled up in me. My stomach nursed a latent terror of the police. I had a feeling that every policeman could see right through me and read the long list of my sins. Every time I got past a police uniform unarrested, I felt as if the old man in Heaven had been especially merciful to me.

We were the people this policeman wanted to talk to. There was no doubt about it. For a moment I thought of running away—right across the street—but I knew from experience that I was not capable of running away from a grown-up person. Besides, even if I was afraid, I would be still more afraid away from Johanne than with her.

Now the big policeman stood in front of us—in all his might and power.

"What's going on here?" he asked, in a not over-friendly tone.

He was very fat—even fatter than coachman Larsen. His face was ruddy from wind and weather. A huge fox-red mop of a moustache hung down over his mouth. His eyes were a watery blue. His helmet was noticeably too small in comparison to his huge bloated cheeks. His white-gloved hands were fingering his heavy leather belt, which was just on a level with my eyes. No wonder he filled me with a sense of my own physical inferiority and spiritual despicableness.

"This lady has been taken ill," Johanne answered. Her voice was calm, but I who knew her intimately, could trace more than a little nervousness behind her calm.

To my horror Aunt Laura suddenly began to sing. At least "sing" is really too strong a word for it. It was some kind of tragic ballad she was trying to intone, but the words were barely comprehensible, for her voice was unsteady, and only occasionally did she strike the right note.

"Ill? Really ill?" the policeman asked. His air was not without suspicion.

"Yes, the lady has had an attack—she has them sometimes ... The lady suffers from this here—falling sickness."

Johanne put great emphasis each time on the word "lady".

"Shouldn't I call the ambulance for her?"

"No, thank you ... the attack's over now. The lady just needs to get home and go to bed—She'll be quite all right in the morning."

"Wouldn't you like me to call a cab?"

"The lady lives quite close here."

Johanne told him the address.

"Oh, there," said the policeman. "Very well, then—just go on—but try not to make a disturbance, or—"

"Yes, Mr. Constable." Johanne suddenly grew bolder. "But couldn't you, Mr. Constable, tell those children and that man with the hand-cart there they mustn't follow us."

The policeman did not need to speak to the children. They had formed a circle round us, excited to see whether we were going to be taken to the police station; but as soon as they heard Johanne's appeal they scattered, frightened, in all directions. The man with the hand-cart, however, remained standing where he was, unmoved. He probably wanted to convey that he had a perfect right to stand wherever he wished.

"Move along there," shouted the policeman. The voice was wholly different from the one he had been using with us. He was now confronting a man in working-class clothes and he knew exactly where *he* belonged in the social scale. My good clothes and Johanne's respectful "the lady" had given him a bit of a puzzle. And, even Aunt Laura, despite her bedraggled appearance to-day, had preserved a certain air of gentility.

"Walk on," whispered Johanne, softly and quickly.

I wasn't slow to obey. Like a guilty dog I shot across the street—followed by Johanne and Aunt Laura.

"A man has a right to stand where he wants to" I heard the man behind us grumble.

"When I say move on, you'd better move!" roared the policeman.

"All right—I'm going," the man answered. On the surface he seemed to be about to follow the policeman's orders quite peacefully, but underneath his voice was full of mockery and malice.

"Stay right here!" shouted the policeman, his voice rising to the top of the scale with anger, "Until the ladies have passed."

The policeman was all the same not so stupid as not to realize that the man secretly planned to continue to follow us.

"What the devil do you mean? First you tell me to move

on; then, all of a sudden, I'm *not* to—!"

The bickering died away behind us. In the distance I heard the policeman threatening to take the man to the station—then they were out of earshot.

"Here it is!" said Johanne suddenly. "It is that door there."

I pushed the heavy street-door open with some difficulty.

"Hold it open for us," said Johanne.

The opening was so narrow that she had to turn sideways, her arm still around Aunt Laura, to get in. Aunt Laura stumbled as she crossed the threshold—and almost pulled her down. They came tumbling in through the narrow opening with a great hubbub.

"Go on up," said Johanne.

I climbed the staircase ahead of them. I could hear Johanne trying to hoist Aunt Laura up the stairs, and how the toes of her shoes kept banging against the runners. It could not have been easy for Johanne, for the stairway was so narrow that it was difficult for two adults to go side-by-side.

"Stop, Soren. It's here."

I stopped on a landing—a little perplexed. There were two doors, and I was not yet able to read names on name-plates.

"Where is the key?" Johanne asked. Her voice was calm, firm and sympathetic.

Aunt Laura repeated rather foolishly,

"Where is the key ... Where is the—?"

Suddenly she seemed to realize that it was a question and that it was directed to her.

"The key? It is ... It is in my ... in my ..."

It was as if she took a preliminary run ... and finally she got out the word "handbag."

Johanne, who had already taken charge of the bag in the park, got Aunt Laura seated on the stairs, the flight leading up to the next floor. Then she began to rummage in the handbag, turning things over in it one by one. Among the numerous objects there was a glass bottle containing a clear, water-like fluid.

Aunt Laura seemed suddenly to become aware of my presence.

"Good *day*, Viggo," she said. Viggo was my father's name and not mine, but there was no doubt about it that she was addressing *me*.

She reached out her hand toward me, but I did not go any closer. I even moved a little further back behind Johanne. I was not only annoyed by Aunt Laura's appearance and behavior, I was, honestly speaking, a little afraid of her.

Her hand dropped. Then she declared profoundly.

"Life is ... success and ... failure. Mos' failure. Mos' failure. 'Member that, Viggo."

Her manner of speaking surprised me. At one moment she couldn't get her words out; the next she slurred three or four syllables together, putting the greatest emphasis on the first—then, she stopped short again and there was another pause. There was something in the way she spoke that reminded me of the way a drunken man walks.

Then she crumpled up and began to weep. Her weeping was a thin, despairing, monotonous kind of crooning.

Johanne found the key. She pressed Aunt Laura's goods and chattels back into her handbag, and unlocked the door.

"Just go in, Soren," she said.

I went in. Behind me, I heard Johanne say cheerfully, "Now let's see if we can climb into the coach!"

It was a curious apartment—there was no entry hall and no corridor either. The sitting-room was only separated from the stairway by a wall and a door. But it was really nice inside with old empire furniture and family portraits—all evidently inherited pieces. In the bay-window there was a little aquarium.

Johanne came stumbling in with Aunt Laura. Aunt Laura was so crumpled up that she seemed almost lifeless. Johanne almost had to carry her.

"I am just going to put your aunt to bed," she puffed

exhausted. "There are some magazines over there that you can be looking at."

She dragged Aunt Laura further in. As the adjoining door opened and shut, I caught a glimpse of a bedroom. It was plain that Aunt Laura only had two rooms: a sitting-room and a bedroom. I suddenly became aware that she belonged to a lower social order—not only than Farmor's and the Agerlins', but also even than Miss Tychsen's. Even if a single lady might be expected to have a smaller dwelling than others, merely one room with a bedroom attached— that was *too* little. And I understood without anyone's having to tell me how humiliating it must be to have a sitting-room and a stairway unseparated by any hall.

My legs steered me straight for the aquarium. It was certainly worth seeing. In the green water, between green grasses, swam big, red-gold fish. There were some queer-looking creatures among them: their eyes looked as if they had shot right out of their heads, and their tails were long like trains, and light and elegant as silk. They were at one and the same time very pretty and very ugly. I should have thought better of them if they had not had long black threads hanging down from their nether regions. Unfortunately, I assumed that these threads meant that they were making gaga and this somewhat destroyed their beauty in my eyes.

Suddenly it occurred to me that the fish might be human beings like Aunt Agerlin's parrots. Perhaps Aunt Laura was really a witch who bewitched people she didn't like— changed them into goldfish and put them down in her aquarium! That bottle in her handbag must be a magic potion! Anyone who drank from it would become a gold-fish. What a pity she had not given the fat policeman a drop of it! In my imagination I could see him putting the bottle to his lips, throwing his big head well back—and suddenly shrinking into a little floundering goldfish. And that particular goldfish I would certainly get permission to take home to an aquarium of my own!

Suddenly—utterly alone though I was—I grinned all over my face.

Notwithstanding my interest in the fishes and the flight of my unbridled fancy my ears were registering very distinctly what was going on in the bedroom. I could hear them moving around in there, and sometimes it sounded as if they were wrestling. Finally the bed began to creak violently.

Then there was quiet—a profound silence.

The door opened and Johanne slipped through on her tiptoes. She stood a moment, her head stretched into the bedroom, apparently observing Aunt Laura. It was dark in there—Johanne had probably pulled down the blinds. All at once a sound of deep breathing came from the room—a sound that plainly came from someone asleep. Then Johanne closed the door—slowly and carefully.

"Now we can go," she said in a low voice.

She came over to the window, where I was still standing by the aquarium. I noticed that she had the bottle with the magic potion in her hand. She stood pondering for a moment—then I could see that she had a sudden idea. She quickly pulled out the cork—and held the bottle over the aquarium, upside down. The clear magic potion plumped down into the water.

"Will they become people now?" I asked.

"What questions you do ask, Soren!" she exclaimed in mild despair. "Sometimes one would think that you were not all there!"

I gave up the idea of telling her what I meant. I didn't have the necessary vocabulary. Still I did not feel particularly injured. I had asked a perfectly natural question, and if she could not understand it, it was she who was stupid—not me!

Johanne put the empty bottle on the windowsill.

"Come, Soren," she said.

We went out. As we closed the door, she noticed that she had left the key in the lock. She turned it, drew it out, and pushed it in through the letter-slit. I could hear it drop on the floor inside.

Then we went down the stairs. Johanne took my hand, evidently for fear of my tumbling down the steep steps.

"Is Aunt Laura very ill?" I asked.

"Ill or unhappy," Johanne answered, a little evasively.

"Why is she unhappy?"

"I don't know, Soren," she answered, gravely and a little sadly. Then she continued slowly,

"There are many people who are unhappy. It is not nearly as nice to be grown-up as you think, Soren. Once I was tired of life—very weary of it all—but then you came along, Soren ... and then I was happy again."

She paused a little.

Then she said in a very low voice,

"And may God keep his protecting arm around you, Soren."

A little shyly, she raised the back of her hand and dabbed her eyes.

I was silent. The conversation had taken a solemn turn that I did not care for. I would really much rather have talked about Aunt Laura's goldfish; but unfortunately Johanne was completely non-understanding in this regard.

We had come down to the street. For a long time we walked along without talking. Johanne continued holding my hand. Though I did not know the neighborhood, something told me that we were homeward-bound.

Suddenly Johanne spoke again—her voice subdued and grave.

"Are you a big boy, Soren?"

"Yes," I assured her. Of course, I was a big boy—going on for seven, wasn't I?!

"A very, very big boy?" she insisted.

I did not answer. I knew from experience that when she said things like that, there was something or other she wanted me to do. However, the flattery did not fail in its effect.

"If you are a *very* big boy, do you know what you will do?"

"No?"

"You will not breathe a word to Farmor or anyone else that we met Aunt Laura to-day. Do you promise, Soren?"

I promised.

I promised not to, and I kept my word.

When Farmor asked where we had been, I answered, "Over there." Nothing more than "Over there."

And with that oracular reply with which I answered her various questions, Farmor had to be satisfied.

And I never broke faith later, either.

Perhaps my silence on the subject was assisted by the fact that Aunt Laura from that day onward disappeared from my life. For some reason she ceased coming to Farmor's and thus vanished from my little world. She only recurred to my memory a couple of years later—namely on the day when I was solemnly informed that she had gone up to the old man in Heaven. Later I found out from the conversation of my elders that she had been burned to death. It was thought that she had been smoking in bed and had fallen asleep with a lighted cigarette in her hand.

Then I wondered with a shudder whether the fire had boiled the goldfish ...

Yes, I kept my word to Johanne.

But, of course, now that I am recording my childhood's memories I am breaking it.

It is a broken promise, however, that does not disturb my conscience. All that remains of Aunt Laura, Johanne and Farmor to-day are some grimy bones in a churchyard and their pale outraged ghosts in my memory. So nobody living need feel grief or pain that I have disregarded my promise and included in my memoirs this odd fragment of a forgotten person's existence.

23

Every afternoon when I left Aunt White's at three o'clock, she remained standing looking over the balustrade until I was all the way down. As soon as Farmor's door was opened, either by Farmor or Johanne, she would call down cheerfully through the bars of the bannisters,

"Goodbye, Soren! See you to-morrow!"

After which her face disappeared and I heard her door being closed ....

One afternoon as I came down the stairs as usual, I heard somebody mounting with a springy step. And just as I reached Farmor's door, Father's shining top hat came up out of the depths.

"Hullo, Soren," said Father, surprised. "Where have you been?"

"Up at Aunt White's," I answered.

I was surprised, for my part, that Father didn't know about my going there.

"Aunt White?" he repeated. "Who is she?"

"The lady upstairs."

My voice was a little impatient. Father's enormous ignorance annoyed me.

"The lady upstairs? Do you mean Mrs. Tychsen?"

I stood there, a little helpless. I couldn't find the right words to explain that it was not Mrs. Tychsen I was accustomed to visit, but her daugher. My difficulty arose from the fact that I had not yet learned when to say "Miss," and when "daughter." I knew both words of course, but it is one thing to know a word, another to venture to apply it.

Before I had succeeded in overcoming my helplessness, Aunt White saved me the trouble.

"Good-day, Mr. Poet," sounded cheerfully from above.

Father and I both looked upwards. The upper part of Aunt White's body was visible leaning over the bannister—

high above us. Seen from below, her doll-face looked even more round than usual.

"Good day, Miss Tychsen," answered Father. "Is it you that Soren has been visiting?"

"He has only been up to hear some stories," Aunt White called down.

Father put his hand up to his mouth,

"Wait a moment—I'm coming up to call on you, too!"

I could tell that he was trying to speak in a low voice and yet distinctly. What he said was meant to be heard by the distant Miss Tychsen—and only by her.

Father seized my hand in his big one and we began to climb. He moved his long legs so impatiently that I had difficulty in keeping up with him ...

I was proud of my father. It was easy to see that he was very distinguished. His top hat rested cockily on his brow. His broad English moustache was cut in the latest fashion—the one introduced by Prince Christian. His black coat with the velvet reverse was so long that it almost reached his ankles. And up under his arm, as if glued there, was a thin, silver-knobbed cane. Even if I was not familiar with the most modern in style, I had no doubt that Father, *my* Father —was one of the most elegant fathers anyone could have.

"Do you often listen to stories up at Miss Constance's?"

I nodded.

"Do you enjoy them?"

I nodded again.

"Is she on the topmost floor?"

"No," I said shaking my head. "Hansel and Gretel live up there." Then I added hurriedly—to allay Father's fears,

"But Aunt White lives just below."

Father looked sideways at me.

Then he observed—with friendly humor,

"Well, so you, too, are a kind of poet!"

We approached the landing of the fourth floor. Aunt White came into view. She looked quite as lovely as a princess in Grimm's Fairy Tales.

"I hear that you often read stories to my little son," said father, still climbing.

"I am teaching him his ABC and a little figuring—that's all. He comes up every day between one and three. And at the end of the lesson he gets a story as a kind of reward."

Aunt White's account was not absolutely true. She gave very little time now to the lessons. Most of the time was spent in reading aloud, probably because we both enjoyed that most.

"How very good of you, Miss Tychsen," said Father. "I hardly know how to thank you—"

"Oh, it's nothing to be thanked for. I enjoy it. Soren is an unusually nice boy. Won't you come in?"

"Well, er ... Thank you," Father spoke hesitantly. "I was really on the way to visit my mother—but, of course, I can do that later."

We went into the hall. Several times Father had to repeat that it must be a short call—a very short call—before he'd let himself be persuaded to take off his coat. But finally he hung his hat on a hook, removed his left glove—he already held his right one in his hand, took off his galoshes, and shrugged himself out of his overcoat. He was wearing a long slinky Prince Albert coat, a silk handkerchief showed in his breast pocket, and the top of his coat was buttoned.

We entered the sitting-room. The fairy-tale book lay open. Aunt White had just been reading me the story about Rapunzel—the lady who lives in a very high up tower where she has been locked in by a horrible witch, but who lets her braids hang down from the window so that the king's son can climb up to her. It was a frightfully thrilling story—and there was a bloodcurdling illustration to it showing the witch with bird's claws on her legs, cutting Rapunzel's hair with a big pair of scissors. Now I come to think of it, Aunt White used to read that story to me quite often.

"How cosy you have it here," exclaimed Father—who evidently had the same taste as I had in these matters. "It's

easy to see that you'll be a splendid housewife when you
marry! Some famous philosopher said once, 'If you want
to know what kind of a wife a young girl will make ... er
... er ... look at her potted plants ...' "

I could tell that for some reason or other Father was
regretting his quotation even while he was making it. He
had begun it fluently—then suddenly stopped—repeated a
word or two, and ended rather flatly.

"Oh," answered Aunt White, blushing a little and with
downcast eyes, "I don't give them so much attention—it is
mostly Mother—"

There was a moment's pause. Father and Aunt White
stood for a moment looking down at the floor—as if they
couldn't bear the sight of each other. Suddenly it occurred
to me that it was because they didn't like each other's looks.
I was a bit surprised at this because Aunt White was so
beautiful, and Father was at least *distinguished* ...

After they had stood silent for a few moments, Aunt White
said,

"May I give you a cup of coffee?"

She meant her voice to sound cheerful and natural, but I
could tell by its tone that she was under a strain of some
kind. This convinced me more than ever that she didn't like
Father. She didn't really want to serve him coffee—but
like all grown-ups she did a lot of things that she didn't like
doing.

Father said, "No, thank you." But Aunt White insisted—
another thing grown-ups always did—so that Father finally
was obliged to say Yes. So she slipped out to the kitchen—
water didn't boil of itself, she said.

Father made himself comfortable on the sofa and looked
at the picture of the witch and Rapunzel.

I wandered about.

I was vexed about it. Vexed because Father and Aunt
White didn't like each other. The people I liked—well,
they must like each other, too!

Father ran over the pages of the book.

At last I couldn't contain myself any longer—

"Father," I said, sadly and firmly, *"You have got to like Aunt White ..."*

Father looked up astonished.

"Do you think I don't like Miss Tychsen? Or what do you mean, my boy?"

"No, you don't like her—and you've just *got* to!" I stamped my foot on the floor. "You *have* to like her!"

"Wherever did you get the crazy idea into your head that I don't like Miss Tychsen?"

"Because you won't look at her."

"Won't look at her?!"

"No, you won't. The whole time you wouldn't look at her."

There was a pause before Father answered. Then he said softly,

"You are mistaken, Soren. I like your Aunt White very much. And I think it is very nice of her to read to you every day."

The kitchen door opened and Aunt White entered quietly.

Father turned to her and broke into a broad smile.

"Do you know what Soren is saying?! He says that I don't like you!"

"No, he *doesn't*," I said vehemently, "and *you* don't like *Father either!* And you've *got* to like each other! I *want* you to!"

Father, laughing heartily, stretched his hand out to Aunt White.

"Well, if Soren insists on it, there's nothing to do but to bow to his will. So shall we agree to like each other?!"

"Yes, let's!" said Aunt White emphatically—and gave Father her hand.

Father turned toward me.

"Are you satisfied now, little tyrant?"

I had won. But the more one gets the more one wants. Besides, I wasn't sure that they were not making fun of me.

They were smiling and laughing too much—perhaps their friendliness was really only make-believe.

"Then you must kiss each other," I cried. When Mother was alive I had sometimes seen Father and her—after a little quarrel—kiss and make up.

Both Father and Aunt White got red in the face.

"No, Soren," exclaimed Father, "Now you really are being *too* demanding! As much as that I really cannot *like* ... Aunt White!"

Tears are often a child's most effective means of getting what it wants. I had rich experience in that respect. So I screwed up my face, with some effort, to weep. At least, perhaps, in saying this, I do myself an injustice. It may be that on this occasion my tears were not pure calculation. It may be they sprang from real sorrow and genuine anger.

"But Soren, now you are being quite impossible!" exclaimed Father.

And Aunt White begged at the same time,

"Be good now, little Soren!"

I answered them by throwing myself into the depths of the armchair and howling as loud as my lungs and my voice permitted.

Father began to laugh—rather slyly.

"I don't see anything else to do but to obey the tyrant ... !"

Aunt White blushed anew.

"Well then ... just on the cheek!"

"Of course."

Father got up and approached Aunt White—

"You have to kiss on the mouth," I cried, "or it doesn't count!"

"But Soren," wailed Aunt White. "What a thing to ask!"

Father smiled broadly. Suddenly he took Aunt White's cheeks between his hands ... and kissed her—kissed her right on the lips.

I stood on tiptoe to see the better. My tears stopped. And my heart was filled with love for all mankind. I had had my way.

When Father had kissed her, he stood for a moment with his hands round Aunt White's face. His gaze was bent fixedly upon her. For a moment their eyes met; then Aunt White lowered hers.

At last Father released Aunt White's face.

"Are you satisfied, Soren?" he asked, in an unusually merry voice, "now that you have had your way?!"

The kettle in the kitchen began to whistle.

"The water!" cried Aunt White—in a tone and with an expression like those of a drowning person catching hold of a plank; and out she flew.

Father began strutting up and down the floor—now and then he whistled as if he were enjoying himself immensely.

I myself crawled up on the sofa, back to Grimm's Fairy Tales.

For five or ten minutes I looked at the pictures while Father walked about.

And then Aunt White came in with the coffee.

We had been sitting a little while in a rather embarrassed silence when Father remarked,

"I can't possibly tell you how nice I think you are to read to Soren. I only wish I could do something in return!"

A little smile brought the dimples into Aunt White's cheeks.

"That would be easy enough," she said.

"So? How then?"

"By reading something to *me!*"

"By . . . by reading to *you?!*"

Aunt White nodded.

"Exactly. From your book of poems, *Violets and Violins.*"

Now it was Father who smiled.

He made a movement as if he were about to feel in his pocket; then he said, still smiling,

"I think, unfortunately, that I haven't the book with me—"

"No? But *I* have a copy of it," answered Aunt White. And she smiled, too. Then she grew serious. "I read in it almost every day. But of course it would be absolutely wonderful to hear the poet read aloud himself!"

She rose, went over to a table—a little round one with mosaic edges and three crossed bamboo legs—and took from it a thin, octavo book, bound in red cloth, with a lot of gold lettering.

"There you are," she said and handed it to Father. "Now you mustn't say No."

"Well, of course," said Father, looking serious, "If it really can give you any pleasure—"

He sat looking down at the gilt edges of the book, without opening it.

Suddenly, he raised his head and looked at me. Then he quickly withdrew his gaze, rather as if he felt embarrassed. I, for my part, at that moment, felt a tiny sense of foreboding— as if something were going to happen which would displease me.

"Well, it's certainly nothing for the boy to listen to," said Father, with a rather foolish little smile. "Wouldn't it be better for him to go down to his Johanne? He wouldn't understand a word of what I read."

I looked at Aunt White. Beseechingly. But she didn't notice my eyes. She sat looking down at the carpet.

"No," she said slowly. "He wouldn't understand, of course . . ."

Then she added quickly,

"Besides, they must be expecting him—it's well past his walk-time."

She turned toward me,

"Come, Soren—You had better go down now."

Then, seeing my downcast face, she added cheerfully,

"Don't grieve, Soren. Tomorrow you shall have a whole heap of stories to make up for it!"

She took my hand and led me to the door.

Father followed us into the hall.

"Don't say anything to Farmor about having seen me," he said to me in a low voice.

And he added, in explanation to Aunt White,

"I think I'm going to cancel my visit to Mother to-day. It was really Soren I came to see. Mother must wait until tomorrow, or the day-after-tomorrow. I have a patient at four, and if I'm going to read aloud now—"

Father bent over me:

"You understand now—not a word to Farmor."

I promised.

Aunt White unlocked the door—it was done considerably more quickly than down at Farmor's.

"Goodbye, Soren," she said, and stroked my head tenderly—"and hurry down."

Then she closed the door.

I stood out on the stairs—alone.

Formerly I had been a little offended that she remained standing on the landing, bent over the bannisters, until the door on the second floor had been opened. So humiliating, really, for a boy of six! But now—now when she wasn't there, I somehow felt strangely abandoned, strangely depressed.

I went slowly down the stairs.

I felt full of sadness. It was like having asked some other children to be allowed to play with them—and not being permitted to. In a way I had nothing to be unhappy about —not, at any rate, directly. But I just wasn't there where they were enjoying themselves ... there where they were being happy.

24

For once, Johanne had had to agree that the afternoon walk must be cancelled. The weather was too awful. A November storm went howling through the streets and parks; bakers' pretzels, barbers' shavingbasins, shoemakers' boots and other shop signs, all swung, angrily screeching, on their iron brackets; and the rain which dimmed the windows looked like cascades of water from a fountain. Even Johanne had to admit that it was no weather for walking.

Neither was it visiting weather. Nevertheless Aunt Agerlin suddenly appeared at the door. I was not present when she was admitted. I was playing on the floor in the dining-room, but from my place there I witnessed her entry in instalments: her soaking-wet shawl, scarf and overcoat were each separately carried in by Johanne and Rosalie, and hung to dry on chairs and screens beside the stove (Rosalie, by the way, was a new maid who had come on the first of the month). The last object to appear was Aunt Agerlin's umbrella. This was brought in like a scepter and carried through the room into the kitchen, where it was to drip into a tub. The storm had turned the thing inside out. And it looked so dirty and distorted that I had to laugh out loud.

Then at last Aunt Agerlin herself entered.

"Heavens—is the boy at home?" she shrieked in surprise. "I thought he always went out in the afternoon ... at this time ..."

"We did not think the weather was good enough," said Farmor.

"Well, no—no, I suppose not."

It sounded as if my presence was not an altogether agreeable surprise to Mrs. Agerlin.

But then she realized this, and gushed,

"But how glad I am to see the dear boy. Does he remember my parrots?«

She stroked the parting in my hair lovingly with her brown hand.

For a few seconds a conflict raged inside me. A conflict between the well-behaved boy and the natural one. The well-behaved boy won it. So I did not lower my head more than half an inch from her touch.

On the other hand, I did not condescend to answer her question. Whether I remembered her parrots! In the first place it was a foolish question, and in the second it was plain to everyone she did not really want any answer. The question was only launched to fill a vacuum which she thought had to be filled.

"I really came to have a little chat with you, dear Mrs. Jensen—so his being at home is a little bit unfortunate."

"I can't see that the boy's being here makes any difference. We can still have our talk."

"Yes, of course ... Indeed we can ... that's evident ...

Mrs. Agerlin's reply was larded with afterthought.

The two ladies sat down. I returned to my toys on the floor.

Farmor and Mrs. Agerlin began by making inquiries about each other's health. Neither of them was well. Mrs. Agerlin was suffering from her old gall-stone trouble; and Farmor, of course, had all the various illnesses which were all shortly going to lay her in the grave ...

When that subject was exhausted, they passed to Uncle Billenstein.

I only half-listened. I was absorbed in my game. The fortress I had received from Father on my birthday was South Africa; my Danish soldiers were Boers, and the dominoes were Englishmen. Every time I said Bang-Bang, a Boer or an Englishman fell. The Englishmen mostly.

Farmor's and Mrs. Agerlin's conversation was not quite as lively as usual. Mrs. Agerlin was nervous and distracted —and now and then she shot a glance down at me that indicated that she found my presence irksome.

Finally she lanced the boil.

"Now there is something I particularly want to talk to you about, dear little Mrs. Jensen," she began.

"Yes, terrible," answered Farmor. Then she went on resignedly, "But we can't expect the weather to be any better, not now it's November."

Mrs. Agerlin raised her voice, though she had not spoken softly in the first place. Though she shouted, she still tried to make it sound deferential and affectionate.

"There is something I particularly want to discuss with you, Mrs. Jensen."

Farmor assumed a surprised expression—

"So?—well, all right."

She leaned forward in her chair, cupped her hand to her ear and assumed an expression of polite attention.

Despite their politeness, these preparations seemed to increase Mrs. Agerlin's confusion.

"Yes, but—the boy!" she shouted.

"The boy?"

Farmor's expression bespoke non-comprehension in the highest degree.

"Well, I'm not very keen to have your grandson hear what we are going to talk about. No matter how good he is, you know that children are not especially discrete ..."

Mrs. Agerlin did not shout quite as loud as before. She probably couldn't continue at the same pitch. To make up for it, however, she bent her body far over toward the cupped hand.

"But, dear Mrs. Agerlin," wailed Farmor, "you wouldn't have me send him out in *this* weather!"

"Couldn't he go into the kitchen for a little while?"

"It's so cold out there—and he's recently had trouble with his lungs—"

This news about my having been ill was new and surprising—even to me.

"Well, then couldn't you and I go and sit in the den?"

"Of course," said Farmor. "Of course. You mustn't be annoyed that I didn't think of that at once. Yes, of course—we can go in there. But I must first get my shawl ... It is ice-cold in there, and you know—my bronchitis ..."

Farmor glided into her bedroom.

She stayed there a long time. Even though she moved slowly she took a surprisingly long time about finding a shawl and putting it on. Mrs. Agerlin sat and tapped on the sewing table with her long nails while she waited. She looked furious—especially when her eyes lit on me.

At last the door opened and Farmor came back, her chest and shoulders wrapt in a ghostly grey woollen shawl.

Mrs. Agerlin's expression once more became affectionate and deferential.

"Right then, Mrs. Agerlin," piped Farmor. "Forgive me for taking so long—I *am* so helpless ..."

As Farmor opened the door, a gust of cold air swept in.

Mrs. Agerlin went into the den, and all followed by Farmor, who closed the door behind her—slowly, coughing all the while.

Their strategy to prevent my eavesdropping was something of a farce. Their conversation could just as well have taken place in the dining-room. The folding-doors between the den and the dining-room were of very thin material, and there was a gap between the doors and the floor; in addition, the lack of a carpet contributed to noises not being softened. Indeed I could not only hear every word they said—I could even hear where they were sitting. Farmor sat down in the chair at her desk—it creaked in a very special way—and Mrs. Agerlin had to take the high, uncomfortable one with a low back which stood next to the desk, its back against the dining-room wall.

There was a silence. Farmor waited. I could imagine her sitting there in her chair, small and helpless, an expression of naïveté, almost of stupidity, on her face ...

Finally Mrs. Agerlin began.

"Well, Mrs. Jensen, it is just that Agerlin has come into a slightly embarrassing position—the whole thing is unimportant, you understand—but ... well ... I must confess we have had a lot of expenses ... and now, in a fortnight, the rent will be due, you know. So that is why I have come to ask you, dear little Mrs. Jensen, if you could do us a favor and lend us 300 kr. Only till the first of January. Then you will get it back again—on my word of honor!"

Mrs. Agerlin's voice conveyed plainly that the whole thing was a mere bagatelle, hardly worth discussing.

When Farmor began speaking, the sorrow in her voice was positively boundless.

"Oh what a great, great pity, Mrs. Agerlin! If only you had come yesterday, or the day before! Think of it—I had 300 kr. right at hand, then. But then came a bill from the plumber's for 280 kr.! How they do plunder me! ... 280 kr.! ... and I paid it ... and now I have nothing left!"

"But, little Mrs. Jensen, you must have some money in the bank—or else your lawyer—"

"My dear Mrs. Agerlin—you must not think I would not help you if only I could. My late lamented husband, now, *he wouldn't have!* He was very close where money was concerned, Jensen was. Indeed he was. He always used to say, "Never lend money for friendship's sake! Either you never see it again or else it's the old story: Lend to a friend, make an enemy." But I'm not like that at all, believe me, Mrs. Agerlin. If I had 300 kr. in the bank, you should have it all—God knows you should. But I really haven't any money to lend. I have only 20-30 kr. and that has got to last us until the first—"

"I understand perfectly, dear Mrs. Jensen! But in that case we could wait until the first to borrow the money—we shan't really be needing it until then."

"Oh, what a shame it is!" Farmor became even a shade more inconsolable. "How very, very sorry I am. The money I get on the first all, every bit of it, has to go to pay off interest."

"No, but really, Mrs. Jensen," Mrs. Agerlin was having more and more difficulty in controlling her anger, "You cannot seriously mean to say that the interest you pay is as much as what you collect in house rents! That would be the same as saying that your property yielded no profit."

"I didn't say that, dear Mrs. Agerlin. Under normal conditions there is, of course, some profit on the houses although not nearly so large as people think. But I have just had to renovate two apartments for new tenants—one of them actually demanded a new stove! The three rooms in the garden house have not been occupied for three months, and the people on the second floor, left, have not paid any rent for over six months. When things like that happen, you can be sure there isn't much left of one's income. Oh, no—it's not all fun to be a house-owner!"

"Dear little Mrs. Jensen," (I could hear Aunt Agerlin rising from her chair), "If I had known you were so hard up, I certainly shouldn't have bothered you."

"You haven't bothered me at all." I heard the writing-desk chair squeak—Farmor, too, was rising. "I am only sorry that I cannot help you. But don't you think—pardon me for mentioning it—that you are paying a little too much rent? If you gave up your present apartment and took one less expensive, then maybe you could manage better with your money."

"Thank you! I know where *that* idea comes from! From your son and your late daughter-in-law. But you mustn't forget that it was my husband who founded the clinic—and even if your son is very clever—and *that*, God preserve us, he *is*—Agerlin himself admits it—Agerlin and I must also be allowed to live in an elegant way. And even to live a little more elegantly then your son does!—without having to put up with sarcasms because of it!"

And Mrs. Agerlin went out, slamming the door behind her.

But at Farmor's any attempt at a dramatic exit was doomed to failure thanks to her locking-up system. And in this case, Mrs. Agerlin not only had to wait for the front door to be unlocked, she also had to wait to be packed into all her wraps which had been drying beside the kitchen stove. I believe it took ten minutes before, bereft of any triumphant last word, she was able to leave the battle-field where she had suffered such an ignominious defeat.

Farmor came gliding back into the dining-room through the door which led into the hall. Her usually so melancholy face was for once wreathed in a smile. It was a cunning smile.

She came right over to me, stopped a little—and stroked my cheek with her cold, crooked forefinger.

"I made a fool of her!" she smirked. "She didn't get any of your money, Soren! No, not one ore!"

25

It was one of the days just after Christmas—perhaps the first or second day—and I was to go up to Aunt White's. I had not been there for almost a week. One day she had come down and said that at times when other children had a holiday, it was only reasonable that I should have one, too. But at the same time she had shot me a secret look to remind me not to reveal the real reason: that she was very busy finishing sewing her Christmas gifts.

But now I was on my way up to see her again. Over my fine party-suit, I was wearing an apron which Mrs. and Miss Tychsen had presented to me. Mrs. Tychsen had cut it out and sewn it and Miss Tychsen had decorated it with embroidery. The embroidery represented Snow White in her glass coffin surrounded by the seven dwarfs. There was a deep pocket in front, and it was on this that the coffin with Snow White in it was embroidered. I had been made to put on the apron—although I was making a call—as a gesture of appreciation to the two donors. They were to see how well it fitted me, how pleased I was with it, and how badly I had needed such a garment.

The call had two objects. I was to hear a Christmas tale, one Aunt White had promised me when she came down on Christmas Eve to leave her packages. And I was to thank them for their gifts. Mrs. and Miss Tychsen had given me, besides the apron, a collection of Christmas poems. Unfortunately, I was not particularly charmed by either gift. I couldn't read the book, and the apron seemed to me to border on the sissy order. Neither Fre'erik, Haralt nor Sophus wore aprons—the very thought of their wearing one had something ludicrous about it. The fact that Johanne had given me a toy cannon contributed to my indifference toward their gifts. That cannon had, in fact, thrown all my other presents in the shade.

Mrs. Tychsen opened the door.

"Good-day, Soren," she said, "and a right blessed Christmas season to you." She put her hand under my chin and raised my face so that she could look the more directly into my eyes. "You haven't forgotten the little child Jesus while enjoying all your goodies and gifts—?"

I seized the weapon to which I always had recourse when strangers tried to penetrate into my soul's privacy. This weapon was extreme politeness. I extended my hand, put my heels together and bowed, putting my head well forward. At the same time I mumbled, gravely and properly,

"Happy Christmas. And thank you for the Christmas gifts."

The weapon worked. Mrs. Tychsen was forced to adopt the same friendly formality which in such an effective way establishes a respectful distance between people.

"Don't mention it," she said.

And then she continued,

"Go right in. Constance is sitting in there waiting. I think in the meanwhile I shall go down and call on your Farmor."

Constance sat by the window in a dark red armchair, in the midst of all the green plants. She held Father's book of poems in her hand and she had a long shawl over her shoulders. The room was brighter than I had ever seen it before. It was the snow outside which was casting a white, solemn kind of reflection way up here on the fourth floor.

I ran straight to her. I think my face must have shone with the joy I felt in seeing her again. At any rate I felt I had been missing her all the week since I had last been with her. Constance evidently read my thoughts in my face—at least she said,

"Have you really missed me so much, Soren?"

I had an impulse to throw my arms around her, but suddenly remembered the instructions I had received when I left the floor below.

I stretched out my hand, bowed, and reeled off all of a piece,

"Many-thanks-for-the-Christmas-gifts-the-apron-fits-me-very-well."

"Oh stop, stop!" Aunt White laughed gently. She put a friendly arm around me, and drew me down on her knee. "I suppose you do not care about the apron. But the book you will enjoy after you have finished the primer."

She removed her arm again.

"But now tell me what other Christmas presents you have received. Bring the cushions over here and then tell me about everything you got."

The "cushions" was a kind of stool or truffet consisting of three thick cushions one on top of the other. They were dark red, with tassels in the corners, so arranged that they could turn in a spiral.

I drew the cushions over to Constance's feet, and began telling her about the cannon Johanne had given me. When one put a pea in the tube in front and then pulled something else behind, the pea shot out just like a cannon-ball. It could even shoot dead. Not the soldiers—they stood their ground—but I had several times shot a domino so that it fell.

"And what else did you get—?"

I could tell that Aunt White did not fully share my interest in the miraculous cannon. I began consequently to enumerate the other gifts—at the same time giving the names of the givers of each object.

All the time I was chatting, I was gazing at her.

She was wearing a white blouse, with a high collar, and, in front, a kind of jabot of white batiste. Her blouse reached deep down to a point in front, overlapping her belt—I had had a doll once on a wooden stick and with bells—a so-called Punchinello—which had been dressed in the same way. But Aunt White's blouse was half-hidden by a shawl, a long white one, into which had been woven small oblong metal pieces which looked like silver. These metal pieces shone and twinkled in the field of white like a fountain in moonlight. For a moment it occurred to me that I had seen this shawl before somewhere—but I did not bother about it, I didn't think about it—I just sat there quite hypnotized by its loveliness.

My torrent of words flowed on.

Now and again Aunt White would exclaim with enthusiasm, "My, what a lot of presents you have!"

Or,

"You don't say!"

As I sat there chattering, a feeling of tenderness welled up in me. I wanted to be with her *always*. For ever and ever. She must never be out of my sight, no not even out of my reach. The feeling became so intense that my eyes filled with tears ...

The enumeration of my Christmas gifts had long ceased to interest me.

Suddenly I stopped talking, seized her hand in both mine, and kissed it. Kissed it again and again; kissed it violently, clumsily, ardently.

She burst out,

"But Soren, what is the matter?"

She was astonished—but she liked this spontaneous declaration of love very much. This was clear from among other things, the way her free hand at once began stroking my neck.

Suddenly I let go of her hand and climbed into her lap. She folded her right arm round my back and shoulders, while her left went round my knees.

"Aunt White," I begged as I looked up into her face, "Won't you be my mother?"

"But Soren ... !—What are you saying!"

She was obviously bewildered and blushed deeply. She looked like someone caught in an embarrassing situation.

"How did you ever get such a—such a strange idea?"

"It is 'cause I like you so much."

"But you can't have everybody you like for your mother!"

"But I like you best of all—"

This last remark was not untrue. I think that at that moment I liked Aunt White better than anyone in the whole world—not even excepting Johanne. That is to say, it is possible that my love for Johanne and my love for Aunt White could not really be compared at all, for they were of two different kinds.

She pressed me to her, and answered softly and slowly,

"I am happy to hear you say that, little Soren."

"Will you be my mother then?"

Again she looked embarrassed.

"But really I don't see how I could be your mother!"

"And then, when I'm as old as you we can get married!"

Aunt White began to laugh:

"If we got married I wouldn't be your mother—then I should be your wife!"

She laughed as if her sides would split.

I reconsidered the matter.

"Yes, but you could be my wife also ..."

Aunt White hugged me tightly.

"What nonsense you talk," she said, "but I love you! you darling little idiot!"

Then she let me go, and said in another tone of voice,

"Well, get the book and we'll read another story."

I crawled down and fetched the picture book. Since our first reading it had never been put back in the bookcase, but had had a special place reserved for it on the round table with the inlay and the bamboo legs. This was so that I could take it whenever I wanted to look at it.

I handed her the book and seated myself on the cushions again. Suddenly I reached my hand out to touch the white shawl.

"It is lovely," I said.

"Don't you recognize it?" she asked, a little surprised.

I shook my head.

"Your father gave it to me for Christmas. It is one that belonged to your mother. Your father bought it once in Capri. Well, which of the stories would you like to-day?"

I asked for the one about the little boy who died but came back at night to beg his mother not to cry.

It is a story called *The Shroud*.

26

Mrs. Agerlin had not visited us for quite a long time, but one day she came back again. Came back shrieking as usual in her gushing, spiteful and hectic manner, as if she had forgotten all about her unsuccessful borrowing visit.

Farmor asked her to come in and soon the two ladies were sitting in their accustomed places: Farmor in her wicker chair by the sewing table and Mrs. Agerlin in the armchair between the windows. And Farmor piped away in her customary helpless, melancholy way, just as if nothing had happened.

The conversation developed along the customary lines.

The ladies began with accounts of the condition of their respective ailments. Mrs. Agerlin, contrary to habit, was in perfect health. She had positively never been in such excellent health and such good spirits as she was today.

Then followed the chapter on Personalities. I remember the rapid malicious sketches they drew of Lillelund, Miss Rosengreen (their Swedish dressmaker), Lotzfeldt (Mrs. Agerlin's hairdresser, whom she patronized whenever she was to attend social functions), Uncle Billenstein, Cousin Christian (who really did look now as if he had consumption) and Mrs. Tychsen. As regards Mrs. Tychsen, Mrs. Agerlin expressed her sincere sorrow that that lady's poverty-stricken condition had made it necessary for her to "take a position". And Farmor, who was in perfect agreement with her on this point, added sadly,

"And she's certainly not getting paid much for it!"

And then it was that Mrs. Agerlin remarked—sweetly and innocently,

"I hear that your son often visits Miss Tychsen—"

The statement hung in mid-air—hovered there in a peculiar way ...

I turned round to listen. Yes, I had been listening already, but only with, so-to-speak, half an ear. Now I not only listened with two ears, but with two gaping ears. At least that's the way I felt.

There was a pause before Farmor replied.

But then, slowly, innocently and without any sign of surprise, she said,

"Yes, he runs up there now and again."

Mrs. Agerlin burst into scornful laughter—

"Now and again! Ha! ha! Do you know what, my dear? You call almost every day 'now and again!' Ha! ha! That really is *too* funny!"

Farmor answered as if she were familiar with the whole affair,

"He comes two or three times a week, and he quite often looks in on her after he has visited Soren and myself. I really don't know whether that should be called "now and again" or "every day" as you put it ..."

But Mrs. Agerlin was far from defeated.

"Evidently you have been kept in the dark about it, little Mrs. Jensen. Forgive me for saying it, but the fact is that your son calls on Miss Tychsen much more often than he calls on you, Mrs. Jensen. And it is somewhat—" Mrs. Agerlin drew in her breath, "how shall I put it?—somewhat *peculiar* that he always comes at times when he knows Mrs. Tychsen will not be at home!"

"From whom have you heard that?"

Farmor made her voice sound as naive as possible. Moreover, her tone conveyed that she was not really specially interested in the answer.

But Mrs. Agerlin was not taken in.

"Well, I have no right to tell you—but I assure you it is the absolute truth."

"Maybe the person who told you this has got bad eyesight?"

"What do you mean by that, Mrs. Jensen?"

"I mean that the lady or gentleman in question has probably confused Viggo with little Soren. It is *Soren* who goes up there each day."

Mrs. Agerlin laughed again—like an affectionate hurricane.

"If you really must know, it was Mrs. Mau-Andersen who told about it to a Miss Holstrup who told it to Mrs. Lowenfeldt, wife of the Chamberlain, who is one of Agerlin's patients (by the way, the wife of the Chamberlain thinks that Agerlin is a little gentler than your son). Mrs. Mau-Andersen has put a chair in her hall so that she can hear both when your son comes and when he goes. And she says she has often thought of complaining to you, because she never dreamed when she moved in here that she'd be coming to live in a house where women of loose behavior ... received visits from strange gentlemen ..."

I did not understand much of what Mrs. Agerlin was saying. But I understood enough of it to *hate* her at that moment. I hated her from the soles of her big, wrinkled shoes right up to her ugly grey-white neck-bristles. I knew, moreover, who Mrs. Mau-Andersen was. She was the woman who lived just above us. Sometimes when I passed her door she had opened it and handed me a little red sugar plum. I understood that the sugar plum was intended for me, but it was always pushed out to me in silence. I had never seen any more of her than that hand and a portion of a thin, blackclad arm. I had not even heard her voice. But at that moment I loathed Mrs. Mau-Andersen notwithstanding her candy—loathed her as much as I loathed Mrs. Agerlin. And I promised myself that the next time she stuck her hand out, I would seize hold of it and bite it as hard as I could!

Farmor began speaking,

"But what are you saying, Mrs. Agerlin! Are you meaning to imply that Miss Tychsen is a woman of loose behavior simply because she sometimes talks to my son? In the first place there's probably no question of any romance between them, and, in the second, if there is, it may be he's going to marry her ..."

Mrs. Agerlin's face assumed a spiteful expression.

"And what a fine match that would be!"

But Farmor was as long-suffering as one of God's angels—

"Goodness, why not? Viggo earns enough to marry again, and once I'm dead—and it won't be long now—he will have all I own; I don't see that it would be such a misfortune for him to marry a wife without a dowry."

"I must say you surprise me, Mrs. Jensen. In the case of little Anette Schultz, you did all you could to put a stop to the match ... because her dowry wasn't large enough!"

Farmor went on, as if she had not heard Mrs. Agerlin's interruption,

"And you must remember this: Constance comes of an excellent family. Her father was a physician—even if he did not practise here in town—and they are sensible people, both she and her mother—people who have not taken a bigger apartment than they can afford."

Farmor stopped short. A little akwardly. Like somebody who had really meant to continue, but suddenly had no more to say.

And there was a pause.

Mrs. Agerlin broke it—dauntless, uncowed.

"Have you heard, Mrs. Jensen, that Pastor Moller ... last Sunday ... at a wedding ... once again had too much to drink ... ?"

When Farmor came back to the dining-room after accompanying Mrs. Agerlin to the door, she directed her steps straight to me.

"Get up a moment, Soren—there is something I want to ask you."

I got up from my cannon on the floor, a little sullenly, rather unwillingly.

"Which day do you suppose today is," she piped ingratiatingly.

I considered.

"It's just an ordinary day," I said.

"Do you think it is Sunday?"

I thought it over. No, it couldn't be Sunday. Sunday felt different from ordinary days. Quieter, duller, greyer somehow.

"No-o—it isn't Sunday," I said.

"Would you like to get a Sunday ten ore even if it isn't Sunday?"

Would I!!

"You shall have a nice new shiny one if you will tell me what I'm going to ask you—and tell me without a single little untruth!"

Immediately I felt a bit uneasy. Maybe I had done something bad which she wanted to drag out of me in this crafty way. But even that possibility did not deter me. The thought of the ten ore was too alluring. For one bright piece of silver I would have been willing to confess all my sins that day—the uncommitted ones as well as the committed.

I agreed to the bargain.

"There, that's a good boy." Farmor stroked my cheek with her cold, crooked forefinger. "Do you like visiting your Aunt White."

I nodded—vehemently.

"Does your Daddy go there too?"

"No-o," I said. I chose to interpret her question to mean: was Father there *every* time that I was and was he there *all* the time.

"Have you never seen him up there at all?"

"Yes," I said.

Farmor looked reproachfully at me.

"Remember you are only to have the ten öre if you are a good boy and tell the truth."

"That's what I *am* doing," I exclaimed, righteously indignant.

"Then your father does go there sometimes?"

I nodded.

"Often?"

I considered the question. Then,

"Does 'often' mean 'many times'?"

Farmor gave up the question.

Then she suddenly smiled—sweetly and affectionately:

"And do you think they like each other, your Daddy and . . . your Aunt White?"

I nodded emphatically and happily. And I added by way of explanation,

"At first they didn't like each other, but later they *did* like each other!"

"And—how do you know that they like each other now."

"Oh but they do—because they kissed each other!"

"Ki-ssed each other?"

Farmor's voice sounded strange—at one and the same time both surprised and sad. What was she sad about? If two nice, jolly people liked each other, it was just something fine, wasn't it?

"You were a good boy to tell the truth. Wait a minute and you shall have the ten öre I promised you."

Farmor's voice was again as usual.

Still, something or other must have been the matter because immediately afterwards she went to bed, and did not get up again that day. Johanne had to serve her supper on the big copper tray and bring it to her in her bedroom.

27

A few days later Father came to visit us again. It was a Sunday and he wasn't so busy as usual.

Farmor served coffee and Victoria kringles. She was as kind and amiable as ever—perhaps even a little more affectionate than usual.

About her conversation with Mrs. Agerlin she said not one word, to begin with. It took quite a long time before she got around to the subject which at the moment interested her more than any other. I think it took a whole hour.

Only then came the little question from her big wide mouth. It came out sweetly and innocently ... and as if it were not at all important:

"Are you thinking of getting married again soon, Viggo?"

Then I knew, more from the tone of her voice than from the words themselves, that something dramatic was afoot.

"No-o," said Father, equally innocently, "How did you hit upon that idea?"

"Oh I don't know—one hears so many rumors."

"Oho!" Father nodded ironically. "So some of the local gossip-bags have been visiting you, have they?!"

Farmor's tactics in the face of unpleasant remarks were simply to pretend not to hear them. These tactics she had recourse to now.

She proceeded, in the same innocent tone of voice:

"Do you often go up to Miss Tychsen's?"

Father assented with a nod.

Then he added—as if his nod were not sufficient,

"I go up there a great deal."

The tone was impertinent. His smile likewise.

A pause followed. It seemed as if the clock on the wall ticked louder than usual. Its ticking was positively painful.

Farmor broke the pause—anxiously and cautiously.

"Forgive me for asking, Viggo—but do you go to see her when her mother is not there?"

"It happens sometimes—yes."

"You shouldn't do that, Viggo. It is not proper."

"Thanks!—but I know quite well what is proper and what is not."

"People are talking. If you won't stop for your own

sake, then do so for hers. You don't want to blacken a young lady's reputation, do you?"

"There are always people with dirty minds. Against such there is no defence."

"I am not discussing what you and she do. That is not the reason why I bring up this subject. I do so only because as your mother I am afraid of your making a fool of yourself."

There was another pause—an oppressive one. However, it did not oppress me so much that I did not seize the opportunity of helping myself to another kringle.

Father was looking down at the table-cloth as he began to speak:

"I suppose I'd better give you the rest of the story since you already know so much." He spoke slowly and gravely.

"Constance and I have got engaged. And we are planning to marry next spring. If we didn't announce our engagement either to you or to Constance's mother, it was because we wished to wait a little longer—not to make it public until a whole year had passed since Anette's death. But now there are not many days left, so—"

Again there was a pause. A long, heavy one.

Then it was Farmor's turn again.

"I can only say, Viggo, that you surprise me. I thought you had been so happy with Soren's mother that you would not think of remarrying for the present—that's what you said, at any rate, when she died. But the dead are quickly forgotten."

Father sat and shook his head—wanly and continuously, like a mechanical doll. A mocking and all-knowing smile lifted the corners of his mouth.

"If I surprise you, I confess that *you*, for your part, do not surprise *me*! It was exactly the kind of hearty congratulation and motherly understanding that I expected from you!"

Farmor answered in her most tearful fashion,

"God Almighty, I think of nothing but what is best for

you, Viggo! Everything I do, I do for your and Soren's sake. And when you marry, I only want you—not for my sake but for your own and Soren's—to make an advantageous match."

"An advantageous match!" Father began to get violent. "Yes—there we have it in a nut-shell! You think only in terms of money. Good Lord, why *should* I make an "advantageous match" as you call it! I don't need more money. I only need a wife whom I can love."

"Money one can never have too much of, Viggo."

"No, *you* can't—that's obvious. But I have more than enough. I earn more than most people in this country, and when you one day peg out, I shall have a private income, too—that's something I can hardly fail to know ..."

"There, you see! You go about waiting for someone else to die!"

"By God, I don't! But when you go about everlastingly telling people about all the income I shall inherit when you die, then I may be allowed to mention it also. Besides, it's nonsense to reproach my not being interested in money and yet at the same time imagine I'm going about waiting for you to die so that I can inherit yours!"

"An advantageous match means something more than money—"

"As to that you can be reassured—Constance is absolutely a proper match. She is quite faultless—*and you know it!*"

Father pounded the table with his knuckles, "And her family is all one could desire. Her father was a physician and her grandfather on her mother's side was a pastor. So let there be no more discussion of *that*!"

There was another pause.

Then Farmor began once more—humbly and submissively,

"You mustn't get angry, Viggo, but aren't you ... a little too ... trusting ... where women are concerned—?"

"Good heavens, what are you hinting at now?" Father's voice was at once mournful, mocking and menacing. There was a hint of fear in it, too. He could evidently sense some new strategy on her part.

"Perhaps it's not you alone. Perhaps all men are a bit naive. They think they themselves choose the girls they want to marry—naturally, they think so, because it is they who propose—but really it is often enough the girls who have said, 'He's the one I want' ... and then spread their net."

Father was getting impatient.

"What are you driving at with all this chatter?"

"I'm not driving at anything—but just open your eyes, Viggo, and you will see how two moneyless women have been sitting, waiting to snare a young widower—one with a large income—and a fortune in the offing, too."

Father struck the table a blow.

"Stop it, I say! Stop all this dirty backbiting—!"

"I say nothing but the truth, Viggo. Can't one once in a while tell the truth to one's own son in one's own sitting-room!?"

"Continue, then with your infernal talk. I'd be most interested to hear how Mrs. and Miss Tychsen went about 'snaring' me, as you put it!"

"Very well then. To begin with, Mrs. Tychsen took a job in town so that Miss Tychsen could be alone at home—"

"Lord, Mother! You know as well as I do that she took the job because she needed the money."

"Do you think it makes any difference one way or the other, that 25 kr., she earns each month? I don't believe it. But even if I'm mistaken on that point, there's plenty of other evidence. Why do you suppose Miss Tychsen kept tearing up and down the stairs to get her hands on Soren? And when she finally did get hold of him, why do you suppose she offered to read aloud to him and teach him figures—gratis! Take note of that: *gratis!*"

"Even if it sounds improbable to your ears, mother, there are people in this world who don't demand money for everything they do for others. If she offered to read to Soren, it was simply because he's an unusually nice little boy."

"Certainly he is a nice little boy—no question about it. But it is a good rule in life always to ask one self, when people give one something for nothing: *What do they expect me to give them in return?* Mrs. and Miss Tychsen have been giving free teaching in the hope of free maintenance. They have thought to themselves: 'He who takes a child by the hand takes its mother by the heart.' That's to say, they have simply substituted the words 'the rich widower' for 'mother'. And they thought right—they have managed to catch a great big codfish in their net without his being aware of it!"

Father stood up—and threw his napkin down on the table—

"Do you know what would have happened if you'd lived three or four hundred years ago? You would have been burned alive! Burned at the stake! It is a hard thing to say to one's own mother—but you are a witch, Mother— and that's the truth!"

"—And now, see to it to have that damn' door opened!"

Farmor, whimpering, got down from her chair and slipped out into the hall. Father followed her, calm but determined, and without a spark of pity or filial love.

Farmor was a witch. If Father said so, then it was true. Moreover, there was no reason to doubt it. Didn't she look like one of the witches in the picture, in Grimm's fairy-tales? She did not have a moustache, true, but that was only because she shaved herself. The way in which she stroked my cheek with her cold, crooked forefinger—was it not just the way in which the witch welcomed Hansel and Gretel when they came to the gingerbread house? And then, too, everybody's being so respectful to her, yes, even afraid of her, although she was so weak—it all added up to the fact that they knew she could work witchcraft. Indeed, everything went to prove it. Simple logic led to the same conclusion. All witches were old women. Farmor was an old woman. Therefore, Farmor was a witch.

I began to smile. It was so funny that she should be a witch. I felt proud that I belonged to a family that possessed a witch—a genuine, wicked, ugly and repulsive witch! There was no reason to be afraid of her, of course. My princely Father and Princess Aunt White should have each other in the end whatever Witch Farmor did—and they would finish by living happily together ever after—that I knew for certain from literature. And as for myself, there was little to worry about. Possibly Farmor did eat children and change people into dogs that she buried in the dog-cemetery. Is was possible, as I have said. But an unerring instinct assured me that she would never devour *me* or change *me* into anything.

When Farmor returned from the hall, I said—inwardly and without words:

"I know very well that you are a witch, Farmor!"

And then I gave her a smile—proud, admiring ... sharing her secret ...

28

Aunt White and I were sitting on the sofa close together. We were reading—that is to say, *I* was reading. Yes, I was actually reading by myself now—only occasionally, when I was in difficulties, did Aunt White have to prompt me. The book that we were reading was the collection of nursery rhymes which she and her mother had given me for Christmas. We held the book between us—just a shade closer to me than to her, while my forefinger crept snail-like under a row of black letters.

I had begun to enjoy reading. It was a kind of research work in my eyes, and like all research work it was full of small delights. There was the excitement of finding out whether one was really capable of solving a problem; and there was the excitement about what the result would be if the problem *was* solved. For instance, all these letters which I was slowly and hesitatingly reading out at the moment— what kind of strange words would they eventually produce? And the words I had read already—when all were put together what kind of funny verse-line would result? And finally, when all the words had been read and one had grasped the meaning, the excitement would culminate in a feeling of delight at having solved the puzzle and at one's own cleverness ...

I had gradually come to like reading by myself almost as much as being read to, even though the first was undeniably a slower process.

The doorbell rang.

My eyes wandered from the book. The bell annoyed me. It interrupted me in the middle of a long word, and I couldn't bear being disturbed when I had to remember the beginning as I approached the end.

Aunt White, on the contrary, seemed pleased at the sound. She smiled. She looked as if she were expecting something delightful.

"I shall have to go to the door," she murmured. She rose and went into the hall. A moment later, I heard Father's voice.

"The whole thing! Yes, almost, about our being engaged, too! But that I told her myself—so that she should not think too badly of you."

Father's voice was quite excited. I heard him hanging up his overcoat as he said,

"But who told her about us? Where the devil did she get it from?"

Aunt White answered something that I could not hear. Then the door opened, and she came in, followed by Father.

"Hello, Soren," he said.

Suddenly I saw a thought strike him.

He came quickly toward me—

"Was it *you*, Soren?" he exclaimed, and he looked fixedly

at me, his eyes hardening, "Did you tattle-tale to Farmor that I came up here to Aunt White?'

My head got hot, my heart thumped. I was absolutely sure that, innocent though I was, I could never convince the others of my innocence.

"It wasn't me," I answered, my voice bordering on tears, "It was—it was Aunt Agerlin—It was Aunt A—a—a—Agerlin!"

"Yes, but how did she come to know about it, Soren?"

It was Aunt White who put this question—asking it with a calmness that communicated itself to me.

"From a lady. It was that Mrs. Andersen who lives on the third floor, who told another lady. And that lady told Aunt Agerlin."

Father looked over to Aunt White.

"There isn't a doubt that the boy is telling the truth," he said. Aunt White nodded. And Father continued,

"I'm the one who has been a fool. I should have been able to guess the whole thing was due to Mrs. Agerlin. Her feelings about me are nothing but a balloon of jealousy. I am not to make more than her husband—as, of course, I do! I'm not to get a reputation of being cleverer! I am not to live in a bigger house! If some day I were to buy myself a landau, you can be quite sure Mrs. Agerlin would get two! It was a terrible blow to her when we had Soren. We had gotten something then that she couldn't get herself. But note this: her jealousy isn't born of love for Agerlin—oh no, she treats him like a worm! No, it springs purely and simply from jealousy—vanity—stupid ambitions—"

Father's eloquence had finally set him striding up and down the floor.

Then he stood still again.

"And then *Mother!* Mother has only one standard in life: *money*. Not because money can give happiness, but because of the power and prestige it gives you. She is really a complete *monomaniac*—"

Aunt White interrupted gently, but without reproach,

"I don't think it's quite right to say such a thing about one's mother."

For a moment her voice sounded quite like Mrs. Tychsen's.

"One certainly *has* the right!" stormed Father. "In the first place, it's the truth; and in the second, it is the only excuse for her—she is stark, raving mad—!"

Aunt White looked a little doubtful.

"What an idea! I think your mother behaves very reasonably."

"Of course she does. Outwardly she is completely normal. But under the surface she's ready to commit any sort of villainy to prevent her son from making a poor match. It was bad enough when I married Anette. Her inheritance was not nearly large enough in Mother's eyes. But now when I am wanting to marry a young girl who has no dowry at all—! I tell you she is ready to do just *anything* to stop me. You should have heard how she abused you and your mother—saying, among other things, that you had spread a net to catch me!"

Aunt White's arms reached up to Father's shoulders and went around his neck. I could see she stood on tiptoe.

"Don't worry about it, Viggo," she said tenderly. "Let your mother talk. Let people say what they will. If we two care about one another, what does it matter what stupid and—crazy—people have to say!"

Father's hands rested on Aunt White's hips.

"You must not be annoyed with me for becoming a little vehement. Even though I know Mother from experience, still her malice yesterday made a certain impression on me. Try to understand—I was just beginning to be happy again, to recover my good spirits. I was happy again—after all the sorrow and misery of the last eighteen months. And then, just when I was getting my head above water, Mother comes and pushes me down again into a dirty pool of gossip and malice and baseness—!"

Father paused. Then he continued, a little bitterly,

"Alas—as soon as one seems to have reached happiness,

something happens to prevent it—something always happens—"

All at once he released Aunt White.

"That, by the way, is an idea for a poem, a good poetic theme—I think I'll just make a note of it."

Aunt White drew back her arms—fearful of standing in the way of an inspired poet.

Father took out his red morocco notebook and wrote in it. His lips moved, softly murmuring something. We others were silent. Aunt White looked as if she were witnessing a miracle.

When he had put the book back in his pocket, she threw her arms about him again.

"Now you must forget your anger!" she said.

She threw back her head and smiled up at him in loving admiration.

Her face was, as it were, radiant.

Suddenly Father bowed his head over hers. I couldn't see what was happening, but I guessed that they were kissing one another. The kiss lasted a long time. I sat staring fixedly at them all the time, and simultaneously I became aware of something happening inside myself. I didn't know what it was I felt, nor why I felt it. All I knew was that it was something that hurt.

When Father at length released Aunt White, his eyes lit on me.

It was as if a wave of irritation and anger spread over his face.

"That confounded youngster! There he sits gaping at us as usual!" he exclaimed, "Or eavesdropping!" he added.

Then he seemed to repent his exasperation. He continued, in a more friendly way,

"Well, go down now to Farmor, Soren—there's a good boy."

Suddenly a thought struck him.

"And for God's sake don't tell her I am up here. You

can say—well, tell her that Aunt White has a cough and so she's had to postpone your reading till tomorrow."

Aunt White took me, smiling, to the door and saw me out.

29

The most painful event of my childhood must now be recorded. I am still—41 years later—so filled with shame —that it is only reluctantly and with an effort of will that I am able to write about it. But there is no alternative. These memoirs would not be honest ones if I omitted an event which left so deep a scar in my memory.

One morning Johanne and I were alone. I do not know where Farmor and Rosalie were—probably they were in town shopping.

Johanne was hanging curtains. Every once in a while— I don't know how often—the white lace curtains had to be washed and fresh ones hung in their places.

It was quite an undertaking. First the curtain pole had to be lifted down from the wall-brackets on which it rested. Then the curtains attached to it had to be unpinned, a very lengthy operation as the tape to which they were sewed was attached to the pole by innumerable pins. Then the freshly washed and starched curtains had to be put on again by means of pins. Finally the pole had to be lifted and hooked on to the aforementioned wall-brackets again.

To accomplish the first and last process, a stepladder was necessary. The stepladder most popular in those days was a patented kitchen chair which could be transformed into a ladder of four or five solid steps. My parents had had such a one—but Farmor preferred another kind. Her ladder was of the kind which can be opened up so that in profile it resembles the letter A. Farmor's abhorrence of idleness and laziness did not permit her to have any sitting-down devices in her kitchen.

While Johanne was busy with the curtains I drifted idly around. Sometimes I watched Johanne, sometimes I fiddled with the playing cards which I had spread out over the table, and sometimes I stood by Piphans' cage amusing myself by blowing his feathers apart. But this was not because I was bored. The reason was rather the opposite. My lively high spirits would not allow me to do anything so trivial as to concentrate on any form of amusement. None of the games I knew were sufficiently stimulating to satisfy my need for fun or provide an outlet for the ebullient vigor which momentarily filled me. I felt happy, that is, but my happiness was not complete. The daily monotony of my life irked me. Perhaps it would be nearer the truth if I say that I was going around in expectation—expectation of something's happening—something quite unusual.

Johanne was just completing the last stage of her task. She set the ladder up in front of the window, and mounted it, balancing the curtain pole. She looked a little nervous—the ladder, which was an old one and a little rickety constantly shook.

She had reached the next-topmost step ...

And then it happened.

Before I knew what I was doing, I had done it.

From high spirits, from sense of fun, from sheer desire for something to happen, I had gone up to the ladder and given it a little push.

Johanne tottered for a moment.

Then she screamed.

And fell.

Terror blinded me. For a second or two I was unable to realize what had happened. It is possible that my inability was due to the rapidity with which the accident had taken place—maybe the speed with which things had happened was too swift for my childish mind to take them in.

But when the first numbness had passed, I perceived what had happened. Johanne lay on the floor—stretched on her back—with the curtain pole on top of her. The ladder also had toppled over, but only half-way. It stood leaning against the armchair between the two windows. And in his cage

Piphans was fluttering about agitatedly so that his feathers fell out ...

Johanne lay there, saying nothing. Her eyes were closed, the lower part of her face was puffed up in a strange, unnatural way, and she looked as if she had ceased to breathe.

A thought, which caused my heart to lose a beat, flashed through me—

"Are you ... dead?" I asked.

She answered me by beginning to weep. Tears trickled from beneath her closed eyelids. And her parted lips began to moan,

"Oh no! Oh no! Oh no!"

The words came at regular intervals. It sounded as if she meant that the suffering was more than she could bear. As a matter of fact, I think these involuntary sounds lessened her pain to a slight degree.

Strange to say I just stood there. It did not occur to me to throw myself on my knees and try to help her—or at least to kiss and comfort her. No, I just stood there on shaking legs, my hands hanging loosely, my head bent forward.

After a little her moans ceased. For a second it looked as if she were sleeping. Then she opened her eyes, slowly, quite slowly.

"Little Soren," she whispered, "Little Soren ... can't you ... take ... the pole ... away?"

The words came jerkily. And with pauses between each. It seemed as if she found it difficult to speak—difficult and painful.

The eyes, veiled, and apparently not looking at me, closed again.

I looked at the curtain pole. I knew that I must get it over onto the table—it was there that Johanne had had it when she was taking the old curtains off and putting the new ones on.

As I lifted the pole, I discovered that I was standing on the curtain. My brain told me that I couldn't move the curtain as long as I stood on it. I put the pole down again and moved a couple of steps backwards. I watched my feet carefully so that I should not step on Johanne's arm which must be somewhere underneath the curtain.

This went all right, but now I had gotten so far from the pole that I couldn't reach it. For an instant I stood in despair. Then suddenly I had an inspiration. If I moved over by Johanne's head, I could reach the pole without stepping either on her or on the curtain.

I walked all way round the dinner table and over to Johanne's shoulder. Then I kneeled and reached over for the pole. I could just reach it; but in this position—with only one hand free—I was unable to lift it. So I had to pull it forward along Johanne's breast, right up to her neck, and then stand up before trying to lift it from the floor.

And I could barely lift it. The pole was heavy, at any rate measured by my strength, and it was hard to move the long contraption in the midst of all the furniture. I strained and puffed and finally raised it breast-high and got a good hold of it. Then I walked backwards slowly, with the material dragging after me. For a moment Johanne was completely buried beneath it.

It was necessary to turn my back so as not to collide with the sidebord. This maneuver, too, proved successful. But when I stood with the pole in my arms, my back to the table and no room in which to turn again, nor strength enough to lift the pole up over my head—then I burst into tears. The problem with which I was confronted—how to get the curtain pole past myself—was too much both for my understanding and my strength.

But my very weakness came to my aid. My arms refused to hold up the pole, which was steadily getting heavier and heavier, any longer. Finally I had to put it down. I tried to lower it slowly, but unfortunately it went down much more quickly than I'd expected and struck the floor with a bump.

But simultaneously I had solved the problem. I floundered across to the other end of the pole and, after a little pause to regain my strength, raised it to the level of the table-top. Thenceforward it was an easy matter to push the pole on top of it and still easier to drag the curtains after. But alas, as I stood there, crumpling their whiteness, I began to think about what Farmor was going to say. Just imagine her coming home to find a pair of newly washed and starched curtains already needing to go into the washtub again! Of all the bad things I had on my conscience I did not doubt but that this business of the curtains was going to be the worst!

"That was well done," whispered Johanne. It was as if she had been following my actions with closed eyes. Yet she lay so strangely—her upper teeth were biting into her lower lip, her eyes were shut tight, and her head was pressed against one shoulder. It looked as if she were suffering in a different way than before.

One of Piphans's feathers fluttered down from the cage and slowly came to rest on her stomach.

A moment later she managed to say something again.

"I must try to get up on the sofa," she murmured.

The words were uttered more to herself than to me.

She pressed the palms of her hands against the floor and raised herself to a sitting position. She stayed so for a moment—not moving—unable to stir for pain or to speak.

At last she recovered her voice.

"Little Soren," she said, "bring a chair to me."

I pushed one of the dining-chairs up to her. She leaned over it and with her hands grasping the seat slowly raised herself. Then she stood there, very bent. I noticed that she stood on only one foot—the other one stuck out a little.

I stood waiting. Stood waiting, unable to help—or at least not knowing *how* I could help. Oh how incompetent I was! If *I* had fallen from the ladder, Johanne would not for a moment have been in doubt how to help me. Awareness of my own incompetency increased my feeling of shame.

Suddenly Johanne tried to stand on the other leg. At that instant a spasm of pain wrenched her body and an invol-

untary cry escaped her. Quickly she limped the two or
three steps to the sofa, let herself fall on to it in a sitting
position, and then fell over. She had calculated her sitting
position so well that her neck came to rest on Farmor's
pillow.

She lay there a while, breathing heavily. Her face was
covered with beads of sweat. I realized that the sweat came
from the pain she was suffering.

"Soren," she whispered, "Can't you get me a glass of
water?"

I flew out to the kitchen, out to the plate rack, where
there were a few cups without handles used for drinking
water. In a flash I was up on the kitchen table at the end
by the sink. The cock was so tight that I had to use both
hands to turn it, so I put the cup in the bottom of the sink
while I pumped. At first I had trouble getting the cup
filled, for the water came with such force that it spurted
out again, but finally I discovered that each time I closed
the cock, a little more water came splashing out, and so
after two or three little after-splashes I could get the cup
filled.

Then I got down from the table, took the cup from the
sink and rushed back into the dining-room. Of course water
dripped all the way there.

Johanne took the cup, lifted her head, and drank the cold
water. A little stream ran out of one corner of her mouth
and down her chin, which she did not try to wipe off, a neglect which made the aesthete in me feel uncomfortable.

"Thank you, Soren." She handed me the empty cup.
"Will you please set it on the table."

When I had put the cup on the table, she said,

"Sit down beside me—and give me your hand, little
Soren."

I pushed the chair by means of which she had risen over
to the sofa. Then I sat down, and gave her my hand. She
closed her big, red, work-worn hand around mine.

"Thank you," she whispered. Two tears broke through her eyelashes.

She lay there a long time, with closed eyes. And her lips pressed tightly together.

And I could see the pain come and go. Her face became still more pinched, while new beads of sweat appeared on her chin, her nose, her brow. Moreover I not only saw her pain, I could also feel it. Every time it was especially violent, she pressed my hand hard.

She lay like that a long time.

I suffered, too. It was as if evil spirits were housed in me—especially in my breast and stomach—pinching me with tweezers. But my physical pain had no physical source. It was—to use a psychiatric term—psychogenic.

Naturally I suffered first and foremost because Johanne was suffering. I loved her. Loved her as much as the ego in me allowed, and thanks to that love I now had to suffer all that she suffered, though of course in a much weaker form.

Together with this *sympathy*—in the word's true meaning—the pangs of conscience were at work. I knew that it was all my fault. My fault that the fine, white curtains were ruined. My fault that my dear, sweet, darling Johanne now lay here on the sofa groaning with pain. My fault! My fault! *Mine! Mine! Mine!*

The pangs of conscience became mixed with anger. Why couldn't she do something to lessen the pains now? Do something to end it—and then get the curtains hung before Farmor got home. If she continued to lie there and twist so, it must be out of sheer malice. She wanted to revenge herself on me by tattling!

And ah! that sympathetic pain and nagging of conscience were both as nothing compared with a third misery: the feeling that all sorts of people were going to know about what I had done. Farmor first, and Rosalie—for they would come any minute now. And then the story would spread, first to Mrs. Tychsen and Aunt White (Aunt White, oh dreadful thought!), then to Father (who of course would hit me with the ruler), then to Pastor Moller, Mr. and Mrs. Agerlin, Uncle Billenstein, Cousin Christian, Lillelund—Oh everybody in the world, without any doubt, would hear about my crime!

The shame in me was so great that it took account in advance of all the penalties I should suffer, and I sat hunched over with the thought of them.

It was then that an evil wish was born in me! I began to wish that Johanne would die! I began to imagine Johanne lying very still ... her eyes strange ... like those of an old carthorse I'd once seen keel over in the street ... Yes, because in the very instant that Johanne became like that, there wouldn't be anyone who'd know that I had jolted the ladder—for naturally I myself would never tell!

But didn't I love Johanne?

How could I love her if I could sit here and wish that she would die?

Certainly I loved her. She was the person I loved most —with the only possible exception of Aunt White. But so overwhelming was my fear of the judgment of others and their condemnation that I really did wish for a little while for her death.

I have no idea how long I sat there waiting—with my hand clasped in Johanne's—but finally I heard the noise of the front door being opened.

In the same instant I became rigid. The moment when my evil-doing would become known to the world was upon me. There was still long to wait, however. Farmor was never one to be in a hurry. Besides, for us human beings, time can be of a monstrous elasticity: in awesome moments, seconds can seem like minutes and minutes, hours.

The clock ticked. A winter fly alighted on Johanne's brow. Perhaps it wanted to slake its thirst from the sweat of pain which was trickling down her face ... At last the handle of the little door to the hall turned.

Farmor plodded in, followed by Rosalie.

Suddenly she stopped short—

"Lord!" she cried, "What in the world has happened—?!"

Her voice was already attuned to the catastrophe.

I did not answer. I sat hunched even lower than before. But Johanne lifted her head—quite easily.

"Madam must excuse me," she said slowly, "I fell down ... while I was hanging the last curtain ..."

Her voice was a blend of respectfulness and pain.

Farmor came right over to us.

"But however could you do such a thing, Johanne!?"

The sympathy in her voice was not so strong but that there was also room left in it for reproach.

"I really don't know. The ladder, you know, is not very steady—and maybe I wasn't careful enough ..."

She closed her eyes and let her head fall back ... on Farmor's pillow.

Her face had become the same color as Father's paper-cutter—the ivory one.

30

Johanne was carried out of my life on a stretcher.

Two men who made me shudder with terror came in with an uncomfortable bed onto which they lifted her, after which they wiggled the apparatus out of the room, came into view again in the street below, and pushed it, with Johanne in it, into an ugly dark-green wagon.

And then they drove away.

But alas! I realize that this is all too condensed an account of what happened. I must go into it in a little more detail, however much it hurts me to recall those hours.

After Farmor had pondered a little, she sent Rosalie down to Lillelund with a message to telephone old Professor Hoystrup, Farmor's own physician.

After about half an hour the doorbell rang and when Farmor opened it a crack, there stood the Professor, carefully wiping his galoshes on the doormat. The old gentleman was quite out of breath due to the speed with which he had come from his house to Farmor's. He was admitted, we surrounded him, and Farmor, Rosalie and I relieved him of his umbrella, his galoshes, his fur cap and his overcoat with the greenish shoulders.

I knew him well from having seen him at my parents' home. "Fessor" as I used to call him, had innumerable times listened to my chest and back with his funny wooden trumpet, and pushed down my tongue with a dessert spoon while ordering me to exhale a prolonged, ghostly "AH-H-H."

The professor pottered into the dining-room, genial and bent-shouldered, with a hearty Good-day to Johanne. We others drew back. Farmor and I slipped into the den, where we shivered with cold; Rosalie, on the other hand, had to content herself with the kitchen, where, thanks to the stove, it was a good deal warmer.

Farmor and I did not exchange many words, and we didn't occupy ourselves, either, with work or play. I believe we both concentrated on listening, Farmor in curiosity, I in terror that Johanne would reveal to the professor how she had really fallen from the ladder.

At length he finished and came into the den. He closed the door carefully behind him, wiped his brow, and looked at Farmor over his spectacles.

"I am afraid," he said, "that the poor girl has broken her thigh bone. At any rate she must go to hospital—it can't be helped."

Half an hour later the ambulance arrived.

I watched its arrival from my place at the window. It was a nasty, dark-green wagon with frosted windows, two horses, and a man standing on a running-board behind. The man behind opened the doors and together with another man who'd been sitting inside carried out a stretcher; then they closed the doors again and disappeared under the window.

A few moments later they appeared up in our apartment. There they lifted Johanne on to the stretcher and packed her in with woollen blankets.

She did not scream, she did not cry either. I heard Farmor and Rosalie whispering something about the professor's having given her an injection so that she could not feel anything. That was perhaps why she seemed to be asleep—without really sleeping. And that is probably why she allowed herself to be carried away by strange men without crying—even without so much as saying goodbye to her little Soren.

But I cried.

I wept silently.

I also watched them drive away.

Through a white veil of tears I saw the men come out from beneath the windows. First they put the stretcher down on the pavement, then they opened the doors, and at last shoved her into the wagon. A big crowd had collected. I think I had never seen so many people in our street at any one time before—there were at least ten. Then one of the men closed the two doors, and stepped up on the running board. The man on the box, who had turned the wagon round while he was waiting, drove off.

It was a bitter sight.

Although I knew they were driving Johanne away to make her well, I felt a dull despair at losing her, and a helpless anger against those who were taking her. Nor did the weather diminish my depression. It was grey and melancholy, rainy and windy. It was the kind of a day which is neither spring nor winter ...

The ambulance turned the corner. It was bound for the hospital on the asphalt avenue, a little distance beyond the church which we saw from our windows. It was no farther than a man could walk in five or six minutes. So I could follow it with my eyes—follow it until some tall trees on the parkway came between. Then it disappeared and I could no longer see it.

For a moment her disappearance became a pain in my

very palms. Alas, I could no longer stretch them out and feel her body, so soft and warm and full of motherly tenderness.

Johanne was carried out of my life, and it was spring and almost summer before she came into it again.

Perhaps I exaggerate a little. She did not completely vanish from my sight and memory. I visited her a few times. And I also thought about her ... a few times.

It was in the hospital I saw her. She was lying in a large room where I think there were twelve other beds. I still remember how I tramped around and let myself be admired by old women and young girls. Once even wearing a paper hat, Napoleon-style, which one of the patients had made for me ...

But these few visits yielded neither Johanne nor myself much pleasure. All my kisses and embraces were strangely unnatural, and forced somehow. She looked so peculiar lying there, in a bed I did not like, with a little house built over her leg, and hardly able to move herself. The twenty-four eyes—or however many there were—which peered at us all the while—did not contribute to a genuine abandonment to affection either.

There was something else, also, which now separated us. It was the fact, that we both developed during this period—developed in experience and knowledge which was not shared. I developed in independence, and Johanne—! Indeed her development was more than surprising. It is true that she came of extremely respected parents—her father had been a ship's captain—but her mother and father had both died when she was comparatively young, and such schooling as she'd had was extremely modest. She had never had time to develop her mind: right after her confirmation she had been pitched out to earn her own living as a servant—which in those years meant very hard work and little free time. Yet despite these early limited circumstances she was seized, now as she lay there in the hospital, with a passionate interest in *astronomy*, an interest which led to her getting possession of a series of popular astronomical books and later saving enough out of her poor earnings as a servant to buy herself a little telescope through which she could study the stars. This new hobby, maybe, did not lessen her love and devotion for her little Soren, but still—I could feel that I was no longer the sole object of her interest.

But what separated us most was the debt that I owed her. Johanne's goodness to me had always been overwhelming. She loved me like a mother—a mother who had neither other children, nor a husband. Indeed she loved me to a higher degree, for how many mothers would have been so self-sacrificing, so self-effacing, even to an only child, as Johanne was!

But all this goodness I had taken as a matter of course. To be sure I had felt that she was good to me, that she had given me much and received little in return, and that I could never repay my debt to her. But this subconscious knowledge had never weighed upon me, had never given me a feeling of *indebtedness*.

Now it was otherwise. The fact that she did not reproach me for pushing the ladder, did not even reveal it to anyone, neither at that time nor later—that was almost *too* great a benefaction, *too* great nobility and self immolation. I am ashamed to confess it, but her withheld reproach and persistent silence awakened, not my gratitude, but my enmity. And the day she came out of the hospital, and I saw her limp, saw her, thanks to my rashness, handicapped, if not crippled for life, then I hated her. Yes, I hated her! So contemptibly is the human mind capable of reacting.

The hate vanished—naturally. Strong passions rarely endure. Nonetheless I felt, as long as our paths ran side by side, a certain bitter, hostile resentment every time I observed her limp.

The poor man who owes a rich man money, money he will never be able to repay, and which in fact, the big-hearted rich man neither expects nor demands back—is hardly

likely to feel unmingled love and gratitude towards his
factor. On the contrary, his feelings will probably all
clude those of inferiority, envy, dislike, resentment.
I was like that poor man in my relation to Johanne.

I have already said that I developed independence whi
hanne was in hospital.

Rosalie was largely responsible for this.

Rosalie was a not-so-young servant who came to us s
after Fernanda. (There had been another one in-bet
but for some reason she had disappeared after only a
taking with her a tattered dog's collar). It was really
trary to Farmor's habit to engage a girl as old as s
was her custom only to employ the very young—but
there was nothing behind this custom beyond the fac
the youngest were the cheapest, if an older woman a
willing to work for the same wage as a newly conf
girl, she was ready for once to forego it.

Why Rosalie was so cheap was explained later. On
day she cut her jugular vein, and the event revealed th
that for 22 years she had been an inmate of an insane as

But while she was with us she was normal enough.
she had a tendency to get cramps in her hands and
things she was carrying. Neither of us attached any i
tance to it. I thought it rather funny, and Farmo
not annoyed since it was her custom to deduct from a
wages the cost of anything she broke.

However, Rosalie did have one major defect in my
her hands were very red and scaly and full of wrink
tiny wrinkles, thousands of them. They reminded me of
slaws. And the aesthete in me found it repugnant to let
hands touch me. So within quite a short time I learn
dress and undress myself, to wash myself, brush my
dress my hair, cut my food, and go alone to the toilet.

Thus the disastrous impulse which made me give J
ne's ladder a little push proved almost as significant a

in my development as the separation of a foster son from
his mother.

31

"Misfortunes never come singly," piped Farmor quoting
the old saying. And even if the saying in question is hardly
the law of nature there seemed to be a certain appropriateness
about applying it in this case: for Johanne's misfortune had
been followed by another misfortune—an even greater one.

Aunt White had fallen ill.

It began with Mrs. Tychsen's coming down one morning
and telling us that her daughter was a bit unwell and therefore she, Mrs. Tychsen, was staying home from work, and
for the same reason I was not to go up there after lunch.
We must wait and see—at any rate till next day.

Farmor expressed sympathy, and Mrs. Tychsen expressed
the hope that it was nothing serious. Then she went back.

But in the evening she came down again. This time she
seemed strangely changed, and her eyes were red-rimmed.
Constance had got pneumonia. Mrs. Tychsen had had a
suspicion of it when her daughter had started having fits of
shivering and coughing—not for nothing had she been a
doctor's wife—but one always, she said, hopes against hope.
But when the doctor came, hope was crushed—his diagnosis
was indisputable. She had hired a nurse and now she and
the nurse would take turns so that somebody should be with
the patient all day and all night. Of course it was going
to be very expensive having a nurse, and they could not
really afford it; but in case of sickness one did everything
in one's power regardless of cost—wasn't that so? Otherwise one might regret it bitterly afterwards—if something
happened . . .

Farmor nodded. She approved all Mrs. Tychsen said to
her.

The two women sat at the dining-room table in the gaslight
speaking in whispers. They whispered about cases of pneu-

monia they had known, about household remedies and professional skill in dealing with it, and about the last hours of
people who'd died of it. Pneumonia was something very
serious, I gathered. Nearly all old people who caught it
died of it. Young people were not so dangerously affected
by it, but even for them, it was a gamble. The most important thing was that a patient shouldn't be moved. Moving
meant certain death. One of Dr. Tychsen's colleagues had
made a farmhand who'd collapsed on a threshing-floor
when suffering from bronchial pneumonia remain lying
there, with only a pillow under his head and a couple of
blankets over him. What worried Mrs. Tychsen most was
that Constance's father had died of pneumonia, and he,
too, caught it at the beginning of spring. Spring was the
most dangerous time of all, Mrs. Tychsen said.

I listened, but I was not really terribly anxious. That
anything could happen to Aunt White—that she, for instance, could fly up to the old man in Heaven—that was,
for me, something completely beyond the bounds of the
probable. Still I felt uneasy. But that was due rather to
the two pale, blackclothed women in the blue-white light and
the way in which they both shrank from and at the same
time regaled themselves with thoughts about sickness and
death.

Then Mrs. Tychsen left.

Farmor went with her to the door and expressed all possible good wishes for her daughter's quick recovery. If she
was not being sincere, then she lied so convincingly that
even I believed her.

A week of anxiety and anguish followed.

Mrs. Tychsen called every day, sometimes several times
a day, to keep us informed. Each time she expressed her
trust in God, but at the same time she became noticeably
thinner, kept bursting into tears, and declared that life
would not be worth living if Constance died.

Father, too, came in now and then, after his visits to the

fourth floor. He sat quietly, completely prostrated for long periods—and then would suddenly jump up and off to his clinic. He never passed me without at least stroking my hair, and in addition he often lifted me up and hugged me close to him, a thing he had not done for a long time—indeed not since Mother's death. But what was most remarkable was that his visits always went off peaceably now. Well, maybe this was because Farmor was at least as much worried about Aunt White's illness as he was. Perhaps she had, in spite of all, become reconciled to the thought of having her as a daughter-in-law ...

And then one day our fears were over.

Mrs. Tychsen came down, her face shining with unearthly happiness, and told us that the crisis had been successfully passed. Aunt White's temperature had fallen from 103.6 to 97.3; her pulse was normal; and at the moment she was asleep—sleeping without any coughing or shivering fits. She was out of danger. It was only a question of time now when she'd be well again.

Farmor piped,

"It was indeed God's mercy! I can't tell you how happy I am."

I had been sitting browsing in one of Farmor's almanacs. But just then I looked up and glanced at Farmor. In that second it had sounded to me as if she were lying. As if she were not really glad at all. As if she had not at all wished for Aunt White's recovery.

I looked at her searchingly.

But her pale, porous, old-woman's face looked just as usual. It was melancholy as always. It wore the expression: "I realize that I am just a weak and unimportant person." And it looked too, as if nothing much were going on behind it.

Mrs. Tychsen replied, nodding her head, and with closed eyes,

"The Lord has been merciful to me ... He has indeed."

And Farmor nodded,

"Yes, our Lord is merciful—that He is."

I turned back to my almanac.

I did not in the least share the exultation felt by Mrs. Tychsen. Why should I? I had never been the least bit worried. Not for a second had I believed in the possibility of Aunt White's flying up to the old man in Heaven. But even if I did not exult, I was nonetheless happy—happy in the thought that Aunt White would soon be able to read to me again.

All at once I lifted my eyes from the book.

"Can I go up to Aunt White's now?"

"Soon, my friend. Soon."

I thought about it for a moment.

"When is 'soon'?"

Mrs. Tychsen laughed,

"In about two weeks—at the most three weeks."

Mrs. Tychsen turned towards Farmor.

"How everybody loves my daughter!" she said.

Although I tremendously loved Aunt White myself, I didn't like Mrs. Tychsen's last remark. For some reason it irritated me, as, too, did most of the things that she said.

Then she went upstairs again.

After Farmor had let her out, she pottered up to the kitchen door and called,

"Rosalie—it is Soren's bed-time now. It is late."

After which she slipped into her bedroom.

Perhaps joys come in the same way as Farmor said troubles do, that is, never singly. At any rate, over and above the happiness I felt that I should soon be able to read with Aunt White again, another and still greater happines came.

The day after the joyful tiding that the crisis had passed Father arrived at Farmor's accompanied by a messenger-boy carrying a large wooden box. When the box was opened, I found in it—wrapped in tissue paper and packed in exelsior

—the fabulous clockwork train which I had once seen in the window of the "Children's Bazar"! It was all there: the locomotive, the tender, the carriages, the rails, the station, the barricades, the bridges, the tunnels, the signals ...

I tore the package open and scattered the paper and excelsior all over the floor. The more treasures I found, the wilder, the more hysterical, the greedier I became.

A few minutes later, after the last item was unpacked, Father and I were lying on the floor playing trains.

32

I think it must have been four or five days after the crisis that Mrs. Tychsen came down one forenoon and asked Farmor if she would look in on Constance that evening. Mrs. Tychsen had received an invitation to dinner, from some friends, which she had really meant to decline, but Constance had plagued and plagued her until she had accepted. As a matter of fact there was no reason for not accepting it— Constance had been out of danger for some time now. But unfortunately the nurse had left the day before. They really couldn't afford to keep her on, nor was there any sense, really, in keeping her now that Constance was so much better. On the other hand Mrs. Tychsen didn't like the idea of leaving her alone for a whole evening without anyone's looking in on her. So she would be most terribly grateful if Farmor would just peep in between eight and nine. That was the time when Constance usually went to sleep and it would be nice to have someone look in and see how she was and whether she needed anything ... and so on. Constance, too, had to have her sleeping drops, and it would be best, too, if Farmor would put out the light so that the convalescent would not have to get out of bed.

Farmor assured her that she would be only too delighted to do her this service, even though her legs and her breast did find the numerous stairs a little bit of a strain; Mrs.

Tychsen for her part could not sufficiently express how touched she was by Farmor's helpfulness; and Farmor protested that such a trifling matter was nothing to be thanked for.

Then the ladies rose.

"Yes, and I had better give you the key right now, while we think of it."

Farmor took the key, tied a piece of pink yarn to it, and laid it on her writing desk in the den.

Farmor unlocked the door for Mrs. Tychsen. Until the door closed the two women continued to assure one another of their mutual sympathy, esteem and gratitude.

I must at this point interpolate a little piece of information that I did not have at that time: Farmor did not really need to borrow the key—she possessed keys to every room in the house!

I discovered this fact one day long after, during my schooldays.

A gas drama had occurred in the "garden house." The police wanted to break down the door, but Lillelund got them to go over to the proprietor's and borrow a key from her. I happened to be visiting Farmor just at the time the officer rang the bell.

Why then did Farmor accept Mrs. Tychsen's key?

I must confess I can think of no other explanation of this but Farmors craftiness. Her tenants were to remain ignorant of the fact that there was not a single place in the complex of buildings that the owner couldn't get in to if she chose...

We had finished supper. We were sitting in the dining-room, Farmor, Rosalie and I, the last hour before my bed time. Farmor was playing patience; Rosalie was embroidering—something at which she had exceptional skill— and I was playing with my train which I had loaded with soldiers and dominoes.

The game of patience came out correctly (Farmor's

patiences nearly always did, because she cheated) and she
was gathering her cards together. Then she looked up at
the clock ... and mumbled, as if to remind herself,

"Now it is time to go and look in on Miss Constance."

I dropped a soldier which was just on the point of killing
a domino.

"I will go too," I said.

"No," said Farmor, "it is too late now. It is past a little
boy's bed time."

"I will go too," I repeated. The determination in my
voice was increased to a higher pitch. In addition, I was
keeping in reserve a fit of weeping if this preliminary de-
monstration of my intention did not prove sufficient.

Farmor reconsidered.

"If you will do as I tell you, and go to bed like a good
boy as soon as we come back ..."

I promised. I was prepared to promise anything in order
to go. I longed to bursting point to see Aunt White again.
Besides, such an excursion was a change—an adventure—
in the daily monotony of Farmor's house.

Farmor went into her bedroom to fetch the brass candlestick. On its round lower edge, she had placed a box of
matches.

I was already waiting at the door leading into the hall.
I was restless with happiness—like a dog who has been
promised a walk.

Farmor took the key from the desk. Then she said to
Rosalie,

"Leave the door open so that I can see to unlock; but
close it as soon as we have gone, to save the heat."

"The door" was the door connecting the dining room with
the hall, the one at which I stood waiting.

Farmor unlocked the front door in the dim light of the
gas from the dining room. She had rather felt her way
there than seen it. By contrast the light out on the stairs
seemed quite dazzling. There was a gas bracket just outside Farmor's door, and its white globe sent forth a light

which, after the gloominess of the hall, appeared cheerful and reassuring.

There was a gas light not only outside Farmor's door but on every floor, however, as a rule only every second was lighted. It was one of Lillelund's responsibilities to see that the stair lights were lit and extinguished at the right hours. People who came home late had to grope their way up in the dark or light their way with matches.

If I had been alone I should have climbed up to the fourth floor in less than a minute. But now instead of springing up like a deer, I had to trip like a foal. Farmor's tempo was even slower than usual. She was not only held up by her asthma and her varicose veins—the darkness also slowed her progress. She climbed with her right hand slowly sliding along the bannisters—a movement which gave her the appearance of sneaking up to perform some nefarious deed. Although she seemed to be feeling her way up, I kept hearing her shoes thud against the stairs' runners.

"The gas seems to be getting poorer lately," she complained ...

Well, finally we got there.

The fourth floor was one of the dark landings. In contrast to the second floor which received a certain amount of light both from above and from below, the fourth one had to be satisfied with only the light that came from below, because of course there was no light on the attic landing— there wasn't even a gas bracket there.

Farmor handed me the candlestick in the dark.

"Hold it, Soren," she piped.

Then she struck a match and held it over the wick.

The flame finally caught on the little twisted string.

Farmor drew me close to the door and warned, "Stand perfectly still now—so that you don't set the house on fire."

She pulled the key from her blouse, fitted it into the key-hole and turned it. At the same time that she gently opened the door she piped out in the most friendly voice she could muster,

"It is me—Mrs. Jensen."

There was no answer. Evidently Aunt White had not heard her. Farmor took the candlestick from me. She slipped in, her hand shielding the flame. Her caution was plainly necessary, for the flame flickered wanly in the open doorway—seemed now and then, in fact, to be losing contact with the wick.

In the hall, the candlestick changed hands once more. Farmor, of course, wanted to take the key out again to lock the door behind us. I began to find the situation a little eery. I had never before participated in breaking into someone else's home and our invasion was not made less nerve-wracking by the fact that the whole apartment was in complete darkness. Suppose someone came—why, they would think we were thieves ... and probably put us in prison!

Again Farmor took the candle-stick from me, and with her hand in front of the flame she stole further in—up to the little door which led into the sitting-room. Perhaps I should explain that Aunt White's sitting-room corresponded to Farmor's dining room on our floor. The room which corresponded to our sitting room (and which the Tychsens called "the corner room") they usually let to some theological student.

Farmor opened the door, carefully, quietly. This time, too, the flame looked as if it would go out.

It was perfectly dark inside, except for a yellow light which shone from the bedroom the door of which was not completely shut. The golden light looked so cheerful—as if something even more than cheerful were inside—it was as if it emanated from a room where *happiness* was dwelling.

"Who is it?" a voice called suddenly. A weak voice, a weak and rather frightened voice, came from the room with the golden light.

Suddenly I realized that the voice belonged to Aunt White. I was happy—but also sad. Sad because it sounded so weak.

"It is me—*Mrs. Jensen*," answered Farmor.

She fumbled her way through the overcrowded room. Her careful movements made her look like someone who has evil in mind. A dark, eery figure . . . in a dark, eery room . . .

Farmor continued,

"And I have taken the liberty of bringing Soren with me. He wants so much to see his Aunt White."

From the bedroom I heard,

"Oh how nice!"

The voice was still very weak, but now a little happiness was blended with it.

We approached the bedroom door. Farmor opened it. I squeezed in behind her.

There lay Aunt White. The golden light from the oil lamp standing on the night-table fell on her. But oh how strange she looked! Pale, waxen-white, with cheeks that were hollow instead of round and with eyes grown very large, while the whites of them shone more than ever like mother of pearl. Still, as she lay there, pale and tired and thin—how beautiful she was! Beautiful—beautiful! Indeed, as she lay there in her white nightgown with its lace-work and puffed sleeves, her hair spread loose on the pillow, she reminded me of the image I had always cherished of angels and fairies . . .

She caught sight of me as I ducked out from behind Farmor's broad skirt. Her eyes with the dark brown irises which looked like chocolate lozenges looked out towards me. Her head was turned to the side—evidently so as to see me as soon as I entered—and one of her arms was stretched out toward me.

Joy at seeing her again bubbled up within me. I hurried forward to kiss her, then stopped suddenly. Something told me that too much emotion would not be good for her. Instead I tiptoed up to her bed, seized her hand and covered it with kisses.

"Goodday, little Soren," she said, with that gentle tenderness which was like a caress to my heart. Then she crooked her fingers round mine and drew me to her, pulling me gently down until I lay in her arm, with my mouth and nose pressed between her bosom and shoulder. It was soft and cozy—and I liked the smell of her.

Farmor, out of breath, had sunk down on a chair next to the bed. Now she put her hand affectionately over Constance's and piped,

"How are you, little girl?"

"Thank you, Mrs. Jensen," Aunt White answered softly, still holding me. "Now I am quite well again. I'm just very tired still—so awfully tired, you see, and so I don't sleep well yet—"

"They will come back soon—both strength and sleep. It is just these first days ..."

Farmor and Aunt White continued talking. I said nothing. It was so lovely, lying there. I should have liked to lie there *always*.

Suddenly Farmor's chair squeaked,

"Now we must not tire you any more," Farmor said, "Now I must see about getting you ready for the night."

"Thank you so much ... if it is not too much trouble ..."

Farmor picked up the candlestick which she had set down on the wash-stand.

"Soren, be a good boy now and go into the other room. Miss Constance and I would like to be alone for a little."

I heard her open the door into the sitting-room.

"Come now, Soren."

It hurt me physically to pull myself away from Aunt White's embrace.

Farmor brought the candlestick into the sitting-room and put it on the oval table.

"Maybe you can find something to look at," she said.

"Soren knows where the book of fairy tales is," came Aunt White's voice, slightly raised, from the bedroom.

"But take care not to jog the candle," warned Farmor.

Then she slipped back to the bedroom. She closed the door carefully behind her.

It was rather dark in the sitting room, which was only lit by the unsteady candle. I turned over the pages of Grimm, but in the weak light I could hardly see the pictures. Instead I sat staring into the candle flame.

Farmor and Aunt White continued their talk. I could hear every word. I could hear as well as if I had remained in the bedroom. The sofa I sat on had its back against the bedroom wall and was close to the door. Besides, the doors up at Mrs. Tychsen's were no more tight than those in Farmor's apartment.

"Shall I smooth the bed a little?" began Farmor. Her voice was unusually affectionate.

"Oh no thank you, it isn't necessary," answered Aunt White. "Mother re-made it just before she left."

"But shan't I shake up the pillows?"

"That isn't necessary either, thank you. I haven't moved at all since Mother left."

"Would you like to use the bed-pan?"

"No, not that either, thanks."

I could tell from the tone of her voice that Aunt White was smiling a little.

"But you will have your sleeping drops?"

"Thank you, yes, please. It is that bottle beside the lamp there. There's a clean spoon in the glass beside it."

"Yes, it must be that. How many drops do you have?"

"Ten, I think."

There was a pause. I could hear the spoon being taken out of the glass, then there was silence for a half or perhaps a whole minute.

"Here you are."

"Thank you."

Another pause.

Then Aunt White asked,

"Wasn't that a little more than usual?"

"I counted ten drops—just as you told me."

Farmor's voice sounded a tiny bit offended.

"Gracious, Mrs. Jensen! I'm not accusing you of trying

to kill me! Maybe it is only eight drops I usually have. Never mind, two drops more or less won't do any harm, I'm sure."

"Wouldn't you like me to wash you?" asked Farmor.

"No, thank you—Mother did that, too."

"Isn't there anything you want—water, or—?"

"No, thank you. Absolutely nothing."

"You would'nt like me to read something to you—from the Bible or the hymn book?"

"No, thank you—I would just like to sleep now."

The door-handle turned.

The golden light streamed out again.

"Soren," whispered Farmor, "Come and say good-night to Aunt White."

I jumped up and tiptoed into the bedroom.

"Good night, Aunt White," I said, at a little distance.

"Good night, Soren," she answered, in the same gentle, tender voice that always stirred my love.

She tried to stretch her hand out, but it fell heavily.

I understood her gesture. I went to her quickly and seized her hand. And covered it with kisses, at once gentle and wild.

"Goodnight," she murmured.

Then she went on, slowly and with closed eyes,

"I have prayed every night that I may be as good to you as your own mother."

"That you certainly will be," piped Farmor.

At that moment I hated Farmor. Hated her for her voice. Hated her for her presence.

Farmor continued,

"Come now, Soren. Now Aunt White is going to sleep . . ."

She put her hand on my shoulder to indicate that we must leave. Both her voice and her movements indicated uneasiness of some kind.

I released Aunt White's hand. It fell wearily back on the sheet.

Farmor plodded over to the night table, held her hand

over the chimney of the lamp and blew. The flame wavered
—fighting for its life. Then it prevailed.

"One hasn't even enough breath to blow out a light,"
whined Farmor. "Ah well, it will soon be over."

Once more she blew into the chimney. This time she was
successful. Darkness surrounded us.

"Goodnight," chirped Farmor, "and sleep well."

"Goodnight," murmured Aunt White, somewhere in there
in the dark. "And thanks for all your kindness."

Her voice was full of the sadness which comes from
weariness.

Farmor answered, sugar sweet,

"It has been only a pleasure to me."

I felt her hand on my back. It pushed me ahead of her
into the sitting room with a speed which was unusual for
her. Then she closed the door to the bedroom—took pains
to close it tight—and picked up the candle which was mir-
rored in the oval mahogany table.

We went downstairs.

Farmor mumbled:

"We could have saved ourselves the trouble of that visit.
Her mother had done everything before she left—made her
bed, washed her hands, given her her sleeping drops—There
wasn't a thing left for me to do. Not a blessed thing."

I did not answer. I just went on longing for Aunt White.
She was so much softer and warmer than Farmor, and her
voice was so much nicer, also. But when Father and Aunt
White were married, then I should go back home again—
Aunt White had herself said so one day when I was up there
with her—and then I should be with her *for ever*.

For ever.

33

I opened my eyes ...

I opened my eyes and knew that it was early, that I had

waked long before my usual time. .

I knew, too, that the sun was shining and that the sky was blue, completely blue.

It was, as a matter of fact, rather surprising that I should know this.

Both the blinds were down, the windows faced north, and I was lying on the box-couch with my back to them.

But there was a kind of brightness in the room that told me that it was daylight—a brightness created by the sun's reflection in specks of dust, the green leaves, windows, and greenhouse panes—a brightness which had partly forced its way through the blinds and partly penetrated the slits on either side of them.

And what I wasn't able to see I certainly heard. The air was filled with bird-song, with that outpouring of bird twitterings of all kinds which is heard in a city's early morning hours before man arrogantly takes possession of the streets.

I lay there a moment happy. Just happy. Indeed happier than happy. It was as if I were lying on my back and floating in air and light ... floating, a disembodied spirit, somewhere where only happiness prevailed.

Then the bell rang. The kitchen bell. It rang again and again, hysterically and steadily, scattering its flat, unbeautiful noise in all directions. I not only heard the bell, I could also hear the rustle of the bell-button each time it was pressed against the door.

Suddenly I realized that I had not awakened naturally—the doorbell had waked me. It had rung once already, but not so insistently as now. Something inside me remembered that first little push of the button.

At last the noice stopped. It was a relief, like liberation from some minor pain. The silence which followed seemed vast and wonderful.

I lay speculating as to who could have rung.

It couldn't have been the milkman—he did not ring, at least, not at Farmor's—he just quietly left his little milk-cans at the top of the kitchen stairs. The milkman rang a bell down in the street, of course, but there could be no question of confusing his bell with the door-bell. The baker's boy didn't ring either. He just put ordered bread, wrapped in thin yellow tissue paper, next to the milk-can. The newspaper-woman, who had the privilege of going up the front stairs, performed her task by pushing the paper through the mail-slit without ringing the doorbell either. The first person to ring it was the postman—he pushed the bell ever so slightly when he delivered morning's mail. But in the first place he rang at the *front* door, and, secondly, he came much later than the others did. If he came at all, that is! Farmor's correspondence was meager and it was far from every day that she received letters. No, I couldn't figure out the source of that ringing at all—It must mean something quite unusual.

The silence was broken by the creaking of a door and the sound of steps dragging across the floor. I was in no doubt as to what was happening: it was Rosalie slipping out of her room and going to the kitchen door.

"Who is it?" she whispered.

I could hear the question, though it came through two doors. On the other hand it was impossible to hear the answer.

But Rosalie heard it. She answered quietly,

"Just a moment—I will call the mistress"

Rosalie had good reason to call the lady of the house. The kitchen door was locked and the key lay with all the other keys beneath the lowest of Farmor's pillows.

I could hear Rosalie shuffling across the little dark corridor and knocking at Farmor's bedroom door. She had to knock a couple of times. Farmor, who was always complaining about insomnia, was evidently sleeping hard at the moment.

At last she piped, heavy with sleep,

"Who is it?"

The voice was frail and helpless. Apparently aimed to

awaken softer feelings in the murderer or whoever it was on the other side of the door.

"It's me, Mrs. Jensen," answered Rosalie. "Lillelund is here and wants to speak to you. He says it's something very important."

There was a pause before Farmor answered. Perhaps she was considering whether it could be a trap. But then it sounded as if she had gathered confidence. Her answer was to request Lillelund to wait—she would come immediately.

I heard Rosalie trudge back to the kitchen and deliver the message. Then I heard Farmor creaking out of bed and donning necessary garments with various sighs and groans. A clinking in a water glass indicated that she was not forgetting her false teeth.

Although it was long before my usual getting-up time, I was now wide awake. So early a call by Lillelund was unusual, thrilling, a sure promise of something out of the ordinary's happening.

A key scraped. Farmor had rigged herself up and got as far as the kitchen. After the rattle of the burglar chain came the squeak of the kitchen door.

Then a whispered conversation began, which, to my disappointment and chagrin, I couldn't follow. Only now and then did I catch a word from the composite buzzing of Farmor's and Lillelund's voices. It was mostly when Lillelund was speaking—a couple of times, for example, I heard him mention Mrs. Tychsen. The mention of her diminished my interest, however. The subject of Mrs. Tychsen's welfare was one that held no interest for me at all.

Suddenly the conversation stopped.

There was a pause.

Then all at once I heard Farmor say—loudly and distinctly,

"Well, tell him I shall come immediately—just as soon as I can get dressed."

"Very well, Mrs. Jensen," sang out Lillelund respectfully. Then I heard his boots trudging down the kitchen stairs—

it sounded as if he were walking upstairs till, a moment later, the sound was cut off by the kitchen door's being shut.

I lay there a little while.

I was both a little bit curious and a little bit uneasy. Mostly the latter. I didn't like the thought of Farmor going away from me—especially at that time of the morning—it was altogether too contrary to the routine of the house.

Suddenly I threw off my sheets and eiderdown, brought my feet down on the cold linoleum, and walked over to her bedroom door. There I turned the handle, drew it towards me, took a pace back—and sneaked into her room.

Farmor was putting something away. My eyes followed the object—it was the razor, the razor from the washstand drawer. That meant that Farmor had "bearded" herself, as I used to say when Father shaved.

"Are you up already, Soren?" she exclaimed.

She was fully dressed. And it was not in her everyday clothes. She was wearing what she wore when she went calling.

"Are you going away, Farmor?" I asked.

"Yes," answered Farmor. "I'm just going up to Mrs. Tychsen's. But I shall be right back, Soren."

"Why are you going up to Mrs. Tychsen's?"

I wondered, puzzled, if they were going to play bezique at this early hour.

Farmor looked hard at me.

Then she came right up to me and said:

"Now you mustn't cry, Soren, but something has happened that you will not like."

I looked up at her questioningly.

I felt my eyes growing big with fright.

Farmor's two cold finger tips stroked my cheek—

Then she said,

"I believe your Aunt White is dead."

I stood for a minute until the words had penetrated to my understanding—until I grasped what had happened.

Then suddenly I realized that Aunt White had gone—gone up to the Old Man—and that I shouldn't see her again. Not today, not tomorrow, not the day after tomorrow, not even when I grew up. She would be away—all the time!—just like Mother.

It took time to understand. My feelings also needed their time. First I had the sensation that something painful was going to happen inside me ... then I felt my lips beginning to tremble ... then tears sprang from my eyes and sobs from my lips. To ease the pain, which seemed unendurable, I threw myself at Farmor, and wound my arms about her.

Of course, she was not nearly as soft and nice as Johanne —still, at the moment there was no one else to cling to.

Farmor stumbled a step backwards from my violent embrace.

Then she recovered her balance and gently stroked the back of my neck.

"There, there, Soren," she murmured lovingly, "Don't cry so, little Soren. Believe me the dead are quickly forgotten. They *are*, dear."

Then she raised her voice:

"Rosalie, come in here and look after Soren."

And when Rosalie came, she added,

"I have to go upstairs to Mrs. Tychsen's."

Rosalie put me back to bed and tucked the eiderdown tightly around me. In my despair I accepted the situation. In spite of her hands.

My sorrow did not abate. I believe my emotions were much more violent than when my Mother died, partly perhaps because I was sixteen months older, partly also because the earlier death had made me more sensitive, given me greater understanding of what death could mean—at any rate for those left behind—and because the comfort I had previously derived from the thought of angels and the Old Man had all at once ceased to exist for me—maybe because

I now no longer had someone whose bright voice could convince me of the consolation such thought can provide.

I lay for a long time, crumpled like one in convulsions and shaken by sobs which gradually turned into a kind of hiccup.

Then Rosalie persuaded me—she sat faithfully by the side of my bed all the while—to close my eyes. And as I followed her advice, the pillow became a boat—a boat that carried me far away from a world where sorrow and suffering are such frequent guests.

When I awoke, the worst of my sorrow had passed. I dressed myself and began to play with my train; and when Farmor came down again, I ate my breakfast—all without thinking overmuch about what had happened.

I was capable in those years of strong emotions. I could feel sorrow that seemed unendurable. I could experience fear so intense that my heart would stop beating—or that, at any rate, was how it felt—and my whole body became cold and knotted. I could get so angry that I would kick and bite. I could be so ashamed that my shoulders would droop and my stomach cave in. I could rejoice so much that I couldn't stand still but had to dance, sing and shout. And I could sink into such a state of happiness that there was paradise on earth. I experienced everything more violently, more intensely then than I can today. But, on the other hand, my feelings were of shorter duration. My violent emotions never lasted very long. Even the strongest of them were only explosions.

If, therefore, I say that I realized vaguely that morning that something tragic had happened, I have expressed all that, after the first outburst, I felt about Aunt White's death.

From the conversations between Farmor and Rosalie and between Farmor and Lillelund, I came in time to understand what had happened. At any rate, to a certain degree.

When Mrs. Tychsen arrived home the preceding evening,

her daughter had been sleeping so soundly that she did not have the heart to wake her. She had undressed in the dark and crept in beside her. But early next morning her daughter appeared so strangely still and pale that she had tried to rouse her. She had even shaken her, but without Constance's giving the slightest sign of life. Then Mrs. Tychsen, throwing on a dressing-gown and a pair of slippers, had rushed down to Lillelund's. After a great deal of effort she succeeded in waking him, and he let her into his shop where she had telephoned the doctor, after which he went back with her to the apartment, where they tried again to waken Aunt White. Till the last Mrs. Tychsen, though desperate (for she realized from her experience as a doctor's wife, what had probably happened), tried to convince herself that her daughter only *appeared* to be dead. But when the doctor arrived, all hope was shattered. He announced that Miss Constance was dead —and had been for several hours.

Of a sudden Mrs. Tychsen had dashed to the window and smashed a pane with the intention of jumping out—but then the doctor and Lillelund had caught hold of her and dragged her back.

As the doctor dared not after this leave her in the room alone, Lillelund was sent down to fetch Farmor. For an hour Farmor and Lillelund watched over her. Only when a nurse, an elderly, stalwart female, one who had been in charge of a mental patient for many years, had arrived, had Farmor and Lillelund been able to go home.

What seemed the most terrible thing about it all was that Aunt White had died *at night.* While she was sleeping! To die in one's sleep seemed to me the most horrible fate imaginable. What did one dream about at the moment one died? And just think of waking up in the morning and finding out that—! But no, that was just talk. When a person died, he or she did not wake up at all ...

Alas! The sorrow I felt then was not on Aunt White's behalf. It was only on my own. But all the same it went deep. For many years afterwards it happened sometimes that when I was going to bed, I would be overcome by a sudden icy fear that I might die in the night. So I would lie there struggling against sleep—naturally without much success ...

But as far as Aunt White was concerned I did not suffer very much—except for that first outburst of grief. What I felt later that morning—alas, I'm ashamed to confess it —was chiefly the gratification that one experiences when one sees somebody else suffer a disaster which one escapes oneself. That gratification which expresses itself in the words,

"Thank goodness it wasn't me!"

34

We had almost finished our soup when the front doorbell rang.

"That is unfortunate," complained Farmor. "Right in the middle of dinner."

She loosened her napkin from her neck and limped out to the hall.

It was Father.

I could hear that his Good-day was short and unfriendly. And Farmor's condolences were interrupted by a menacing,

"I've got to talk with you, Mother. About something serious."

Farmor tried to coax him to the dinner table.

"We are having duck—you're so fond of that—and you could have a nice plate of soup also."

But Father was adamant.

"No thanks, I have come just to talk to you and nothing else. Let us go into the den."

His voice sounded as if he had forced himself to throw off despair. On the other hand it was curt, severe—almost brusque—and full of energy.

"All right," said Farmor.

Her voice was innocent, humble, obedient.

I heard the door between the hall and the den open. Then the door to the dining room opened a crack and Farmor stuck her head in.

"Rosalie," she piped, "Go out in the kitchen. Don't go on with dinner till I come back."

"Very good, Mrs. Jensen."

Rosalie shuffled obediently out into the little back corridor, and beyond it into the kitchen. Then Farmor closed the door into the dining room.

"Please sit down," she said plaintively.

I snatched a piece of sugar from the blue bowl—it had been brought out for after-dinner coffee—and turned around 90 degrees on my chair, the better to listen.

"Thanks, I prefer to stand," answered Father; "but sit down yourself if you feel the need."

I could hear by the well-known creak of the desk chair that Farmor took advantage of the suggestion.

As she seated herself she lamented sorrowfully,

"I can't tell you, Viggo, how grieved I am over what has happened—not so much for my own sake as for yours."

Father ignored her condolences.

Instead, he began in a magisterial tone—it was devoid of all filial feeling, yet not excited or uncontrolled,

"You went up to Constance's last night?'

"Yes, indeed. Mrs. Tychsen had asked me to look in on her."

"You were to make her bed and—?"

"Oh it was already made when I got up there. Mrs. Tychsen is always so tidy, so finicky."

"And then you gave her some water and ... her sleeping drops?"

I could hear that Father was bent over toward Farmor—looking her straight in the eyes.

"Oh no, she would not have any—she wouldn't even let me give her the bed pan—Mrs. Tychsen had seen to everything before she left. I said to Soren, when we came downstairs, afterwards, we could have saved ourselves the effort of the visit."

Father sat down. I could hear the creak of the delinquent's chair, the tall, uncomfortable one with the low back —designed, I imagine, to prevent tenants sitting long enough in it to get to the subject of repairs.

"Was Soren with you?" asked Father, a little surprised.

"Yes, he wanted so much to see her. It was such a long time since he'd been up there and so I thought it would be a pity not to let him."

In Farmor's voice there was plainly an admission of having done something wrong. But also a plea for forgiveness.

"Yes, of course," answered Father. "That is of no importance."

There was a pause. It was so quiet I did not even dare to suck the sugar.

Then Father said,

"Do you know what the doctor is saying?"

"No," answered Farmor innocently.

"He says that Constance died of an overdose of sleeping drops."

Again a tiny pause.

Then Farmor exclaimed,

"But what a dreadful thing!"

Father continued,

"He cannot say it for certain. Not before they've carried out an obduction. But he is quite convinced that that was how it happened."

Farmor wailed,

"An accident! A frightful accident! However can it have happened?"

There was another little pause.

I wasn't wholly clear what it was Father and Farmor were talking about. I only grasped that it had something to do with Aunt White's death and that it was something very bad and nasty—

Father asked,

"How many drops did you give her when you were up there?"

"I didn't give her any—I have already told you."

"But somebody gave her some. The spoon which stood in a glass of water on the night-table had been used. There was some medicine in the water and it could only have got there from the spoon."

"It was probably Mrs. Tychsen?"

"No, Mrs. Tychsen didn't give her any. She left before six, and so thought it too early."

"Well, then it must have been Miss Constance herself."

"There are *three* persons who may have been responsible: Mrs. Tychsen, Constance, and *you*. *You*, Mother. Mrs. Tychsen certainly had no wish for Constance to die; nor had Constance herself. She was just looking forward tremendously to getting well again and getting married, and ... but you, on the contrary, Mother—"

"But Viggo, you are not suggesting that your Mother *murdered* Constance—?"

"*Yes.*"

Father's voice was hard, severe.

In a moment I understood everything. It was Farmor who had killed Constance! It was Farmor! Hate and fury began to seethe in me, like steam in a covered kettle.

I say that I understood the whole matter. This I believed then. But now, forty-one years later, when I think back to this little drama, I realize that I did not really understand the cause of Aunt White's death, that I did not perceive the connection between it and the sleeping drops at all. I did not at that time reflect on the connection. But if I had been forced to do so and had had words to express my thought, I should certainly have described what had happened as *witchcraft*. And I would not at all have marveled. For me witchcraft was just as real and just as natural as the gas in the gas-pipe and the water in the tap.

Farmor whined,

"That is a dreadful thing to say to one's mother. But it confirms what I so often used to say to your Father: 'Viggo is not quite right in his head'. And when your Father got angry and said I should not say such a thing about my own son, I used to say 'Yes, but it is the truth, and one must always be allowed to say what is true, and it is the only possible excuse for his behavior'—"

Father's tone was icy.

"All that is beside the point. All that is something you just say in order to evade the fact that you were the only person who wished Constance dead. You did not want her for a daughter-in-law because she had no dowry and no inheritance in view. And so you acted like rich peasants still do in your native village with old people, you killed her! You killed her—*with poison!*"

"You forget, Viggo, that there is something called a mistake, an accident. Mrs. Tychsen may have given her daughter a dose before she left. They both forgot it, maybe, and then a little while later Miss Tychsen took another, or maybe your betrothed herself may have taken two doses herself, forgetting she'd already had one."

There was another pause.

Then Father said—still 'cold as ice—but continuing to exercise control:

"It is possible. It could have happened that way."

Then he added, slowly and with great emphasis:

"*But I do not believe it did.*"

I could tell from the scraping of the chair that he got up. For the first time there were tears in his voice.

"May God forgive you if you did it. *I* cannot.'

From the creaking of the floor I could tell that he went toward the hall.

Farmor followed him.

The anger which had begun to seethe in me was close to explosion point. When Farmor came back to the dining room, I stood in the middle of the floor with clenched fists.

"Well, now we shall have our dessert," she piped, and closed the door to the hall.

"I don't like you," I said staring at her. My eyes smarted with hate, and I could feel how the skin on my forehead became tight with rage.

Farmor turned.

"Do you not love me, Soren?"

"No," I hissed through my teeth. "It was you who made Aunt White dead!"

A hint of anger and impatience sounded in Farmor's inveterately long-suffering voice:

"So little Soren is going to be just as boorish as his father, is he!?"

"You are a witch," I said. "I know that you are a witch."

Farmor tried to calm me by stroking my cheek, but it was just what she should not have done. I felt the caress just as Hansel and Gretel must have felt the witch's fingerings when they sat in the pigsty being stuffed. First I struck at her hand, and then when she gently tried to stroke me again, my rage exploded: I threw myself at her; struck her wherever I could; bit and spat and kicked. At the same time I shrieked out:

"It is you who made Aunt White dead! It is you who made Aunt White dead! It is you who made Aunt White dead!"

I was the stronger. Farmor tried for a few moments to defend herself, but I broke down her weak defences. Her helplessness did not restrain me. She tried to slip out of my reach—she took a few steps backwards—but the result was only that I forced her toward the door to the hall. And there she was caught in a corner, unable to escape and with neither Rosalie nor Lillelund in reach to help her.

"But little Soren!" she gasped repeatedly—in a voice trembling with fright.

Even her fright did not move me. Perhaps I was in the grip of the same kind of frenzy which made our Viking forefathers go "berserk". I remember that it was precisely this word "berserk" that the grown-ups used to describe my fits of rage as a child.

Suddenly Farmor began to weep. Really weep.

But not even her tears could have aroused my compassion and held me back. What stopped me was what she then said and the voice in which she said it. I had never before heard that voice—and I have never heard a voice like it since. I can only describe it as *naked*.

"Little Soren," said that naked voice, "Can't you understand that everything I do—every single thing—I do for your sake."

The voice and the words stabbed me. Yes, I knew it was the truth. I knew that what she did she did for my sake. My arms sank, paralyzed.

The naked voice continued,

"*If* I have killed someone, Soren, it is so that some day you shall be a great and rich man. I have done it so that your children, those I shall never even live to see, shall be great and rich and powerful, like yourself, Soren."

My rage had forsaken me. Bewilderment and depression invaded me. What confronted me was something too big and complicated. I would go to pieces if I tried to face up to it. Involuntarily I seized upon the defence nearest to hand: I burst into tears. I clothed myself in tears as one might in armor.

Farmor tried to stanch my tears with promises: a visit to Johanne, an extra ten ore. All in vain. But finally she hit upon the right thing.

"Come and rest on the couch here, Soren—then perhaps you can get a little nap."

I followed her obediently.

Farmor spread the big, crocheted coverlet over me.

Then I lay there, hiccuping, my face toward the Pompeiian-red wall. I could hear Farmor and Rosalie whispering behind me—saying that they could warm up the food when I woke.

For the second time that day I let sleep carry me away from this world of sorrow and adversity.

35

How much did I understand of what Farmor said that day in that *naked* voice? Naturally, very little. And yet perhaps more than many might think. Children often understand in their own way, their *inarticulate* way, much more than grown people realize.

However, when I think about it today—ponder what she said on that occasion and compare it with her actions throughout the years—then I find an explanation for those actions.

Farmor lived for an idea—the idea of founding a dynasty.

And so vital, so mighty was this idea that she was ready even to kill a fellow human being for its sake.

Farmor, who physically was so small and fragile, was spiritually cast in the same mold as the wicked queen in *Snow White*, the witch in *Hansel and Gretel*, *Bluebeard*, the wolf in *Red Riding Hood*, *The Devil's Great Grandmother*, and similar grandiose figures in the Grimm's Fairy Tales of my childhood.

Or perhaps it would be more correct to associate her with all those queens, mistresses, sultanas, women of the nobility, wealthy city women, and rich peasant women in history who have not flinched from any means to secure the order of inheritance or to assure their successors power and riches and position—women who seem not to have had much joy themselves from this dynastic urge. Nature's stern law has only permitted them to behold a little fragment of the gene-ological tree for which they battled. They doubtless acted from instinct—the same instinct which makes a female insect protect her egg despite the fact that she will never see the child that issues from it—and the joy such women have experienced has probably been just the primitive satisfaction that anyone feels when following his or her instinct.

Are these women wicked? Many of them, to be sure, are murderers—quite a few of them, *poisoners*—murderers who have destroyed their own breed, their own children, even, simply so as to advance their dynastic plans.

Ah no, they are not wicked. They are not conscienceless furies. Neither, for that matter, are they declamatory martyrs of their consciences à la Lady Macbeth. All that is romantic fiction. Nor is it just a question of crazy sadists or emotionally frustrated imbeciles—statements to that effect, despite the claims of modern psychiatry—are just fiction also. No, they are people just like you and me, people like millions of others.

Gentle reader! Let me use a simple image that can aid understanding:

Have you ever seen a rabbitbreeder? *A rabbitbreeder who loves his rabbits?* Seen him when he was exhibiting them to his friends and acquaintances; seen him when he lifted an animal up in his arms and scratched it lovingly behind its long ears; seen his happy smile when he fed his animals and the greens in his milk-pail vanished into their twitching mouths; seen his sorrow when one of them died from some unknown cause or was bitten to death by a dog? Or have you ever heard him say to visiting children,

"You may look at them, but you must not do them any harm. One must always be kind to animals."

Yes, indeed, his affection for the little flock of small, pretty, plump little fellows is genuine enough.

But then comes autumn. He calculates how many of the rabbits he will keep over the winter. One male and two females will probably suit him best ... And it is *Oscar* who shall live, for he is the best breeder ... and of the females, *Snow White* and *Miriam*—they are both of the right age; and Snow White is so good to her young and Miriam's brood is always the biggest.

And so every now and then—with suitable intervals—the

fancier goes into his garden, catches one of the rabbits by the hind-legs and swings it against a post ... after which he cuts off its head with a large kitchen knife.

Some of the animals are sold; others are eaten by him and his family for dinner—while they smile happily over the delicacy of the meat.

Economies ... including one's daily food ... these matters, just have to take precedence over other feelings, don't they!

And when Queen Livia dealt out poison right and left and when Farmor gave Aunt White too many sleeping drops, they were not being any more wicked than that breeder of rabbits. They acted as he did in accordance with a considered plan and the procedure they followed was the one they regarded as the best, if not for themselves, then for the family. The FAMILY.

The ordinary man is a goodnatured murderer. A murderer who clears everything out of his way—and does the clearing along such lines as he thinks the right ones.

36

In the preceding chapters I have talked as if I were quite certain that Farmor deliberately killed Constance Tychsen, but I have to confess now that I am not certain at all.

The event took place when I was going on eight years old. Then I "forgot" it—"forgot" in quotation marks—for many years until, at the age of puberty, the memory of it rose to the surface again—romantic and captivating and surrounding Farmor with the heroic nimbus of an impressive criminal. Since then my memory has often evoked it again for scrutiny. Among other things, I remember it ran like an obbligato to the pastor's address at her funeral— his address about the good and pious woman whose earthly remains were here brought to rest. And, not unnaturally, during these last days when I have been recording my memories of Farmor's house it has more than ever occupied my thoughts.

But now it occurs to me that every time that I ponder the event, I find it a little changed. Memory—which certainly is endowed with poetic qualities—has rounded off, adjusted, filled in, rubbed out. In the interest of truth, therefore, I must say that, even though I have taken great pains to remember as honestly as possible, nevertheless I have the feeling that what is told here is *still* not 100 % true. I know, moreover, from earlier experiences that my memory is often unreliable.

This confession must be supplemented by still another avowal, namely that I do not know the result of the post mortem on Constance Tychsen. Nobody told me, and I never heard the grown-ups discuss it.

To sum the whole thing up:

I *believe* that Farmor killed Aunt White, but I do not *know*. I do not *know* because among other things I am not sure whether my memory of what happened is precise or reliable.

37

In Farmor's house everything slipped back into its customary tranquil routine.

I forgot Aunt White—at least on the surface of my memory —forgot her a day or two after her death. I also forgot my accusation against Farmor, forgot my rage, forgot my urge for revenge, forgot Farmor's defence—the days rolled by with their regular meals, their games, their walks, their baths, their getting dressed and getting undressed, their duties and their sleep.

But one day Father came again. A day when summer was already some way advanced.

It was not a desolate man who came, not even a sorrowing one. It was a man abrupt, energetic and authoritative, a man who seemed to have forgotten all his grief. At the same time, one felt that his curtness, his energy, his decisiveness were the result of the two hard blows fate had dealt him.

"I am going to the country on Wednesday," said Father, in a voice that excluded all objections, all opposition. "I am going to the country and I shall be taking Soren with me. And when I return home I shall keep Soren with me. In other words, Mother, you need not expect to have him again. I thank you for the time you have kept him, but I think it is wisest to bring it to an end. It is not right for a boy to have no other companions but two or three women who spoil him—it would end with his becoming a sissy. Besides I have entered him for a school. He will be starting there in the autumn—and so it will be much more practical for him to live with me. And you'll have to do without Johanne, also. She will be coming home to Soren and me as soon as she leaves the hospital."

Farmor piped,

"Very well, yes—yes, just as you decide, Viggo."

And as Father decreed, so it happened.

38

Farmor lived a long time.

She outlived not only my Mother and Aunt White, but also Aunt Laura, Cousin Christian (who died quite young of tuberculosis), Dr. Agerlin, Pastor Moller, my Father, Mrs. Agerlin and Mrs. Tychsen ...

Indeed she lived long enough to see me matriculate and enter the university, and also (and it must have been an indescribable triumph to her) become *the only surviving heir to her fortune.*

She must have died happy, too, if one can use so strong a word about a person whose voice implied perpetual melancholy. Perhaps I should content myself, in the circumstances, by saying that she died *contented*.

But what has happened since her death would *not* have contented her.

In the course of six or seven years I ran through her entire fortune. Not wildly and foolishly, but by spending it on long, luxurious sea-journeys and gratifying my epicurean tastes. My task was, of course, made easier by the fact that in the so-called inflation years money lost much of its value. Only when the fortune was almost exhausted did I resume my studies. And on the day I had passed my final examination (the law one) I went up to the tower of the City Hall and let my two remaining ten kroner notes flutter down over the city. I have rarely felt in so hilarious a mood as I did when I saw the wind catch up the two little brown bits of paper and carry them far out of sight. And when I later in life got married, I married a woman without either money or any prospect of inheriting any. And as if deliberately to foil Farmor's dynastic plans I begot three girls and no boys!

Strangely enough I should like to feel that Farmor has witnessed all of this. I should like her to have been sitting somewhere in Heaven or Hell or on some planet—and seeing how I was squandering her fortune, watching how the house she had built with such toil, was, thanks to the third generation, all laid in ruins.

Yes, I should like that.

But I'm not sure whether my wish stems from a childish love of teasing—like the times I ran upstairs and told Farmor that there was a mess under the stairs when there really wasn't one—or whether it derives from a still stronger wish: the wish that there exist a justice beyond all understanding which determines our human destiny.

BIOGRAPHICAL NOTE

Agnes Camilla Hansen, the translator of Soya's "FARMOR'S HOUSE", died in 1963. Though born in California, she must have felt herself partly European for both her parents were Danish and she spent many years in Europe, living and studying in Copenhagen, Paris, Rostock and other German cities. She spoke and read, not only the Scandinavian languages, but French and German as well, and also had a reading knowledge of Russian and Spanish. Educated at Reed College and the University of Washington, Miss Hansen received her library traning at Pratt Institute. After acting as head of the foreign department of the Seattle Public Library she was for some three years—1924-1927—on the staff of the American Library in Paris, that rendezvous for the cultivated of all nationalities. Miss Hansen was Associate-Director of Pratt Institute Library School in Brooklyn, New York until 1944 when she retired, and she has been translating since then, eager to introduce Danish literature to Americans.

The manuscript has been revised and edited by Mr. Alan Moray Williams.